AN UNUSUAL PROPOSAL

All Lucas Garrett longed for was a good night's sleep. But as the last able-bodied, hot-blooded man left in a town full of lonely women, he hadn't had a moment's peace since the Gold Rush had lured all the eligible bachelors westward. Now he's just plain exhausted. So he turns to the only person he can trust—pretty, proper Priscilla Wentworth. If she would agree to pose as his future bride, then the fluttering flock of amorous ladies would finally leave him alone.

A TEMPORARY
ENGAGEMENT

Priscilla agrees to pretend to be Lucas's fiancée in exchange for one thing only: he must help her find a husband of her own. Of course, Lucas is completely unsuitable—he's too handsome, too charming. But then he takes her in his arms, tantalizing her with unforgettable kisses . . . and so much more. And suddenly Priscilla is wondering if the last man in town is really the only man for her.

If You've Enjoyed This Book,
Be Sure to Read These Other
AVON ROMANTIC TREASURES

BECAUSE OF YOU *by Cathy Maxwell*
HOW TO MARRY A MARQUIS *by Julia Quinn*
ON BENDED KNEE *by Tanya Anne Crosby*
SCANDAL'S BRIDE *by Stephanie Laurens*
THE WEDDING NIGHT *by Linda Needham*

Coming Soon

TO TEMPT A ROGUE *by Connie Mason*

Susan Kay Law

The Last Man in Town

An Avon Romantic Treasure

AVON BOOKS  NEW YORK

This is a work of fiction. Names, characters, places, and incidents either are products of the author's imagination or are used fictitiously. Any resemblance to actual events, locales, organizations, or persons, living or dead, is entirely coincidental and beyond the intent of either the author or the publisher.

AVON BOOKS, INC.
1350 Avenue of the Americas
New York, New York 10019

Copyright © 1999 by Susan K. Law
Inside cover author photo by Kit Rogers
Published by arrangement with the author
Library of Congress Catalog Card Number: 98-94815
ISBN: 0-380-80496-4
www.avonbooks.com/romance

First Avon Books Printing: June 1999

AVON TRADEMARK REG. U.S. PAT. OFF. AND IN OTHER COUNTRIES, MARCA REGIS-TRADA, HECHO EN U.S.A.

Printed in the U.S.A.

WCD   10   9   8   7   6   5   4   3   2   1

To the newest man in my life,
Garrett Martens Law
We waited for you a long time, sweetheart.
Welcome to the world.

Acknowledgments

Authors are magpies, collecting bits and pieces of ideas and inspiration wherever we go. It is rare that I can point to a single source as sparking the idea for a novel. But in this case I am indebted to Linda Peavy and Ursula Smith, authors of the reference work *The Gold Rush Widows of Little Falls*. While I had to create my own town in order to get rid of *all* the men, the spirit and fortitude of my characters owe much to the women who were left behind in Little Falls.

Chapter 1

August, 1860

Late summer held the town of Maple Falls in a sweltering grip. Night air hung heavy and damp, ripe with the scent of hot earth and river water. It was the kind of night that beat thick and low in a man's blood, making him dream of rumpled sheets and sultry women, of flesh going slick beneath the stroke of his hand.

Lucas Garrett flopped onto his bed, blissfully, gratefully alone.

He gave a relieved groan, sprawling over the full width of his specially made extra-wide mattress.

Such luxury! No one to prod him awake just as he drifted off to a well-earned sleep. No soft voice to politely request a blanket when the night was clearly too damn hot for it. No knee, however shapely, to be suddenly drawn up a little too close to areas he'd rather be protected from stray extremities. No reason to wake up spitting out the hank of silky hair that had ended up in his unsuspecting mouth.

1

Just for a moment, he wondered if his sharp relief meant he was getting old. Surely not; he was only twenty-eight. Even Lucas Garrett needed some time to himself, an occasional night off. Heck, he *loved* women; everyone knew it. After a night or two alone, he'd undoubtedly be back in the saddle with his usual vigor.

He frowned when the prospect didn't provoke a single twinge of anticipation.

Maybe three nights.

Lovely, solitary sleep was just drifting over him when a brisk knock rattled his door on its hinges.

Husband! Father! was his automatic, instinctive response, bringing him up sharply until he remembered. There weren't any husbands and fathers in Maple Falls, not anymore, at least, none worth worrying about. He started to relax.

But the bright, cheerful "Lucas?" that followed the knock had him wondering if an enraged father wouldn't be preferable after all.

"Lucas? It's the third Thursday of the month. Wake up and let me in, darling."

Damn. Flora Fergus, whose anger at her absent husband translated into luscious—and extremely exhausting—enthusiasm. He hadn't actually forgotten that Flora claimed alternate Thursdays, though spending an hour gently chasing off Letty Monroe at sunset had distracted him from the date. And he'd tried to drop enough subtle hints when Flora had visited his store yesterday afternoon to make sure she'd skip their usual rendezvous tonight.

Unfortunately, Flora had never been a terribly subtle woman.

He briefly considered letting her in and just as quickly dismissed the thought. He could try to explain to her that he just wasn't interested, not tonight. But knowing Flora Fergus—and he did know her, intimately well—she'd promptly burst into abundant tears. If there was one thing in the entire world that terrified Lucas Garrett, it was a weeping woman. He'd have her in his arms to comfort her before the first tear finished rolling down her lovely plump cheek. And then he'd *never* get any sleep.

"Luuuu-cas," she called, cajoling and seductive. The doorknob jiggled loudly.

Lucas rolled over and pulled a limp pillow over his head, trying to blot out Flora's voice, telling himself there was absolutely no reason to feel guilty or obligated or any other damn thing.

A feather quill poked through the slack casing and scratched his cheek. The pillow effectively cut off his air, wrapping him in suffocating heat. Unfortunately, it didn't do nearly as good a job at muffling sound.

Hell! He yanked the pillow away, sat up, and groped around on the floor beside his bed. For once, without a woman there to insist on showing off her feminine skills by picking up after him, he'd been able to leave his clothes conveniently nearby.

He hopped into his pants and tugged on a shirt. The only doorway that led to his rooms over the store sat at the top of the outside staircase at the back of the building. Flora blocked that escape route, but these were desperate times. He tiptoed through the sparsely furnished parlor and poked his head through the front window, left wide open in the vain hope of catching a humid breeze from the river.

A big, blurry moon sweated yellow light over the town, revealing the broad, empty street below. He hesitated only long enough to hear the falling tones of Flora's disappointed sob. Lucas swung his leg over the windowsill and dropped the few feet onto the porch roof.

The corrugated iron bowed beneath him, a telltale metal twang ringing into the night. He stilled, certain he'd been given away, but from the back of the store drifted the sound of Flora's wail, now steadily theatrical. Thank God the other businesses nearby were empty; she'd have raised a crowd in no time.

Lucas bumped slowly over the heated metal and lowered himself over the edge of the roof. He swung there, waiting for his momentum to slow, and wondered how he'd ever explain this if someone came across him right then. The truth—that he was fleeing from what every healthy young man in America dreamed of finding, a town full of willing, attractive, and downright eager women with no other men to turn to—sounded preposterous even to him.

He let go, bending his knees as he hit the ground to take the force of the fall. A sharp stone bit into the side of his foot, and for an instant he regretted not taking the time to yank on a pair of boots. But the lock on his door was somewhat less than sturdy, and Flora definitely was not.

Jamming his hands into his pockets, Lucas automatically turned north, parallel to the river, and headed for sanctuary.

Wide, straight streets led past the sturdy

buildings of a town built in a wild burst of giddy boom-town optimism. But now, abandoned businesses blinked hollowly behind broken windows and doors badly in need of fresh paint. The sagging porch tacked onto what had once been Boswell's Emporium, the fading gilded letters on the cracked office window of the *Maple Falls Frontiersman*, and the fallen-down sign that used to proudly announce Tuttle's Boardinghouse all clearly told of forsaken hopes, shattered dreams, and a failing town.

But the depression that had emptied the town and reduced Lucas's business had also eliminated his competitors, leaving his store alone ready to profit when the town recovered. Not to mention that when he'd had enough of quiet solitude, as he undoubtedly would soon, he'd once again relish being surrounded by an entire town of charming and delicious women who could scarcely wait to be led astray. Yes, he was clearly a man who had everything, he reminded himself firmly, made all the more delightful since he'd been the only man in the area who'd had enough sense to realize it. This oddity of mood that made it seem as much a burden as a pleasure would surely burn off tomorrow as easily as a remnant of morning fog.

Moonlight sluiced off the placid, glassy surface of the Mississippi. A shadowy tumble of useless rubble hugged both shorelines, all that remained of what had once been a strong, well-built dam. Hard to believe the water that looked so sluggish now carried enough force to do such damage.

He turned a corner, away from the fickle river. Up ahead, a light burned steadily in Louisa

Rockwell's small cottage. Kept lit to guide her father home, he supposed. Obadiah was no doubt rolling on his pins again, slumped somewhere between home and the entrance to the bar of the Great Northern Hotel. Save Lucas's own, it was the only other surviving commercial establishment in Maple Falls.

On another night, he would have gone in search of Obadiah and lugged him home. He'd done it a dozen times before. But then there would be Louisa's generous, and undoubtedly physical, thank you to deal with, and he'd just . . . rather not.

He sighed deeply. The endless obligations . . . no, the *expectations*, wearied him. Even more so, the continuous gratitude shown him, the necessity of living up to what was anticipated of him, and the responsibility of giving fair and unselfish return for the favors given so freely to him.

Something simply had to be done. He was only one man!

Around one more corner, there was his mother's place. Small and simple, decidedly unprepossessing, it could not have been more different than the graceful brick home they'd occupied in Illinois. The house huddled demurely under the sheltering arms of the great white oak that Lydia Garrett had taken pains to save when she'd had the place built.

Lamplight glinted in one window, speckling delicate patterns on the ground where it fell through a swath of lace curtain. Lydia was still awake, as he'd known she would be. But he never considered stopping. He'd made that mistake only once as a child, going to his mother's room late at night for comfort after a particularly gruesome dream, and he'd learned things about his mother that no nine-year-old should even know existed.

He passed the carefully nurtured hedge of young lilacs and turned, slipping along the edge of the bushes and around the side of the next house. All the windows were dark, but Lucas knew exactly which one he wanted.

First floor, rear corner, overlooking the herb garden. Lucas swung lightly over the sill, brushing aside a filmy cream-colored curtain panel, and quietly entered the room.

His eyes had already adjusted to the night, and he picked out the familiar furnishings, shadowy forms lit by a thin gauze of moonlight.

An oak dresser sat against a nearby wall. He indulged himself, running a finger over the glassy-smooth finish, tracing the frilled edge of a hand-tatted dresser scarf. He lifted a cut-glass bottle, toyed with the gleaming silver of a hand mirror. Familiar, all of it, and yet it still caught him, the essential female mystery. Useless frippery and silly confections, the kind of thing no man would ever bother with. But they always intrigued him, in the way they said *woman*, hinting at things he could explore for a lifetime and never fully understand.

He walked over to the bed. She was fast asleep, of course, and he took a moment to admire the faint gloss of light on clean hair, the pearly sheen of pale, fine skin against a crisp white pillowcase. Even in the heat, she was fully covered, the lacy edge of a sheet tucked high across her chest and turned precisely square over the crazy quilt he knew she'd stitched herself.

Even the air smelled of her, a little spice, a hint of flowers, a lot of good clean soap. He shifted, uncomfortably aware that though his favorite hobby had long been appreciating women and all their unfathomable, secret, and utterly erotic ways, he'd never focused so exactly on *this* particular female.

Just one more sign of how truly addled he was tonight, and more evidence of why he must get his life back in order as quickly as possible. If he kept looking down at her in the moonlight, he might do something truly insane.

"Pris," he whispered. "Wake up, Pris."

She didn't move, but he heard her quick intake of breath, saw the gleam of her irises when her eyes fluttered open.

"I've got to talk to you," he went on.

"Oh," she said, a distinct note of disappointment in her voice, as if she'd just unwrapped an exceptionally promising looking package to find nothing more than a plain pair of cotton stockings, "it's just you."

Chapter 2

Lucas grinned. This was what he liked best about Priscilla Wentworth: she reacted to things, and particularly to him, in a completely different way than any other woman he'd ever known. Their friendship went back nearly as far as he could remember, interwoven as tightly and irrevocably into his life as taking breath. Usually he gave it no more thought, for it was simply *there*, a relationship that had nothing to do with sex, something that was always simmering between him and any other woman whether he lay with them or not.

"Who were you expecting?" he asked. "You were hoping some *other* man was going to sneak into your bedroom in the middle of the night?"

Though her answer was light and teasing, she waited a beat too long to be convincing. "No one but you."

Well, well, he thought, what's this? It would never have occurred to him that Pris would be intrigued by some mysterious man climbing through her window on a sultry summer night. He wasn't sure he approved. Didn't she know a woman could get in all kinds of trouble that way?

"Now see here, Pris—"

She sat up abruptly. "Don't call me that! I am *not* prissy!"

He blinked at her sudden and completely unprecedented vehemence. "But Pris, I've been calling you that for darn near twenty years now, and you've never said a word about it be—"

"Well, you can just stop it. I'm *not prissy*."

"Of course not." He looked at how, even on the hottest night of the year, the crisp cotton of her nightgown bunched high around her neck, the frilled wrists demurely hiding her hands. Her sheets were tucked securely beneath her mattress, so she barely made a ripple beneath their taut surface, as if she hadn't twitched a muscle all night. He doubted so much as a single unruly hair dared to escape its tight braid, and he swallowed an amused smile. Pris was the prissiest woman around, but Lord only knew what she'd do to him if he even hinted at such a thing. Guess he wasn't the only one in an odd mood tonight.

"What am I supposed to call you, then?" he ventured cautiously.

"You can call me Priscilla, like everyone else."

"I don't know," he said, perching himself comfortably at the end of the bed. A ribbon-bedecked three-legged stool was the only other place to sit in the entire room, and he didn't trust the unstable thing to hold him up. "I'm not sure I can do that. Old dogs, and all that. Once I get in the habit of something, I have an awfully hard time changing."

"Make an effort," she said dryly.

"But Pris—"

She raised one warning finger. "—Cilla," he finished quickly, and narrowed his gaze at her. She looked the same as always: eyes calm, mouth prim, face composed, her manner and expression as smooth and undisturbed as her bedclothes. "Is something wrong?"

"Of course not." She selected a match from the tiny floral dish resting on the carved bedside table, flicked it to life, and touched the flame to a lantern. The new light chased shadows and gold into the corners of the room. It should have replaced this unsettling hint of intimacy with their accustomed, friendly ease. Instead, it only made them seem all the more . . . alone.

Lucas frowned. They'd been unaccompanied a thousand times, but they'd never been *alone*.

"So," Priscilla said, her brisk, everyday tone of voice coming as a distinct relief, "what's the problem?"

"What makes you think there's a problem?"

"Of course there is."

"There has to be a problem for me to come see my closest friend?" He didn't want her reading him so easily. Not when he was suddenly having such a difficult time doing the same with her.

"For you to come creeping into my room in the middle of the night, there does."

"I've done it dozens of times before."

"Not for quite some time." She pulled up her legs and tucked her arms around her quilt-covered knees. "Not since you scraped your shin climbing out of Pamelia Fletcher's barn loft and came looking for a bandage because you didn't want to drip blood all the way home. That was nearly a year ago."

So long? There'd been a time when he'd sneaked into Pris's bedroom at least a couple of times a week, his day somehow seeming less than complete if he hadn't seen her. Because he was more comfortable here than almost anywhere else, and because no one else knew him like Pris—or asked less from him. When had it become a rare occurrence? When his nights became more and more occupied with other things ... other women? Or had it simply started to seem less appropriate since his family had followed hers to Maple Falls four years ago, when even he'd had to admit that late-blooming Pris could no longer be considered the little girl next door?

And when had he ever cared what was *appropriate*, anyway?

Her casually spoken words finally sank in. "How did you know it was Pamelia? I didn't tell you whose window it was."

"Of course I knew," she said. "I almost always do."

An undeniable flush scorched the back of his already sweating neck. Not that he was ashamed of anything he'd done. He'd never made a great effort to keep the way he lived his life a secret. But having Pris know it in an abstract and general way seemed very different from her having intimate knowledge of the details—the who and when and how.

"So," she went on, "what's the problem?"

"It's not a problem, exactly." He was not yet

so desperate that he would call being surrounded by eager women a *problem*. It was simply a ... momentary inconvenience. Like the
way even a man who loved his work needed an
occasional Sunday afternoon off. "Did you
know, I had seven invitations to go to the Literary Society tomorrow night?"

"You poor thing." Sympathetic words, but
something airy shaded her tone. He frowned at
her, just to make certain she understood the se-
riousness of his prob ... inconvenience.

"And when I turned them down, though I was
tactful as I could possibly be, four of them
started to cry."

"Oh, dear. I bet you had a terrible time cheer-
ing them up, didn't you?"

"I did!" he said, brightening. He'd *known* his
Pris would be properly sympathetic, once she
got a good picture of the situation. "And on
Wednesday, at least five different women
brought pies to the store, and not a one of them
would be satisfied before I ate a piece right then
and there, while they were watching. I thought
I was going to lose my apples all over Dorothea
Tuttle's shoes."

"I'm sorry I missed it."

"I have three engagements for Sunday dinner.
I couldn't get out of them, no matter how hard
I tried. One at noon, the next at one thirty—three
miles away!—And then—"

Her burst of laughter stopped him cold. He'd
come up with a plan as he'd wandered through
the town, but how was he going to talk her into
helping him if she didn't appreciate the nature
of his dilemma?

Not that it wasn't nice to hear her laugh like that, he thought, distracted. Usually all anyone got out of Pris was a pleasant little trill, something that conveyed contained amusement and cool good manners in equal measure. He always counted it a triumph when he could surprise a really good guffaw out of her, one that made her eyes shine and her chest—what there was of it— jiggle, like now. Still, it wasn't exactly what he had in mind at the moment . . .

"Now, Pris," he began, assuming what he hoped was an irresistibly mournful expression, trying to focus on the issue at hand before the situation got completely out of control. She wasn't going to feel nearly sorry enough for him if it all simply amused her. But at least she'd given up her insistence on having him call her by her full name. "You don't know what I have to put up with!"

Her smile flashed, a gleam of white in the night-shadowed room. "Oh, come now. All those free meals! How fortunate for you. And you can't tell me that when every other man in Maple Falls went running out of town with a pickax over his shoulder and a whiff of gold dust in his nose, you didn't stay behind in good part because you knew precisely what would happen."

"Well, maybe I had a bit of a suspicion. Maybe." Was it his fault he hadn't thought it through completely, hadn't looked beyond dozens of empty beds and empty arms, all just waiting for him? Any man would have had his brain temporarily scrambled by the temptation. "I didn't know how . . . *relentless* they could be."

"Why don't you just go ahead and get married? That'd get rid of them." She paused, reconsidered. "Most of them, anyway," she allowed.

Well, hell. This wasn't going at all the way he planned. "M-m-married?" he managed. "Me? For God's sake, Pris, can you think of any man in the entire state who'd make a worse husband?"

She pressed her lips together so tightly the dusky rose color disappeared into a thin line. "Not necessarily. You're presentable enough, and you make a decent living. If you found a woman who knew what she was getting into, who didn't care about fidelity and commitment and details like that, who wouldn't ever fall in love with you, it might work."

Presentable enough? He decided to let that pass for now, because he was too shocked by the rest of what she was saying. "And where, exactly, am I supposed to find a woman like that?"

"You want me to do everything?" She looked him up and down, as if studying him for possibilities, and he resisted the urge to sit up straight and square his shoulders. This was Pris, damn it. Who was he showing off for? It wasn't as if she'd never looked at him before. He just couldn't remember her ever studying him quite so closely, eyeing his shoulders and his legs. He could almost imagine a gleam of appreciation in her eye, a gleam he was well used to and usually enjoyed thoroughly. But the prospect of it coming from Pris unsettled him, leaving him restless and downright jumpy.

"All right," she admitted. "Maybe it would be difficult to find a woman who wasn't going to fall in love with you. Doesn't mean it would be impossible."

"Now that you mention it," he began, mentally running down the arguments he'd planned to talk her around to his position. Her idea and his weren't all that far apart, if you looked at it the right way.

"Surprised you haven't been caught by now, anyway," she broke in.

"Caught?"

"You know." Her lids lowered over her eyes, as if she were too embarrassed to look at him directly, and he was vaguely relieved. If she'd kept staring at him like that much longer, he'd have started twitching. "Caught. So you had to get married. Like your mother and father."

"Not a chance." He'd made absolutely sure of it, and Pris should have realized it. It was widely known back in Chicago that the only reason William Garrett had married Lydia was because Lucas was on the way. It was even less of a secret how the marriage had worked out, turning into years of infidelity and bitterness and hatred. Or rather, a decade of hostility, followed by years of resigned, resolutely separate lives, capped by a surge of caustic anger when his father's final, lewd, wildly embarrassing act had made it impossible for Lydia to stay in Chicago after his death.

"Certainly there was a *chance*, Lucas, after all—"

"No." The word came out as almost a growl. "I wouldn't let it happen."

"I don't see how you can say—"

"There are ways, Pris."

"Really?" Intrigued, she sat up straighter, leaned his way, her mouth parting as if she were waiting for a kiss. "What ways?"

"Oh, for God's sake." His bare feet thumped against the smooth wood floor, and he sprang from the bed like a scalded bullfrog. So much for Pris being the prissiest woman he knew. The August heat must be melting her brain. "I am *not* discussing this with you."

"Who else would tell me? I might need to know this someday, Lucas. You never know when the information might come in handy."

"No!" He didn't care if he shouted it loud enough to bring Mrs. Wentworth running. Maybe *she* would rescue him.

Priscilla and *sex* were two thoughts that had never knowingly occupied his mind at the same time. Now she'd lodged them both there, right up front, and it made him feel . . . weird. Hot and itchy and a little dizzy. He went to stand by the window, hoping the heat and night would blast the idiotic notions right out of his head, counting on the scent of night-blooming flowers to replace the faint hint of powder and soap that he knew came from her.

It didn't work nearly as well as it should have.

"Lucas?"

He ignored her, blowing air in and out of his lungs, thinking of the most sexless things he could come up with. He began tallying the spools of thread he'd sold that week, calculating the number of barrels of flour he should pick up in St. Cloud, running down his entire stock of farm tools. Finally feeling steadier, more like his usual self, he turned toward her.

It took only one good look at Pris with that bright, questioning look on her face, all neat and shiny and clean, to start him wondering what she'd look like delectably mussed up.

Oh, God. He closed his eyes in self-defense. If he had any sense, he'd run out of here right now and not come back until he was completely back to normal. But then he thought about tomorrow and tomorrow night, and the day after and the night after that, someone always there, always wanting something from him, until he'd given out every last drop of himself. He imagined walking home, women leaping out at him from behind every bush, and decided to stay where he was.

It's just Pris, he told himself. Just Pris. He conjured up a picture of her the first time he'd seen her, poking her nose through the hedge that separated their houses, a skinny six-year-old with wiry braids and thick spectacles and a serious, all-grown-up look on her face. Then, she'd been the only female the scabby-kneed nine-year-old he'd been could tolerate. That had changed quickly enough, but their friendship had never wavered.

Cautiously, he cracked open his lids, and the relief rushed out of him. Now this was his Pris, still looking an awful lot like that odd-duck six-year-old.

But he stayed where he was, with the width of the room safely between them. No reason to push his luck, especially when his luck seemed pretty precarious at the moment.

Time to get back to his original plan. "Actually, Pris, I had sort of the same idea you did."

"You *are* thinking of getting married?" Though it was *her* suggestion in the first place, her words were clipped. Miffed, even.

"Not married, exactly. Just . . . obviously promised to one woman. For a little while, 'til things settled down some."

"Promised? To whom?"

It was so obvious, he couldn't believe he had to be the one to suggest it. "To you, of course."

She went so stiff he was surprised she didn't pop right out of the bed like a broken spring. "To *me?*"

"Who else?" More comfortable now—he'd figured this part all out—he crossed the room and hooked the flimsy stool with his toe, dragging it toward him. He wasn't quite ready to chance the bed again, where too many weird thoughts had jumped into his head, but he guessed he could sit down. "Not a real engagement, of course."

"Of course," she repeated flatly.

"Just pretend. Until everybody gets used to—" *Doing without*, he'd almost said. Stupid, but he'd stopped himself in time. "—Gets used to me being otherwise committed."

"Of course."

Certain he was on the right track now, he plunged on. "There's nobody else I'd trust like you, Pris. Nobody else that I could be sure wouldn't get, um, caught up in the whole charade and get carried away."

"Or that you'd be tempted to, *um*, give up a precious night's sleep for, with all the time you'd be spending together, and all."

"Well, yeah." Though he hadn't planned on mentioning that detail, Pris could always be relied on to see a situation clearly. Eagerly he bent toward her, anxious to explain the rest of his plan, and nearly tipped the useless stool over. "Damn it!"

"Don't swear," Pris said reflexively.

"Sorry," he said, his apology as automatic as her protest. "Besides, Pris, who else would work as well as you? Everybody in town loves you, so no other woman would even think of poaching on your territory. Saint Priscilla."

"You don't think so?"

"Of course not." Time for a little flattery. No woman was completely immune. Not even Pris. "All those things you do for everybody else. Teaching the children after Mr. Babbit ran off. Sewing quilts for the flood victims. Bringing food to darn near everybody. Sitting with anyone who catches a sniffle, especially since Doc Nickerson lit out for Pike's Peak. Bringing—"

"Enough!" She flung up a hand to cut him off. "You make me sound like the worst kind of self-martyring do-gooder."

"Of course not." Hell, he'd been praising her, couldn't she tell? She sounded almost offended. "Everybody adores you for it. I hear it all the time. 'That Priscilla Wentworth, have you ever known such a wonderful girl? Always helping others, she—' "

"Enough, I said." But this time amusement bubbled through. "Dear me, am I that bad?" She shook her head, then dropped her chin to her knees. "Lucas, didn't you, of all people, ever suspect why I do all those things?"

From the way she was eyeing him, he figured

"out of the goodness of your kind and glorious heart" was the wrong answer. "Why?"

"Because I couldn't stand just sitting around anymore! I was desperate for something, anything, to *do*."

"You were *bored*?"

"Yes. Not very noble of me, was it?" She smiled, unrepentant. "Oh, I'm not saying it doesn't have its rewards. But I was going out of my mind. Mother would never have let me get an actual job; it's simply not ladylike, not for the daughter of Levi Wentworth. I'm having a terrible time convincing her she should let me help with Maple Falls Manufacturing, despite my offering at least a hundred times. Bad enough that *she* has to pretend not to be running it. It's only been recently that she's allowed me even the slightest of roles in the company. And there were people who needed help, and there I was with nothing else to occupy me, and all in all it's worked out fairly well."

"Jeanette doesn't seem to need anything to do."

At the mention of her sister's name, Priscilla sighed. "Yes, well . . . I'm not nearly pretty enough to spend all my time simply being decorative."

"Not pretty enough!" Outraged, Lucas came to his feet, sending the stool spinning away. Hell, he'd stand. "Who says you're not pretty enough?"

It had been years since he'd really looked at her, he realized, in more than the most superficial of ways. Why should he? He knew what she looked like.

She looked like Pris.

He would have bet his next year's profit that
Pris considered her beauty or relative lack of it
a triviality unworthy of attention or concern.

She has nice skin, he thought, studying her
now. The low lamplight gave it a soft and delicate sheen. Nice eyes, too. A bright, vibrant
green in daylight, in the semi-darkness they took
on the color of spring leaves as dusk slid into
night. Too bad her spectacles usually distorted
her eyes, making them appear to bulge out in an
unfortunate way. Still, her eyes were warm and
pretty underneath; it didn't take much brains to
see that, did it? And she didn't wear her spectacles to bed.

She did have a lovely mouth. Plump, plush-
looking lips, a luscious peachy-rose color, they
curved so gently—he might have said kissably,
but he'd never thought of kissing her, had he?—
when he could get her to really smile. But a lot
of foolish men probably never got around to no-
ticing her mouth, because they were too distracted by Pris's nose. And there was no getting
around it, Pris's nose was . . . he stopped short of
the word *big*. It wasn't big. It was . . . impressive?
Distinctive? Generous?

What the hell difference did it make, anyway?
Any man worthy of Pris should know exactly
what kind of prize he was getting, or he didn't
deserve her in the first place.

"Who said you're not pretty enough?" he demanded again.

Her smile softened, part resigned, part grateful. "It doesn't matter."

"But—"

She shook her head slightly, dismissing the subject. He'd rather have pursued it, convinced her of her own appeal. Making a woman feel good about her attractiveness was one of his more obvious talents, and he enjoyed it. But he found himself surprisingly uncertain. This was Pris, and the usual words and phrases might not have the same effect on her as they did on most women. Or they could work entirely too well, and he was unwilling to risk anything that might change a relationship that had functioned very well for years just the way it was.

"So, you want us to pretend to . . . court?" she asked. "You think that'll be enough to get them all to leave you in peace?"

"I think so. If you make it clear that you don't want anyone drinking at your well." He grinned, imagining it. Pris, set on a subject, was something to see. "We'll probably at least have to imply there's a wedding upcoming. Maybe even more than imply, if it comes to that."

She tilted her head, considering. "For how long?"

"I don't know. A month or two, maybe three at the most. Just until I've had a fair stretch of peace and quiet." Or I get tired of sleeping alone, he thought. "Maybe only a couple of weeks," he added quickly.

"And then?"

"I guess you'll just have to jilt me, you heartless wench."

"And you'll just have to put up with those sympathetic women waiting to console you?"

"What can I say? I'll be heartbroken."

Priscilla drummed her fingers against her knees. "On one condition."

"Condition?" He'd fully expected her to agree without a murmur. Pris could never resist anyone who really needed her help. She'd certainly never turned him away when he'd needed her. But she sure as hell had never before put any *conditions* on her assistance, either.

"Yes," she said, as businesslike and determined as Levi Wentworth had ever been. "You have to find me a husband."

Chapter 3

"**A** husband?"

Lucas's bark of laughter made Priscilla want to shrink beneath her covers. Was the thought that she might find a husband so outlandish?

And who was he to laugh at her, anyway, considering the suggestion he'd made only a few minutes ago? "What's so all-fired amusing about that? At least I want a real husband, not just a fake sweetheart."

"Hell, Pris, why now? If you really wanted to get married, why didn't you just pick a fellow and be done with it years ago? It's not like you never had any chances."

"Don't swear. And don't remind me." Even now, her own foolishness astounded her.

There had always seemed to be plenty of time and opportunity. Oh, maybe she wasn't particularly pretty, but that had never seemed to matter so terribly much. She was pleasant and personable—at least, she always tried to be—and reasonably healthy. Not to mention that her father's businesses had always prospered, and

25

he'd made it clear he'd be happy to have a son-in-law join him in his ventures.

Back in Chicago, there'd seemed to be little rush. She'd been young enough, silly enough, to want to wait for a man who looked at her like— well, the way they always looked when they first laid eyes on Jeanette. Like heaven had dropped an angel right in front of them and they could hardly believe their own good fortune. Now Priscilla understood what she'd been too childish to realize then. That they could no more stop that look from crossing their faces when they saw Jeanette than Priscilla herself could keep from smiling on the first truly glorious day of spring. And that it wasn't how a man looked at a woman the first time he saw her that mattered, but the expression in his eyes after he knew her a month, six months, six years that made all the difference.

But before she'd figured all that out, her father's entrepreneurial eye had been caught by the challenge of building a business and a town, perhaps even an empire, out of nothing, and they'd moved here. At first, there'd been a hundred men for every woman, and the wealth had overwhelmed her. She couldn't blame herself for that too much. What woman wouldn't have been a little dazzled by all those strong young men, loggers and millers and fur traders, all competing for the prize of just a snippet of a woman's time?

It was harder to admit that she'd been waiting. Waiting to meet a man who'd make her heart beat harder just by walking into the room. Whose smile would make her breath stutter in her chest, whose mere existence would make her feel like she did on that first spring day. Before she'd had a chance to outgrow those girlish dreams, they'd all vanished under the sorrow of her father's death, rapidly followed by the death of his dream for Maple Falls. Just when Priscilla had finally come to her senses, had realized that settling for shared goals and mutual respect was an acceptable, even desirable, trade for the opportunity to begin the family she'd always wanted, the male population of Maple Falls had been swept with a disease more powerful and contagious than any she'd ever encountered: gold fever. And all those men had abandoned Maple Falls.

All those men but one. The one who was now standing by her bed, staring down at her with clear shock, and more than a little distaste, written across his familiar features.

"Why would you want to go and do a thing like get married, anyway?"

"I just do." There seemed no point in trying to explain it to him. Not when just the mention of marriage caused him to shudder in revulsion. Not when he'd grown up with such a terrible and painful example of the institution, and he was obviously as miserably unsuited to it as the father he resembled so much had been. Had she grown up in the Garrett household, she might well have the same opinion.

But she hadn't. Her own parents' marriage had been everything Lydia and William Garrett's had not: loving, solid, and supportive. She'd always assumed she'd have the same someday. But her impatience had been sparked only a year ago, growing more insistent, stronger, with each change of the season. The drive to simply *get on* with it, to build a home and life of her own. She was tired of waiting, filling empty days with other people's children and other people's problems.

"Where'm I supposed to find you a husband, anyway? The only man around is Obadiah Rockwell, and I'd marry you myself before I'd let you stoop that low."

"Don't even say that." She grimaced.

"Was that frown for Obadiah or for me?"

"What do you think?"

He grinned at her, with a smile that transformed him, turned him from a pleasantly nice-looking man to the most appealing one she'd ever seen, even when there'd been hundreds of attractive men in Maple Falls.

Oh, he wasn't plain. Far from it. His hair, dark and glossy as her mother's mahogany sideboard, almost matched his eyes. His features were even and strong. But she'd known more handsome men.

No, it was his smile that did it. Even she, who should have become immune years ago, felt its temptation, how it promised, *You'll never have as much fun as you will with me.* And if she sometimes suspected that Lucas's smile hid as much as it revealed, she was certain she was the only one who did.

His grin faded slowly, dimming until it was only a shallow remnant of itself. "You're serious, aren't you?"

"I've never been more serious in my life. And you know that's pretty serious."

"I wouldn't even know where to start," he

said. "I've never put much thought into how someone would go about finding a husband."

"I didn't think you had." She'd expected Lucas to be more entertained by her wish to get married than anything else. But after his initial laughter, he now seemed almost concerned. Shadows had blotted out the usual twinkle in his dark eyes.

Likely it was a trick of the dim light, she decided. Or perhaps he didn't like the idea of losing his co-conspirator too quickly. "However, you must know a *few* eligible men. Merchants you've dealt with, or businessmen in St. Cloud. Old friends of yours. You have access to men that I don't. Not to mention that you'd have an easier time finding out about their, ah, personal habits than I would. And, of course, since you know what makes a bad husband, that should give you *some* insight into who might make a good one."

"Of course," Lucas agreed flatly. He didn't understand why her last line twinged painfully in his belly. He'd always known full well he'd make an abysmal husband. But there was something about hearing her state it so matter-of-factly, as she sat in her virgin-white bed, eyes gleaming with nerves and anticipation like she was already waiting for her worthy bridegroom, that made him want to start throwing things. Mess up her perfect little room and her perfect little dream of marriage.

He was used to being the one to make her smile like that, damn it . . . not some fantasy husband she'd conjured out of a young girl's plans and an old maid's hopes.

"So you're really not going to help me out if I don't promise to start scrounging you up a husband?"

"Only some reasonable candidates," she pointed out. "I'll take it from there."

"That's not fair," Lucas complained. "All you have to do is pretend. I've got to dig up a real live man willing to marry you when every man in town headed for Jefferson Territory six months ago. That's *much* harder."

"Oh? You think so?" she asked, in a tone that could have iced the Mississippi over in an instant.

"That's not what I meant," he added hastily, realizing what she must have thought. "It's not that I don't think that dozens of men ... thousands of men, *millions* of men would be eager to marry you. I'm just not sure where to begin looking for one that's nearly good enough for you."

Now that he thought of it, that was going to be a real problem. He tried to picture Pris with any one of the unmarried men he knew and all he got was a vaguely sick feeling in his gut. There was a terrible flaw with every single one of them. Oh, they were good enough fellows to bend an elbow with in a saloon, but there was no way in hell he would consider letting Pris actually *marry* one of them.

"Besides," Pris went on, "what makes you so certain anyone will believe that you and I are sparking? I imagine most everyone will think that if we were really going to fall for each other, it should have happened years ago."

"There's their faith in your impeccable honesty," he said. "And then, of course, there's this."

He moved so quickly she never saw it coming. He was sitting beside her on the bed with her hand in one of his, the other cupping her cheek, before she had time to so much as blink.

Oh my, she thought shakily as her thoughts began to cloud and swirl, is *this* what it's like? His hand around hers was big, hard, strong . . . and terribly gentle, making her feel fluttery and feminine and young. His thumb traced her jaw, whisked the tip of her chin, rubbed down her neck to where her pulse beat hard against his touch. She caught herself just before she tilted her head right into the heat of his palm. Why, when she was already so hot, did that warmth draw her so much? He had one long leg pulled up on the bed, his bare foot dark and very male against the neatly embroidered patches of her quilt, his knee brushing her thigh, and the blankets between them felt much thinner than they should have. Had any man's leg ever touched hers before, she wondered wildly? How terribly wasteful if it hadn't.

And his face; dear Lord! His expression of utter focus and complete appreciation was the most tempting thing of all. The look that said that there was no other woman in the world nearly as interesting, nearly as fascinating, nearly as desirable as she was.

She'd seen him wear that look so many times before, gazing at other women, and often wondered why it always seemed to work. It wasn't that there was anything false about it. She was certain that, every time, Lucas meant it absolutely. But Lucas's attention was both temporary and non-exclusive.

"I don't think," he murmured, each syllable a seduction, another spur to senses already reeling, "that making anyone believe it will be a problem."

"I—" She couldn't make the words come out right, and slid her tongue over lips that suddenly seemed too dry. His gaze fell there immediately, eyes dark with what looked distinctly—impossibly—like speculation. Like anticipation. "I—"

"That's really good, Pris," he said, his voice still that low, slow whisper fairly vibrating with sex, "the stuttering. You sound just like a young girl caught in the grip of her first passion. No one will ever suspect you're faking it."

Faking it? She wasn't sure if it was hurt or anger that saved her, and she didn't care. Straightening abruptly, she knocked aside the hand still stroking her neck. "It's too hot to have your sweaty hands on me," she snapped. "Get away."

His expression vanished as if it had never been. Which, Priscilla reflected, was true. It had never existed, not really. It had only been an illusion built from Lucas's years of experience and his current desperation.

"Of course," he said, swiftly rising from the bed. Even with his wrinkled pants and unbuttoned shirt and bare feet, he stood formal and remote as a well-trained butler, giving nothing of himself away. She felt a totally foolish pang of regret, even as she forced herself not to try and see through the shadows to what lay under that loosely hanging shirt panel. "Do we have a deal?"

There was still another possibility, she reminded herself. But that chance was distant and uncertain, while Lucas was right here, and very real.

Even so, the answer came surprisingly hard.

"Yes," she agreed. "Go ahead. Make everyone believe we're in love."

Everyone but me.

Chapter 4

The silvered glass hanging over her bureau, as spotlessly clean as the rest of her room, reflected her face with ruthless accuracy. Priscilla wished that for once she'd done a less perfect job of cleaning, so a few smudges and streaks would soften her image.

She tugged at the waist of her sleeveless jacket, her fingers leaving damp ovals on the black corded silk. It was her best dress, brown Irish poplin trimmed with darker brown velvet. It was only three years old, bought just before the initial flood swept away the dam meant to power the mill and factory, causing her father to suffer the first of what proved to be several financial setbacks.

She'd never worn it to a Friday Literary Society meeting before. Would her mother and Jeanette even notice, and would they comment if they did? Lucas would probably prefer that, right from the start, they give the impression that *this* Friday, as he escorted her, was different from every other time he'd done so. But she'd rather begin the charade with someone other than her family.

Peering closer into the mirror, she tried pinching some color into her chalk-white cheeks. Oh, what was the use? She could gild all she wanted and she'd never be a lily.

It shouldn't matter. It *didn't* matter, she told herself, except that she'd agreed to the bargain and so was wholly committed to furthering its success. Therefore she must appear to be a woman who could permanently fix Lucas's attention.

Not that Lucas was only seen with the loveliest women. He appreciated women of all varieties, found beauty in women less than conventionally pretty. But surely the woman who captured his heart, not merely his momentary regard, would be someone quite spectacular.

Oh, *why* had she ever thought this could work? But then, she hadn't really thought, had she? She'd been seduced, first by the prospect of having Lucas dig up an eligible man for her to marry, something she'd nearly given up hope on. And then by Lucas himself, in that instant he'd sat beside her on her bed and laid his hand against her throat.

She'd always prided herself on being different from the other women in his life. And here it had turned out that she couldn't resist him, either. How utterly ridiculous of her!

"Priscilla?" Jeanette called from the hallway. "Are you ready to go? Lucas is coming up the walk."

Priscilla pressed a hand to her chest to still her fluttering heart, afraid its hard, erratic beat could be seen beneath the dark fabric. She was so terribly nervous. Not because Lucas was escorting her; foolishness that could be excused during a hot and moonlit night would simply not be tolerated in daylight. But she was completely unaccustomed to this level of subterfuge. How on earth was she to manage such a thing?

She reached for the hat she'd chosen for the evening. A veiling of lace overlay the straw base, almost hidden beneath silk fuchsia peonies and clusters of bright green grapes. There, she thought, settling it firmly on her head. Who would notice her nose when she was wearing such a glorious creation?

"Didn't you hear me?" Jeanette burst into the room with her usual flourish. "Lucas is looking remarkably fine tonight, even for him. If you don't hurry up, I might be tempted to steal your escort."

Eyes trained carefully on her reflection, Priscilla poked at the blue-winged butterfly that was the magnificent grace note to the milliner's art. Jeanette hadn't meant anything by that last comment. No more than either Jeanette or her father's assistant, Robert, had meant to fall head over heels in love the instant they'd laid eyes on each other.

It had been no secret when Levi Wentworth had hired a bright young Northwestern graduate, Robert Stephens, as his assistant, and brought him to Maple Falls that he'd hoped he'd found a husband for his older daughter. At first, Priscilla had resented him, for she'd dearly hoped to join her father's business herself someday. But she'd had to admit that her parents wouldn't allow such a patently improper thing, for business was an unfeminine endeavor. And Robert had been so kind and charming, so interested in her ideas and opinions, that she had begun to envision . . . not the future, precisely, but possibilities—vague nascent dreams of their working together both in and out of the office.

But while Robert had respected Priscilla, it had been Jeanette he had loved. Now, as Priscilla turned to face her sister, she wondered if Jeanette had ever regretted it. It could not have been easy for her when Robert had decamped for the goldfields soon after their marriage. He'd abandoned their father's business in the face of so many difficulties after Levi's death. As close as she and Jeanette were, they'd never discussed it. Certainly Jeanette seemed as always; the sparkle in her bright green eyes hadn't dimmed one bit. Her smile still seemed to light the sun.

"For heaven's sake, Priscilla, aren't you ready yet?"

Her musings had distracted and calmed her. Hands steady now, Priscilla tugged on a pair of spotless cotton gloves. "How do I look?"

Tilting her head, Jeanette appraised her seriously, for appearances were serious business. She eyed Priscilla's hat but nobly refrained from comment, having learned long ago that Priscilla didn't take well to criticism of her headgear. "You look well, though I don't know why you insist on wearing such colors. I've offered you my green muslin more than once. The color would suit you as well as me. You could change right now."

"I thought I was running late as it was."

"There's always time for a little primping," Jeanette said, dimpling prettily. "The fact that there are no men around to appreciate it doesn't mean it's not still worthwhile."

"No men?" Priscilla headed for the hallway. "I'm going to tell Lucas you said that."

"Lucas doesn't count," Jeanette said, falling into her usual position two steps behind. Jeanette claimed Priscilla always walked too fast. In return, Priscilla insisted Jeanette simply liked to make an entrance.

"First of all," she continued, "you've known him forever. It's not the same. I'm not sure he ever noticed you grew up. Which is strange, come to think of it; he notices everything else. And even if he did, it's still Lucas. When was the last time he didn't appreciate a woman? Where's the challenge in that?"

He never noticed me.

Priscilla came to a halt just outside the doorway leading to the parlor. From within came the low murmur of voices, her mother's precise syllables followed by Lucas's low rumble, and the gentle clink of china—ever the thoughtful hostess, her mother had no doubt offered tea when her daughter had been slow to appear.

Drawing a shaky breath, Priscilla tugged again on the bottom of her vest. How was a smitten woman preparing to meet a suitor supposed to look? She pasted on a nervous smile.

"Are you all right, Priscilla?" Jeanette asked. "I didn't mean it like that, you know. It's not as if he ever noticed me either. Just watch. He'll glance our way, and say something routine about how delightful we look, three such lovely ladies in the same family, and that will be the end of it. I swear, it used to make me feel downright plain."

"You've never felt plain in your entire life."

"It's as close as I ever want to come."

She was stalling, Priscilla realized, standing here teasing Jeanette. She never stalled, preferring to complete unpleasant tasks as quickly as possible. But then, neither had she set out to perpetrate a lie on her family, much less the entire town. Once she stepped through that door there'd be no more opportunity to back out gracefully.

Why had she ever let him talk her into this? She drew on the dreamy image she'd been carefully building for years, that of a man—not handsome, perhaps not even young, but kind and respected and well dressed—taking her hand to pull her beside him, watching together as their children played in the yard of their house.

That was why, she reminded herself. It was a good reason, a well-considered one.

Lucas and her mother occupied two chairs near the carved mantel on the far side of the room. A fine blue-and-white china cup cradled safely in his big hands, Lucas sprawled comfortably, one knee bent, looking all the more big and male in the delicate floral-patterned chair. Her mother bent to refresh his tea, beaming at him as few proper and concerned mothers ever did, for they were the one species of female immune to his charms because they were so deeply worried by them.

But Clara Wentworth had always been fond of

Lucas. Perhaps because she'd seen him grow up,
perhaps because he was the son of her oldest
friend. Or maybe because Clara understood that
he posed no danger to *her* daughters, and so
she'd treated him much as if he'd been her son.

The instant Priscilla stepped into the room,
Lucas looked up, his gaze unerringly finding
her. She waited for his expected reaction, the cur-
sory glance and the automatic, glib compliments.
Jeanette had made no great prediction, for his
reaction was always the same.

But not this time. He looked her over, tip to
toe, his gaze sliding over her slow as winter
syrup. Just for an instant, their eyes met, his dark
with distinct alarm. He whipped his gaze up, fix-
ing it over her left shoulder.

His Adam's apple bobbed against the crisp
edge of his shirt. And then he smiled, lazy and
fully appreciative, and rose to his feet as if he
had all the time in the world.

Usually, Lucas moved quickly, all crackling
energy and quick purpose. But when he set himself to wooing a woman, everything changed, his
voice and manner becoming as easy and unhur-
ried as a long summer afternoon. She'd asked
him about it once; he'd just grinned and said no
woman liked a man to rush. She supposed it
made a woman feel important, as if he would
rather spend time with her than hurry off to do
something else.

It was a good thing, she'd decided long ago,
that people got married. If they spent all their
time wooing, nobody'd ever get anything done.

"Pris."

That was it. Just "Pris." But somehow he

seemed to put all sorts of nuances into the single syllable of her name, so that it meant a hundred wonderful things, as if he couldn't think of any other word that was nearly good enough. As if any easy compliments were just too trite and shallow to use, so he'd just whispered her name.

My, oh my, she thought. He is *so* good at this.

"Are you ready to go?"

"Yes," she said, and she didn't even have to work to get the breathless quality in her voice. Perhaps this would be easier than she'd expected.

"If you'd wait just a moment," Jeanette put in from beside her, "Let me find my hat, and I'll be able to walk with you."

"Well, actually," Lucas said smoothly, "I'd promised to get there a bit early tonight. Gotta check the rigging on the stage curtain. So I'd like to go right away . . . if you don't mind."

"Of course not." Clara transferred teacups to a tray. "Jeanette and I will meet you there."

Just like that, he'd maneuvered so the two of them would be seen walking alone together, arriving at the schoolhouse as a couple. Neither Jeanette nor Clara showed the slightest bit of suspicion. Even her own ever-proper mother had never seemed at all concerned to find Priscilla alone with Lucas. Priscilla might have been insulted if it hadn't been so convenient. And if she hadn't chosen to believe that it was tangible proof of Clara's faith and trust in her rather than indication that even her own mother thought her incapable of attracting Lucas's attentions.

He stepped forward, and it was obvious that Lucas, too, had taken pains to appear as if this

were a night out of the ordinary. In deference to
the heat he wore no jacket, but his collar was
crisply fresh against his tanned neck. A perfect
crease bisected the line of his trousers, and his
polished brogans winked at her as he moved.

But his attention, oddly, was still focused on
the air above her left shoulder. Did he think she
had so little control that if their eyes met, she'd
give the whole thing up? Perhaps he had some
slight justification for thinking that. Once, when
they'd dropped a fat little frog in Jeanette's milk
cup, they'd been unable to stop giggling at each
other over the table and Jeanette had been
warned before she'd even taken a sip.

That was years ago, though. She had pounds
of self-control now, tons of self-control, more
self-control than most anyone she knew. Obviously far more than he had.

As she slipped her arm through the crook of
his formally offered arm, however, she had to
fake a little cough to cover a betraying hitch in
her breathing—due entirely, she assured herself,
to concern over their forthcoming "debut," and
not at all to the feel of his hard-muscled forearm,
shifting smoothly beneath her palm.

But wasn't it convenient, she thought, as they
made their way out into the sun-ripe evening,
that all that lugging of boxes and barrels Lucas
did made such a very *nice* arm to hold on to?

The first women descended two blocks before
he and Pris reached the schoolhouse. Lucas
never saw them coming.

He'd been understandably preoccupied. For
who would have expected that just having Pris's

small, well-kept hand resting lightly on his arm would send him into reams of heart-pounding fantasies, damn near overwhelming *paroxysms* of fantasies, of a soft white hand sliding over his chest and his thighs and his crotch? So many images, so vivid, that he had one hell of a time walking straight? After all, he'd surely walked down Center Street, her arm linked with his, a hundred times before, yet he'd never felt like this. He was sure he would have remembered.

He'd been so certain that last night, in her room, was some strange aberration. A brief, very temporary madness caused by the heat and Pris's absurd fixation with marriage.

But he'd glanced up as she'd entered the parlor and it had hit him, *boom*, like a stick of dynamite had exploded beneath his chair. That drab brown-and-black dress just made him want to rip it off; she'd look so much better without it. The chalky pallor of her skin only made him long to kiss her, good and hard, to bring her color up.

He hadn't even dared look at her again. Still hadn't, though thankfully he'd gotten his brain to function well enough to put on a little show for Pris's family.

It wasn't as if Pris was even sexually appealing. She was a managing kind of female, appallingly neat, and downright picky about some things. She was also unexpectedly funny, had more temper than most people suspected, was three-quarters heart and all female, and . . . well, all right, she *was* sexually appealing. Head-spinningly so. So what? It hadn't just happened overnight. He'd overlooked it completely for at least a decade. Surely he could continue to resist for another ten years. By then, he or she or both of them would be too damn old for it to matter anymore.

So he'd decided, turning the fantasy that he couldn't quite rid himself of into someone else entirely. As they turned the corner in front of the pathetic shack Herman Meirdorf had abandoned six months ago, he was breathing much harder than the stroll called for, deep into a vision of himself and someone who resembled but certainly was not Pris, who wore the shredded remains of a nightdress almost exactly like the ridiculous tent Pris had been wearing last night.

So he'd not seen them coming. The Sturgis twins and Sarah Jane Bosworth had all set upon him at once. He must have been further gone than even he'd realized, because while he might not have seen them coming, he sure as hell should have heard them, for they arrived with a nerve-shredding screech of laughter like the scream of a red-tailed hawk falling on its unsuspecting prey.

None of them was more than seventeen. Flush with the novelty and power of new womanhood, all they really wanted was a little male attention and admiration, something in frustratingly short supply. He was usually content to give it to them; it was easy to do, far less than most asked from him, and it made them so happy. If only they didn't express their pleasure in such shrill tones, he'd be even happier.

But this time he'd just mentally peeled back the last ragged ribbon that hung straight from his imaginary lover's collarbone to her toes, fluttering between her breasts and coyly hiding the good parts, so the girls' arrival came as a rude and unwelcome shock.

A pang of guilt for what he was about to do hovered as he waited for the opportunity to pounce. It wouldn't take much—a warm smile and a couple of compliments, and the three girls would be happily debating whether it was better to be called *lovely* or *delightful* for weeks. But for their plan to succeed, he had to give clear notice that from now on, all his time and energy and enthusiasm were reserved for Pris and Pris alone.

Frances Sturgis, the smallest—and quickest— of the three, swiftly appropriated his right arm. Sarah Jane took up a station right in front of him, scuttling backward as they walked, nattering on about the new bonnet she planned to buy next week. Nellie Sturgis hovered to Pris's left, her head cocked and eyes bright as a robin ready to pounce on the first juicy worm of spring. Except that the worm she coveted was Pris's choice position on Lucas's arm.

He gave a distracted "hmmm" and bent what he hoped was an obviously lovestruck smile on Pris. His back teeth ground together and he was afraid he looked more like a raving lunatic than an enamored suitor; hell, it wasn't as if he'd had any experience with the emotion. He might be a world-class lover—something that could be attributed, he figured, as much to other men's short-sighted concentration on their *own* pleasure as to his own innate gifts—but he'd no experience at all at being in love. He'd not even particularly made much study of the subject. He suddenly, and somewhat belatedly, wondered if he'd be able to put on a convincing show.

Pris's answering smile was far more genuine than his, though hardly lover-like. She was too busy being entertained at his expense, clearly waiting to see how he'd handle the girls. Then all three laughed at once, a noise that would have made nails on slate sound positively melodious. Pris winced, her amusement turning rapidly to pity.

He bent to whisper in her ear—closer than he should have, for his lips brushed the warm curve of skin. But the girls were watching, and that was the point, wasn't it? "I told you it was a terrible burden."

"Lucas?" Frances gave a firm tug to his sleeve.

"I hadn't fully considered," Pris whispered back, "precisely what you've been so cheerfully enduring all these months." Her eyes sparkled behind her lenses, brilliant green under glass. The practice must have helped, for this time his besotted expression came much more easily.

"Lucas!" Another yank, one that damn near popped the stitches on his shoulder seam.

"What?" He reluctantly turned to Frances.

"I—I was asking, which do you think would look better for a new dress, the sky-blue silk, or the dark green serge you got in last week?" She peered up at him hopefully, teeth worrying her bottom lip, eyes pleading for him to say "Either one, for you'd look pretty no matter what you wore."

Intending to brush her off, he opened his mouth to spout something discouraging . . . and found he couldn't do it. Particularly not when they all knew full well Frances wouldn't be able to afford a new dress anytime soon. It was too much like kicking a puppy. What would it cost him to flatter the girl a little?

In the back of his mind somewhere, he knew that wouldn't bode well for his dream of peace and solitude. That it might well be like giving Obadiah Rockwell a few swallows of whiskey, making him crave it all the more. But the habits of a lifetime were hard to ignore, and he couldn't bring himself to be that cruel.

Against his side, Pris took a firmer grip on his arm and snuggled up close. One breast pressed firm against his biceps, and for a moment he forgot everything but that softly resilient warmth. Old habits again; just the prospect of making do without touching breasts—surely one of God's finest creations—for a few weeks, and already he was fixating on the nearest ones handy. Much nicer ones than he'd ever realized, too. He came back to himself just in time to catch the last of Pris's words.

". . . We do dearly appreciate your indulging us in this matter. I *knew* I could count on sophisticated and experienced young women such as yourselves to understand the difficulty in our finding a few moments alone, and that you would be kind enough to grant us this precious time."

Bless her magnificent heart, Pris was rescuing him. He considered kissing her right then and there, full on her glorious mouth—purely out of gratitude, of course—before deciding that was tempting fate. The last thing the Sturgis twins needed were more ideas.

The girls, clearly befuddled, glanced back and forth between Lucas and Pris as if the truth of this odd turn of events might be written on their foreheads. He could almost see the thoughts whirling in their young heads. *Lucas and Priscilla Wentworth? Alone? Whatever for? Surely not that.*

But they could hardly refuse a request from Pris, even one so delicately put. Hadn't she stayed all night with Sarah Jane when Mrs. Bosworth had been forced to travel down to St. Paul, trying to extend the notes her husband had left when he lit out for Gambol Gulch? Sarah Jane had been afraid to be alone because Sioux war parties were crossing just north of their place, heading for Chippewa land. Didn't she give the twins her copy of *Godey's Lady's Book* just a week after she'd received it and when she probably hadn't even read it yet? Not to mention the dozen other things she'd likely done for them that he didn't even know about.

As soon as Frances heaved a disappointed sigh and released his arm, Pris towed him off down the street, leaving the bewildered girls behind.

"I thought I'd never get you away before you said something stupid!" she snapped.

"I wasn't going to—"

"Oh, yes you were. I could tell. You would have said something to Frances about how there wasn't a length of cloth in your entire store that could ever do justice to her coloring, tactfully giving her a way out, since you know she couldn't afford it anyway, and you wouldn't have been able to pry her off your side all evening."

She was right, of course. So much so that he didn't dare admit it to her.

From up ahead came the clatter of arriving wagons, the vibrant soprano trill of female laughter, and the murmur of conversation. In a town where entertainment had mostly succumbed to survival months ago, the Literary Society meetings were a cherished and much-anticipated diversion. Since the Reverend Dada had left, too, ending church services in Maple Falls, Lucas and Priscilla could not have picked a more public and well-attended occasion to unveil their new "relationship." By tomorrow, every woman in Morrison County would know that Lucas Garrett had finally been caught.

Priscilla stiffened beside him, her grip on his arm cutting off the circulation from the elbow down.

Time to start the show, he decided, and gently drew his finger along the edge of her set jaw. She just stared up at him, looking more like a woman preparing to undergo surgery than show off her newest conquest. "I'm going to owe you *two* husbands before this is all over, aren't I?"

The lines of her face eased. Color blushed lightly over her cheekbones, as if she'd been nipped by a cool wind.

"One good one will do," she said softly.

Chapter 5

❧⟪⟫❧

*F*inally. Priscilla plopped on a schoolhouse bench beside Lucas and removed her hat. She thought they'd never get here.

Unfortunately, it turned out the other women of Maple Falls were much harder to dissuade than a trio of twittering adolescents. Half a block from the schoolhouse, Lucas and Priscilla had been engulfed in a flurry of bright dresses and bright smiles and bright expectations.

And they all wanted Lucas. Oh, in different ways, for different reasons, but they wanted him just the same. So much so that despite what even Lucas had to admit were Priscilla's best efforts, they were mostly oblivious to her presence by his side.

Some of the thin, tense women, worry lines etched into prematurely aging faces, depended on Lucas for their families' survival. Priscilla knew Lucas extended more credit than good business dictated, and made many an unnecessary trip to St. Cloud, peddling their butter and eggs. Since he was "going to town anyway." At least these women acknowledged Priscilla, giving her a quick smile and greeting after the hesitantly grateful one they gave Lucas.

Not so for the rest. Women hoping for a little male attention simpered and flattered Lucas so outrageously Priscilla thought his head might swell too big to get through the front door. Others clearly wanted something much more personal from him. They gave him secret smiles and pointed their bodices in his direction with such single-minded enthusiasm that Priscilla had to practically plant herself in front of Lucas and shout "Hello" into their faces to gain their notice.

And there were those who'd apparently decided that a faithless man was preferable to no man at all. They invited him for walks and offered him food, trying mightily to prove their domestic skills. Priscilla might have laughed, embarrassed at her own sex's machinations, amused by the way they skirmished over Lucas as if he were the last blueberry tart, had their actions not cut painfully close to home.

For in the end, weren't they after the same thing she was—*a man*? A man to give them all the things they couldn't give themselves.

Priscilla shuddered. Lucas slipped his arm around her waist and pulled her closer to his side. "Surely you're not cold?"

"No. Of course not."

Fingering the bright peony petals on the hat resting in her lap, she forced the doubt away. Her search for a husband was not an impulsive move nor a greedy one. She couldn't afford to falter now. She'd just make sure that the man she married was getting a fair bargain in the process, one he'd sought with as much forethought and anticipation as she had.

And doubt was the least of what plagued her. There were also Lucas's hands. On her. Constantly. The first time had been a shock, for in public Lucas was always properly circumspect, even with his lovers. His eyes, his smile, were something else entirely, but he'd always kept his hands well within the bounds of propriety. So she hadn't expected it when, just as they'd entered the schoolyard, he'd reached over and, with slow deliberation, tugged the cotton glove from her hand before pointedly enfolding it in his. It was a more obvious gesture than she'd ever seen him use. But then, no one had noticed the more subtle ones.

A shock, yes. As if she'd been scuffling on carpet before he'd touched her. A vibration began in her palms and thrummed its way up her arms, reverberating in her flesh and heart.

His arm was draped warm and heavy around her back. Too public, too . . . *there.* She edged away, hoping he wouldn't notice, and tried to concentrate on her surroundings rather than on the man beside her.

Cloth-covered tables laden with plates of cookies and sandwiches stood beneath the tall windows. The four huge pitchers made her smile; they held not lemonade, but simply water, from the spring her father had discovered when he'd first explored the townsite. The first thing he'd done was negotiate to buy it from the Chippewa; the second was to deed it to his planned town.

A wire, stretched across the front of the room, sagged, lopsided, beneath the weight of a dark calico curtain, drawn to one side. Flora Fergus, who stood in the center of a stage thrown together of rough lumber, had begun an enthusiastic reading of "Curfew Must Not Ring Tonight." If Flora's voice didn't carry so well, no one would have been able to hear a thing above all the sniffling going on, for most of the women present could imagine only too well the prospect of losing a lover.

In the sea of worn calico and faded cotton, the only males present besides Lucas were either under the age of sixteen or over the age of seventy. And few enough of the latter, for more than one man whose legs were scarcely spry enough to carry him had followed the siren call of gold.

A burst of enthusiastic applause followed Flora's recitation. She flashed a proud, intimate smile in Lucas's direction. He ignored her, bending even closer to Priscilla.

"It's not working, you know," Priscilla told him. The few discerning women who'd even noticed her presence by Lucas's side sent pitying looks her way, as if unsurprised that she, too, had finally fallen beneath Lucas's spell. *Welcome to the club,* they seemed to say.

"It will," he said, full of so much male confidence that she wanted to dump a pitcher of water over his head. *He* wasn't the one being dismissed as too uninteresting to capture the attention of Lucas Garrett.

Instead, Priscilla fixed her mouth in a loverly smile.

"*Must* you lean so close?" she whispered through set teeth.

"Yes," he answered, practically nuzzling her neck. The man was taking shameful advantage. She'd agreed to fake an intimate relationship; she hadn't agreed to let him practically smother her in front of the entire town.

"I can hardly breathe."

"If you faint, I'll catch you. I promise," he said. "Might be a good idea, anyway. Show just how overcome you are by my charms."

"Lucas, if you don't back off, I swear, I'll hand you off to Flora without—"

"By the way," he broke in cheerfully, "did I tell you about my old friend Calvin Putnam? Owns a flour mill down by Sauk Rapids. Decent fellow, widowed almost two years now. But then, I'm sure he's too dull for you. Probably shouldn't bother—"

"I like dull. I *adore* dull. Excitement is highly overrated, as I'm sure you are only too painfully aware. So transitory. So . . . *insubstantial.*"

He narrowed his eyes at her. "Enough."

"So trivial."

"Enough, I said." He squeezed her waist lightly. His hand came to rest by her hip, brushing up against her rump. The intimacy caught her off-guard, made her breath catch in her throat. It was so easy for him, and so entirely new to her. "I promise to find you someone so dull and dependable and downright reliable you'll sleep through the wedding."

"Good."

"Not to mention the wedding night."

She slanted him a sidelong glance. "You know, the Sturgis twins have been standing there by the refreshment table for quite a while. I'm sure they'd like to sit down. I'll just go ahead and change places with them, shall I?"

"You know something, Pris?" He reached up, smoothing a damp strand of hair off her forehead, his touch light and sure and somehow more genuine than any that had come before. "You're a wicked woman underneath all that starch. And I'm the only one who knows it."

"Well." She cleared her throat, touched and a little dazzled by the thought. Wicked? *Her?* "You'd best remember that, then."

"Oh, I'll remember."

Priscilla was relieved when Louisa Rockwell took the stage, giving her an excuse to turn away from Lucas's unsettling gaze. Polite, resigned applause greeted the announcement of the upcoming recitation, for while the sentiments were certainly admirable, "Lips That Touch Liquor Will Never Touch Mine" somewhat lacked entertainment appeal, particularly after Mrs. Fergus's heart-tugging selection.

But Louisa had the fire of her convictions, her pretty face growing pink and glistening with her exertion. Lucas could hardly help but notice, Priscilla supposed, glancing his way.

But Lucas wasn't looking at the stage at all. His dark eyes still studied her intently, sparking with wickedness and promise. How *did* he manage that expression? If she could pull it off, she'd catch a husband in no time.

Had he been watching her all this time? Had she scratched her nose or breathed with her mouth open or done something equally unattractive?

"So? Is it true?" she whispered, just to distract him.

"Is what true?"

She tipped her head toward the stage. "Do lips that touch liquor never touch hers?"

"I'll never tell," he said, roguish smile flashing another answer.

Any other time, she would have laughed. His entanglements had been a source of endless amusement to her, for she'd been secure in the knowledge that while other women flickered in and out of his life like a firefly's light, she alone remained.

But this time she saw it, saw his mouth coming down on Louisa's, saw his hand stroke Louisa's face with the same tenderness and awe with which he'd stroked hers. *Hers.*

It clutched in her stomach, cold and painfully new. She circled the emotion, prodded at it like a sore tooth. Jealous? Was she *jealous?*

Bitterness ate through the jealously like acid. Surely she wasn't stupid enough to build hopes around Lucas simply because he was so knee-weakeningly good at touching her. She'd always known he could seduce. He'd been born to it, had inherited the talent along with his dark good looks. She'd been smug, secure in her own immunity.

Except it had turned out she wasn't immune at all, and she'd best remember it.

"Shhh," she scolded him under her breath. "Be quiet. Some of us would like to listen."

Lucas contemplated Pris's profile for a moment, trying to decide whether he should point out that she'd been doing every bit as much talking as he had. But the prim and ladylike Priscilla Wentworth had returned, her attention firmly to the stage.

He decided on discretion. Why take the risk when he'd finally wrestled his passions firmly under control? He'd been sitting beside Pris throughout Flora's gawdawful performance and hadn't had one unsettling fantasy. Well, hardly a one. A flash or two here and there didn't count. They could have been about anybody, couldn't they?

Thankfully, Louisa was almost done. Only the debate was left, and then he could skeedaddle out of here and figure out what to do next. Maybe Pris would take pity on him and let him sleep in her stables. Nobody'd look for him there.

Mrs. Pugh, the acknowledged champion of the debate, sailed up to the stage, the glint of battle in her steely eyes.

"Now," she said, her voice ringing clearly from a truly substantial chest, "we move on to the centerpiece of this evening's entertainment. My own beautiful daughter, Harriet, has agreed to argue in favor of the resolution."

Harriet, a pale, inconspicuous replica of her formidable mother, like a figure printed by a press running out of ink, scuttled up.

"The topic I've selected for this evening is a particularly interesting one, which I'm sure you'll all find both entertaining and enlightening," Mrs. Pugh continued. "Resolved: That married men are more beneficial to the community than bachelors."

"Uh-oh." Months ago, Mrs. Pugh settled on Lucas as the desperate solution to the horrible fate awaiting her daughter—spinsterhood.

"Have we volunteers for the defense?" Ruthless as an eagle's, her sharp eyes scanned the crowd.

"Come on." He jumped to his feet, yanking Pris up beside him.

"There you are, Lucas! I was hoping—"

"Sorry." Dragging Pris along in his wake, he plunged for the door. "Pris's awful dizzy. Must be the heat. Gotta take her outside for some fresh air."

"But surely she'll be fine," Mrs. Pugh protested. "I know that Priscilla wouldn't want our program interrupted—"

"Oh, dear!" Pris slapped a hand to her forehead and staggered.

"There, you see?" He scooped her up just as she started to topple. As such things went, it was the most unromantic carry he'd ever performed. Her head flopped over his left arm, her legs dangled limply over the right, and her skirts tangled up around his neck, damn near choking him. Still, a ripple of blissful, wishful, feminine sighs followed them as he charged through the mass of bodies.

He set her on her feet right outside the door. Silence reigned briefly inside the schoolhouse, chased by a bubble of frothy, excited voices. He knew in a moment the audience would stream out to check on Pris's welfare. Somehow he had to make damn sure they understood that from now on he belonged to Pris. *Only* Pris.

"I'm sorry," he said.

"Oh, that's all right. I wanted out of there, too."

"Not for that." They were almost to the door now; the muffled clatter of bootheels was getting louder. "For this."

He hauled her up against him, clamped his hand on the back of her head to stop her from struggling, and planted his mouth on hers.

And right then he had a moment of clarity, when the world froze into a perfectly preserved instant. Pris's gasp, the exclamations of startled women as they spilled out of the schoolhouse, the burning red glare of the setting sun that seared his eyes before he closed them. And then, as his brain began to blur and melt, to surrender to the feel of Pris's mouth under his, her body beneath his hands, he had one last, conscious thought: Now he'd gone and wrecked it all.

Chapter 6

They'd been friends for a lifetime. To stay that way, he'd made sure—they'd *both* made sure—that they'd never wanted anything from each other than friendship. Sex, for all its wild and wonderful intensity, always burned out, and quickly enough at that. To keep her in his life, he'd never wanted her.

Or so he'd always thought. Now he knew it had always been there, solidly dammed up behind a wall so thick and impervious he'd never even suspected its existence. Hidden, growing, waiting.

Pris threw her arms around him, clutching his back so hard he knew her fingers would leave imprints, badges of her response. God help him, he wanted her mark, longed to put his own on her. Her mouth moved under his—eager, warm, more exciting in her unskilled impatience than any expertise he'd ever known. Their chests pressed close together, and Lucas could swear he felt her heartbeat, fast and hard, calling his own heart into a matching, painfully wild rhythm.

The blow caught him across the back of the

neck, sending his head jerking back in reflex, tearing his mouth away from Pris's.

Women swarmed around them, thick as bees on the stairs and in the doorway. He had hazy impressions of their faces: eager, confused, hurt, surprised. But only Pris's image was clear, her eyes soft and dazed, lips parted and gleaming from his kiss. He forced himself to let her go. Knees nearly buckling beneath him, he grabbed for the iron stair railing to steady himself.

"Oh, for heaven's sake, Lucas, what *were* you thinking?" Her arm cocked for another blow, Mrs. Wentworth firmly gripped her handbag, her otherwise unruffled appearance in sharp contrast to her warrior pose.

Lucas winced, gingerly probing the lump growing at the base of his skull. What the hell did she keep in there? He supposed he should be grateful; nothing less forceful would have ever induced him to stop. "I wasn't," he admitted.

"Obviously not," Mrs. Wentworth said briskly. "If nothing else, at least your discretion has always been admirable. And you know perfectly well that Priscilla should not be allowing such liberties to a man to whom she is unpromised. Her foolishness is appalling."

Priscilla flinched, her face paling.

"Who says there are no promises?" Lucas asked.

A few women gasped. More snickered.

Mrs. Wentworth turned to her daughter. "Priscilla?"

Mutely, her stunned gaze never wavering from Lucas, Pris gave a tentative nod.

Had he one shred of decency, he'd have dragged her out of there, begged her forgiveness, and forgotten the entire plan. But he had no decency, for if he *had* gotten her away, he had no doubt that he would immediately have taken up where that kiss had ended. And this, he reminded himself, public and unmistakable proof that he belonged to one woman now, had been their intention from the first.

"What promises?" Jeanette squeezed between two sturdy and very interested farm wives, who reluctantly surrendered their excellent view to someone who was, after all, family. "Don't you tell me, Lucas," she said fiercely, "that—"

"Jeanette." Mrs. Wentworth's soft interjection stopped Jeanette immediately. Only the reflexive tightening of her fingers around the silken rope handle of her bag betrayed any emotion other than complete calm. "I believe it is time for us to return home. Lucas, I shall expect your explanation first thing in the morning."

"There's no need." Priscilla said, as crisply as though she were negotiating the price of a dozen eggs. She seemed a different woman than the deeply sensual one he'd held in his arms a few seconds ago, and he had a brief, dangerous notion to kiss her again, just to see if he could bring that other woman back. "I'll tell you what I told Lucas: despite his flattering efforts, I've yet to make up my mind. When and if I decide to accept his suit, we'll inform you immediately."

He swallowed his surprised laughter. Only Pris! A minute ago she was so lost in a sensual fog she couldn't even speak. Now she was deftly implying that he was practically begging for her attention, that *she* was the one resisting a formal announcement, who had him on his knees before her like a heartsick fool. He couldn't even contradict her, not without giving too much away.

He grinned. "I'm doing my best to convince you."

Her mournful expression cast clear doubt on the quality of his *best*. "I'm sure you are."

While Mrs. Wentworth and Jeanette hustled Pris away, Lucas ducked into a nearby copse of trees and made his escape. He'd almost made it home before he remembered.

If he'd really been head over heels in love and planning marriage, surely his mother would know about it.

Hell! His mother was not part of the usual gossip rounds in Maple Falls. Most of the residents thought she was more than a little odd—"What *do* you suppose she's doing in there, with the lamp on all night long?" Not to mention her well-known habit of disappearing for weeks at a time. Little did they know that the truth was far more shocking than anything they'd dreamed up. For she left town to visit her . . . to see George Russell, who'd been hovering around her for years. And as for what she did all night long—well, he was sure that even Clara Wentworth had little idea of his mother's vocation, not to mention her avocations, or the women would no longer be friends.

However, his mother frequently took walks in the early afternoon, just after waking, and passed a word or two with the people she met. For a town already somewhat doubtful about the true nature of his relationship with Pris, his mother's ignorance would only confirm their suspicions.

So now he stood outside his mother's house and tried to figure out how to tell her he'd fallen in love—with Pris, no less—and that he had every intention of marrying her.

Damn it! Marriage. His mother, with good reason, was no more fond of the institution than he was.

He knew little of how his parents' marriage had started. But he knew too well what it had become. He still couldn't imagine how they'd ever tolerated each other long enough to conceive him in the first place. How was he supposed to tell her that he planned to get married, a state she'd left behind with nothing short of jubilation? No doubt about it, he was going to get his ears boxed.

Stalling, he let his gaze slide over to the Wentworths'. Lamps burned in the kitchen window; Pris had some explaining of her own to do.

Maybe he should go and check on her. Make sure she was all right, after their kiss and its aftermath.

That was all it took, one stray thought about kissing her. Blood roared in his ears, beat in his groin. His hands flexed, remembering the slender, firm slope of her waist and back through the thin poplin of her dress. He was instantly hard, violently aroused, so much so he was grateful she was out of his reach. Because he knew, if she'd been near and alone, it would take far more than a simple whack across his head to stop him this time. And *then* where would he be?

Clearly, he would have to stay far, far away from Pris—for however long it took to get himself back to normal, though at the moment that seemed an impossible task. How he was to give the impression of enthusiastically pursuing her without ever being in the same room with her was a problem that at the moment was beyond him.

First things first—and that meant his mother. He banged on the door before he could change his mind. At least if he were talking to his mother he couldn't go climbing through Pris's window the instant the lamp was extinguished in the Wentworths' kitchen.

No answer.

"Come on," he muttered, pounding harder. Lydia was prone to ignore such extraneous things as someone knocking on her door when she was lost in her work. Though how such a thing required so much concentration eluded him.

Finally Lydia tugged the door open. Dressed as usual in a limp cotton dress that hung on her spare frame, her graying hair scraped back, she looked older than her years. Twenty years with William Garrett had done that to her, he supposed. But traces of the pretty girl she'd once been remained. He wondered what her readers would think. He'd bet that every man who'd panted over the words of Madame Michelle, the woman whose imaginative, blatantly erotic, and enticingly crude fictional diaries outsold even the ever-popular Anonymous's, had never pictured her as resembling a genteelly aging schoolteacher. He shuddered away from the thought; she was his *mother*.

"Lucas! What a surprise. Come in." She stepped aside to allow him entrance, her attention returning to the slender vase in her ink-stained hand. Perhaps seven inches in height, flowing blue glass spiraled up to a scalloped edge.

"I hope I'm not interrupting your work."

"It can wait." She tilted the vase, measured the circumference with her thumb and forefinger. "Do you think this would fit—"

"I don't know!" he shouted.

"I was only going to ask if you thought it was too tall for roses. The crimson ones will be blooming next week."

"Oh." He sagged against the wall. Thank God that was all. His mother took great pride in her work. She'd enjoyed beating his father at his own depraved game, using the lurid knowledge he'd forced upon her to earn financial independence from the man she despised. But Lucas still did his very best to ignore her books and lived in terror that she might mention to him the details of whatever scene she was working on. "I guess so."

He knew that he was something of an aberration in his family. His father had first taken him to Lucinda, one of his favorite whores, on the occasion of Lucas's thirteenth birthday. William had beamed with paternal pride when Lucinda had reported that Lucas possessed great enthusiasm and natural talent.

William Garrett had clearly hoped that his son would follow in his father's debauched footsteps, joining him in his pursuit of unusual pleasures. But Lucas's tastes had proved to be a lot more traditional. Oh, sure, he'd been known to make good use of a few feathers now and then, maybe a swath of silk. But all the other toys and props and scenarios that Lucinda kept coming up with—hell, they just seemed to get in the way to him. Not to mention that having two or three women there, to his mind, only meant you were doing a half-assed job of concentrating on the one.

"What brings you here tonight, Lucas? You rarely come this late."

"Got something to tell you."

"Hmm?" She weighed the vase in her palm. Now that he'd mentioned it . . .

". . . And so, we're going to, well . . ."

Lydia's head snapped up. "What did you say?" When lost in a train of thought, she tended to be inattentive to everything around her, and she'd caught only a phrase.

Jaw set, Lucas glared over her shoulder at what was really an inoffensive landscape. "I said that Pris and I, well, we're probably getting married." His frown deepened. "*Thinking* about getting married."

"Oh!" Lydia bobbled the vase, then grabbed it by the neck before throwing her arms around him in a tight hug. "It's about time!"

"What?" Lucas unlocked her arms from around his neck and set her back so he could look at her. Maybe his eyes worked better than his ears. For damn certain he couldn't have heard her right. "You *like* the idea?"

"Of course I like the idea. It's the best news I've had in years."

"But . . ." Rather than have his mock engagement dig up memories better left buried, Lucas had just about decided to tell her the truth—though how he was going to tell her and still ask Pris to keep it from *her* mother, who wouldn't and couldn't lie to save her soul, he hadn't quite worked out yet. But now she was looking so damn happy he was afraid the truth would break her heart. "You always said you'd rather starve to death than consider getting married."

"True."

"And you like Pris."

"I adore Pris."

"Then why the hell would you ever want to do that to her?"

"I want grandchildren."

"*What?*"

"Remarkably conventional of me, isn't it?" She shrugged, smiling in anticipation. "But there it is. Make me beautiful grandchildren, Lucas."

Chapter 7

Priscilla spent the first night after Lucas had kissed her lying wide awake, listening to the fierce rumble of thunder in the distance, her emotions roiling just as violently. She studied a solitary crack in the pristine white plaster of her ceiling, thoroughly, inextricably confused.

How on earth had *that* happened? Why hadn't she ever suspected? In a few seconds Lucas had turned everything she'd ever thought about herself upside down. She was *not* proper. Not immune to baser, decidedly unladylike urges. Not nearly as reasonable, thoughtful, and ruled by her intellect as she'd always so pridefully assumed.

Instead, she was hungry and wanton. *Weak.* Weak enough practically to fall all over Lucas just because he gave her a little kiss.

Well, not a *little* kiss, she amended. A big, juicy, wonderful, amazing kiss. But, dear heavens, if she was that easily swayed, who knew what she might do under the right—or, more precisely, the *wrong*—circumstances?

She spent the next day at home, painfully mortified, futilely trying to occupy herself with meaningless tasks. There were things to be done around town, but she was too cowardly to face those knowing and speculative smiles. Or worse yet, to run into Lucas himself.

How could she have been so foolish? For of course Lucas was not attracted to her. Completely *unattracted*, in fact. If he'd had the slightest inclination toward her, surely she'd have known it by now. When had Lucas Garrett ever tried to resist his carnal urges? If he'd felt even a stray whim in her direction, he'd have tried to seduce her long ago.

And she'd been too senseless—all right, she admitted, too stunned, too *lusting*—to make even an attempt to hide her own response. It must have been obvious to Lucas that she was wildly attracted to him. That if he'd crooked his finger she'd have run off with him into the night, found the first comfortable bed, and done anything he'd asked.

She wasn't even entirely sure she would have insisted on comfortable.

Likely her response had repulsed him. The last thing he wanted from Priscilla was *passion*. He asked her for a respite from all that, for heaven's sake. They'd remained friends for so long precisely because she'd wanted nothing from him. And now, despite her best efforts, she wanted, all right.

God help her, but she wanted.

By the third day, Priscilla was downright mad. She was still closeted in her room, fashioning a quilt for the McCanns' youngest child, cursing Lucas Garrett all the while.

He'd left her alone, the inconsiderate bounder! Alone, to chafe and fret and stew. To reassure her painfully concerned mother, who'd done nothing to earn such worry. To deal with all the avidly curious women who'd just happened to drop by the Wentworth house, all their subtle— and not-so-subtle—questions, and their rampant curiosity about what was clearly the best entertainment to come along in Maple Falls in many a day.

Lucas had not even had the decency to visit, allowing her to pretend that nothing untoward had happened and that the kiss had been a simple and unemotional act purely for the benefit of their audience. Failing that, at least he could have let her act as if she'd gotten over it already. That it had been an aberration born of her surprise, caught off-guard as she had been. She'd been working up to it for two days; she was quite certain she could give the impression that she had no wish to kiss him ever again.

After all, it was entirely Lucas's fault.

He was the one who'd kissed her in the first place. He'd certainly not *needed* to use all his skill and talent, to put all those little tricks with his tongue and his lips into that one kiss. He should know full well the effect it would have on an unsuspecting and unprepared woman. But he had done it anyway! Probably couldn't resist showing off, the conceited lout.

Thank goodness she'd managed to shake herself clear of her daze quickly enough to imply that she was the reluctant one in this relationship. She refused to appear to the town as just another interchangeable way station on Lucas Wentworth's freight line.

But if they weren't seen together soon, everyone would suspect he was just kindly allowing her to salvage her pride. That he'd kissed her and moved on, just as he had a hundred times before. Even worse, for he'd *only* kissed her. Lord knew, most of them got more out of it than that!

If Lucas Garrett wanted everyone to think he was besotted with her, he could certainly put a little more effort into proving it. Maybe she'd make him grovel.

Priscilla jabbed the needle through layers of flannel and batting. She'd had enough of waiting for life to come to her. What had waiting ever gotten her? If she'd been less patient, had gone after what she wanted, she'd be married by now. Or be running Maple Falls Manufacturing. Preferably both.

Well, no more would she allow the winds of life to blow her where they would. She stuffed the quilt aside and went to her dressing table to prepare herself for battle.

From now on, Priscilla Wentworth was a woman of action.

Jeanette was the very last place in the entire world she wanted to be, and it was all her husband's fault. The Gold Rush Widows of Maple Falls were meeting at the Wentworths' home tonight. They were supposed to have met at Dorothea Tuttle's, but she'd claimed that her youngest, Timothy, had a slight sniffle and she wouldn't want to expose the other women. It was very considerate of her.

Jeanette huffed. It was a crock! Dorothea would never have left an ailing child; she'd hovered over Timothy for three whole weeks when he'd suffered from the mildest case of chicken pox in town. No, Dorothea, and all the other women stuffed into the Wentworths' parlor, were here to ferret out some snippet of information about Priscilla and Lucas.

Oh, God. Priscilla and Lucas! It only went to show how truly mixed up the world had gotten. Her husband had left her, and Priscilla had taken leave of every one of her usually reliable senses and gotten herself tangled up with the last man on earth who could give her what she deserved.

Pamelia Fletcher nudged Jeanette's left elbow and passed her a platter holding a scattering of crumbs, one lone remaining example of Louisa Rockwell's delectable butter cookies, and a full dozen of the gingersnaps Jeanette had spent the entire afternoon in a sweltering kitchen to bake. So what if they were a mite crispy? Defiantly, she snatched one and bit down before passing the plate on.

The group had formed nearly a year ago. In the beginning, only her mother had been a true widow—until the collapse of a mine shaft in Gold Dust had crushed Orson Farnham. Then Doc Nickerson had died of illness—an unexpected fever, his wife insisted, though Jeanette suspected his illness had been contracted in the bottom of a whiskey bottle.

Many others simply didn't know. It had been so long since they'd heard from their husbands, they were unsure whether they were merely victims of the painfully slow and unreliable mails, had been permanently abandoned, or were truly widows, after all.

Jeanette knew which category she fell into. Damn it.

Across the room Emma Metcalf droned on, reading the most recent missive from her husband, who was the most faithful correspondent. The women often shared their letters, for the men who fled Maple Falls sometimes stumbled across each other in Gambol Gulch or Mountain City or whatever other godforsaken place they wandered through in their idiotic search for gold.

In a way, the entire fiasco could be laid on Emma's shoulders. It had been her wandering younger brother who'd struck it rich and written his sister about it; her brand-new husband Henry, recently laid off from the chair factory, was the first to head west.

And as the chair factory, and the sawmill, and finally the flour mill, had closed, the other men had followed. Even Robert.

Especially Robert. Robert, whom she'd fallen head over teakettle for the instant she'd met him, when she'd been completely unmoved by the men who'd vied for her hand before. Robert, who was so clearly intended for her sister. At the time, she'd been half certain she would die from the pain of it, from loving him and knowing she could never have him.

Now, Jeanette wished she'd never met him, because he'd left her when she was practically still a bride. But it wasn't just her.

He'd abandoned them all. Her mother, to try and sort through the carcass of the business. The town, too, which depended upon Maple Falls Manufacturing, a town built around Levi Wentworth's dream. The slow exodus of men had multiplied unbelievably after Robert left, and who could blame them? What man wanted his livelihood dependent upon an already shaky business now run by a woman?

"Oh," Emma was saying, pink and flustered, fluttering the letter in front of her face, "that's it, I guess."

"Come, now," a woman called. "Read us the rest. Let us poor old married ladies remember what it's like to be newly wed. Though you were hardly married long enough to get used to it, were you? Surely you can't miss it as much as we do."

Yes, she could, Jeanette thought. Even if he'd done something unforgivable.

"I . . . couldn't," Emma repeated, eyes flicking in Jeanette's direction. And then Jeanette knew. Emma wasn't hiding any newlywed billing and cooing; she was hiding more rumors about Robert's carousing in the goldfields.

"There's no more letters?"

They looked at each other in silence, hoping, wishing, unwilling to let go of this tenuous ink-and-paper thread that bound them to their men so far away.

They were all so careful not to look at Jeanette. She, who'd had only one letter since her husband had left, and that more than four months ago. When they all *knew* the letters were stolen or just slow, for surely no man could forget *her*, could he?

She didn't want his letters anyway. She just wanted them all to stop pitying her, to stop wondering what she'd done to drive away her husband so quickly.

The next bite of cookie turned to sawdust in her mouth. Catching her mother's eye, she mimed that she was going for a drink, and darted out of the room and down the hall.

Once inside the kitchen, she braced both arms on the table, her head drooping, and took the first deep breath she'd managed in an hour. It was so damn hot in there. All those clinging, desperate, lonely women. She didn't belong there. Damn them, damn Robert. Most of all, damn herself, for falling in love with him in the first place.

And now Priscilla was on the verge of making the same mistake. If a man like Robert, who'd appeared to be all that was desirable and dependable in a husband, could do what he'd done, how much worse could Lucas, the most unrepentantly unfaithful man in the entire state, be?

She wouldn't stand for it. If she hurt this much, how much worse would it be for Priscilla, whose heart was so big and so generous?

Jeanette marched out of the kitchen, down the hall to Priscilla's room.

And found it empty. Priscilla had slipped out

while they were occupied in the parlor. And not just to the garden or the necessary; an open hat-box rested on the bed. From the top of the dressing table Jeanette lifted a cut-crystal bottle, its teardrop-shaped stopper shattering light like a diamond. Jeanette had special-ordered it from Chicago and given it to Priscilla for Christmas nearly three years ago, the last time there'd been ready cash to buy frivolous presents. The light, pretty scent suited Priscilla, but she rarely bothered with it; the amber perfume rippled as Jeanette set the bottle nearly two-thirds full, back down.

But a hint of scent still clung to the air, the smell of spring blossoms, a garden spilling with a luxurious medley of flowers, their smells jumbling together.

Which meant she'd gone to Lucas.

Priscilla's causes had always amused and perplexed Jeanette, who'd been half-admiring, half-jealous. For Priscilla often whipped things back into shape before Jeanette even noticed there was something amiss. And she'd envied Priscilla's dedication and passion, wondered why she, Jeanette, hadn't gotten her share of those qualities.

But apparently she'd simply never been confronted with the right problem before. And the right problem was Priscilla, falling—*running*—headlong into pain and disaster. Priscilla had never learned to handle men, never learned to guard her heart. And if Jeanette could make such a horrible mistake, how much worse would it be for Priscilla?

Jeanette to the rescue, she thought, whirling for the door. What a novelty.

Chapter 8

A cubbyholed oak barrier, in a place of honor just inside the front door, sectioned the post office off from the rest of Garrett's Dry Goods. Lucas stood behind it, shuffling through a handful of letters, pausing as he came across a particularly bent and stained specimen. No doubt it had taken a long and indirect route to Maple Falls. Jenny McCann would be so pleased to hear from her husband. The last time Lucas had seen her, she'd been so worn down with work and worry and her new baby, there'd barely been anything left of her.

With the front door to the store propped open, looking for a breeze, he didn't have the warning tinkle of the bell hung over the door. Only the slight scrape of a heeled shoe on the sanded pine floors alerted him, and he looked up to find Flora Fergus almost upon him.

Damn. It had been going so well. Oh, there'd been a few curiosity seekers, but he hadn't had a single proposition in three days. "Mrs. Fergus! What can I do for you today?"

Bad choice of words. Her smile was slow, seductive, thoroughly pleased. "I imagine I'll think of something."

"No mail, I'm afraid." He waved the packet of letters. They fluttered in the air like a white flag of surrender, and he quickly stuffed them into a wooden box, letting the lid fall with a resounding crack.

"Oh, dear." She pouted prettily, but her eyes were anything but disappointed. "I suppose you'll have to find some way to cheer me up, then."

Her fingers trailing on the polished oak of the counter, she rounded the corner.

"You can't come back here. Postal regulations."

"Really? Since when have you ever bothered with silly little rules?"

Her skirts frothed over the tips of his shoes and he took a quick step back. "The law's the law."

"Oh, I like laws." Her fingers had found a new path now, slowly walking down his shirt front. "The laws of nature, for instance. Wouldn't want to go against them."

"Mrs. Fergus." He caught her wrists just as she reached the last button showing above the waistband of his pants.

"Oh, it's Mrs. Fergus now? Isn't that a little formal, all things considered?" Obviously intent on continuing down the trail she'd begun, she tried to tug her hands free. "Let go, Lucas. You're holding on too tight."

"Sorry." But he only gripped tighter, his thumbs pressing hard against the inside of her wrist where the blood ran close to the surface, and her pulse quickened.

He was so strong, so forceful. He had such passion in him; she knew that well, and figured he'd had no release for days. Too many other women had believed that ridiculous farce with Priscilla Wentworth, and God knew that prissy little woman couldn't give him what he needed. It was only a matter of time before he'd crave a woman of experience and passion, a woman who could match him. A woman like her.

Anticipating it, dreaming of what Lucas would be like after a few days of denial, she'd hardly been able to sleep. So today would be the day. Her impatience growing, she'd lugged buckets of water from the spring rather than use plain old well water, washed her hair and her skin until they both gleamed, put on her prettiest underthings, and waited until she was sure they'd be undisturbed—all those other fools were over at the Wentworths'.

She was certain he couldn't resist her.

"Is that how you want it, Lucas?" she purred. "I don't mind, you know. Go ahead." She leaned into him, so he had to constrict his hold to keep her from toppling forward. "Force me."

The tendons in his strong hands flexed as he fairly lifted her off the floor and set her away in one quick motion. Lordy, but he had lovely hands! Just the thought of what they felt like on her body had her gasping.

"Mrs. Fergus." A barrel of salt sat not three feet away, and he dived for it like a lifeline, hefting it to his shoulder and heading for the back counter. The salt didn't need to be moved, but even Flora Fergus wasn't fool enough to accost a man holding up a fifty-pound barrel.

He hoped.

Carefully, he set the barrel down between one filled with molasses, its sides sticky and dark, and a smelly case of oil-packed sardines. He straightened. Flora was stalking him across the crowded store, her eyes alight with anticipation, and he quickly put the sturdy width of the display case between them.

He'd always entered into his liaisons easily, simply. They had all ended the same way. He never seduced a woman unless he was certain she wanted to be seduced, and that she wanted nothing more from him than he was willing to give. If any of them had been hurt, he hadn't noticed.

Flora Fergus was no different. But their entanglement hadn't run its natural course. He'd chopped it off publicly by kissing Pris Friday night, and so he chose his words more carefully than he otherwise might have.

"Flora," he began. "This isn't fair to you—"

"Make it up to me, then." She grinned, making a dash for the left end of the case. He headed the other way.

"That's not what I mean. I have all the respect in the world for you. Too much respect to continue on as we have been, especially now. You deserve more than I can give you, and it would be unforgivable of me to do anything else. Considering the esteem in which I hold you."

There, he thought. That was pretty good, even if he did say so himself.

Flora didn't seem to agree. "What?" she

shouted, slapping both palms down on the counter hard enough to cause Lucas to fear for the inset glass top he'd shipped in from St. Anthony at such expense.

But at least she'd stopped moving.

He must have lost his touch. His usual charm and glib tongue weren't having their customary effect. Perhaps they'd flown out the window with his good sense on a hot August night.

"You're a married woman, Flora. And I know that you're a woman of honor and integrity. It was inexcusable of me to take advantage of your loneliness and your natural warmth. And now that there is Priscilla, well, I can't ask this of you. It wouldn't be fair."

"Lucas, please." She laughed, cackling as heartily as an old setting hen. "You don't expect me to think that this . . . whatever it is between you and *Priscilla Wentworth* is what's stopping you?"

If a man had said Pris's name in that tone, he wouldn't have been able to say another word for a week.

"I am promised to her," Lucas said solemnly.

"Promised?" Her eyes narrowed, darkening the summer-sky blue to thunderstorm navy. "Since when do you make promises?"

"Just because I haven't made them before," he said, "doesn't mean that I *can't*." Now, *there* was a lie. Promises that lasted longer than a night weren't in his repertoire. "Given the right incentive."

Her lids lowered, veiling the flash of anger as her lips curved seductively. "You made promises to me, Lucas."

"Never." Never had, never would, had never been the slightest bit tempted.

"Yes, you did." She advanced again, slowly this time, her hips swaying as vigorously as a saloon dancer's. A shudder of revulsion gripped his spine. Another new experience; a woman's advances occasionally might not have interested him, but he couldn't recall ever being repulsed.

"Oh, maybe you didn't *say* them," she went on. "But your lips made promises, every time you kissed me. Your hands, whenever you touched me. And each time you entered me, your cock—"

"Mrs. Fergus!" Priscilla swooped in like an avenging gull, the long white feathers on her hat sprouting between gobs of fake cherries. "His—" Color climbed, spreading slowly up from her neck like pale fabric dipped into strong scarlet dye. "—*male chicken* part is no longer any of your concern. Nor any other of his parts, for that matter."

"Well, well." Flora turned, planting one fist on her ripely curved hip. "If it isn't the happy bride-to-be."

"I specifically recall mentioning that whether or not I shall be a bride is not yet settled to my satisfaction."

"Oh, please." Flora flicked her a glance, top to toe, amused and unimpressed. "Never figured you for stupid. You know as well as I do that one woman couldn't hold him—it just ain't in his nature. But if there *was* one who could, can't see how it would be you."

Pris drew herself up, gloves and starched blouse gleaming pristine white, the fake cherries bobbing merrily as her chin pointed ever higher. All furiously affronted lady, easy to dismiss if you'd never tested the steel supporting that ramrod-straight back.

"Who better? For you see, Mrs. Fergus, I already have." Though she was a good four inches shorter, Pris seemed to tower over Flora. "I've held his friendship quite firmly for almost twenty years. If I haven't held him in certain other ways in that time, it's only because I haven't *chosen* to do so. There are unique advantages in allowing a man time to sow his wild oats, as I'm sure you realize."

By damn, Pris! If Lucas hadn't known better, he might have believed her himself. That she'd merely been waiting—he bit his cheek to keep from laughing—for him to *practice* on other women until his skills became worthy of her . . .

Flora blinked as if she'd just emerged from a dark cave, unable to credit that those words were coming out of the thoroughly proper Priscilla Wentworth's mouth.

"Oh, by the way," Pris went on briskly, "I'm sure you're aware Mr. Fergus still holds a few shares in Maple Falls Manufacturing. It's necessary to write to him occasionally with an appraisal of our progress. I would hate to slip up and mention the methods you use to . . . entertain yourself in his absence."

Flora's soft, rounded features sharpened abruptly. "Are you threatening me?"

"I believe that I am."

Flora only huffed, blowing in and out like a winded runner.

"Now, I'm certain you don't mind if I have a

moment alone with my . . ." Priscilla searched
for the appropriate word, settled on the simplest.
"With my Lucas."

The implied claim hung in the air among the
three of them, tangible as the dust motes dancing
in the light that poured through the front windows. Flora looked at him expectantly, awaiting
his denial.

Her Lucas. To his knowledge, no woman had
ever called him "her Lucas" before. But it
seemed natural now, mostly, he figured, because
he knew that Pris hadn't meant it. Not at all.

No more than he would have. He met Flora's
glower. "I'm sure you understand, Mrs. Fergus.
I am always at the whim of—" he smiled—"*my
Pris.*"

Flora shot a last glare in Priscilla's direction
and flounced out in a flurry of blue lace.

Pris's confidence left with Flora. Her shoulders
drooped like those sorry cherries. Her head
swiveled, inspecting the barrels of whiskey and
flour and smelly kerosene oil, wheels of cheese
and bolts of calico, boxes of spices, the well
buckets and coils of rope hanging from the ceiling, as she looked anywhere but at him. He
hadn't seen her this uncertain since she'd been
waiting for Andrew Berry to pick up her up for
her first real dance, and he'd come over to tease
her out of it—and check out Andrew. He hated
being the cause of it now.

All he'd wanted was a few weeks of uninter-
rupted peace. He hadn't expected to sacrifice the
ease and comfort Pris and he had always had
together, a comfort born of a firmly held certainty that no matter what they did, no matter

how they changed, nothing would alter their friendship. Somewhere deep inside he would have mourned the loss, if he hadn't been absolutely sure they could get it back.

"Ah . . . how are you?" she ventured, studying a display of hat pins with extreme and unnecessary interest.

"Good." He would be better if she'd just stop skittering around the store as if she expected him to pounce on her like a randy goat. The woman knew damn well the whole thing had been for show.

Well, it was *supposed* to have been just for show.

"Your week has gone well thus far?"

His week had been great. He'd finished the inventory he'd been trying to get done for three months. Everything in his rooms was in a logical and readily accessible spot, right where he'd left it. For dinner he'd eaten a handful of crackers, half a small cheese, three slices of cherry pie, and not one single damned tasteless vegetable. Last night he'd even managed to sleep for three whole hours without his brain conjuring up visions of Pris, deliciously naked.

Come to think of it, his week had been goddamn perfect.

"I came here to . . . to—"

Since when did Pris need an excuse to come see him? If she hemmed and hawed one more time, damned if he wouldn't give her a reason to feel awkward.

"To discuss my future husband."

"Me?"

"No!" She didn't even laugh, just twittered

every bit as awkwardly as Sarah Jane Bosworth. "Not you, of course not. My potential husband. The candidates you've come up with."

Uh-oh.

"You have come up with some appropriate possibilities, haven't you?"

Shit. "Absolutely."

"Wonderful! I'd like to hear about them."

"Can't." Because he hadn't given one single thought to the matter since the last time she'd brought up the fool notion. "I haven't"—he drew circles in the air—"checked them out thoroughly yet. Wouldn't want to get you all hepped up about one who turned out to be an ass."

He waited for her to lay into him. He hadn't kept up his end of the bargain. Pris had never been one to let someone weasel out of his obligations.

"Oh." A disappointed little sigh. "I understand perfectly." She backed toward the door, flicking her hand in an awkward wave.

Enough was enough. "Pris," he said, determined not to dance around the issue anymore. What the hell good had that ever done? It's not like women ever just forgot about things.

"Lucas, I was wondering . . . do you ever get in any more of those cove oysters? Mother did so enjoy—"

"The hell with the oysters!"

"Lucas, don't—"

Relieved, he didn't bother to listen to the rest of her routine admonishment. This, at least, was familiar ground.

"About that night. When I kissed you, I—"

"It was nothing," she put in quickly, waving

her hand as if shooing away a bothersome gnat.
"I've already forgotten about it."

Nothing? He had half a mind to show her
nothing. She'd practically ignited when he'd
kissed her, her mouth hot enough to burn. He
could still feel the pressure of her nails in his
back as she'd tried to pull him closer, closer. If
they hadn't been standing on the school steps
with an audience full of women, she'd probably
still be wrapped around him. And if he hadn't
owed her for chasing off Flora, he'd prove it to
her right now.

"Unless, of course, it wasn't effective in convincing everyone of our ... attachment," she
went on.

"I don't think it was effective at all." Just exactly when had he lost his mind entirely? Was it
when he kissed her, or when she tried to pretend
it hadn't affected her at all? "Might be forced to
repeat it, just to make sure everyone got the right
message."

"Repeat it?" She couldn't let him kiss her
again. She'd escaped total humiliation by the
skin of her teeth—and by her mother's timely
arrival. Lord knows what foolishness would
seize her this time.

It had been a tactical blunder to call that kiss
nothing, she realized, watching in fascinated
horror as he rounded the counter and advanced,
his brows lowered, eyes dark and intent.

Her rump bumped against a barrel of vinegar,
halting her retreat. Her feet refused to move any
further. Lucas was giving her plenty of time to
escape; his saunter was slow, easy, deliberate, a

big cat stalking his prey, and she was as help-lessly captivated.

"No reason to repeat it," she said quickly. "There's no one to see us now."

"Practice," he drawled. "To make sure we get just the right amount of enthusiasm in it."

He was only three feet away from her when he caught her scent. He shouldn't have; the store seethed with smells: peppermint, leather polish, salt meat, and a hundred others. But hers caught him just the same, the soft scent of soap and a sweet, barely perceptible hint of flowers. Just like her, all everyday practicality on the surface, al-most hiding the core of thoroughly luscious fem-ininity.

Almost.

Blood roared in his ears. Deserting his brain, rushing to another region, which was why ra-tional thought was quickly abandoning him. Losing ground to the relentless, powerful drive to put a claim on this woman in the oldest way of all.

"Priscilla! I didn't expect to see you here."

Damn it! Who now?

Jeanette skidded to a stop, her heaving chest and flushed face betraying the speed with which she'd covered the distance from home to the store. She'd forgotten her hat, so damp strands of rich brown hair clung to her sweat-beaded brow and neck, and still she was one of the pret-tiest women he'd ever seen. Odd, how he'd never been tempted.

"Mother sent you," Pris accused.

"Of course not."

"So you just decided to follow me on your own?"

"Why would I follow you?" Jeanette could lie to a man without a blink, but she wasn't nearly so good at deceiving her sister.

Lucas grinned, waiting for Pris's affronted explosion.

"Oh."

Not the anger he'd expected. Distinct hurt instead, lurking in Pris's soft answer, in the bowing of her head over the loss of her family's trust.

So he found the anger in himself. Pris had never given anyone reason to question either her choices or her actions. And even if she had, who was Jeanette to do the questioning? It wasn't as if Robert Stephens had been a blameless choice.

"Isn't that closing the barn door a bit late, Jeanette?" he asked.

"A horse can be shooed back in, can't it? And then I can put a big sturdy bar across the door and nail it shut."

"I do *not* appreciate being compared to a mare by either one of you."

"Oh, not a mare, sweetheart," Lucas said with a smile, relieved to see quick pride replace the hurt. "I'd compare you to a sweet lil' filly, at least for a couple of years yet."

That earned him a glare, as Pris marched toward the front of the store. "I'll be going home now. *Not*, you can be sure, for any other reason but that I am ready to do so. And you, Lucas Garrett, I believe have some investigations to do. I shall be anxiously awaiting your findings." The door banged shut behind her.

"Oops." Jeanette contemplated her toes before tilting a glance his way. "Investigations?"

Chapter 9

~~~ ∽⊙⊙∽ ~~~

Lucas managed to steer clear of Pris for four more days. Not entirely, he knew, due to his own skill at evasion. If Priscilla really wanted to corner him, she'd have done it.

No, obviously that expectant moment, that "would've-been-should've-been" kiss, had rattled her. Proved to her that the wisest course would be to avoid dangerous situations such as being alone with him. And Pris had ever heeded the wisest course.

Unfortunately, these last days and nights weren't nearly so peaceful as the three previous ones. For if Pris had disturbed his sleep before, now she absolutely haunted him. Pris, and the lewd and wonderful things he longed to do to her. *With* her. It was all he could do to keep from racing across town, clambering in her window, and keeping her in bed until he could at last sleep without dreaming of her, because he would then have lived out every single one of those fantasies.

For all his faults, he'd never fallen prey to wanting the one woman he couldn't have. But now that this particular folly had arrived, so late and unexpectedly in his life, it appeared with a fierce and relentless vengeance.

In desperation, he resorted to the tried-and-true method of clearing a man's brain of a woman he doesn't want there.

He turned to drink.

And so Friday afternoon found him hunched over the bar in the back of the Great Northern Hotel, staring into the liquid promise of a glass of whiskey and water, aiming for oblivion. Halfway through his fourth one, he still hadn't drowned his brain enough to stop remembering the feel of kissing Pris. All he'd managed to wash away so far were the reasons why he couldn't do it again.

Slatted shutters, closed tight over the two narrow windows, blocked most of the afternoon sun. The room smelled less of booze than the soft soap Temperance Churchill was using to scrub down the tables. Not that anybody'd sat there in a week. The only other customer in the place was another man, thin and taut as a fence wire, sucking down his own drink two paces to Lucas's right.

"Well." Mrs. Churchill left off scouring the table and flipped the sodden cloth over her shoulder, spraying a mist of lye-scented droplets on the wall behind her. "Guess I'd better be checkin' on supper. You two need anything else, you just holler."

Lucas lifted his glass in salute. "Will do, Mrs. Churchill."

Soon as Mrs. Churchill had disappeared through the swinging door to the kitchen, the stranger wheezed a heartfelt sigh. "Thank Jesus," he said. "All that cleanin' was getting on my nerves. Half afraid that, if I dared to spit, she'da taken that rag to the inside o' my mouth."

"She's enthusiastic, isn't she?"

"No shit. Never been in a bar so clean in my whole life. It's unnatural. Where's a man s'posed to relax if it ain't in a bar?" He took a swig, bulging out cheeks thickly prickled with fading red whiskers. "Sure do have good whiskey, though. Best on my whole route."

"Whiskey's same as anyplace else. It's the water that makes it go down so smooth."

"The water?" The stranger gave his glass a suspicious sniff. "Oh, yeah. Comes from some spring, don't it? Heard somethin' 'bout that last time I was here. Was a fella here then, though. *He* just poured. None o' that cleanin'."

"That was Amos Churchill. Owns the place. Been gone almost six months now."

"Sorry to hear that. Seemed healthy enough. Accident?"

"He's not dead." Now why, Lucas wondered, was he getting drawn into this conversation? He'd been content to enjoy his drink in peace. He certainly wasn't lonely. He hadn't spared his usual companions a single thought.

Maybe he'd missed Pris once or twice. Maybe. Just because he was used to having her around yammering at him, scolding him to stop swearing, and his ears weren't accustomed to the silence. "Left town. Like everybody else."

"Everybody else? Got in this mornin'. Seems to me there was a few people around."

"See any men?"

"Well, no, but—" The man hunched over his glass, drawing in his head like a turtle seeking safety, afraid that whatever malevolent phantom had snatched the men of Maple Falls would get him, too. "What happened?"

"What didn't?" Though he'd been here to witness all of it, Lucas could still hardly believe that so much bad luck could descend at one time onto a town that had begun with such immeasurable promise. "Droughts, grasshoppers, blizzards, floods. Then all those banks failing back east that were supposed to invest here. The chair and sash factory went first, then the sawmill."

The stranger nodded. It wasn't an unfamiliar story.

"Then Mrs. Metcalf got a letter from her brother. Set the whole thing off. As she tells it, he hit it big out in Jefferson Territory, found one hell of a vein of gold. Still, a few might've stuck it out, but Mr. Wentworth, who'd founded the whole town and been just barely holding it together, died." They both observed a respectful moment of silence. "Don't know if the worry finally got him, or if the rest collapsed because he did. Either way, that was it. A chance out west seemed better than no chance here, I expect."

"But not to you?"

Now why the hell had *that* been? He was having a hard time remembering. "Never was much of a gambler." Half the remaining whiskey in his glass went down in one swallow. "Better ways to make money, anyhow."

The man squinted at Lucas, eyes disappearing behind a net of deep sun-spawned lines. He let loose a creaky laugh, rusty as the thick layer of freckles under his tan. "You telling me you're the only man in this whole damn town?"

Lucas had to admit he was.

"And all those women are still here?"

"Most of 'em."

"Whoo-ee!" The man slid down the bar and clapped Lucas heartily on the back. "You old dog! Forget the gold! That's enough to make even an old traveler like me hang up his hat in one place for a while." Lucas's drink sloshed when the stranger grabbed his hand and pumped enthusiastically. "Gotta shake the hand of the luckiest man in the whole state! I'm Harlo Dillon. Hell, I'll even buy you a drink."

"This one's fine." Lucas retrieved his hand, wrapped it back around the glass that he sud-denly wished had a whole lot more whiskey in it, and tried to recall how, not all that long ago, he'd considered himself the luckiest man in the state, too. "Lucas Garrett." He eyed Dillon's eco-nomic leanness, the clothes and features worn from years of hard travel, and the thick pack that slumped on the bar, safely close at hand. "Indian agent?"

"Yup." Harlo patted his leather pack. "Got April's treaty payments right here."

And it was August now. "Prompt this time."

Apparently Harlo wasn't much offended by sarcasm. "Damn right!"

"Well." Lucas polished off the rest of his drink and swung away from the bar. "Best get back to it."

"Lucas?" Mrs. Churchill poked her head through the doorway. "You up to your old tricks again?"

"Me? Tricks?"

"Don't you try that smile on me, Lucas. I'm wise to you." But she couldn't help smiling back just the same. "I went out to the side yard to take down some wash. Saw Priscilla headed this way at a mighty good clip. Looks like she's got a bee in her bonnet this time for sure."

And it looked like his reprieve was over. Lucas wheeled back to the bar.

"Lucas." Mrs. Churchill waggled her finger at him. "She's a nice girl, that one. I don't want to find out you're hurting her, you hear me?"

It was easiest to simply agree. "Yes, ma'am."

She gave him a warning glare before disappearing back into her kitchen.

Dillon clucked in sympathy. "Wife?"

Lucas grabbed the bottle and sloshed whiskey into his glass. Forget even Maple Falls' excellent water. "Nope."

"Well then, why so glum? I'd be downright gratified to have a little filly chasing me." Just to be companionable, Harlo refilled his own glass. "Lessen she's ugly?"

"She's not."

"She one of those Bible-thumping types?"

"No." Inspired by a good third of a bottle of Old Pepper, Lucas gave Dillon an appraising once over. Harlo was over sixteen, under seventy, and male. He'd do. "Want to meet her?"

Harlo lit up like he'd just struck gold. "You mean it?"

Lucas would have been happier with a little less enthusiasm. Still, it was the best he could do on short notice. "Sure."

"*There* you are!" Priscilla careened around the

corner, her skirts swinging hard enough to send a chair skidding. "Lucas Garrett, we need to talk. *Now.*"

Lucas winced out of pure reflex. Was there a man alive who didn't dread hearing those words from a woman? *We need to talk* never boded well.

"Pris! Perfect timing. Saves me a trip to fetch you."

"Oh?" she said, with a distinct note of suspicion.

"Yup. Got someone I'd like you to meet." He waggled his eyebrows meaningfully. "Mr. Harlo Dillon, here in Maple Falls on business."

A man. Lucas had found her a man! And here she'd been thinking the worst. She'd avoided him for days because she needed to be certain she wouldn't be one bit tempted to kiss him. Until it had occurred to her that she was doing exactly what he wanted. She was not only warding off all the other women, she herself was leaving him alone, too! And in the process, allowing him to shirk his responsibilities to her. While she had never known him to let down his end of a bargain—he was far too much the businessman for that—he was not being too prompt about this one. After waiting half her life already, she wanted prompt! She was aging by the day.

Determined to make a good impression, she snatched off her eyeglasses and stuffed them into her handbag. "How silly of me, neglecting to take these off after sewing. I need them only for very close work, of course." She smiled winningly and turned to the man who hovered at Lucas's elbow. Intent on cornering Lucas, she'd given the man only a passing glance when she'd entered the room, and her first impression had been less than . . . impressed. She squinted now, trying to make him out more clearly. Unfortunately, he did not improve upon a second, albeit very blurry, look.

Now, don't make precipitous judgments, she scolded herself. Surely she, of all people, had learned to overlook such shallow concerns. Likely Mr. Dillon had many fine qualities to make up for his somewhat unkempt appearance. In fact, his neglected grooming only proved how desperately the poor man needed a wife.

"Why, Mr. Dillon." Aping the graceful gesture she'd seen Jeanette make with such effective results, she extended one hand, smiling up at him beneath her lashes, "I am so very pleased to make your acquaintance."

"Yes, ma'am." Harlo stared at her hand for a minute, then grabbed it enthusiastically. "I mean, I'm surely happy to meet you, too."

Lucas frowned as Pris's delicate hand disappeared into Dillon's grimy, bony paws. Now, what the hell was he doing touching her? Her gloves would need bleaching for sure.

But then Dillon, encouraged, stepped just a little too close. Pris's nose wrinkled like someone had just dropped a horse apple on her toes. That was more like it, Lucas thought. He'd had a whiff of old Harlo himself.

Priscilla disengaged her hand and stepped furtively back. "Have you been to Maple Falls before, Mr. Dillon?"

"Sure have. I'm an Indian agent. I travel around a lot. Checkin' on things."

"I see."

Harlo made a valiant attempt to puff out his narrow chest. "Negotiating treaties, ya know. Keepin' the red savage in line's a nasty job."

"I . . . see," Priscilla said with a puzzled look. Obviously Pris knew that a low-level agent like Harlo wasn't running around negotiating treaties.

"And a *lonely* job."

"Of course it must be."

Why was Pris flapping her eyelashes at Dillon like that? Lucas wondered. She *couldn't* be interested in the old geezer. Unless Lucas had seriously underestimated her desperation.

"Not that the squaws aren't accommadatin'."

"Wha—?"

Better and better. If Dillon kept talking like that, Pris might even give up the whole damn fool idea. Realize that the selection of men was kind of limited right now, and stop trying to find someone to marry, at least for a while.

"Usually happy to share blankets with a white man, they are." Harlo hitched up his pants for emphasis, just in case the lady didn't catch his meaning.

"Mr. Dillon!" Lucas made a choking sound, and Priscilla shot him a glance. His face was completely sober, but his eyes danced with glee. Now, why was he so delighted this meeting was fast going sour? He'd only have to find her more candidates.

Unless he thought that one nasty experience would be enough to put her off her plans entirely. Well, they'd just see about that.

"I'm certain that they are always pleased to . . . make *your* acquaintance," she said sweetly, winning a pleased smile from Harlo. Who she was surprised hadn't been murdered in his sleep by one of those poor Indian women long ago.

"But it ain't like havin' a fine upstanding white woman. No, indeedy."

"I suppose not." Under the shielding cover of her hat brim—convenient things, hat brims—she peeked at Lucas, who looked like he might explode at any moment if he kept trying to keep his mouth sealed shut like that. Served him right.

"Hell, I remember one time—" Harlo was going on.

"Aren't you going to tell him not to swear?" Lucas burst out.

Priscilla leveled him an even stare. "I am confident Mr. Dillon is well aware that the civilizing influence of—" Priscilla held onto her temper, but just barely "—*white women* includes a certain restraint in his language. When upon our further acquaintance I ask him to refrain, I am positive he will do so. Which is more than I can say for *some* men."

"*When* you ask?" His brows climbed to his hairline. "Are you out of your mind?"

"Now wait a minute," Harlo said. They ignored him.

"You can't possibly be considering spending one second more with this—"

She rounded on him, arms planted firmly on her hips. "Why did you introduce me to him, then?"

"Ah—" Shit. "Pris, I didn't really *know* he was such an ass." Weak, but true enough. "Besides, who'm I to make decisions for you? Figured you'd rather check all the possibilities out for yourself." Better, Lucas congratulated himself.

"In the future, perhaps your—what was the term you used? Oh yes, your *investigations* should be slightly more exhaustive." Priscilla dug into her handbag, removed her spectacles, and placed them firmly back on her nose, magnifying the effect of that accusatory green gaze. "There is much we need to discuss, Lucas. I suggest we leave Mr. Dillon to his own company, adjourn to the front room, and commence with it."

"Just hold on." Harlo shuffled forward, attempting to regain the lady's attention. "We was just gettin' acquainted. Mebbe we could just go on up to my room, and—"

"Mr. Dillon!" He had Pris's attention now, all right. Lucas half expected to see ol' Harlo shrivel down to nothing in the glare of Pris's full *attention*. "We are not now, nor are we ever, going to be any further acquainted than we presently are. In fact, I shall do my very best to *forget* that I ever met you. You are disrespectful, ill-mannered, coarse, and ... and ..." Priscilla searched for a sufficiently vile word. "... Quite unsanitary!" she finished on a furious note. She wheeled around and marched from the room, pausing only once to call back over her shoulder.

"Now, Lucas," she ordered.

Full of admiration, Lucas watched her go. She sure did get a lusty little twitch to her walk when she got riled. And she was the only woman he knew who got more and more ladylike the madder she got, pulling out fancy speeches and sticking that nose in the air like she was a princess. No wonder he had such a hard time resisting any opportunity to tease her.

Dillon whistled through his teeth. "Thought you said she wasn't the Bible-thumping type."

"Didn't hear her mention God once. Did you?"

"She would, though. You just know that kind would." Harlo rocked back on his heels, pondering. "Feisty one, though. I like that. Don't it make your pecker stick out when they get fiery like that?"

A perceptive man might have noticed that Lucas's eyes went dangerously cold. Harlo, however, was going blithely on. "Might even be enough to make a man overlook that nose."

"I'd better see what she wants," Lucas said quietly. Although the floor appeared level, he stumbled badly. And unfortunately for Harlo, Lucas's elbow snapped up as he tripped, smashing into Dillon's nose.

Blood geysered.

Lucas sidestepped quickly, though not fast enough to avoid gaining a smear of blood on his white shirt sleeve.

"Thon-ob-a-bith!" Dillon's hands whipped to his face. "My nothe!"

"How clumsy of me." Lucas fetched a stained, damp rag from behind the bar and tucked it into Harlo's crimson palm. "Here you go," he said. "Better not get any blood on Mrs. Churchill's clean floor. She wouldn't like it."

Whistling, he went to find Pris.

The front room of the Great Northern harkened back to grander times in Maple Falls. Plush velvet the shade of goldenrod draped over the wide front windows and covered two deep chairs. The oak front desk gleamed like glass.

Her back to him, Pris stared out a window, her toe tapping smartly. While she was dressing him and Harlo down, anger had flushed her cheeks and snapped in her beautiful green eyes, and now all Lucas could think was that there were a half-dozen private, comfortable beds conveniently up the length of the stairway.

"There you are!" Pris whirled on him. "Lucas! Your arm is bleeding! What happened?" She was beside him in an instant, rolling up his sleeve to check for injury.

Lucas considered lying, the touch of her hands felt so good on his skin. But he guessed she'd notice he was in one piece and that would come to an end quickly enough. "I'm fine. Mr. Dillon had a bit of an accident, and I just happened to be in the way."

"Oh." Chagrined at how abruptly her fury had submerged beneath concern over his welfare, Priscilla dropped his arm and stepped back.

"It occurs to me," she said, "that when we first entered into this agreement, we should have spelled things out a bit more precisely. Call it carelessness on our part."

Call it madness, she thought. A madness born of the overwhelming, and agonizingly persistent, feelings sparked when he'd sat on her bed and laid his hand against her throat. A madness she was determined to overcome.

It was clearly not going to be easy. She'd thought herself over it completely, but she'd walked in and seen him staring into his drink, handsome and alone, a remote set to his broad shoulders and a deceptive air of sadness around him, and all she'd wanted to do was kiss him again.

She'd have to set boundaries. Clear, precise, unbreakable ones, so they'd both understand what this would be.

And what it absolutely would not.

"Go on." Lucas crossed his arms over his chest.

"First, in order to facilitate the appearance of our new relationship, you will escort me twice a week. Somewhere quite public, and with due attentiveness and consideration."

"Agreed."

"Agreed?" she repeated, his ready consent clearly catching her by surprise.

"Agreed." Particularly to the *public* part. How much trouble could they get into there?

"There will be no more kissing," she said severely. "Under any circumstances."

He stifled an automatic, emphatic protest. No more kissing was undoubtedly a good idea, and his head knew it, even as his body screamed in protest. If their single kiss had scrambled his brain so much, what might happen after one more?

Worse, what might happen to Pris? If he, who had experienced and forgotten a thousand kisses, had been unable to forget that one, how much worse would it be for her?

Because Pris was the last woman in the world he wanted to fancy herself in love with him. It would ruin everything.

"That's fine, too."

"It is?" She was not disappointed that he'd agreed so easily, Priscilla told herself. She *refused* to be disappointed. "Of course it is. Now, on to your part of the bargain."

"Yeah, about that. Pris, I'm sorry about Dillon. But you've got to give me a little slack here and admit the pickings are kind of slim."

"That is no longer my problem, Lucas. For now, you see, it is yours. And if you wish to continue to sleep undisturbed, you will understand that right now."

Sleep undisturbed? Hah, Lucas thought. He *wished* he were sleeping undisturbed. Hell, dreaming about having sex with her was turning out to be more exhausting than the things that had driven him to this bargain in the first place. He might have called the entire thing off and gone back to his old ways . . . except, for some reason he couldn't quite figure, he really did not want to do that.

"You will introduce me to one eligible man per week."

"One a *week?*" Okay, now she'd really gone 'round the bend. "Where the hell am I supposed to find that many men?"

"As I said, that is no longer *my* problem." She dusted her palms together in good riddance. "And please refrain from using that vulgar term, or you shall be exploring its environs more closely than you wish to."

He was going to be dragging corpses from the cemetery to come up with enough men to meet her ridiculous demand. This, all because Pris had gotten it into her head that she wanted to get married. *He* wasn't married, wasn't ever going to get married, and he was perfectly happy. He was so goddamn happy he might just choke on it.

"These men will be gainfully employed, and—"

"Dillon was gainfully employed."

She scowled at him, which only made her mouth draw up into a very delectable pucker. "There was nothing at all gainful about Harlo Dillon."

"That's not entirely true." The man bled pretty satisfyingly, for one thing.

"I have no intention of wasting any more time discussing that man. Now, then—"

"Where's your list?"

"My list?"

"Seems to me you made yourself a list. Why don't you just give it to me, and we can both go on our way?"

"I don't need a written list. *I* can remember my requirements quite well without one. I assumed you could do the same," she said, her tone implying that perhaps she had overestimated. "I could write you one, if you'd like."

"I wouldn't like."

"Good. Also, I require that the candidates be of good moral fiber and in reasonably good health."

"Wouldn't do to have bad moral fiber, would it?"

"It would not," she said, ignoring the gibe beneath his cheerful comment. "And as to his age—" Here her recitation stumbled. Her gaze dropped to her toes, presenting Lucas with a good view of the crown of her hat, aging yellow straw encircled by a bounty of frayed blue ribbons. "It is only important that—" Her head tilted, exposing the side of her neck and the lower curve of her cheek, fine, clear, and glowing bright pink. His anger surged.

"Has to be young enough to put on a good show in the sack, is that it?"

Her head snapped up. "I want children, Lucas. What is so remarkable about that?"

"Fine. You'll get your children and your healthy, moral, employed husband, and your precious marriage, if that's want you want. Now, I've had enough of this foolishness. Some of us have work to do." He strode toward the door.

"There is one more thing."

"What *now?*" he asked, without turning.

"Next time, I require that the man be clean."

Chapter 10

⁓◯◯⁓

So gently the air didn't stir, Clara Wentworth closed the ledger book, centering it
on the big wooden desk. No one, she thought,
had they seen her at that moment, would detect
the roil of anger and grief and dejection churning
so painfully, so newly familiar, within her. Presenting the world with a calm and contained ex-
terior was one of the dwindling sources of pride
and comfort she claimed.

The room she occupied was clearly a man's,
all dark colors and heavy furniture. Leather-
bound books tightly packed the bookcases, and
the records of her husband's many successful
businesses filled a row of cabinets. A tooled
leather box, still holding his favorite cigars, sat
on a small table next to his favorite wing chair,
the mahogany-colored leather of the arms and
seat worn smooth from years of use. Even the
cut-crystal decanter was still half-full of the
French brandy he favored; how could she possibly pour it out?

Once this room had given her much comfort.
She'd sat in his chair, placed her arms where his

had lain, and felt both swallowed up and sheltered by the big piece of furniture that had fit
him so well. She'd felt close to him, imagining
that he would at any moment walk in, scoop her
up, and settle back in the chair with her in his
lap. And kiss her, and perhaps even more,
though she'd scold him for his wickedness before giving in, laughing, as long as she'd known
for sure their girls were safely out of the house.

She pressed her fingers against her temples,
trying to forestall the headache that lurked there,
waiting to claim her. Already this morning she'd
spent two hours poring over the books again,
trying to find a way to make it all work.

She was failing. Failing Levi, failing her
daughters, as she had failed the town, unable to
make Maple Falls Manufacturing once again a
viable and profitable concern.

She pushed away from the desk and wandered over to stare out the window, leaning one
hip against the sill. The weather had finally
turned, the air cooling, bringing in a hint of fall
beneath the ripe, blowsy scent of full summer.
Hollyhocks and dahlias spiked along the edges
of the grass. Asters turned brilliant petals to the
morning glory-blue sky. It was her joy and sol-
ace, her garden, where she could lose herself
among the earth and the flowers.

It still stunned her that she'd been brought to
this turn. She'd been a good wife, properly respectful of her husband's wishes and comfort.
She'd tended their home and daughters as he'd
tended his business. Although she'd always regretted there'd been no more children, and she
knew Levi longed for a son. But he'd never made

her feel like an inferior wife even for that failing, had always seemed pleased with her efforts.

How had it come to this? They weren't destitute. She should be grateful for that. But at times that made it even harder when she saw the desperation that hovered like a specter around so many of her acquaintances. Surely she should suffer as the people who'd depended on them did.

But as always, Levi's foresight had prevailed. He'd transferred many of the assets of Maple Falls Manufacturing into Clara's name before his death. The creditors who'd descended like vultures within a week of his death had been unable to touch most of it. That hadn't stopped them from trying, hounding her relentlessly. But she could no more pay off the notes the company owed than she could force its debtors to pay her, and which of them would feel compelled to pay a mere woman? None.

She whirled back to the room, eyes searching its familiar corners, half-expecting Levi to appear so she could accost him—shout at him, as she never had in life, for leaving her this mess. Without instructions or hints, none of the direction she'd depended on. All he'd left her with was Robert, who'd turned out to be no help at all.

Tears burned like acid. Levi should have prepared her, should have taught her!

And he shouldn't have left her. She snatched up the decanter of brandy and whirled, heaving it out the window. It landed in a clump of dirt at the base of her roses, and she sobbed. She couldn't even break the stupid thing. It lay on its side, the crystal globe of its stopper beside it.

Old brandy leaked onto the dry earth, spreading a dark stain like puddled blood.

Well, perhaps the spirits would do her roses good.

"Mother?" Priscilla said softly behind her. "Are you all right?"

Clara took a quick, surreptitious swipe at her cheeks and eyes, then pressed her palm down the front of her skirt. "I'm fine, of course," she said, pleased with the steadiness in her voice, and turned to face her daughter.

Priscilla pursed her lips, drawing her brows together. "What's the matter?"

Her Priscilla. Always too quick for her own good. And, often, her parents'.

"It's nothing." She gestured toward the desk with its neat stack of books and correspondence, the closed ledger. "It's simply the books again. You know trying to decipher your father's handwriting always gives me a headache."

Priscilla smiled fondly. "He did tend to scrawl, didn't he? Thank goodness that's one thing I didn't inherit from him."

"You should smile more, Priscilla."

The smile remained, but Priscilla's eyes clouded. "There hasn't been so much to smile about recently, has there?"

"No." Less all the time, Clara admitted to herself. She'd always worried about Jeanette, her tendency to let pride and impulse rule her. She'd never worried about Priscilla. That had been a mistake, she realized now. But her elder daughter had always seemed so certain of herself. So bright and proper and giving. What had there been to worry about? Even her friendship with

Lucas Garrett had never given Clara more than a moment's pause. Priscilla had been too intelligent to allow it to become a problem, and Lucas had simply *liked* her daughter too much to sleep with her.

Or so Clara had always believed.

She watched Priscilla move about the room, clicking shut the drawer on a cabinet that was open a fraction, aligning a book more evenly with its neighbors. She lifted the lid of the cigar box and sniffed before letting the cover close again with a soft snap. Seeking her father's presence, Clara supposed.

"We'll have to do something about that, then, won't we?" Priscilla said. "Soon, perhaps there'll be reason to smile. Celebrate, even." When she found a husband, Priscilla thought. And gave her mother grandchildren to dote on and fuss over. Then, perhaps the perpetual worry that marked her mother's face would ease.

She approached the desk and reached for the ledger book. Here, at least, was something she could do to help. The numbers came much more easily to her. "You should have called me."

"No." Clara placed her hand on the ledger. "I've been thinking it over, and I've come to the conclusion that you shouldn't be involved in the business, after all. You're too young, too inexperienced, and it's not a fit occupation for you in any case. It was wrong of me to lean on you for my own convenience."

Priscilla fought back a wave of hurt. "You didn't think so before."

"I've changed my mind."

"I may be inexperienced, but I'm not unskilled. Nor am I all that young," Priscilla said. "I absorbed a lot during the time I spent with Father."

"Obviously, that was a mistake. I wondered at the time, but bowed to your father's wishes, since he had no son to keep him company as he worked. I should have insisted you occupy yourself with more suitable pursuits."

"More suitable pursuits? Cooking and cleaning and sewing, you mean? I can do all those. Quite well."

"Yes, you can." It gave Clara no joy to see Priscilla blinking rapidly. But Clara had never shirked unpleasant duties when they were necessary. Better to mend what she could, salvage whatever was possible out of this predicament. "But you never enjoyed them as you should. If you had, perhaps your life would be very different now."

"I'd be married by now, do you mean?" Pride was an inconvenient and demanding master, Pris reflected. It would not allow her to so much as hint that she wanted that, too, very much. "Even if that's not what I want?"

But pride wilted beneath the concern in her mother's expression. "I wish only the best for you," she said softly.

"I know," Priscilla whispered in return. For she did know that Clara worried for her every bit as much as she herself worried for her mother. Threads of gray dulled the warm brown richness of her mother's hair now, and her elegant slenderness had, sometime in the years since her father's death, crossed over into drawn thinness.

But there were a few things she could do to help, and she was determined to do them. "We've been through this before, Mother. Do we really have to go through it again? Please let me continue to help you with the business."

"It is too much responsibility for you. It was a mistake of me to permit it."

"You no longer trust my judgment."

"No." Narrow shoulders trembled beneath the fine white lawn of Clara's blouse, as if she carried too much weight for her small frame. But there was little use arguing further; her mother's will was far less fragile than her appearance. "Not when you give me reason to doubt it."

Hurt hovered beneath Priscilla's breastbone. Perhaps her judgment *was* impaired, for she had never foreseen this when she'd agreed to what had seemed such a simple plan.

No more than she had predicted that it would endanger a friendship she would have sworn could withstand anything.

Oh, if only Lucas had never kissed her! She was sure that had been the genesis of the problem.

Blinking rapidly, she tried to focus on her father's books, his chair, hoping his things would give her the strength his presence so often had. For once, she was at a complete loss as to what to do. Hoping for distraction, she turned to leave.

"I'll be back by supper," she said.

"Where are you going?"

"Afraid I'm going to Lucas?"

"Yes."

Well, what had she expected? Her mother had

never been one for prevarication. Surprising, how it could still bother her, even when she knew it was coming. There were things, she'd learned, that were impossible to steel yourself against.

"I'm not. I thought I'd go out to the McCanns', watch the baby for a while so Jenny can have a little break." Easier to lose herself in the problems of others than dwell on her own; she'd discovered that years ago.

"That's fine, then. Please give them my best."

"I will."

Blindly, she walked from the room by instinct, brushing her fingers over the back of her father's chair. She'd gone twenty years without a loss before he'd died. That had blindsided her, turned a bright and promising world into something much bleaker. But she hadn't suspected that loss would be the first of so many. Her mother's respect and trust. The dreams for her future she was terribly afraid she would have to relinquish, no matter how hard she was trying to make them come true. And Lucas, whom she counted on in more ways than she realized, his importance in her life made brilliantly clear by his absence.

It would be all right, she told herself. She'd make it all right.

Lucas lay sprawled on his bed, flat on his back, alone and none too happy about it. And temptingly aware that had it been any other woman, in any other circumstances, he would have been doing his damnedest to end his solitude in a satisfyingly physical way.

The lone window, open and uncurtained, threw a rectangle of silver moonlight on the bare wall opposite his bed. Darker patches mottled the light, and he occupied himself trying to guess which blotches were caused by the thin clouds dribbling across the face of the moon, and which were due to the streaks on his window.

That worked for all of about thirty seconds. Until it occurred to him that the oval blot in the upper left corner had a sweetly gentle curve to it, almost exactly matching the curves that a lifetime of practice told him lay under Pris's bodice.

By damn, but he had it bad!

He was not going to sleep with her. He was *not*.

He knew Pris. Knew well that she wasn't the kind of woman to work off an urge and then forget it. She'd been raised to believe that sex should occupy a certain position in her life. A private and vaguely embarrassing place, safely within the cage of marriage, a means of procreation and a way to please her husband. Perhaps even a bit of restrained entertainment on alternate Friday nights, if you got really lucky in your match. It was a hundred and eighty degrees from his own opinion.

He flopped over, belly down, one wrist dangling over the edge of his big bed. He couldn't help but imagine what good use they could put it to, should Pris suddenly take it into her head to corner him and force herself upon him.

He was obsessing over this. Over *her*. Only because, he figured, he'd had so little practice at denying his own desires. It was undoubtedly a good character-building experience.

A thump echoed below him, and he gratefully latched onto the distraction. It sounded like it had come from the back of the store, just under his bedroom. The wind might have blown something over, except he was sure he'd shut the windows. Maybe a hoe had slipped off the hook used to affix it to the wall.

But *that*, now *that* was not such an innocent sound. The unmistakable clatter of a tipped-over barrel proved someone was rummaging around.

Damn! He hoped it wasn't the molasses barrel; he'd just tapped a new one this morning, and it would be hell to clean up.

He clambered off the bed, waded through the laundry he'd left piled on the floor, and pulled on a pair of pants.

The stairway tacked to the back of the building led down to the rear door of his store. He inched the door open and eased inside.

Two small rooms occupied the very back of the store. He used the first small cubbyhole as his office, which opened into an equally tiny storeroom. There were no windows, leaving it black as the devil's heart as soon as the door swung shut behind him. But it also meant, as he wound his way through his office and into the storeroom, that there was no chance the prowler would see him. Plus, he knew the space too well to bump into anything, even if he couldn't see.

Light leaked from the main room, clearly delineating the rectangle of the open door. He edged along the wall lined with stock and peered around the doorframe.

He'd installed two large display windows facing the street, and moonlight poured through, cool and clear as spring water. It reflected off tin containers of tea and spices, bounced off jars and the glass case, filling the room with shadows, doubling its usual appearance of clutter.

His gaze searched the store, hunting for a bulky shape that didn't belong, the flutter of motion. Nothing. But then a faint rustle stirred on the far side of the room, followed by the scrape of feet against the wood floor.

There—a small, slender form silhouetted in silver as it skittered in front of the front windows, head jerking in the furtive alertness of a wary animal.

Not a stranger. Nor one of the impoverished women of Maple Falls.

A child.

Lucas crossed the floor in a half dozen quick, silent steps. He swooped from behind, catching the thief around his middle and scooping him up. A bulging flour bag thumped to the floor, toppling a keg of nails. Beneath his forearm Lucas felt a skinny chest through thin fabric, the corrugation of bony ribs. The child flailed wildly, bare heels drumming a frantic tattoo on Lucas's shins.

"Easy there. Just calm down—ouch!" He carried his captive, struggling silently but furiously in his hold, back across the room. Judging from the light weight, Lucas guessed the kid couldn't be more than five or six. But he had wiry strength, and every now and then, a heel landed a lucky enough strike to be painful.

Behind the display case in the rear of the store, he set the child on his feet. "Don't move," he ordered, reaching for a lantern and matches. "Damn it!"

The child was both quick and desperate. But Lucas had the advantages of familiarity with the room and long arms, and he recaptured his young prowler in an instant, looping one arm around his waist and dangling the squirming child from his right hip.

"Now, what am I going to do with you?" he murmured, half to himself. He wanted to see who he was dealing with, but lighting a lantern with one hand—while holding a struggling prisoner who just might knock it over, sending them all up in flames—looked to be a bit of a trick.

"Let me go!" the child squeaked.

"Oh, so you can talk? No, I don't think I'll be doing that."

His office, then. He hitched the junior thief higher and strode through the building to the office packed with extra stock and piles of paperwork. He dumped the still-wriggling child into his desk chair, which tilted back with a shriek of protest.

Lucas's wide frame blocked the only escape route, allowing him to fire up quickly the lantern hanging above his desk. Light flickered to life, an insubstantial illumination that reached just far enough to reveal the papers scattered over his desk and the child that huddled in his chair.

He'd expected to recognize his intruder. But this wasn't a child he knew, and he was older than he'd first thought, maybe eight or so. Small for his age, with hunched, narrow shoulders and a body that had gone past thin, verging on painfully gaunt.

His hair was dark, absorbing the weak light. The sharp nose and cheekbones, honed to a hungry edge, spoke of Indian blood. But there was something familiar, too, in the square chin that promised to grow into a heavy, prominent jaw. And in the wide, tilted set of the dark eyes, furtively darting from side to side, searching for a way over the boxes and out the door.

"I wouldn't try it, if I were you," Lucas advised. "I'm a lot faster than you, and I'm a tad grouchy about being dragged out of bed. If I have to chase you around some more, I might just call the law and be done with you."

The boy snorted, unimpressed. "Ain't no law. Not anymore."

"That's true. Guess that makes me sheriff, judge, and jury. How convenient. I can do whatever I want with you and nobody'd stop me."

The kid's brave front wavered. His eyes widened, measuring the formidable width of Lucas's bare chest, and he swallowed. "I'll stay."

"That's good." Lucas settled himself on a nearby barrel of coffee beans. "Mite young to be embarking on a life of crime, aren't you?"

Shooting Lucas a sullen glare, the boy poked a finger through one of several holes that scattered like buckshot over the front of his stained knit shirt. He pulled his feet up on the chair, revealing bony legs almost to the knee. But the child appeared clean, his thick hair cut crookedly short from a recent trim.

"Who are you?"

"You gonna tell my ma?"

"That depends."

"Don't." He twisted his finger, wrapping a

wad of shirt around his hand. "She cries all the time already." He wiggled. "You should let me go now, 'fore she gets worried."

"Not so fast. Not until you tell me who you are."

"Mick." Mick thrust his chin out. "Mick *Fergus*."

"Ah." That explained much. When trappers and traders had first come to this territory, female companionship had been hard to come by, and more than one man had taken an Indian woman to "wife." But when white women began arriving, those same men quickly abandoned the women they'd lived with for years and the half-breed children they soon managed to forget. Some of the women returned to their tribes. A few settled west of town in a small collection of wretched huts, a pitifully poor community that the other good citizens of Maple Falls contrived to overlook as much as possible.

Apparently Tom Fergus had been one of those men. He wondered if Flora knew about her husband's half-breed son.

"Your English is good."

"My ma, she makes me practice all the time." He snuffled, wiping the side of his hand beneath his nose. "For when my pa comes back."

"Hmm." Mick stated the last by rote, as if he'd repeated the line a thousand times, though he'd stopped believing it years ago. "I'll expect you back here tomorrow morning. Eight o'clock sharp. You can tell your mother whatever you want, but if you're late, I'll come looking for you. What she finds out then is your problem."

"Eight . . . o'clock?" he repeated, confused.

"Yup. Be ready to work."

"A job?" Fragile hope mixed with well-ingrained suspicion. "You're giving me a job?"

"How else am I going to make sure you don't run all over town, taking things that don't belong to you?" And make sure the kid got enough food to flesh out those ribs. "Don't have a jail to lock you up in."

"Yeah. I guess."

"First two weeks I get for free, in repayment for dragging me out of bed in the middle of the night. Lunch comes with the job. After the two weeks are up you'll have to take your pay in trade. You can pick what you want out of stock. Whatever you can talk me into, that is."

Dazed, Mick could only nod in agreement.

"Be ready. I'll work you hard." He fixed Mick with a severe look. "No more stealing, or it'll come out of your hide the next time."

Mick edged forward in the chair, his butt in danger of sliding off. "All right."

"Sir."

"All right, sir." Something tugged at the corners of his mouth—not quite a smile, but maybe the promise of one.

Lucas stepped aside, clearing the way. "You go on, now. And go straight home—no side trips."

Mick hopped out of the chair and scuttled for the door, glancing back once over his shoulder as if he couldn't quite believe that Lucas really meant to let him go.

Lucas poked his head out the door to watch him leave. There was enough moonlight to see Mick slip between the side of the store and the empty boardinghouse next door, the bulk of the two buildings making him look even more small and frail.

Lucas frowned. The kid was too young to be out wandering around in the middle of the night. Deciding there was no time to grab more clothes, he followed, hoping no one would see him.

Unless it was Pris, of course.

Mick wasn't trying to hide, nor was he looking around much, so Lucas had no trouble following him without being seen. He waited until Mick crept into a tiny shack that looked no more substantial than a peach crate, and watched a little longer, just to make sure, before he turned for home.

Chapter 11

Lucas left his store at 5:45 and flipped over the neatly lettered sign to "Closed." Pris had given it to him shortly after he'd opened Garrett's, on the correct assumption that any sign he painted would be all but illegible.

He was supposed to meet Pris at the Great Northern, and he counted it unfortunate that they were likely to be the only customers in the dining room this evening. Being left alone with Pris might just do him in. He'd much prefer to avoid temptation than count on his little-tested ability to resist it. He wondered if they could just be seen coming and going—which was the whole point, after all—and skip the dangerously cozy dinner in between.

Strolling past Luella Rice, who was sweeping the porch in front of the tobacco shop her husband had closed a year ago, he waved cheerily. She and her children still lived above the store, and she survived by taking in laundry, though Lucas figured he was the only customer she currently had. Which is why he'd used her services, even when he'd more than one offer to have his wash done for free. Her youngest daughter, Anna, a cheerful and out-going three year old, stirred the dust next to her with her own small broom. Lucas picked a coneflower and handed it to the child, earning a dimpled smile.

Luella straightened, beaming at him. "Hear you're having dinner with Priscilla tonight."

"You're well informed, Mrs. Rice."

She didn't even bother to look embarrassed. For what was there to be embarrassed about? Taking an interest in Priscilla Wentworth's welfare was tantamount to a civic duty in Maple Falls. "Temperance bought one of my hens this afternoon. Needed something special for dinner, she said."

"Roast chicken then, is it? Don't know anyone who makes it finer."

"No, indeed." She nodded. "I'm happy for both of you, Lucas. Didn't know you had the sense to settle down with such a fine woman."

"She's the only one who'd put up with me."

She waved off the absurdity. "Never saw a woman more suited to being a wife and a mother than Priscilla. Just can't help fussing over people. Was starting to get afraid she wasn't going to have the chance, though."

Lucas kept his smile steady, but he winced inside. What, exactly, was everyone's fixation—Priscilla's included—with getting her married? "Yes, well, I'd best be going. Wouldn't want to keep the lady waiting."

"Got you toeing the line already, hmm?"

He laughed and dipped his chin in her direction. "Good afternoon to you, then."

The rest of Center Street was deserted. No doubt the good townspeople were at home, preparing for their cozy family dinners, or as close as they could come with Papa gone. If Lucas's parents had ever attempted one of those nice family suppers, it was before he was old enough to remember. Thank God for small favors.

However, Pris really wanted those family dinners. In all fairness, he should probably put a little effort into helping her get them. He tried to envision a smiling Pris in a high-necked apron, sitting down to a food-laden kitchen table with a clutch of children. Yep, he could see that all right. But then he tried to see the man, presiding over the opposite end of the table, and his mind balked.

He just couldn't picture it.

But he had four days before Pris was expecting him to come up with someone. He'd have to do better than he had with Harlo Dillon.

Down in St. Anthony there was Philo Camp, his old school friend. But he was too damn good-looking . . . every woman wanted to be the prettiest one in the marriage. Or Lewis Hull, who sold Lucas farm implements, but he was going to get fat in ten years or so; Lucas was sure of it. James McGuire? Naw, he liked whiskey a little too much.

And then there was always Dan Cardinell. A possibility. His own store in St. Paul was prosperous, and he was a truly good man.

Lucas took a quick look down the street before he angled across toward the hotel on the opposite side.

In fact, Dan's only flaw was that he was deeply in love with a married woman who, for her children's sake, wouldn't leave her husband. The affair had been quietly going on for years and wasn't likely to stop. However, if Pris didn't demand fidelity, Dan was as good a catch as there was.

But hell, if Pris didn't care about fidelity, she might as well marry him.

Whoa! His thoughts screeched to a halt as he stopped dead in the middle of the road.

Where had *that* come from?

He'd thought he'd reached the heights of idiocy when he'd conceived this unimaginable, and apparently persistent, lust for Pris. But that was *nothing* compared to the zenith of stupidity he'd just reached.

For marrying Pris, a notion obviously spurred by that same outrageous passion and the tempting possibility of indulging it to his heart's content, would no doubt end with her feeling about him exactly the same way his mother had felt about his father. And there was one thing he knew: having Pris look at him with that same mix of bitterness and hatred would just about kill him.

Maybe he'd better get Pris safely married off after all. At least she'd be in no further danger from him.

"Whoa! Watch out!"

The shout came from just behind him, and he whirled to find the six o'clock stage from St. Cloud bearing down on him, its driver yanking hard on the reins, battling his team to a stop. Lucas jumped right, the stage careened left and raced by, the blast of wind in its wake buffeting him.

The stage pulled to a stop right in front of the Great Northern. "Mister!" the driver shouted, scrambling down from his perch. "You okay?"

"I don't know," Lucas muttered. He'd known Pris was a threat to his sanity; he hadn't realized she was a threat to his life as well.

The driver sprinted the half block to Lucas, his hat flying off and swirling behind him to land in the street. "I been shoutin' at you for two blocks, don't know how you missed hearin' us comin'—" He got close enough to get a good look at the man he'd almost run down. "Mr. Garrett?"

"Yeah, Johnny, it's me," he admitted. Johnny fell into step beside him. "Sorry about that."

"Beggin' your pardon, Mr. Garrett, but that's a damn fool place to take a reverie, in the middle of Center Street when I'm due in. You know the stage ain't been late since I started, 'cept last winter when the February blizzard clogged up the road."

"You've got me there."

Johnny Merced had taken over the stage route more than eight months ago, when the driver who had done such good business ferrying men out of Maple Falls on their way to the goldfields had decided to join them himself. Johnny couldn't be much over seventeen, his lanky frame and bony features still holding the sharp, clean edges of youth. But he was a good driver and unfailingly cheerful. Though the company no longer made much money ferrying passengers to—or from—Maple Falls, it was a convenient stop on the way to more affluent towns.

Johnny scooped up the battered felt hat and jammed it back on his head. "You got woman trouble, Mr. Garrett?"

"What makes you say that?"

Johnny paused beside his stage, checking that he'd set the brake properly, running a calming hand over the back of the nearest gelding to make sure the close call hadn't given him a fright. "Be a bit unusual for you, that's for sure. But I don't know what else'd make a fella overlook a stage coming up on his back."

"True enough," Lucas admitted. The horse lifted his tail, plopping a steady stream of horse apples in the middle of the street.

"Got me a few of those myself."

"Women troubles? You, Johnny?" He couldn't recall women being a problem when he was that young. More like the answer to his prayers.

Johnny shook his head regretfully. "They just don't seem to be takin' me all that serious, Mr. Garrett. Not looking at me like a man." He cocked his head hopefully, the hat slipping down over his right eye. "You got any advice for me? Can't think of nobody better to ask."

"Nope, not me." Lucas slapped Johnny's shoulder companionably. "Except no one should be pondering women on an empty stomach. Come on, let me buy you dinner."

Temperence Churchill would probably wonder why he'd let Johnny come along to what was supposed to be a romantic dinner. At least this way he wouldn't be all alone with Pris and maybe suggest something that would either get him laughed at or ruin both their lives.

Johnny's eyes lit up like Roman candles. If there was one thing as guaranteed to get the full attention of a young man as the topic of women, it was food. "Well, yeah! Thanks!"

Johnny, at barely seventeen, Lucas guessed, was scraping the bottom end of Pris's age requirement, no doubt about it. But maybe he would buy Lucas some time to find someone more suitable.

As long as Pris didn't like him too much. Sure as shootin' the pup would be handsome enough, once he grew into his face. And he sure as hell was healthy, and hardworking, and morally sound . . . in fact, he was far too close to Pris's requirements for Lucas's piece of mind. No telling just how desperate she was. And as for Johnny . . . well, being seventeen and having your blood runnin' hot had made more than one young man hitch up with a seductive older woman that he shouldn't've.

He pushed aside the lingering thought that Pris'd be better off marrying just about anyone than risking Lucas's touching her again.

"By the way," he said, "we're meeting a lady. An old friend of mine. A really *old* friend of mine."

"Mr. Garrett, you can't want me along then, muddying up your waters."

"Yes, I do. I want you to be nice to her, too. Just not *too* nice, if you know what I mean."

Johnny threw back his head, nearly spilling his hat again, and laughed. No doubt about it, the kid had a handsome smile. And he was even pretty clean. Shit!

"Mr. Garrett, you can't be worryin' that a woman'd be more interested in me than you."

"Hmm." His gaze shifted from the kid, to the big front pockets in his blue cotton shirt, and then the pile the gelding had made. He grinned.

"Johnny, I'll buy you the biggest steak Mrs. Churchill can fry. But you gotta do one more thing for me."

"She's a nice lady, your Miss Wentworth," Johnny said around the hunk of meat he'd just stuffed into his mouth. "She listens to a fella like he's got something worth sayin'."

Lucas all but growled, gulping down Mrs. Churchill's strong, bitter coffee instead. It was no surprise that Johnny considered Pris a "nice lady." She'd obviously set herself to charming the boy. Who'd have thought she'd be so dad-blamed good at it? Sure as hell she'd never tried it on him. Lucas figured that, after one more fetching smile or flirty glance, Johnny was going to throw himself at Pris's dainty feet.

"And that little Churchill kid—did you see the way he giggled when she stopped to talk to him on her way back to the kitchen?"

Yeah, he'd seen it, though he hadn't been looking at Ernie Churchill. He'd been looking at Pris, at the way her face glowed like a just-opened morning glory, like you'd see every bit of happiness in the whole world if you just kept looking at her. And wondering why he never noticed that the blue blouse he'd seen her wear a hundred times made her look so darn pretty.

"You got to know she'd be great with a whole gaggle of them. Reminds me of my own ma."

Good. No way Johnny was working up a good case of puppy-love on Pris if she reminded him of his mother.

"I'd almost be tempted to make a run at her myself. A man couldn't do much better."

Sound rumbled low in Lucas's throat.

"If she wasn't already taken, I mean. Of course. Sir."

"She's not," Lucas snapped out.

"Really?" Speculation gleamed in his eyes. "You think she'd—"

"No," Lucas snarled, with a warning glare for good measure.

"Here she comes!" Johnny scrambled to his feet. "I gotta go out back to the necessary, and I wouldn't want to mention it in front of her. Gotta protect a lady's sensibilities, you know."

He waved eagerly at the returning Pris, then all but ran for the rear entrance. No doubt in a hurry to get his business done and get back to drooling over Pris, Lucas thought sourly.

Pris slid into her chair and looked at him expectantly. Lucas, staring broodingly into his coffee, said nothing.

"Mrs. Churchill is fine," Priscilla said at last. "Since you so thoughtfully asked after her. Ernie seems fully recovered from his chill. And she's made a lovely apple pie for dessert."

Lucas grunted in response.

"You know, you could at least make an attempt to hold up your end of the conversation. Merely for politeness' sake, Lucas."

He arched an eyebrow at her. "More amendments to the agreement, Pris? It's getting so I can barely keep track. I'm not sure you're worth the effort."

Stung, Priscilla blinked. He'd been grouchy throughout dinner, and the more she'd tried to be amusing, the more effort she'd exerted to cover up his uncharacteristic silence, the more he'd glowered at her.

And—oh, foolish heart—the more she'd wanted to kiss away his black mood. It really was a good thing, she decided, that he was usually quite even-natured. Because Lucas, angry or unhappy or whatever he was that put that bleak intensity into his dark eyes, might have caused this ludicrous, purely physical infatuation even earlier. Before she'd been mature enough to resist it.

"Fine, then," she snapped. "Sit there and mope into your coffee. I won't expend any more energy trying to jolly you out of whatever's got you so glum."

"Glum?" No one had *ever* called him glum. Why, he was one of the most entertaining men in the state; he knew dozens of women who'd attest to it.

"Yes, glum." She looked him up and down. "What's gotten into you tonight, anyway? Look at you!"

"Look at what?"

"Those clothes! It looks like you've been wearing them all week."

"Hey! They're clean."

"Clean?" she repeated, dubious.

"I know they're clean. I took a good sniff before I put 'em on, just to make sure."

"Lucas, there is no way that Luella Rice re-

turned your clothes in that condition. She irons
them within an inch of their life.''

"Well, yeah," he admitted. "But after they sit
around on the floor for a few days, they get nice
and crumpled up. Comfortable.''

"On the floor? Don't you have a . . . bureau, or
a closet?''

Now, why didn't she know that about him?

She'd never been in his rooms. Had never before even thought about whether that was odd,
given that he'd been in hers so many times.
Strange that she'd never been curious.

Had she known even then, without con-
sciously realizing it, what a risk it would be?
That his rooms were much more dangerous than
her own, a place designed for seclusion and sin?
But that would mean that this . . . passion, this
desire for him, had existed far longer than she'd
realized.

She wondered just how long she'd been stupid. Or perhaps she'd merely been blind.

It's just Lucas, she scolded herself. To confirm
this, she took in all his familiar features, the
spark of devilment in his eyes and the mouth
that always seemed on the verge of sliding into
a smile—or a kiss.

Just Lucas. Not a compelling stranger or a
cherished lover. Just Lucas, who she longed with
all her heart would reach across the table right
now and kiss her again.

Nope, not blind. Stupid, for sure.

"Now, why would I want to go through all
the work of putting them away, when you just
gotta take them back out again when you want
to wear them?''

"Oh, Lucas." Priscilla shook her head, laughing softly. "You do need a keeper."

"Are you offering to keep me?"

And there it was, released by one quick, thoughtless comment. It charged the air, crackling between them. In the past, Lucas might have called it lust, but no mere lust had ever pulled at him like this.

She stared at him over the width of the table, the line of her mouth softening, parting. Her eyes went slumberous with promise, a beckoning glitter of green beneath thick dark lashes drooping low and sleepy. Her whole posture eased, her neck and back relaxing, as if she were ready to tumble right into bed.

Lucas's hands fisted, nails biting into his palms. Wanting to touch her. Not wanting to touch her. Not knowing whether that touch would break this link between them or strengthen it into something fast and unbreakable. Not sure at all that he wanted either one.

"Lucas? Priscilla?" Priscilla jerked, startled, at Mrs. Churchill's call from the kitchen. As if someone had just broken into her dream, and she couldn't quite bring herself to the surface of full wakefulness. "Can I bring you anything else right now?"

Lucas sucked in a deep, steadying breath, tempted beyond reason to toss Mrs. Churchill out of her own inn and lock the door behind her.

Uncertainly, Priscilla met his gaze.

"Lucas?"

A million questions resided in that one utterance of his name. Questions he couldn't, didn't want to, wouldn't ever answer. So help him God.

Please help him, God.

"Look, Pris," he said, propping both elbows on the table and leaning her direction. "Don't do it."

"Don't do what?"

He nodded in the direction Johnny had gone.

"If you're bent on doing this, give me time to do it right. To find someone who you'd at least have a fair chance with." He swallowed. "Someone who you could . . . care for."

"Are you telling me that you didn't bring Johnny here to meet me?"

"I did, but—"

"That's good."

"But I don't think that—"

"So don't think."

Only Pris could twist him around and back on himself until he couldn't even find the right words, ones that would make her see it all correctly. That would make her see it *his* way.

She was going to marry someone she didn't love. And she was going to be as miserable as his mother had been, as so many women he'd known were, and he wasn't going to be able to stop her.

"Shit, Pris! And don't you dare tell me to stop swearing, or I'll bind and gag you and *then* you'll let me finish what I've got to say without interrupting me!"

"I don't have time!"

"Because you won't be reasonable and agreeable and just a little bit patient and give me time to come up with the right man!"

"It's not your function to come up with the right man," she objected. Lucas guessed she'd used that exact same expression and tone lecturing disobedient boys at school. "You are merely to come up with possibilities that meet my requirements. It is my decision from there."

Lucas wondered how he could simultaneously have an overwhelming desire to make love to her until they both expired from the exertion and an equally powerful urge to wring her pretty neck. "If your reactions so far are any indication, Pris, maybe you could do with a little advice."

Ice and fire. Even though he knew he was going to be the recipient of both inside of two minutes, he couldn't help but admire the effect. Everything that was male in him responded to the challenge of the ice in her manner, the promise of the fire in her eyes.

"And exactly which decision of mine are you questioning?"

"There's this whole ass-backward idea of deciding to get married and hunting up a man to do it with, rather than the other way around." Her hand hovered over her knife, fingers flexing. Let her try, Lucas thought. It'd give him an excuse to put his own hands on her, and whatever happened then would be on her head. "Not to mention that, if you're seriously considering that young pup, you'd better listen to *somebody* who has some sense."

"Oh?" Priscilla asked, imagining how well Lucas would look with the remains of her chicken over the top of his head. They'd gone from friendly to furious so fast her head was spinning. But her heart was pumping hard, her breath coming fast, and heavens, but it felt good. "What is wrong with Johnny?"

"Nothing's wrong with Johnny."

"Then something is wrong with Johnny and *me?*"

Her eyes dared him to imply that she was too old for him. But while Lucas was willing to admit that most of the good sense he owned had disappeared the night he'd crawled through her window, he still wasn't that dumb.

"He just doesn't fit your list, that's all."

"You don't think so? He's healthy."

"He was coughing his head off right before I brought him in here. I swear, Pris, I thought he was going to leave a lung right out there in the street. Can you imagine what Mrs. Churchill would have thought of that? Such a mess to clean up."

"Hmm. He seems to have recovered well."

"And he sure's been out back an awful long time," Lucas went on. "Intestinal difficulties, I bet. Probably why he's so skinny."

"He seems of good moral fiber."

"Well now, Pris, I didn't want to say anything, but—" His voice lowered, drawing her into his confidence. "I have it on good authority that he's got a whole box full of liquor and cigars and lurid magazines back in the stage."

"You don't say." She would not smile at him, the irredeemable bounder. "He's gainfully employed."

"Only until the stage company finds that box. And finds out about the . . ." He stopped. "I promised I wouldn't tell anyone. In confidence, you know. Sorry."

"I understand." The laughter simmered between them, waiting impatiently for release, every bit as compelling and seductive in its own way as the passion. Every bit as hard to resist. "Well, he's certainly not too old."

Lucas leaned comfortably back in his chair, linking his hands behind his neck, as if the answer was too obvious to even bother with speaking it out loud.

"And he's clean."

"Clean? You sat by him all dinner. Couldn't you smell him?"

"That's merely a symptom of his job. Surely he'll clean up properly, given the chance." Priscilla eyed his clothes again and tried for an obviously disdainful expression, implying that he was hardly the one to question another's grooming habits. She had to admit to herself that it was made more difficult by the fact that his rumpled appearance had a strange appeal. Her hands practically itched to start smoothing out wrinkles and doing up buttons. And maybe touch a few other things beneath the clothes in the process.

"Anyway, I like him."

Lucas sighed, reluctant to start going around on the same topic again. "Pris—"

The bell over the front door tinkled, and Pris looked over his shoulder into the hotel foyer. "And so will she, don't you think?"

"Who?"

He twisted around. Sarah Jane Bosworth was hurrying toward them, prettily disheveled by her rush, her smile nervous and eager. "I'm not too late, am I?"

"No, of course not," Priscilla replied. The grin she flashed Lucas was pleased and more than a little smug. "I sent Ernie to invite Sarah Jane to join us. After all, I'm sure that that delightful young man would be pleased to have someone to talk to who wasn't as *ancient* as we are."

In acknowledgment, he refrained from uttering the first word that came to mind. "I suppose this means I'll have to spring for *four* dinners now."

Chapter 12

The small farm, five miles north of Maple Falls, was carved from the border where the prairie met the woodlands. Great oaks and maples sheltered the log cabin, while the broad, empty stretches of land to the west shone with sunshine and wildflowers. The burble of a small stream, hidden within the line of trees, whispered beneath the wind-spawned rustling of leaves and tall grass. What should have been fields had shrunk to nothing more than a large garden, as the prairie and forest showed every intention of reclaiming their land.

Lucas pulled his wagon to a stop. Shouting a greeting, he vaulted from his seat. A dark-haired boy of six charged from the back of the house. Two smaller children tumbled out of the front, setting the flap of oilcloth that served as a door swinging. A fragile-looking woman with a toddler propped on her left hip followed.

"Got any eggs for me today, Mrs. McCann?"

"Don't I always?" Her smile was worn, tired as the rest of her. By Lucas's reckoning, Jenny couldn't be but a few years over twenty; she'd come to Maple Falls four years ago, just before the birth of the twins, full of dreams and love for her equally young husband. The youth had faded quickly; the dreams had taken longer, but they were going, too.

The boy reached Lucas's side and latched on, giving a sharp tug to Lucas's sleeve. "Bring me anything?"

"Kevin!" his mother said sharply.

Lucas shot her a quick smile. "It's okay." He knelt down to bring the youngster to eye level. Kevin had the pale skin and big blue eyes of his mother, eyes that still held some of the excitement and promise that had once shown so clearly in his mother's. "Hey, you know the deal."

Kevin nodded solemnly. "You're a businessman."

"Yup. And businessmen don't give anything for free." Lucas frowned, as if thinking hard, and Kevin curled his mouth down, trying to match Lucas's stern expression. "I could probably use an assistant right now, though. I've got a lot of work to do today. Hard for an old fellow like me to unload everything by myself."

"I could help!"

"Could you?" He inspected his young applicant. "Let me see."

Kevin shoved up his sleeve and flexed his arm, his face scrunching up fiercely as he struggled to produce a muscle.

"Well, would you look at that!" Lucas poked at the tiny biceps. "Bigger'n mine, I bet."

"Yup!" Kevin agreed proudly.

"Tell you what," Lucas said. "You help me

unload the stuff from the back of the wagon, and get your mama's eggs and cheese loaded up, and there might be a couple of peppermint sticks in it for you."

"Three sticks," Kevin bargained.

"Three?"

He nodded. "For Katie and Rose, too." He hooked his thumbs in the waistband of his pants, aping Lucas's stance. "Mary can just have a taste of mine," he allowed.

"Three sticks, then."

Lucas balanced a small bag of white beans over Kevin's skinny shoulder, then hefted a barrel of flour. "Show me where they go," he told the boy.

Jenny stood beside the front door, and as he passed, she lightly touched his arm.

"I wasn't sure what you needed," he said, "so I took a guess. I brought flour, and beans, and a sack of sugar. Some oats, too. If there's anything else you need, I'll be back in two weeks."

"No, that's fine." She took a fortifying breath. "It's too much. I know the eggs don't bring in anywhere near what you've been giving us, and I don't know how to . . ." She trailed off. The baby, unused to strangers, buried her face against Jenny's neck and she rested her cheek against the child's downy head. Pride demanded a fair trade, but pride didn't feed her children.

Lucas rushed in before she could say anything more. "Don't worry about it. Your credit's good."

She wavered for an instant, then gave in. "I don't know how we'll repay you."

"When Michael comes back, I'll expect you to

be the most loyal customers I have. If I hear about you running off to buy your seeds at some fancy new store, I'll be here demanding your business so fast your head'll spin."

She laughed, more relief than amusement. "You've got it."

"There's some hay in the back of the wagon, too." Lucas gestured over his shoulder. "A friend of mine who farms near Sauk Center had so much he didn't know what to do with it. Practically forced me to take some off his hands. Figured we could stack it right around the cabin—be good insulation for the winter. And you could feed it to the livestock if you start running short before spring."

"I—" She closed her eyes, swallowing hard.

"You've got to take it," he said quickly. "Don't know what else I'll do with it, and I'm not much in favor of turning my place into a hayloft."

"How much did the hay cost you, Mr. Garrett?"

"Nothing." Nothing but two kegs of whiskey and the promise of an introduction to a certain dancer in St. Anthony—neither of which he intended to mention.

Jenny gave a sad little chuckle, not fooled for a minute, but too grateful to protest further. They both silently agreed to let the matter lie. Relieved to have the tricky part done, Lucas set himself to unloading the supplies and piling hay around the foundation of the cabin. All the while, Jenny McCann stood silently in the sunshine and watched, swaying back and forth with the baby nodding off against her shoulder.

He loaded a crate of eggs and two ball-shaped

cheeses into the wagon bed, bolstering them with old gunny sacks.

"All done?" When Kevin stood on his toes, his eyes were just high enough to peer between the lowest two boards of the wagon's sides.

"All done." Lucas jumped down and handed Kevin his pay, slipping him a fourth red-and-white stick for a tip.

"Would you like a cup of coffee?" Jenny offered. "Please?"

Though he didn't want to impose, he respected her need to make the gesture. "That'd be appreciated."

"Kevin, I want you to take the twins out back to the shed and do your chores. Don't come back to the house until I call you." Jenny McCann normally had one of the kindest, softest mother-voices he'd ever heard, and the thread of not-to-be-disobeyed steel in her tone caught him by surprise. The only thing he could think of was she had something to ask him she didn't want the children to hear, and tension coiled painfully between his shoulder blades.

He followed her into the dimness of the cabin. Stark and painfully neat, the room held only a bare minimum of furniture made by an inexpert hand; Jenny's life didn't allow either the money or time for niceties of decor.

"Excuse me," she said quietly. "I'd like to put the baby down." She ducked behind the faded, striped blanket draped in the far corner of the single room. He heard her croon to the child, a low, soothing, wordless sound.

Too jumpy to settle in a chair, he wandered over to the single front window, poking aside the scraped and oiled hide tacked there to peer outside. The garden held a patch of straggly potato plants, rows of pale corn and weedy beans. A lean pig rummaged at the edge of the woods.

"I apologize for taking so long," Jenny said, moving by him to the corner of the room used as the kitchen.

Lucas prodded at a loose flap of the window-skin. "This has torn free of the nail here. I could pound it back in for you. Wouldn't take more than a moment."

"Perhaps later," she said, brushing aside the faded calico curtain hiding the cupboard. Her hands shook as she removed a cup, rattling it against its saucer.

"Mrs. McCann?" He was at her side in a moment. He raised a hand meant to comfort, then lowered it again. "What is it?"

She set the cup back before she dropped it, then gripped the edge of the cupboard, fingers curling into the splintery wood, her head bowed.

"Is it the Indians?" he asked. "It's been quiet, I hear, but if you are frightened, I could move you in to town right now. Take you all back into the wagon with me."

"No." A slight shake of her head, the merest ripple of her dull gold hair. "I mean, I hear them sometimes, war parties crossing north of here. But they're far too busy fighting each other to bother with us."

"That could change. If it does, you shouldn't take any chances. Lord knows there's plenty of empty rooms in town. There'd be no problem finding you a place to stay."

"It's not a problem."

"Promise me," he said, feeling the weight of responsibility. Her husband was miles away, and there was no one else to ensure she'd come if the need arose.

"I promise." Her shoulders stiffened, a meager vestige of resolve and determination. "I don't know what we would have done, Mr. Garrett. If you didn't come out here to fetch the eggs and butter every other week . . . I couldn't get them into town myself. It's too far, there's too much to do here, and with the children . . ." Her voice threaded.

Ah, damn, Lucas thought, rolling his head to ease the tightness in his neck and shoulders. He didn't mind the doing; it was the gratitude he couldn't deal with. Especially when he so plainly didn't deserve it. All he was doing was trying to take care of his customers, and they persisted in seeing generosity in it. Lucas wondered if Pris ever felt as unworthy as he did when she lent a hand, or if she managed gracefully to deflect the acknowledgment.

He'd have to ask her . . . if they ever again had a conversation that was more than the stilted, sniping ones they'd been managing lately. He hadn't realized how much he'd depended on her good sense and companionship until they'd so unexpectedly tumbled into lust, which seemed to have deafened and blinded them both.

"I was in the area."

"No, you weren't." She folded both hands together into one fist, and tapped it against her chin. "But I appreciate you trying to make me think that you were."

She stared at him, huge blue eyes searching

deep into his own, as if she were hunting for something. Finally she gave a brief nod, as if she'd found what she'd been looking for.

Deep cracks and pale white scars marred her long fingers, dark brown from a summer of working outside. Those fingers fumbled at her throat, undoing the first button of her graying blouse. Too shocked to register her actions, he merely stared, watching the now-open collar tremble against her neck as her quaking fingers worked the next button.

She moved on to the third, exposing the thready, lacy edge of her undergarments.

"Wha—what are you doing?" The words burst out of him.

Her hands stilled for just a moment, then slid the pale disc through its hole. "I think that's obvious," she said evenly; having struggled with the decision, she didn't want to give in to second thoughts now.

"Stop." He took the hand that was now plucking at the fourth button and enfolded it in his own. "Please stop."

"Oh." Her breath began as a gasp, turned into a sob. "You don't want me." She averted her eyes, resignation and embarrassment stealing the last of her beauty.

"No." She flinched at his denial, and he swore at himself. He was botching this so badly, adding to burdens he'd meant to lighten. But he'd never expected it, not once. He would have sworn that Jenny McCann was too deeply in love with her Michael ever to notice another man. "That's not what I—" He tugged on her hands to bring her closer, and slipped an arm around her back. "That's not how I meant it. Not 'No, I don't want you,' but 'No, this isn't right.' You don't want me."

That brought her gaze around to him again. "But I do!"

He rubbed small circles on her back, hoping to soothe and support, better with touch than he was with words.

"I don't think so." He knew the difference between a grateful woman and an eager one. He'd never taken advantage of the former.

Or had he? She sagged into his touch, a weary surrender to someone else's strength, and he felt a faint stir of sympathy.

Yes, he knew the difference now. But had he always? When he was young and flushed with the power and wonder of sex, when it had seemed to consume him and his life, would he have known the difference between healthy desire for him and any one of a hundred other, lesser, more complicated reasons a woman might have to lie with him?

Revulsion curled within him for the man he'd been then. And regret, for the women he might have hurt, by accepting offers that should never have been made. He struggled to hide his reaction, not wanting Jenny to think the revulsion was for her.

"But I do," she whispered. "You don't know— it's so lonely. Never doing anythin' that's just for me, never feeling anythin' that's not worry." Her hand curled around his collar. "You could make me forget. Just for a while."

"You wouldn't forget." He gently tucked a strand of hair, the texture dry and rough, behind her ear. "You'd just put it off for a while. And then you'd have one more thing you wouldn't want to remember." He set her away from him. "I know where your heart belongs, Jenny McCann," he said. "And so do you."

She smiled, a real one this time, and Lucas was relieved to see that some of the desolate edge was gone.

"And what about you, Lucas? Where does your heart belong? It's a good one, you know. Better than you realize, I think."

"Well . . ." To his surprise, the quick denial he would have expected didn't come. Only for safety's sake, he told himself. While Mrs. McCann got into town only rarely, it was possible that someone might tell her of his new relationship with Pris. "I have a few ideas about that, myself."

"Really? I'm pleased to hear that."

A small cry came from behind the blanket divider.

"Short nap," he commented.

"He's decided he only needs one a day. I don't agree, but—" She shrugged, moving toward the back of the cabin. "If you'll excuse me."

"I'll show myself out," he said. "And I'll be back in two weeks, of course."

She lifted her shoulders with the determination that had brought her this far. "I'll see you then," she said, and disappeared behind the blanket.

Chapter 13

The break in the heat proved to be nothing more than a tease, seductive and meaningless as the flash of a flirt's eyes behind her fan. September rolled in with an unseasonable wave of heat and humidity that had crops drooping low in their fields, an exhausted posture echoed by the townspeople. The air seethed with the portent of violent storms lurking to the west, waiting for the worst possible moment to strike.

There was no energy to be wasted on frivolities, none to spare for haste. Which made Lucas and Priscilla's afternoon parade through town a painfully slow amble rather than a stroll.

She'd met him in the road in front of her house, bursting out from the garden where she'd been tugging absently at a weed in a way he took as evidence she'd been waiting for him. He might've been flattered. If he hadn't been convinced that she was standing out there, broiling, specifically to ensure that he couldn't march up to the front door and ask for her. As if, after all this time, she was ashamed to have her mother know that she was going out for a turn with *him*.

Though they were only planning to parade through town, Pris was rigged out like she was going to church, in a striped, starched blouse that had to be choking her; a big, floppy hat buried under billows of ribbons and fake flowers that provided less shade than weight; and a pair of gloves that probably made her hands feel like she'd just stuck them into dishwater. Served her right, he thought, if she collapsed from the heat.

Of course, then he'd be forced to carry her home. And it'd probably be a good idea if he loosened her clothes, just to make sure she could breathe. His own breathing quickened, and the temperature notched up several degrees. The air temperature, he told himself, not just his, and he reached up and thumbed open another button on his shirt. *He* was not going to pass out in the middle of town just to keep up appearances.

Priscilla had heard Lucas coming. An enthusiastic, off-key whistling of "Camptown Races" preceded him, and she hurried out from her post in the garden where she'd been pretending to thin the pansies.

She would not have let her mother dissuade her from strolling with Lucas this afternoon, she told herself firmly. Why put them through a painful confrontation when it was so easily avoided? So she'd waited for him in the steamy, fragrant garden instead. It wasn't cowardice but expedience.

He was ambling down the street as if he had all the time in the world. Irritation flashed, and she tugged on her hat, settling it more firmly on her head. He'd been holding up his end of their bargain in only the most nominal of ways, and still he couldn't be bothered to dress properly for their date. No suit, no tie, no hat, just a soft pair of canvas pants and a loose shirt. Open at the collar, no less, with the sleeves rolled up to his elbows; he looked like he was preparing to cultivate a field, rather than escort the woman he'd set his heart on.

It was all the more annoying that he looked so . . . heavenly that way. If she were dressed so casually, no doubt people would wonder if she'd been called away from wash day, or if she'd gotten any sleep at all the night before. Lucas, however, only looked twice as attractive as usual. How had she managed to overlook all these years how terribly vexing that was?

Lucas started up the phlox-bordered brick path.

"Where are you going?"

"Don't you think I have any manners at all? I'm going to give my respects to your mother."

"She'll understand. She's very busy. Trying to make her way through all that correspondence. You know it can take hours to read a single letter from the lawyers."

"Thought you'd finally talked her into letting you handle it. Nothing you like better than trying to wade through all that fancy language."

"Yes, well . . ." She made a show of inspecting a droopy petunia, checking for signs of insect infestation. What was the point of telling him about her mother's decision? If she started dwelling on it and Lucas made those nice, sympathetic sounds he was so good at it, she'd be weeping all over him in no time. Just like all the other women who found his shoulder so irresistible to cry on. And while it may have turned out that she was every bit as susceptible to his physical charms as everyone else, she refused to be lumped in with them in all ways. "Some things she prefers to do herself. You wouldn't want to distract her in the middle of things."

She'd gotten about as much mileage as she was going to out of studying that stupid plant. She looked up to find him watching her every bit as closely as she'd inspected the leaf, doubt furrowing his brow.

"Shall we go?" she asked quickly.

He stared at her a moment longer. "Your mother doesn't want you to go walking with me, does she?"

"What mother would?"

"I always thought she liked me," he said, his patently false injured air drawing a smile from her, as she knew he'd intended.

"She did."

"Does this mean we're going to be accidentally running into your mother or your sister somewhere along the way?"

"Probably both," she advised.

He sighed deeply. "Don't suppose I'll ever get her to make me a blueberry pie again, will I?"

"When you've been a faithful husband to me for forty years, and not a day sooner."

She heard the words before she even realized she'd opened her mouth. Horrified at her own foolishness, she pressed her gloved fingertips to her lips, as if she could put the silly words back where they came from. She'd meant it as joke.

Instead, the words sounded wistful and yearning even to her own ears, the expression of a dream that she'd been certain even the deepest recesses of her heart and mind would have been too smart to indulge in. But apparently not.

His jaw tightened, and she wanted to shout that she hadn't meant it, never wanted it, knew far better than to ever mention it again. "I guess I'll just have to find someone else to make them for me," he said flatly.

"I'm sure you won't have any trouble."

"We'd better get going." He spun on his heel, striding off at a healthy clip while she stared at his retreating back.

Well! He hadn't even bothered to offer her his arm. Lucas might be a lot of things, but she couldn't remember him ever being rude before.

It wasn't all her fault. If he wasn't so blamed prickly about the topic, he wouldn't have taken a simple, silly comment as something more. She grabbed her skirts and scurried after him.

He slowed the moment they hit Oak Street and caught a glimpse of Margaret Farnham stirring a vat of soap in her side yard. He waved a greeting and stuck out his elbow in Priscilla's direction. It was a sop to convention, nothing more, and he couldn't have kept her any further distance away without holding his arm straight out. Priscilla swallowed the hurt that was becoming all too familiar. She rested her fingertips lightly against his forearm, the muscle bunching up into a hard swell the instant she touched him. He adjusted his pace to a decorous stroll that had them inching through town, allowing everyone a chance to view them, promoting the impression that he moved so slowly because he couldn't bear to end their time together. Priscilla had to fight not to break into a run, to get it over with so she could go back to her room alone and have a good, weepy sulk.

Oh, it served her right, for having let herself fall in lust with Lucas.

This was, in all likelihood, the most proper stroll they'd ever had, Lucas reflected. Her hand barely hovered over his arm, their only connection; her wide skirts didn't even brush his leg with each careful step. And yet, damned if it didn't make him want her even more. The thin layer of cotton between her palm and his skin was surprisingly erotic. Instead of the barrier it was intended to be, it was a tantalizing reminder off what was forbidden, more seductive than the more blatant and common inducement of bare skin. Images kept flashing in his brain of her gloved hands running over his naked body. The eyes turning their way as they wandered down the street seemed a terrible intrusion, as if they were spying on a private intimacy. Unlike his father, he'd never been one for spectators.

He nodded politely at Dorothea Tuttle, then called a brief hello when Mrs. Rice stuck her head out her kitchen window. He'd never before felt so obviously on display, like a bear caged for the amusement of the humans who came to poke and peer and comment.

"Lucas?"

"What?" he snapped.

"You made a sound."

"I did not." He was sick of it all. Tired of having to watch every single thing he said and did, and so very tired of trying to stay away from Pris. Of being afraid that if he were ever alone with her, if he put his hands on her, he'd wound her in a way that neither one of them could ever forgive.

And by protecting her, he was hurting her anyway. He could see it, how trying to stay safely remote from her, the only way he knew to protect her, was bruising the very woman who'd always been so secure in his friendship and respect.

Damn, but he hated this!

"Yes, you did. It was sort of a . . . growl." They veered around the corner from Oak Street to Center, which was blessedly free from onlookers. The tall false fronts of the newspaper office and empty mercantile cast deep rectangles of shade across the dusty road.

"Hell."

"Don't—" He grabbed her hand and tugged her forward. Her jaws clicked together, clipping off her imprecation.

"Let's get out of here."

She hesitated only a moment, her newly impulsive heart quickly overruling her rational and cautious head.

She grabbed a good handful of skirts, lifting them up and out of the way. Turning her hand in his to get a good hold, she laughed and broke into a run.

Lucas settled into an easy lope beside her. They ducked through the narrow canyon formed by the empty shells of the two saloons that once held court over Chestnut Street, dashed behind the remains of Kidder's Stables. Turning north, they hurried along a line of trees. A wagon rumbled by, and they huddled behind matching oaks, silently laughing at each other until the danger of discovery was past.

Once beyond the densest part of town, their pace slowed, giving Priscilla a chance to catch her breath.

"You used to be able to keep up with me better than this," he said.

"I didn't used to have to wear a corset."

His gaze raked over her, eyes as hot as the sun burning overhead. How long had she been waiting for him to look at her like that?

"Can't imagine that you need one now."

To her surprise and mortification, she blushed. Even more surprising, he didn't laugh at her embarrassment. He gently squeezed her hand, as if making a pact.

The line of trees thickened into woods, the dense green leaves holding the air in place, muggy and still. Here and there a tall pine studded the hardwoods; further north, the evergreens would take over completely.

They'd walked this way a hundred times before; he'd held her hand a hundred more. And those times were *nothing* like this one. She felt the crackle of uncertainty, of breathless anticipation. The frightening, exciting freedom of having turned her back on what was wise and circumspect and familiar, in favor of endless possibilities, thrummed through her veins. In taking that first step away with him, she'd committed to a path she could not see the end of, one with no safe and appropriate conclusion she could conceive of.

And she was doing it anyway.

They stepped into a clearing, the merry trill of running water welcoming them. Shafts of sunlight shot through the leaves, dappling small patches of moss and grass, and the larger areas of gray earth, scoured bare and packed from constant trampling. The spring burst out of a deep cleft that split a tumble of dark rocks as if they'd been cleaved by a giant's pickax. It bubbled into a small stream, flowed through a thicket of dense, emerald ferns, unraveling into a net of rivulets before disappearing back into the boggy ground.

With a reluctance that should have frightened her but thrilled her instead, Lucas released her hand. Priscilla walked to the spring, tugging at the fingers of her gloves.

"Here," Lucas said roughly. "Let me." He unpinned her hat and tossed it aside. "You must be hot." Then he cupped his hands together and dipped them into the shallow current just where it spilled from the gleaming rocks. He held his hands, brimming with water, up to her mouth.

She brought her own hands beneath his and touched her lips to the rim formed of his fingers, which radiated warmth, a sharp contrast to the teeth-chilling cold of the water. The icy water shocked her less than the intimacy of the gesture of drinking from Lucas's palms. It ran over his fingers, wetting her chin, dripping on her bodice until his hands were empty.

"More?"

Wordlessly she shook her head.

He bent again to drink himself, his strong throat working as he swallowed, damp hair curling long against his neck. When he was finished, he sat back on his heels and simply stared at her.

She knew his face better than she knew her own. Knew every line, every angle, the chicken pox scar that marked his left temple. Why did it feel as if she'd never seen him before? Her heart pumped wildly, as if it knew that it was balanced on the sheer precipice of something entirely new.

Slowly, he rose to stand before her. It should have been too close; it didn't feel nearly close enough. She wanted his hands back, cool water and hot flesh against her own. His head drifted down, toward her, until she could feel, each time he exhaled, his breath brushing her lips.

He was going to kiss her, for real this time, for the two of them and no one else. And this time there'd be no one to stop them, no one to make sure she didn't fall right into Lucas and drown.

Lord help her, she wanted to drown.

"So pretty." With one finger he traced the curve of her eyebrow, drew a gentle line over her cheek. "Pris, you're so damn pretty in sunshine."

"Oh, Lucas," she whispered. "I've missed you."

His eyes flashed. Pain or pleasure, she couldn't tell. Maybe some tortuous combination of both. But it was something strong, making his jaw tighten and his throat convulse, forcing him to step back, to look away from her and focus instead on the crystalline flow of the spring.

"Might as well get used to it."

Dazed at the abrupt change of mood, mourning the loss of something she could barely grasp, she could only repeat his words. "Used to it?"

He shrugged, a careless gesture. "After you find this immaculate husband of yours. It's not like he's going to want you to go wandering off into the woods with me."

"Of course he'll—" Her protest was swift and instinctive. And, she realized quickly, almost certainly untrue. What husband would allow her to spend great amounts of time, alone or otherwise, with someone as justifiably notorious as Lucas? She could no longer even protest with a clear conscience that their relationship was entirely platonic, almost fraternal. Not when she could so easily recall the hot press of his mouth, the delirious temptation of his body close and hard. Not when she knew that so much of her longed to feel it again, right now, with a deep and drunken craving that sapped the strength from her limbs and the will from her mind.

Stunned, she wrapped her arms around her waist. She truly had never realized what her impending marriage would mean to her friendship with Lucas. If she'd thought about it at all, she'd envisioned him perhaps as an indulgent uncle to her children, a cherished family friend who would visit her perhaps less often but certainly held in no less affection. And of course that was impossible. Of *course* it was.

She'd not thought of the changes her marriage would inevitably bring because she hadn't wanted to acknowledge them. She'd wanted it all, even though she was surely old enough to know that everything had its price.

The water dribbled steadily over the rocks, a soothing sound. A thin, tenuous shaft of sunlight skated quickly across, dashing gold over the gleaming black.

"I remember when my father acquired this spring," she murmured. "He came home so pleased with himself, happy he could do this for the town he planned, sure it was one more sign that Maple Falls was destined to be a rousing success."

How little anyone could foresee the future. Or affect it. People plotted and planned, sifted through possibilities, and chose with deliberate care. And all it took was one random act of fate, like her father's sudden heart seizure. Or one thoughtless, seemingly innocuous misstep, like agreeing to a simple bargain with an old friend, and there were undreamed of consequences, and her world tilted from the axis it had spun on for years. She'd simply have to be far more cautious in the future.

"He thought it would be such a wonderful gift for the town, to have this spring," she went on.

"It was." Lucas dipped his hand into the water, letting it slide through his fingers. "It is."

"Nothing else turned out the way he wanted, though. It's hard even to walk through Maple Falls today, to see what's become of it, and wonder how long whoever's left can manage to hold on."

"Not very." Lucas couldn't look at her. He didn't dare. The hand he'd plunged into the spring still shook with his need to touch her; every muscle in his body hurt with the effort it took to hold himself still, to keep from reaching out to her.

He'd almost given in. But then she'd said,

"I've missed you" in that lost, wistful voice, and he'd known he couldn't do it. Because he still hoped that somehow they would salvage something of their friendship. He had to believe they would. But if he'd gone ahead and kissed her, had pulled her into the trees and made love to her on the moss, it would have been the beginning of the end.

And then he would have missed her always.

He forced his thoughts away from how her mouth had gleamed with water she'd sipped from the cradle of his hands. Safer for both of them to think about the town's problems instead. He stood up, wiping his hand on his pants. "There's a lot of families pushing close to the edge."

"There must be something we can do." Unable to stay still any longer, she began to pace, skirts swinging with each step. Her mouth pinched in concentration, energy crackling off her as it always did when she was confronted with a problem. "If only we could get the mill going again, something that would bring in some money, some decent jobs. We couldn't manage the sawmill, of course, but perhaps the chair factory." Coming up against a sturdy oak, she turned, crushing a tangle of weeds beneath her heel, and marched back to the spring. "The work's not as heavy, and—"

"You'd need wood, and funding. And orders."

"None of which we have," she admitted.

"You need something that can't be easily bought somewhere else. Something that doesn't take much physical labor, doesn't require a huge investment up front." He watched the water flow and swirl over the rocks, let it soothe him while his mind worked.

And maybe, he thought, it was as simple as that. "What about the water?"

She glanced from him to the spring and back again. Her eyes widened with dawning comprehension and hope. "It's cheap."

"It already belongs to the town, so there'd be no question of charity."

"We could start as small or as big as we'd like."

He nodded. "We'd have to hand bottle at the beginning. But the only real expense would be the bottles themselves, at least to start. I could take them along whenever I go to pick up supplies, see if I could find some regular customers."

"I bet we could get Johnny Merced to give us a good price on shipping, as well."

"Especially if Sarah Jane asks him."

"True." Hope lifted inside her, airy, frothy emotion that had been absent for so long she almost didn't recognize it. "We'd need labels."

"The presses are still in the office of the *Frontiersman*. Mrs. Chapman would open 'em up, I'm sure. If we can figure out how to use them."

"We'll figure it out." She started formulating mental lists, counting off on her fingers. "Do you think we can sell it?" she asked. But he knew she'd already committed wholly to the idea; the question was merely a formality, asked for the pleasure of hearing him answer.

He didn't disappoint her. "Of course we can."

"Who's ever come to town and *not* said it's the best he'd ever tasted?"

"Not to mention drinking the stuff is obviously what makes all the women here so beautiful." He waggled his eyebrows at her like a hopeful lecher, and she burst into laughter, giddy with fresh possibilities.

"We could put a picture of Jeanette on the label. You know, the sketch Mother had made just before the wedding?"

"Hell, I can sell a trainload down in St. Anthony in no time then. Know exactly where to take it."

"Don't swear." She was too happy to really frown at him, though she gave it a good shot. "And don't tell me where. I don't think I want to know."

Damn, but it was good to have things back to normal. He almost swore again, just to see if he could get her to *really* scold him.

"Now for the big question: can we get the town to go along?"

"How can they not?"

"Oh, they can *not*, all right." He tapped his hand against his leg, trying to decide the best way to present their proposition. "We have to get going right away, if there's any hope of having some money coming in before the snow does. There isn't time for letters to get back and forth to the goldfields. That could take months. And you know they're all going to want to wait for their husbands' advice."

"We'll just have to convince them." Her spectacles slid down her nose and she jabbed at them with her thumb.

"Okay. We'll call everyone together, lay the whole thing out. I'll say that I know their husbands would approve, and that the risk is really very small." He'd been expected to substitute for lots of those husbands in one way or another, anyway; now they'd take advantage of it.

"I think I should do it."

She spoke carelessly, tossing off the line. But the undercurrent caught his attention, a slight, husky quaver that told him that this was somehow very important to her.

"Why?" he asked, watching for her reaction.

"Heavens, we've gone through a great deal the last two weeks in order to get all those women to leave you alone. Why risk making them depend on you again?" She flashed him a teasing grin, but her eyes were very serious.

"Thank you for thinking of me."

"Don't I always? Also, I think it is very important that these women learn that they can survive and prosper without relying on a man. Depending too much on their husbands, having no say in family decisions, is what got many of them into this dilemma in the first place. What good is it simply to switch their dependence to you? We'd be passing up an excellent opportunity." She took a deep breath and lifted that wonderful proud nose into the air. "Don't you agree?"

"I don't disagree," he said carefully.

"Good," she said, smiling upon him like a pleased tutor. "Think what a wonderful example it would be for women everywhere to see that a venture formed and managed entirely by women can succeed."

He had no doubt that Pris believed every word she'd said. He was equally convinced that she had a far more personal reason for wanting to do this.

"Not that I would not value whatever advice and assistance you could give me," she said quickly. "Your experience and business acumen would obviously be invaluable."

"You don't have to try and soothe my pride, Pris. I'm not insulted, only curious."

"Oh." She had the grace to look abashed.

"You sure do spout a mighty convincing spiel for female independence, Pris. For someone who's hunting high and low for a husband, that is."

"There are some things women can do alone, and some she can't." She flushed. "And there's a vast difference between *can* and *have to*," she added softly.

For an instant he could have sworn she looked lonely. But what did Pris have to be lonely about? There were people all around her, all the time, enough to send most people running headlong for solitude. And she had him, didn't she?

"So what do you think?" she said, her fingers fluttering at her sides, gaze flitting around the clearing as if she were afraid to have it settle on him. "You would have equal say in every way that matters, of course, but it would be best if I were at least the figurehead of this cooperative venture. For all the reasons I gave previously, and it is not as if I have not had *some* training in business practices."

She was trying to pretend that his answer didn't matter to her, but was failing quite miserably. Her eyes blinked rapidly, her mouth pursed up into a rosebud, and he had the most absurd urge to throw himself at her feet and tell her he'd do anything, everything, she wanted, if only she wouldn't cry.

"Lucas?" she said softly. A cloud shifted and sunshine illuminated her, glinting off her eye-glasses, catching highlights in her brown hair, showing off the soft sheen of that pretty skin. And Lucas knew that all his good intentions were on the verge of snapping like a broken clock spring.

"Yeah. Sure. Whatever you want." He looked around wildly. He spied her hat, scooped it up, and tossed it on her head. "We gotta go."

With maddening slowness, she tied the ribbon beneath her chin, a big, loopy, blue satin bow that sagged almost to her chest while he was plagued with graphic visions of wrapping that same ribbon around her wrists, pulling them up over her head, and . . .

"Come on, come on, let's *go*."

"Oh, all right. I'm coming."

He gave her back a nudge, just to get her started in the right direction, and his fingers somehow managed to prod her far lower than he was *sure* he'd aimed them. He snatched his hand back and jammed it deep into his pocket.

"For God's sake, Pris, stop dawdling and move!"

"I'm moving," she said, sashaying across the clearing like she had all the time in the world. Damn it, he couldn't follow her; how the hell would he ever explain that he kept running into trees because his eyes were glued to her lusciously swaying backside rather than the path?

"Wait!" He plunged after her.

"Wait?" She stopped, hands on hips, and tilted her head. The weight of the flowers piled on top caused her hat to slide to the side, over one eye, and she flicked it back up. "I thought you told me to go."

"I did. I, uh, just think it would be better if you let me walk in front you. Push the branches out of the way, and watch out for poison sumac, and all that."

"And I thought chivalry was dead." She eyed him suspiciously as he veered around her, giving her a wide berth, and took a position a good three feet in front of her. "You know, you're really going to have to get over this."

"Over what?" he asked, half-listening. Better, he thought, and focused on a wild grapevine choking a smokebush up ahead. Much safer than watching her butt.

"This regrettable tendency to agree to whatever a woman asks without even thinking about it, just because you're afraid she might cry on you."

He stopped dead, spinning to glare at her.

"Come now, Lucas," she said smugly, shooing him on with her hands. "Stop dawdling!"

Chapter 14

A nother of the great unexpected drawbacks of Lucas's scheme was that without the convenient excuse of several other engagements, he couldn't avoid his mother's invitation to Sunday dinner.

Lydia Garrett, regularly and with vast enthusiasm, devoted herself to learning to cook. Unfortunately, something about all those shiny utensils and bubbling pots seemed to spark her muse, and when she went running for paper and ink, she tended to forget those same simmering pots entirely. Which meant when dinnertime arrived, the food was usually either hopelessly overcooked or had never made it into the oven at all.

Today, however, Lydia had asked Clara to come over early and give her a cooking lesson, to ensure the food was worthy of this auspicious occasion. So when the Garrett and Wentworth families gathered around the table and gingerly cut into chicken and dumplings, they were pleasantly surprised.

"Hey! Not one spurt of blood." Lucas happily

sawed into his chicken. "Good job, Mother."

"Watch your mouth, Lucas. Or I won't give you a single piece of pie for dessert, and Clara made it, so you know you're safe."

"Pie?" Grinning, he looked up from his plate. "Blueberry?"

"No," Mrs. Wentworth said darkly. "Vinegar."

"Oh." Lucas shrugged. "That's almost as good."

The look Clara shot him said clearly that she'd hoped he hated vinegar pie.

And that was starting to look like the high point of the afternoon.

Lydia had obviously planned the dinner to celebrate Lucas and Priscilla's upcoming nuptials. And despite—or perhaps because of—Clara's carefully neutral manner, it was painfully apparent that she was as upset by their plans as Lydia was delighted. Conversation jolted from topic to topic, stilted as an arthritic horse. Even Clara was roused from her thoughtful contemplation of a carrot stick to turn puzzled stares on her old friend.

Too jittery even to think of eating, Priscilla chased boiled beets around her plate and trailed streamers of creamed spinach over her doughy dumplings. Lucas and she had decided to use this dinner as a trial run for their bottling proposal, springing the idea in a smaller and more friendly setting—though the *friendly* was looking a mite overly optimistic at the moment.

To her left, her mother tapped her knee under the table. "Stop that," she ordered quietly. "I taught you not to play with your food when you were four."

Priscilla balanced her fork on the edge of her plate and folded her hands in her lap.

Beneath the table, Lucas's hand covered hers. He gave her hand a supportive squeeze and smiled warmly. Tension drained from her. His forearm lay heavy across her thigh, the edge of his hand nudged close to parts of herself precariously protected by layers of fabric, and tension of another sort entirely spiraled slowly in her belly.

"Oh, would you look at that!" Lydia said from across the table. "See how they look at each other?" She sighed. "I've been trying to capture that expression in words for three days. Haven't come close."

Lucas snatched back his hand.

"Blushing, too, both of them. Lucas, I don't think I've seen you blush for over ten years. I've missed it."

"Pris?" Lucas said. "Didn't you have something you wanted to tell everyone?"

"Oh . . . of course!" In an instant, the demurely blushing bride-to-be transformed into a determined businesswoman, and Pris launched into the speech that Lucas knew she'd started forming the instant they'd left the spring.

He'd never been prouder of her, or more intrigued by her contradictions, the different women who all resided in one small body. For all that he would have said he knew Priscilla Wentworth better than anyone else on earth, there were layers and hidden secrets in her that were entirely new to him. He wondered if he'd just overlooked them before, or if they were being formed now, new and fresh and waiting for him to discover.

"Well?" Priscilla said, having laid out all her points and plans with military precision. "What do you think?"

"Hmm?" Lydia, who'd disappeared into her usual fog, resurfaced briefly in support. "I think it's brilliant, dear. Just what the town needs."

"It's risky." Mrs. Wentworth's posture was punishingly rigid, her mouth frozen in a frown. "If Maple Falls Manufacturing was struggling so much while your father was here, how do you think the town can possibly make a go of it without him?"

"I think we have a good chance. As I said before—"

"Please tell me you are not implying that you have skills and insight that your father did not."

Priscilla paled, head jerking back as if she'd been stricken. Lucas grabbed the edge of his chair and hung on, to keep himself from spiriting Priscilla away right then and there. Nothing, but nothing, was worth seeing that expression on Pris's face. But he knew she wouldn't appreciate his rescue, and so he stayed put.

"I am saying no such thing." Priscilla chose her words with obvious care, the faint quaver giving her away. "Father, and this town, had a run of terrible luck, the kind of thing no one could plan for. If things had gone differently, none of this would have been necessary at all, and I would be as happy about it as you would."

Hoping for support, she glanced at Jeanette, who smiled briefly but remained silent, no more accustomed to disagreeing with their mother than Priscilla was.

She turned to Lucas, and there it was again, shining from his eyes and his smile. All the faith and conviction and unwavering support she longed for, ready to spring to her defense, and she wondered why she hadn't turned to him first. But she knew that from now on she would, and though that thought should have terrified her, instead it warmed her, calmed her, strengthened her, gave her so much more than a mere look should have.

"I can make this work," she said. "I know I can. But it would be so much easier with your support, Mother."

"I'm sorry. I can't give it."

Priscilla felt Lucas tense beside her and knew that he was ready to jump in. But this was a family matter, something she needed to do alone.

"I don't see that the town has much choice," she said. "Or that there's much to lose."

"It could be the last straw if it fails," Clara warned.

"I realize that." And it had already kept her up nights. "Which is exactly why we don't intend to fail."

"Do you mean to go on even *without* my consent?"

She couldn't recall ever openly defying her mother. Had never found a reason to before, had always tried to be a good and dutiful daughter. But there'd always been her mother's respect and pride in return, something that the last few weeks had stripped from her, and she was tired of trying to win it back. "Yes. I do."

Priscilla's chair shrieked over the wood floor as she slid it back and stood up. "And since I am, there's a lot to be done before broaching the subject with the rest of the town. I'd like to get started. Lucas, would you join me?"

"Of course." He stood beside her, tall and broad and familiar, and it was all she could do not to sink into the strength she knew was there, waiting for her. "If you'll excuse us?"

Hand hovering at her lower back, he guided her from the room.

Back ramrod stiff, Clara stared blindly at the remains of her dinner, wondering how she'd gotten to this point.

"Jeanette?" she asked, "would you please go home and check to see that all the windows are closed? It's getting dark out. I believe the storm that's been threatening is finally blowing in."

And make certain that Lucas and Priscilla aren't left alone, it was unnecessary to add.

"I—" Jeanette drummed her fingers on the edge of the table.

"Jeanette?"

"Heavens," Lydia put in. "You can't leave me alone with that pie. I'll have to spend the next week letting the seams out on my dresses. Jeanette, be a dear and go fetch us some, would you?"

Only a daughter, Jeanette thought, would discern the subtle marks of worry on her mother's carefully serene face. A good daughter would have scurried to do her mother's bidding, especially when she was no happier about her sister's relationship with Lucas.

Except she'd been running after them for days, and she'd come to the conclusion that it was useless. If Lucas and Priscilla were determined to . . . well, she knew from experience that they'd find a way somehow. It was going to take a lot more than careful chaperoning to stop it. All it was doing was annoying Priscilla, which in Jeanette's opinion only threw her more firmly into Lucas's arms.

"Of course," she said, rising to fetch the pie.

"I'd like some tea, as well. If you don't mind."

"I don't mind." She turned for the door, avoiding her mother's eyes because she was too unsure of her decision to deal with disapproval, or worse yet, hurt. "Is it on the stove?"

"Actually, there's none made. Kettle's in the cupboard next to the stove, and the tea's right beside it."

"Fine," she responded, escaping to the kitchen.

"Now, then." With everyone finally out of the way, Lydia turned to her oldest friend. This was why, she thought in resignation, that she preferred to spend so much time in an imaginary world. The real one was just so much more difficult to bend to her will. "I'd like to know what *that* was all about."

Clara propped her elbow on the table and dropped her forehead to her hand, as much a gesture of weariness and despair as Lydia had ever seen from her. "All I've ever done is try to do the right thing, Lydia. I don't understand why it stopped being enough. I know when, but I don't know why."

"Life's messy. Complicated, too. Yours stayed simple a lot longer than most."

Clara's head snapped up, a slight burn of anger kindling in the fine green eyes she'd passed on to both her daughters. Good, Lydia decided. You could live on anger a long time, if you had to. She had.

"You don't understand any better than she does," Clara accused her. "I'm just trying to do what's best for her in the end, even if she doesn't see it now."

"And you're so sure what's best? She's a grown woman. Been one for quite a while, seems to me."

"Of course I know what's best. I'm her mother."

Not even a flicker of doubt, Lydia thought. Ah, well.

"I don't know why she won't listen anymore," Clara continued. "She used to be such a good girl."

"She's still a good girl."

"Not since—" Clara stopped, averted her eyes from Lydia's.

"Not since this courtship began with Lucas, is that what you mean?" Careful, Lydia told herself. "Now we're at the heart of the problem, aren't we? And I must admit it's beyond me why you persist in seeing it as a problem."

"Beyond you? Priscilla and—and—" She stopped, swallowed, as if she couldn't even stand to link their names in one sentence. "It's absurd."

"Clara." Lydia sighed. "Do you know what I've always admired most about you?"

"Admired?" A little bewildered by the change in topic, and equally flattered, Clara touched her fingers to her chest, where a creamy cameo held together a triangle of lace over her bodice. People had always admired her husband; she'd never thought someone might do the same for her.

"Oh, yes. Very much so." China and silver tinkled gently as she moved aside her dinner service, clearing the space between them. "For all your personal correctness and unimpeachable deportment, you've never been at all judgmental. That's very rare, you know."

"Oh." Uncomfortable, she fingered the silver handle of her dessert fork, and Lydia gave her hand a quick, affectionate squeeze.

"What other proper young wife would have ever thought to make a friend of someone like me?"

"Lydia, you sell yourself short. You were young, and caught in a situation worlds beyond your experience, or what any of us were taught to handle."

"Don't make excuses for what I did. And do. I'm no longer young, and I don't regret most of it anymore. It made me stronger than I'd ever have thought I could be. The point is, most women would have condemned me, would have swum across the Chicago River rather than risk being contaminated by me. You looked beyond it."

Clara's shoulders lifted and fell. "You have a good heart. That was always obvious." Her mouth curved, and Clara was immensely relieved and encouraged to see a hint of the humor and warmth that had been noticeably absent for the past few years. "Besides, knowing you was always vastly . . . entertaining."

Lydia laughed. "Oh, so I was your look at the wild side of life, was I?" The thought delighted her. "Why can't you extend that same understanding to your daughter and my son?"

"You, of all people, should know what a bad marriage can be, can do to the people involved. How can you possibly want that for Priscilla? Even for Lucas?"

"Why are you so sure it would be a bad one?"

"Oh, please." The words had a bitter edge. "You know I love them both. But I'm also not blind. Lucas, for all he's inherited your good heart, is just not the kind of man to be held by one woman. And even if he were, Priscilla is not the kind of woman to hold him."

"Hmm." Lydia folded a smudged square of linen napkin, creased the edge, and folded it again. "Seems to me it's not such a bad basis for a marriage, a friendship like theirs. No one could ever know and understand each other better than the two of them. And Lucas would cut off his right . . . arm rather than hurt her."

"Which is why I've always approved of their friendship. And that's what it should have stayed, for both their sakes. Anything else is rushing straight into utter disaster. I'm trying to protect them both, Lydia."

"And I don't happen to agree." Setting aside the napkin, she met Clara's gaze squarely. They'd both dug their heels in and there was no use discussing it anymore. But there was one last point to be made. "Either way, you really should think about easing up on Priscilla a little. Speaking as someone who once expended a great deal of energy chasing after forbidden fruit, with disastrous results, I can tell you that you're doing an excellent job of making Lucas seem all the more intriguing."

Clara huffed. "That's ridiculous. Priscilla was never the sort to do something just because I told her not to."

"So she came to it later than most."

"Jeanette? Tell Mrs. Garrett that she's wrong about your sister."

"I—" Jeanette stepped out from behind the door where she'd been hovering, eavesdropping. "I don't think she's cozying up with Lucas because you told her not to, no," she hedged.

"There you go!"

"But I don't think what we've been doing has been very helpful, either," Jeanette added.

Clara bristled, but before she could respond, Jeanette raised the tray she'd brought from the kitchen, laden with thick slabs of pie, a steaming pot of tea, and an etched silver bowl piled with lumps of sugar. "Are we staying for dessert?"

Outnumbered, Clara looked at Lydia and sighed. "We're staying."

Chapter 15

They'd made it only ten feet from Lydia Garrett's door before the first raindrops fell, big, heavy globules that hit the skin and spattered. Sometime during dinner, the sky had turned, going dark as dusk, shading the street with gray-green shadows.

One bright spear of lightning snaked across the sky, bleaching color from the world for a silvered instant. Thunder followed hard on its heels, a crash loud enough to bruise eardrums.

"Here it comes," Lucas shouted. The sky opened up, spilling rain like a swollen waterfall, the hard, hot, lush downpour of a late summer boomer. They dashed through the rain, tumbled through Priscilla's front door, laughing.

"Jeez, it's really coming down." He shook himself, spraying droplets in all directions, and slicked his wet hair back with both hands.

"Good. Maybe the heat will finally break for good."

"I'm sure it has."

Pris's hair had come undone and lay thick against her cheek, tangling damply around her neck. Her formerly crisp blouse clung to her shoulders, the lace frill trimming drooping limp and soggy against her breasts. Beautiful breasts, sweetly curved in a way he just knew would fit his hands perfectly.

"I'm sorry," he said. "You're soaked."

"You should be," she said briskly. "Sorry, I mean, for letting it rain like that. Lord knows it's all your fault." She smiled, her lips wet and gleaming. Like he'd just kissed her, he thought, and felt his clothes start to steam.

"Oh, for heaven's sake, Lucas," she went on. "I'll dry. Luckily, I forgot my hat, so it won't be ruined."

"Too bad."

"What?" She looked up from trying to pluck the sagging ruffle into some semblance of its former state.

"Ah—" He cleared his throat. Wet fabric had gone transparent over her collarbone, revealing a hint of skin beneath filmy white. He wanted to peel it away, put his mouth right there and finally find out what she tasted like. "I said, it's too bad. That you're so wet."

"And I said I don't mind." She pushed at the dark, wet ropes of hair clinging stubbornly to her cheek.

"Here, let me." Bad idea, he told himself. But his fingers seemed to have a mind of their own, lifting the strands and tucking them behind her ear, staying to stroke down the line of her jaw. Her skin was slick and smooth, warm as the rain. He let his fingers fall further, skating down her neck to hover above where the damp cloth kept him from her flesh, and his hand trembled, just a little, before he found the strength to pull it back and tuck it safely into his pocket.

Her eyes went wide, her mouth soft.

The air was charged, crackling with lightning and promise. One wrong move, one spark, and they'd both go up in flames.

"You could stay for a while," she said softly. "You shouldn't be out in weather like this."

She was flirting with danger as surely as if she were out dancing in the storm, waving a steel pole over her head. She knew it, couldn't seem to stop herself.

Their eyes held. Rain drummed on the roof, rattled the window glass. Thunder rolled again, a deep, insistent voice urging him to stay.

"No," he said, his own voice low and unsteady. "I can't stay."

"We've got a lot of work to do, and not much time to do it in." She heard the words coming out of her mouth even as her brain shouted, "*Fool.*"

"Speaking of which—" He shifted, spread his feet wide, and crossed his arms over his chest. His hair was sleeked straight back from his face, dripping onto his shoulders, and his shirt clung to his chest, revealing muscle, showing her his strength. It stripped the civility from him, made him look harder, harsher, and her heart beat as furiously as a captured bird's. "How long has that been going on?"

She considered sidestepping the topic. It was a private matter, between her and her mother, and there were more interesting things to consider at the moment.

"And don't you even think," he warned her,

"of trying to avoid this topic one more time. Obviously I let you get away with it too long already."

"Let me get away with it?" she repeated. Oh, *why* were they talking about this *now*?

"Don't get your hackles up. You know what I mean. And you're not going to distract me by sucking me into another argument."

Lucas was slow to anger, always had been. She could count on one hand the number of times she'd seen him truly mad. Now she watched in unwilling fascination as his temper came up, like a spark slow to catch that finally burst into a bonfire. His jaw hardened, his brows snapped down. His eyes darkened, burned, the expression so close to passion, as intense and strong as he'd looked at her when they'd first come in the door, that her response was exactly the same. Excitement speared into her chest.

"Ever since I kissed you. That's it, isn't it?"

Kiss me now. She pressed her hand to her chest to keep the plea inside, to still the blade-edged, fluttering wings of desire.

"Your mother's suddenly decided to treat you like a brainless twit taken leave of all sense, just because you fell in love with me, hasn't she? And you didn't think to *tell* me this?"

He didn't stop for her answer, her excuse. Fortunate, because she wouldn't have been able to manage one. She was too busy dwelling on the *fell in love with me*. He'd meant to tack a "pretended" in there; of course he had. But the words echoed in her mind anyway, resonating like they meant to stay. Oh, please God, she hadn't been that stupid, had she?

"Nope, not Saint Priscilla. You'd just go on letting her shut you out of your father's business, letting her *hurt* you, because you'd given your promise to me."

"It's not that important."

"Not that important?" He glowered at her. Any other man, and she might have been frightened. But this was Lucas, a wild and tempting Lucas, and excitement streaked like lightning, burned just as hot. "This is your *family*. My convenience is *nothing* compared to that."

He stepped closer and she forgot to breathe. "It hurt you, Pris." Lightly, as if afraid the slightest jar would break her, he laid his hand along her cheek. "I would never let anyone hurt you."

"It's all right," she said. She was a grown woman.

"I know you, Pris." His fingers brushed between her brows, smoothing away the lines that lodged there when she worried. "Don't you think I can tell when you're hurting?"

Abruptly he dropped his hand and turned away, the sudden withdrawal of his touch leaving her gasping and bereft.

"Where are you going?"

"I'm going to stop it."

"Wait!" she cried, causing him to freeze with his hand on the doorknob. "What do you mean?"

"I'm going to tell them the truth, of course."

"Don't do that!" Her vehemence surprised them both. "I mean, if you do that, you'll be right back where you started." She tried to lighten it, forced a smile. "Or are you tired of trying to cook and clean for yourself?" She didn't know why she didn't want the charade to end yet. There was no denying she enjoyed the envy and speculation running rampant in Maple Falls, having people look at her as if there were obviously more to her than they'd suspected. Or maybe it was just that her and Lucas's friendship had foundered, and she was afraid they'd never put it to rights again; if this pretense was all they had, she didn't want to lose it, too.

"Jesus, Pris, how selfish do you think I am?" At that, he yanked open the door. Rain gusted through, wetting the polished floors and spraying her mother's pretty blue moiré wallpaper. He lowered his head against the wind, charged across the porch and out into the storm, big long strides splashing through pooling water.

Oh well, Priscilla thought. She was wet already. Clutching her skirts in both hands, she dashed after him.

Lucas stopped cold in the middle of a big puddle. "Are you crazy? Get back in the house!"

"Only if you come back with me," she shouted over the barrage of the wind and the rain. The air had a bite to it, warning of coming hail.

"It's storming out!"

"I don't care!"

Lucas bent, planted his shoulder against her belly, and lifted. Her head dangled down his back and her knees banged against his chest with each step. Reaching the partial shelter of the porch, he dumped her back on her feet.

"Idiot woman!"

"Idiot?" she screeched. It didn't matter that she'd called herself that a hundred times. But hearing it from him was another thing entirely. It would serve him right if she sent every simpering, husband-hunting, shrill-voiced woman in Maple Falls to dog his footsteps.

"Hasn't got enough sense to come in out of the rain."

"I don't see you heading for shelter."

"I've got something to do!" His hand fisted, one finger extended. He longed to wave it under that proud nose, if he wasn't afraid she'd be tempted to give it a nip. While he rather cherished the idea of Pris giving him a little love bite here and there, he'd rather it be a tad more gentle than what he suspected she had in mind right now. And in a lot more interesting place than his index finger.

"You don't have to do it now!" she shot back. "Let's go in, dry off, and talk about it."

Talk about it. Terrible female phrase. "I don't want to talk about it. I know you. You're going to talk about it until you talk me *out* of it, and you'll be the admirable martyr again. I can do what's right once in a while, too, you know. Now stay here!"

He was so adorably frustrated, Priscilla reflected, wondering what he would do if she just grabbed him and planted a kiss right on that set, furious, sexy mouth. Only the memory of how cold and distant and aloof he'd been after the last kiss kept her from diving right in.

"Why are you so set on coming along?" he asked. "Figure you gotta listen to what I say, in case I muck it up?"

"Smart man."

He sighed with frustrated gusto. Then he

paused, looking her up and down, hot speculation glinting in his eyes. "I could tie you up, you know. Then you'd have to stay."

"You wouldn't dare," she said. But she didn't sound too sure.

"You're right, I wouldn't," he admitted finally. Oh, not that the thought of it didn't have a lustful appeal. But if he tied her up, for damn sure it wouldn't be so he could walk out the door and leave her there alone.

"Wait here." She opened her mouth to protest. "I'm just going inside," he finished quickly.

He yanked the door open, spewing more rain into the foyer. He stomped down the hallway, muddy prints on the cream-and-gold carpet runner marking his path.

Her mother might have eventually forgiven him that kiss outside the schoolhouse. But there was no way she was ever going to forgive him the mess he was making in her house.

She heard him rummaging around in the back of the house, a couple of doors slamming, a curse. Hail started dinging off the roof and bouncing in the yard. Then he returned, still scowling, the bright log cabin quilt they saved for guests draped over his arm.

"You shouldn't use that one," she said. "It's—"

"Not another word," he growled, and she obediently shut up.

For all the fierceness of his expression and voice, a harsh facade that would have sent children running for their mother's skirts, his hands were gentle as he laid the soft quilt over her head and around her shoulders.

"It's hot," she complained.

"Can't have hail ricocheting off that hard head of yours. Be dangerous, that. Probably shoot right through me." And then he bent down swiftly and kissed the very tip of her nose.

He'd never done that before. Never, ever. She stood rooted to the floor and gaped at him, wondering how she could feel a brief peck on her nose all the way down to her toes, and how that simple, affectionate gesture could marry all the friendship and all the passion she'd ever felt into one wondrous emotion. And telling herself that if she allowed herself to dwell on it, she'd be even more foolish than she'd already been.

"Well? Are you coming?" He lifted an arm, making room to tuck her quilt-draped form in the shelter of his body.

"I'm coming," she said, and as they dashed through the beating rain and hail, through the clammy air that made her sweat and shiver at the same time, she tried to forget how perfect she felt right there next to him.

"So that's the whole story," Lucas finished. He and Priscilla had caught the rest of them still in the dining room and he'd managed to sneak in a slice of pie during his recitation.

Jeanette was directly across the table, her thumb tracing the rim of her teacup, her gaze going back and forth between him and Priscilla, her expression thoughtful. Pris was still looking a little disgruntled, but he figured she'd get over it. He'd done the honorable thing; how could she argue with that?

As for his mother, well, she was obviously a

tad disappointed, the same sad droop to her mouth that she'd had when he'd finally admitted he really didn't like her special sugar cookies. He shrugged apologetically, tried a lopsided smile. No dice.

And then there was Mrs. Wentworth herself, who should by all accounts be jumping up and down in celebration. Instead, the frown she aimed in his direction was every bit as frosty as the one she'd given him after she'd bashed him with her handbag.

"There, you see?" he said. "Nothing for you to worry about. Priscilla was just helping me out a little, the kiss was all for show, and her judgment is unimpaired. You can stop treating her like she's not to be trusted. It's not fair to her at all."

"I'm not convinced of that," Clara insisted. "Her judgment had to be somewhat suspect for her to agree to such a foolish and inappropriate plan in the first place. You've always been able to talk her into things that would never have occurred to her by herself."

Exasperated, Lucas huffed. Stubborn woman; now he knew where Pris got it. Wrong, as well; Pris had been as likely to think up escapades, though she wouldn't propose them outright. It had taken him years before he'd figured out her little comments and hints had been calculated to get him to suggest exactly what she wanted to do in the first place. "I played on her sympathies. You know Pris never could resist someone who needed her assistance."

"Still—"

"You should be proud of her, that she would

go so far in the name of friendship. I've never known a woman as loyal, as thoughtful and generous and—"

"Oh, please!" She'd had enough. Priscilla brought the flat of her hand down on the table, rattling teacups in their saucers. "I did it for my own reasons, which Lucas knows perfectly well, and because I thought it might be amusing. Which it was." Not entirely true, she reflected. It had been unsettling and frightening and downright painful. But there was no person in this room that she was willing to admit that to.

"Now Lucas's guilty conscience has caused him to spill it all, over my objections." She didn't dare look at him, for fear he'd see that, though rightfully she should be annoyed at his highhandedness, she was also deeply and quite inordinately touched that he would so quickly surrender his precious freedom and privacy simply because her mother's disapproval pained her.

"I would appreciate it," she went on, "if you would all keep what he's told you confidential. There is no reason for anything else to change, and I do not want to be responsible for Lucas's expiring from exertion."

"I couldn't lie." Clara's mouth was drawn into a thin, disapproving line.

"I would never expect you to. But you don't have to say anything at all. Everyone knows how you feel about keeping family business private. And if someone asks, oh, what our plans are or when the wedding is, just say that you don't know. That's the truth."

"But—" It skated awfully close to the edge, to Clara's way of thinking, and she always preferred to be firmly in the center of correct conduct.

"Please?" Priscilla was not above using guilt when the occasion warranted. "Since you doubted me before, perhaps you could find it in you to trust me on this matter."

"I suppose so," she agreed reluctantly.

"Jeanette? How about you?"

Jeanette tapped her forefinger against her mouth. "Not a word. I always did like being in on a secret."

"Good." While she was on a roll, she might as well keep going. "Now, Mother, as to the spring water venture. Your support would mean so much. We have studied it carefully, Lucas and I, and are convinced it's the only hope, and that we can make it work. Isn't that right, Lucas?"

He nodded. "Your husband taught us both well, Mrs. Wentworth, and I'm sure we can carry on much in the manner that he would have. In fact, if he were here, I believe he would have made the exact same suggestion. The only reason he did not exploit this resource sooner was that he had so many other things already in the works."

It was all Priscilla could do not to applaud. Brilliant touch, bringing her father in like that. It was likely to convince her mother the way nothing else could.

There was one other thing she'd learned from her father—not to push too hard, when to back off and let your point settle. "It seems the storm has lightened up a bit. We should take advantage of the lull. Lucas, perhaps you would escort us home? I have an idea or two I would like to discuss with you."

"Of course," he said, coming to his feet

"We can't leave Lydia with all the dishes," Clara protested.

"Oh, I don't mind. In fact, I like it. Having my hands busy with something simple lets my mind spin." As the four of them reached the front door, she called after them. "Lucas, there are umbrellas in the front closet."

He poked his head through the dining room doorway, looking so handsome and grown-up she still couldn't believe he was her son. "Sorry, Mother. No wedding, no grandchildren," he said before disappearing again.

She pondered the clutter on her table, the violet-painted dishes and the remains of what she'd planned to be a betrothal meal. "No wedding, no grandchildren. *Yet.*"

Chapter 16

Once they'd gotten over the idea that the reason Lucas and Priscilla had called them all to the schoolhouse hadn't been for a surprise wedding after all, the women of Maple Falls were agreeable to the new plan, if not entirely enthusiastic. There'd been the expected reluctance to take such a step without their husbands' advice. But Priscilla had been convincing, Lucas firmly and confidently supportive. Clara's public approval had been the deciding factor. And Priscilla had to admit that, whatever her mother's private reservations, she knew how to present a united front.

A full, voting share in the newly formed Maple Falls Bottling Cooperative was set at ten dollars. Those who couldn't afford to invest that much, and there were many, were allowed to make their contribution by promising future labor. When all was said and done, though, their capital was considerably short of the first, quite conservative, budget Lucas and Priscilla had drawn up. Lucas quietly contributed the rest of the money, including a full share in the name of Jennifer McCann.

Priscilla threw herself into the fledgling company, delighted to at last have a project that promised a more permanent solution than the temporary aid she'd been able to give the last few years. It had the added benefit—or drawback, she couldn't quite decide which—of throwing her into frequent contact with Lucas. In private he was stiff with her, painfully remote, as formal and distant as a self-important stranger. But it was better than not seeing him at all. And sometimes, as they argued over how to proceed, he seemed to forget himself and she'd be filled with a buoyant, thrilling bubble of hope that she wouldn't lose him after all.

Lucas, too, gave every spare moment to the fledging company. It was tortuous to spend time with her, but trying to stay away wasn't helping, either. And at least there was something productive to work on and distract him from Pris's body. Except then he kept getting fixated on her mind. He'd always known she was bright, but watching her work through problems was fascinating, and turning out to be just as likely to make him burn as glimpsing the curves beneath her bodice.

One Wednesday in mid-September, the bell over the door jangled, and Lucas looked up from stacking bags of dried beans. Pris and Jeanette entered, laughing, cheeks wind-stung. Pris had a fuzzy wool shawl wrapped around her shoulders, the dark red setting off her complexion nicely and clashing with the ugly bright green feathers sprouting raggedly from the crown of her hat, and just seeing her took his breath away. Funny, how that kept happening.

"Brrr." She shivered, cuddling deeper into the soft-looking shawl. "Autumn came late enough, but it sure feels like winter's not going to be as considerate." He'd put a kettle of cider on the stove for the first time today, apples and spice adding a sharp tang to the store's usual smells.

"Well, shoot," he said.

Priscilla stopped in her tracks. "What's the matter?"

"How's a man supposed to get any work done?" he groused. "When such lovely distractions as the two of you come wandering through his door?"

"Oh." Her color deepened, and he found himself searching his brain for more silly compliments. He'd never had much trouble coming up with them before. But then, they'd never really mattered before.

Jeanette made a sound of disgust. "I'm the only one here. You two don't have to put on a show for me any longer, remember?"

"Oh. Of course." Embarrassed to be so easily drawn into something that was merely for display, Priscilla fumbled in her handbag for today's schedule. The intricacies of beginning a business had taxed even her ability to keep mental lists, and she'd taken to writing them down, giving her new respect for what her father—and Lucas—faced every day in running their own enterprises.

A display of satin ribbons caught Jeanette's eye, and she wandered over to them. "By the way, Lucas, has there been any mail for me? I've been waiting on the newest issue of *Peterson's*." She fingered the ribbons lightly in a show of intense nonchalance.

"I'm afraid not."

Her fingers stilled, then resumed stroking a gleaming length of sky-blue satin. She was finding it harder and harder to chalk up Robert's neglect to unreliable mails or overwork. Unfortunately, he didn't have the excuse of being dead. He turned up too often in the letters of other prospecting husbands for that to be the case. "What do you think, Priscilla? It would go well with my hair."

"Hmm? There it is." Priscilla came up from digging in the bottom of her jammed handbag, clutching a folded paper. "The kelly green, don't you think? To match your eyes?" She moved on to more crucial topics. "Lucas, I've been looking over those bottle samples you picked up. I wanted to talk to you about—"

"If you're going to talk about business, I'm leaving," Jeanette said. "I could have just as well stayed home."

"No, you couldn't. Mother would have you beating rugs by now, and you know how that ruins your nails."

"True," she admitted. "And I do owe you. Just not big enough to make me sit through one more conversation with numbers in it." She shuddered. "Talk about a choice between two evils. Lucas, Mother's on her fall cleaning spree. Priscilla kindly insisted that she had desperate need of my assistance, saving me."

"She saves me all the time."

Jeanette watched the two of them making

moon eyes at each other, and it didn't look much like practice. All the vague suspicions that had been percolating the last few weeks reared up with a vengeance.

Priscilla was perilously close to falling madly in love with Lucas. She lit up like a kerosene-soaked torch every time he got within twenty feet of her. And Lucas wasn't helping any, shooting her heated looks and smooth compliments at any opportunity. One who didn't know Lucas, hadn't seen him charm ninety-nine percent of the women in Chicago, Maple Falls, and all parts in between, might even believe he returned Priscilla's feelings.

Fools, both of them. Jeanette knew, better than most, what a seductive mirage love was. And what it left in its wake. She'd do just about anything to spare Priscilla that agony. Unfortunately, her sister didn't seem inclined to listen to wiser heads in the matter. Whoever did, when the siren call of "true love"—hmph!—was singing?

"I'll just go hide out in the hotel, maybe have a cup of coffee. You can fetch me when you're ready to go home. All right, Priscilla?"

"Yes, fine." She waved vaguely in Jeanette's direction. "Whatever you want."

The bell jingled again, the door slamming shut behind her, but neither of them moved.

How long had it been since he'd touched her? He tried to think, to remember. But there was nothing to recall; he'd never touched her, not the way he longed to now.

She wouldn't stop him. He knew it; it showed in the way her body swayed toward him, how she looked at him every time she thought he wouldn't notice. He could take her right now, sate himself with Pris, and finally be free of the seductive dreams that had obsessed him since one steamy August night.

He'd gain one night, but he'd lose a lifetime.

And so to keep from reaching for her, he busied himself with the beans instead, stacking and rearranging bags as if he were building a cathedral.

"Pris?" he said at last. She was staring at his hands as he worked, her eyes unfocused and dreamy, a faint smile on her mouth. "You mentioned something about the bottles?"

"Hmm?" Pris and her "hmms." They'd always seemed to Lucas to be the sign that her brain was whirring around. Except lately, they'd gotten lower, throatier, and he'd kept imaging how she'd moan, low and slow, when he sank into her. "Oh yes, the bottles. I like the shape of the brown ones, and the green are certainly fine as well, but I really think clear might be best, to show off the unusual clarity of our product. I—"

"Mr. Garrett?" Mick popped in from the storeroom and with relief, and more than a little regret, Lucas turned his attention to him. "Got the fishhooks all sorted. Whatja want me to work on next?"

"Already?" Lucas was afraid that the boy was working off every bite of food he managed to stuff into him, but the kid wasn't happy unless Lucas found something for him to do. Finding tasks that kept him occupied without being too obviously made up just for him was becoming a challenge. "You could wash the front porch, I guess; there was some rain last night, bound to be muddy out there."

His dark eyes gleamed like Lucas has just offered him a piece of horehound candy from the glass jar on the counter. "Gotta have a clean 'stablishment if you want to keep your customers, right?"

"That's right. You know where the bucket and mop are?"

Mick's head jiggled up and down. "Yup."

"Lucas? Aren't you going to introduce me?"

"Introduce you?" Pris bent a brilliant smile on Mick, who grinned back. "Forgive my manners. This is my new employee, Mick. Don't know how I ever got along all these years without him."

"I am very pleased to meet you, Mick. I am Priscilla Wentworth, a very old friend of Lucas's." With a gracious air worthy of meeting one of the country's finest citizens, she extended a hand. Mick glanced questioningly at Lucas, who nodded. He reached out, then thought better of it, scrubbing his palm down his shirt front before grabbing her white-gloved hand and pumping it enthusiastically.

"Pleased to meetcha, too." He squinted up at her. "But you don't look so old to me."

Priscilla chuckled. "Thank you very kindly for the compliment, Mick. You do know how to charm a lady."

"Yeah?" Dazzled, Mick shot Lucas a smug glance. "Told you I could wait on the customers."

"Not until you can count change, you can't."

Which Lucas had every intention of teaching him, along with everything else he could think of. The boy had too quick a mind to waste.

"Aww." He bumped his toe against a nearby barrel, ready to protest.

"The porch, Mick," Lucas ordered.

"*Then* can I wait on customers? I could do everything but the money part."

"No."

Mick heaved a persecuted sigh and disappeared into the back, quickly followed by a metallic clang and a loud clatter. Lucas winced, wondering what sort of shape the storage room would be in by the time Mick found the bucket. Oh, well. It would give him one more thing to clean up.

"How long has he been here?" Pris asked.

Lucas rubbed a finger across his chin, thinking. "Three weeks, maybe."

"Why didn't you tell me?"

"Never came up."

"It was kind of you, to give him a job." When Pris looked at him like that, admiration shining clear in her eyes, Lucas felt like he'd hung the moon. And it was exactly why he hadn't told her. Her eyes brimmed with hopes and admiration, all the things to which he could never live up.

"What else was I supposed to do after I caught him stealing from me? Haul him off to jail?"

"He was stealing from you? That sweet child?"

"That sweet child," Lucas affirmed. "I didn't want to waste a whole day hauling him off to Ft. Ripley. Don't make any more of it than it is, Pris.

I'm not kind and you know it, so don't start forgetting it now."

"But he—" She stopped in mid-sentence as Mick came back into the room, a limp rag mop propped over one skinny shoulder, a bucket sloshing water in hand.

"Careful with the water, Mick."

Mick nodded, bending his head, lower lip clamped firmly in his front teeth in concentration.

The front door opened and Flora Fergus flew through, market basket over her arm, and charged full-bore into Mick. He yelped and fell hard on his rump. The mop flew and hit the floor with enough force to snap the handle in two. The bucket swung forward, dousing Flora's skirts.

Shrieking, she jumped back. "Look what you've done!" She honed in on the boy who hunched frozen on the floor in front of her. "Why, you—" Her hand snaked out, fingers curled into a claw, and seized his upper arm, so thin and fragile in her grip Priscilla feared it would snap in two.

"Easy, there." Lucas rounded the back case. "It was just an accident. Neither one of you was looking where you were going."

"I'm sure it won't stain," Priscilla added helpfully. "He hadn't even used the water yet, so it's perfectly clean."

Flora nearly snarled, yanking Mick to his feet. "You careless brat—" She stopped, her eyes narrowing as she studied his face.

"What is this dirty little bastard doing here?"

Lucas's hand whipped out, peeling her claw off Mick. Resting a protective arm on the boy's shoulder, he drew him to his side. "He's my employee." He smiled at Mick, who looked up at him, set face betraying no emotion; clearly, he'd had practice. But his shoulder quivered beneath Lucas's palm. "My *best* employee."

"Don't be ridiculous," Flora snapped out. "He's an affront to all decent people. I want him out of here."

"Mick?" Priscilla asked softly, "Would you like to go back into the storeroom with me? Lucas set aside a few special materials for me, and I'm going to need someone to wait on me. You can be my own personal salesperson."

"No." Lucas knew Pris wanted the child out of the room before he heard any more of Flora's invectives. But the boy had heard them before, and would again; better he also hear that there were those willing to stand up for him. "He stays." He glared meaningfully at Flora. "Now and tomorrow. For as long as he wants."

Scarlet burned up Flora's neck, and colored her cheeks. "What kind of customers do you think you're going to get with him here?"

"The only kind I'm interested in."

Flora gaped, her mouth working like that of a landed fish. She whirled, bumped a pile of horse collars, and gave them a vicious kick before sailing out.

Lucas knelt. "You okay?"

" 'Course," Mick said manfully, the shimmer of moisture in his eyes belying his assurance.

"Good."

"You think maybe—" His breath hitched. "I could stay in the back, maybe? So nobody ever saw me?"

"Now, why would you want to do that? I need you here."

"Don't want to. But the customers. You said, s'posed to do what you can to make 'em happy."

"The stupid ones don't count."

Mick's eyes widened and he snorted. "You called her—"

"Stupid. Yes, I did." Lucas tried to look stern. "And if I ever catch you calling anyone that, I'll tan your hide."

"Yes, sir," Mick said smartly.

"Good. You ready to get back to work?"

Mick straightened, thin chest puffing out in pride. "Yes, sir!"

"How about cleaning up this mess? There should be another mop back there. And some rags in the corner of my office."

Mick snapped off a quick salute and scampered toward the back of the store.

"You like children," Pris said softly, wonder threading through her voice like sunshine.

Damn. Caught, Lucas pushed up from the floor and sighed. "Never said I didn't."

"I know, but—" Her heart felt tender from seeing the two of them together, the boy and the man. One more thing she hadn't known about Lucas, about whom she'd thought she'd known everything. "This isn't just not *disliking* them, and don't try and tell me it is." The way he'd bent down to comfort Mick, his easy and deep understanding, it was clear Lucas would make an excellent father. She rolled the concept over in her mind a little, finding it unexpectedly bright.

"Yeah, I like them," Lucas admitted. He

grabbed a box from a high shelf and plunked it on the counter. "So what?"

"You never said anything."

"What was I supposed to say?" He poked through the contents of the box with his finger, started sorting the nails within into piles by size, metal rattling on glass. Plink, plink. "Always knew I was never going to have any, so what was the point?"

"Lucas." He was trying so hard to show that it didn't matter. But the corners of his mouth pulled down, and his brow furrowed in more concentration than the task warranted. "What do you mean, you always knew? You still could."

"Pris, don't start that." Plink *plank*. His movements had more force now, throwing the nails into piles with enough impetus to make Priscilla wince, fearing for the glass countertop. "I'm not getting married. You know that, you know why, and you should know enough not to talk me out of it."

She did. Oh, she did, but she also knew what it was to long for a child. "You wouldn't have to get married. Not strictly speaking."

That shocked him enough to get his attention; his head snapped up, his gaze arrowing to hers. "Tell me you're not considering that."

"No!" She pressed her palms to cheeks that flamed with heat. "No, of course not. But you're not me."

"I wouldn't do that. To do that to a child, just because *I* wanted it . . ." Anger glinted in his voice, soft and fierce. "I wouldn't do that."

"I'm sorry," she said.

"Don't be. I've always known, and I've gotten

over any regret a long time ago. It doesn't matter anymore.''

Doesn't it? she wondered. Twin lines furrowed between his dark brows, and she longed to reach over and soothe them away, uncertain whether she should curse or be grateful for the width of the case separating them. Oh yes, he'd make a wonderful father, all the more so for what he'd just said, putting the needs of a child before his own wants. And deep within her a fragile, glittering tendril of hope twined stealthily around her heart and took firm hold.

Chapter 17

❧〰◗◖〰☙

Flora Fergus marched down Center Street, heels stabbing deep depressions into the softened earth with each step. A mangy, gaunt cat meowed hopefully in front of the restaurant Mr. Peterson had closed down three months earlier. The cat took one look at Flora, hissed, and smartly flew out of her way.

"Good riddance," Flora fumed. If Peterson hadn't had such a soft spot, the flea-bitten creature wouldn't still be hanging around. "Find a mouse like you're supposed to!" she hollered after it. If everyone just did what they were supposed to, by God, the world wouldn't be such a miserable place. And she, Flora Fergus, wouldn't be trekking through this godforsaken town alone, a penny shy of flat broke, with no man around with whom to work out her frustrations. Not to mention she'd just been confronted with living evidence of how her husband had spent his time before marrying her.

Not that he would give his *wife* a child, Flora thought, spitting out a curse. Oh, he could give one to that squaw quickly enough, but not her,

even though she'd pleaded for one. He'd
claimed that he wanted her all to himself for a
while, and she'd believed it, along with all the
other things he'd said as he'd sweet-talked her
into marrying him. But he'd sure left her quickly
enough when the smell of gold had started
blowing through town.

No doubt he was doing the same thing out
west. Her Tom was not the kind of man who'd
go long without a woman, and he'd likely found
some other dark-skinned witch to curl up with
on those cold mountain nights. Maybe he'd give
her a child, too, the lowdown rat.

A small, flat rock glinted in the road, shiny
flakes glittering in dark gray, taunting her with
the sparkling promise of all those things Tom
had vowed to her. She snatched it up and
heaved it at the crack-webbed window of the offices of the *Maple Falls Frontierman*, viciously
pleased at the crash of shattering glass. Broken
splinters showered on the wood floor inside the
building, and she imagined those piercing
shards raining down on her husband's head.
Slicing over him, and all faithless men.

Like Lucas Garrett. Oh, it had started out well
enough. Though she'd enjoyed relations with her
husband, Lucas had been a delicious revelation.
That practiced skill, combined with his slow and
obvious enjoyment of the entire act, what led up
to it as well as the deed itself . . . well, just the
thought of it made her privates tingle. She supposed the fact that she was doing something so
taboo, cheating on the husband who'd deceived
and cheated her, was part of the thrill. Not to
mention she enjoyed knowing she had a part—

even such a small part—of a man that every other woman wanted.

And it had eased her mind about the future. Lucas was a shopkeeper, and a shrewd and prosperous one at that. Even if his business had fallen off, it was common knowledge that he'd put enough away in the flush times to get him through the lean ones. Knowing that if times got hard enough she could get what she needed from him had been a comfort. She'd almost relished the idea of working it off in trade.

But that was before Miss-Holy-Sainted-Good-and-Proper, who was obviously not nearly as pure and respectable as everyone believed, had gotten her claws into him. Now what was Flora supposed to do? Depend on Priscilla Wentworth to sell *water*, for God's sake? A spurt of hysteria bubbled into laughter even as desperate worry churned in her stomach.

She needed a drink. Tom had been right about that, that was for sure; the liquor he kept in the kitchen cupboard went a long way to making all kinds of things easier to bear. But, though she'd been rationing the stuff, her supply was disappearing even faster than her money, and now she sure as hell couldn't wheedle some out of Lucas.

The Great Northern loomed across the way, looking a far sight better than most of the buildings on the street. The paint was peeling some, but the windows were whole and clean, glimpses of drapes showing through them.

If she went over there and ordered what she wanted, Temperance would serve her a hefty dose of disapproval along with her whiskey. She could just hear the whispers that would ratchet around town. *Imagine, ordering spirits in public in the middle of the day.* The unfairness of it burned in her dry throat; Tom could have strolled on in, ordered anything he wanted, and nobody would have thought twice. Just like all the other things he could do that she couldn't just because he was a man and she wasn't. Well, she'd already gone and done lots of things she wasn't supposed to, hadn't she? And she wasn't one bit sorry for them, either.

Temperance wouldn't dare refuse her if she claimed it was for medicinal purposes, would she? And it wasn't as if the innkeeper wasn't in sore need of the business. Flora thought of the few coins rolling around in the bottom of her purse, about how she shouldn't spend them, and it depressed her all the more, something she knew only the whiskey would help soothe.

Flora lifted her skirts and dashed for the inn.

Two really lovely slices of green currant pie and six cocoa-nut jumbles had smoothed out the rough edges of Jeanette's mood. She sat alone at a table in the back of the Great Northern—no reason to open up the dining room just for her, she'd said, and besides, she'd been a little curious to see the room the men always disappeared into—when there'd been men to disappear, of course, before they'd disappeared for real. Temperance had winked at that and cut the first slice of pie extra-big.

She'd also taken pity on Jeanette and left a pot of coffee right on the table, along with a little pitcher the color of the cream it held. Jeanette freshened her cup, coffee first, breathing in that fragrant steam, three scoops of sugar, and then stirring in a rich swirl of cream and watching it fade into the dark brown coffee.

She wished she could stay right here in this nice warm bar, eating sweets and sipping coffee. She supposed men felt the same way, except it wasn't coffee they were drinking, and that's why they spent so much time here. Life wasn't so bad when viewed from the bar of the Great Northern.

"It works better," a voice said behind her, "if you put something stronger than cream in your coffee."

Jeanette stiffened. Flora Fergus. Wonderful. All the good those cookies had done was going to be undone just as quickly by that woman's presence.

"Temperance is in the back. If you want something."

"I can get it myself. Especially since the coffee's already here."

Flora trotted around to the back of the bar and returned clutching a tall, clear glass in one hand and a bottle full of dark amber liquid in the other while Jeanette tried to think of an escape. But it was too chilly to be wandering the streets, she didn't want to go back to the store, for Priscilla would think she was checking up on her again, and if she went home, her mother would put her to work. Besides, damned if she was going to be run out of a spot she was enjoying by the likes of Flora Fergus.

Flora yanked out the chair next to Jeanette's and plopped down. Jeanette clenched her teeth rather than mention there were plenty of empty chairs around; her mother had taught her well that a sour mood was no excuse for rudeness.

Flora's pale, plump hand hovered over the handle of the coffee pot. "Do you mind?"

"Help yourself."

Flora sloshed a healthy dram of coffee into the glass, adding a heaping scoop of sugar. Then she uncorked the bottle and dumped a good dose of whiskey in as well. She tilted the bottle in Jeanette's direction. "How about you?"

For a moment, Jeanette was tempted. Only the knowledge that she'd be using the same method as Flora to drown her problems held her back. "No, thank you."

"Suit yourself." Flora shrugged and replaced the cork, tapping it in with the side of her fist. She picked up the glass by the rim and took a big swallow. "Ahhh."

The sound was so relieved, so satisfied, that for an instant Jeanette devoutly wished she'd taken a dose of the liquor herself. That thought worried her enough to reinforce the idea that it was probably better she hadn't given it a try.

Flora swallowed and lifted her head. "I saw your sister at Lucas's store, just a few minutes ago."

Jeanette barely managed to stifle a groan. The last thing she wanted was Flora's opinion on something she had serious doubts about herself. "I know she's there. I walked over with her."

"Do you think it's proper for her to be there with him unchaperoned? What would your mother say?"

Laughter burst out before she could stop it.

"You're worried about whether it's proper or not? Please."

Flora smiled wryly, a bit of amused self-knowledge Jeanette wouldn't have expected of her. "Things are different if you've been married a spell. After your husband's been gone a while." She flicked a sideways glance at Jeanette. "As I'm sure you know very well."

"He was hardly here long enough for me to miss him," she admitted, then wished she could snatch the words back. Why in heaven's name would she spill such a thing to Flora Fergus, of all people?

Flora nodded sympathetically. She contemplated her glass for a time, then set it aside, folding her hands together on the table before her. "He's going to hurt her, you know."

"I don't know what you're talking about," she lied.

"Lucas. I know him very well," she said, in a knowing tone that would have infuriated Jeanette if her words hadn't been the truth. "And he's no more likely to be true to one woman than he is to learn to fly. That ain't a criticism, now. He can't help being who he is, and there's a fair number of us grateful about that. But there's no changing it, either. And I can't imagine your sister being the sort to turn a blind eye to her husband's dalliances."

Jeanette took refuge in her coffee, hiding behind her cup as she sipped, afraid her expression would give away that she harbored nearly the same opinion.

"It'd be a shame, to have a fine woman like your sister stuck in a situation like that."

Jeanette nearly choked on her coffee and came up sputtering. Now, *there* was a little creative shading of the truth if ever she'd heard it; Flora had never been a great admirer of Priscilla's. "I have to agree with you there, Flora. My sister is a fine woman, one of the best. Lucas'd be lucky to have her."

"Of course," Flora forced out, and Jeanette could tell the words nearly gagged her. "But it's too bad, really, that something can't be done before things go too far. Priscilla won't discover Lucas's true colors before it is too late."

"Oh?" Jeanette asked, with an encouraging lift to her eyebrow. Where was Flora going with this? If nothing else, it might be entertaining to find out.

"If she would see him with another woman, perhaps that would be enough to shock her to her senses."

"Accidentally, of course."

"Of course."

"I don't see how that would happen," Jeanette said. "Lucas has always been very good at not being caught."

"I suppose someone would have to . . . help things along. Purely for Priscilla's own good. Someone who cared about her enough to do such a thing."

Dear God, Jeanette thought, unable to credit that even Flora was making such a suggestion. She actually thought that Jeanette might seduce her sister's fiancé? And arrange to be found out?

Although he really wasn't Priscilla's fiancé, was he? And, if God were kind, he never would be.

After another big swig of her alcohol-doused coffee, Flora stared into it without speaking, leaving Jeanette immensely relieved that she'd dropped the topic.

Her relief ended quickly, however, when Flora spoke again. "Talked to Louisa Rockwell today; she'd got a letter from her brother. Said he ran into Robert in Gold Dust."

Jeanette's stomach clenched violently. "I see."

"I really hate to be the one to tell you this," Flora said without a whiff of regret in her voice. "But I would want to know."

"So you're taking it upon yourself—in all kindness—to tell me that Robert's spreeing all over the Jefferson Territory, is that it?" She wondered how much tighter she could clamp on to her cup without shattering it. "How stupid do you think I am? Do you really think I didn't know already? And how . . . thoughtful of you to tell me."

"As I said, I would want to know." For the first time, Flora met Jeanette's gaze fully, revealing all the bitter rage that burned in her eyes. "I *did* want to know."

"I—" At a loss, Jeanette gulped her candy-sweet coffee. She didn't want to have anything in common with Flora, but pity and unwelcome understanding rose anyway.

"It's better to know, isn't it? To know what he's worth, and what you do—and don't—owe him."

It was something she'd tried very hard not to think about. Robert was her husband; they'd taken vows. If he wasn't living up to his, what did that make of hers?

Flora gave up any attempt at subtlety. "You could kill two birds at once, Jeanette. Save your sister. And take revenge on Robert at the same time."

Surprised to find herself making the effort, Jeanette laid a consoling hand on Flora's. "He must have hurt you very badly."

Flora snatched her hand back. "Lucas? Don't be ridiculous. The man didn't pretend to be something he wasn't, I'll give him that. More than I can say for most."

"No," Jeanette said softly. "Your husband."

Raw pain tightened Flora's round features, drew her mouth back, and swallowed up the anger. "You'd know all about that, wouldn't you?"

Jeanette had knit her own pain behind a web of righteous indignation and tight control. How strange that Flora would be the one who would unravel it all, pull out those carefully held threads so that the agony was finally released full force. It churned in her chest, pushed high in her throat, and she wondered what Temperance would do if she were sick right on the glossy pine floor.

Flora fought for control, found it. "Tom did me a favor, actually." She shrugged. "If he hadn't, I would have been faithful to him. And then I would never have found out what I was missing."

Against her will, Jeanette felt an impermissable stir of curiosity. Flora sloshed more whiskey into her glass, this time forgoing the formality of coffee.

The alcohol she'd been downing all seemed to hit Flora at once, and her eyes crossed. "Yup, Mr.

Fergus, he thought he was a great lover. The member of a bull, that man. But Lucas . . ." She smiled blissfully, sighed the same way. "Oh, my Lucas. He has the hands of a God, that one." She waved the bottle in the air, decided it was easier just to drink it straight from the source. "And the rest of him . . . a god would be jealous of the rest of him."

Jeanette's own experience had been . . . brief. Brief and temporary, and too long ago for her to remember much but a few pleasant sensations and a few deeper urges that might have turned into something good, had they been given the chance. But Flora's face radiated something else entirely, something Jeanette couldn't even imagine. Not quite.

She'd heard rumors of Lucas Garrett's prowess since she'd been old enough to understand them. She'd struggled to ignore them even as she'd struggled to contain her rampant curiosity now, and was mortified when a "You mean that he's—?" burst out before she could stop it.

"More." Flora rose to her feet. "And even more than that." She stabbed the air with her forefinger. "Remember. What's good for the gander . . ." Cradling the bottle to her breast, she turned unsteadily and lurched for the door. "Tell Mrs. Churchill I'm gonna take this with me. I'll settle up later."

Twenty minutes later Priscilla found Jeanette there, still staring into a cup of coffee that had gone cold long ago, glancing up only when Priscilla bustled to her side. "Are you ready to go? I've got so much to do, I'd really like to get started."

Priscilla's eyes were bright and eager, her cheeks almost matching the red of her shawl. Even with that awful outsized bow cinched too tight under her chin, she looked as good as Jeanette had ever seen her, and she realized just how much a woman's mood had to with her appearance. Considering that, Jeanette figured she was looking far from her personal best.

"That didn't take long."

"No. The mail came, and he needed to get started on that—you know how everyone shows up right after it gets here and hovers around, waiting for it to be sorted. It wasn't conducive to doing business," Priscilla said happily. "Did you know, Jeanette, that he's ... well, I guess you could say he's taken on one of those children, though the boy's not living there." Her voice lowered. "You know, from down by Miller's Hill? Isn't that kind of him? I've been terribly remiss. I haven't done nearly enough for those poor women and children, other than deliver some food and blankets now and then. I was wondering, though, if the bottling enterprise begins to profit, whether I could talk them into—"

"You're falling in love with him," Jeanette said flatly.

Priscilla froze. Then she laughed lightly, falsely, her gaze sliding away from Jeanette's probing one. "Mick? A little, I suppose. He's really a charming child, so eager and—"

"No," Jeanette said, too sharp, frustrated by Priscilla's avoidance of what they both knew was the real question. It wasn't like Priscilla to dance around the truth. "Lucas."

"Lucas?" Her laughter trilled again, brittle as a dried flower left too long on the stalk. "Don't be ridiculous. It's all an act, you know that. It's natural to be caught up in it a little, I suppose. But I am certainly not falling in love with him."

But her voice trembled a bit on the last words, as if even she knew they were false.

"I should hope not," Jeanette said darkly.

"Why? Because you, like everyone else, is convinced that I could never hold him? Is it so hard to believe that a man would want me and only me?"

"Not a man, Priscilla. Lucas."

Priscilla found something fascinating to stare at on the empty wall behind Jeanette, her mouth firming into a mutinous line. A few strands of hair had tugged free of their anchor, slipping loose against her neck, and it occurred to Jeanette that she couldn't remember the last time she'd seen her sister with a hair out of place.

"He kissed you, didn't he?" she accused.

Priscilla's gaze swung back to Jeanette, her mouth popping open. She clutched her handbag tight against her waist as if it would shield her. "You know he did," she managed at last. "You saw it. You and everyone else in town."

"Not then. Today."

The color in her cheeks deepened. "He did not!" she denied hotly.

Ah, but you wanted him to, didn't you? Jeanette thought. More than anything. And a whole lot more besides, though maybe Priscilla didn't even realize it herself.

"Besides, I don't see how it would be the worst thing in the world. A woman who reaches my age naturally wants to be kissed now and then." She plucked at the fringe of her shawl. "Would it be such a terrible thing?" she asked, as uncertain as Jeanette had ever heard her, and Jeanette's heart cracked in anticipation, knowing that her sister's was inevitably going to be split wide open, if she stayed on the path she seemed set on.

"Yes, it is."

Priscilla jerked. "I just want . . . something. Someone," she said. "It's not that it would have to be Lucas."

"I know," Jeanette said, even as she doubted it was the truth.

"Could be anyone. He's just the one here," she said, trying as hard to convince herself as to persuade Jeanette.

"Guess we'll have to find you someone else to kiss, then." But even as she said it, more drastic measures tickled the back of her brain, tempting Jeanette with a more definite and final solution before it was too late.

If it wasn't already.

Chapter 18

❧

Lucas rapped on the Wentworths' front door. Without waiting for an answer—why put them out by making them rush to the door, he reasoned—he walked right on in, whistling a merry rendition of "Jim Crack Corn."

Having learned his lesson, he stepped around Mrs. Garrett's wool runner and hurried down the hallway, his booted footfalls echoing, hoping to find Pris quickly. Anxiety and anticipation nagged him, which was a ridiculous reaction, but there it was. But he hadn't seen her for two whole days, having been occupied with helping Jenny dig her potatoes, and he'd gotten back in the habit of seeing Pris every day. Plus he was looking forward to seeing her face when he told her he had two hotels, a saloon, and three restaurants in St. Anthony all interested in buying their water.

"Pris!" he bellowed, wincing as the sound bounced off the plastered walls and shiny wood floors, feeling like he'd just muddied the rug after all.

"Hello, Lucas," she said behind him. His

stomach lifted into his chest, and he spun to find
Jeanette standing in the doorway to the parlor.

"Oh. Hello, Jeanette." He yanked off his hat
and stood there crushing it in one hand, weight
on one leg like he was ready to dash off again.
"Never realized how much you sound like your
sister."

"You're not the first to notice," she said,
amused, and maybe a little insulted, to see how
deflated he was to have found her instead of
Priscilla.

He lifted his chin, craning his neck to look behind her. "She here?"

"Not right now." Falling into old habits, she
leaned against the doorway, angling her body in
the way that showed her profile and waist to
best advantage. It felt good, she realized, to try
and make herself appealing to a man. She wondered vaguely why she'd never tried it on Lucas
before, if only for the practice.

"She said she was going out to the spring.
Something about testing mineral contents, I
think." She didn't tell him that Priscilla had left
nearly two hours ago, and she expected her back
at any time.

He nodded knowingly. "She figured that if we
were going to put claims of healthfulness on the
label, we'd better know exactly what's in there."
He shook his head, grinning. "That woman is
honest to the end. She wouldn't sell a horse without telling the buyer it had stepped on a pebble
a month ago."

"That's true," Jeanette said. "Except when *you*
talk her into lying."

Lucas winced. "She's never seemed to mind."

"That's unfortunately true. But it doesn't make it right."

"Did you get your letter?" he asked, wisely changing the topic. "I gave it to Pris to give to you."

"I got it." For all the good it did her. Six months she'd been waiting for word from Robert, and what did she get? A page of smudged, cheap paper, barely half-filled with a rushed scrawl. Not one word of missing her, or promises to return, or hopes for the future, or a hint of apology. Just a few grandiose statements about the wealth to be found in the mountains, a halfhearted congratulation on her twenty-second birthday—which had been five months ago—and a warning not to attempt to contact him at this address, because he was moving on.

She'd rather have not gotten it at all. Though shredding it into a hundred pieces, dousing it in kerosene, and dropping a match to it provided her a measure of satisfaction.

"Would you like to come on into the parlor? I was just about to sit down to some tea." She gave him a soft smile, pleased when he blinked, caught off-guard.

"I wouldn't want to impose," he said. "And I really must get going."

"Please?" She looked up at him, using her bright green eyes to her greatest advantage. "I've been feeling a little low lately, and I'd really rather not be by myself. Who better to cheer up a lonely lady than Lucas Garrett?"

He narrowed his eyes at her, clearly trying to figure out her sudden change in manner. Good. She wanted him confused.

"There's blueberry pie. I won't tell, if you won't."

She saw him waver, as if he were wondering why she was trying so hard to get him to stay.

"I really should be going," he repeated.

"I know that Priscilla would appreciate your indulging me. She worries about me being alone so much."

It was a calculated trump card, and it worked exactly as Jeanette had expected. Lucas gave a winning smile, no less effective for its being thoughtlessly automatic, and followed her into the parlor.

He took his customary place on the settee—he was too big a man for the delicate pieces of furniture that clustered about the rose-patterned rug. Her father had been the same; he'd allowed Clara free rein in decorating this room, though Jeanette guessed he'd always regretted it when it had turned out there wasn't one comfortable place for a man to sit.

She poured Lucas a cup of tea, balancing it on a blue-painted plate with a hefty slab of pie. Presenting it to him, she bent lower than normal, allowing him a brief glimpse of her cleavage. Lucas startled, scooting his gaze away like a shot, and shifted in his seat.

Flora was right about one thing, she decided. A flirtation with an attractive man went a long way to soothing pride bruised by an inattentive husband.

Perhaps she was right about other things, as well. They certainly agreed on the disastrous potential of a union between Lucas and Priscilla. What else might she be correct about? Jeanette wondered, both repelled and unwillingly intrigued by the idea.

She arranged herself in the chair nearest Lucas, spreading her blue-flowered skirts wide enough to allow a glimpse of ankle beneath, lying back languidly against the pillows.

He ate with good appetite and obvious enjoyment, to be expected, of course; he'd always had a reputation for enjoying pleasures to their fullest. He looked up from his plate now and then, shooting vaguely suspicious glances her way.

His hands were quick and sure, dark and sinewy against the pale, delicate china. Big, strong, steady hands, hands that had pleasured many women. She swallowed hard, shocked that she was having such thoughts about Lucas, and the shock itself was a strange and unfamiliar excitement.

"Priscilla is beginning to have . . . expectations, you know."

Lucas, a forkful of pie halfway to his mouth, fumbled his plate and had to scramble to recover it. "Expectations?"

"Yes." She looked at him steadily, daring him to pretend that he didn't know what she was talking about.

Lucas opened his mouth to deny the very idea of it, say that Pris would never expect—never *want*—more than friendship from him, and found he couldn't do it. He had known, somewhere deep inside, where he'd being trying desperately to ignore it, that Pris had begun to believe in the illusion. But he hadn't wanted to admit it, for if he acknowledged it, he would have to deal with it. And he was enjoying her infatuation, he thought with a guilty start, waiting each day for her to look at him in that way that made him feel like the king of the world.

"What are you going to do about it?"

Enjoy it until she comes to her senses was probably not the right answer. But it was what he wanted to do. He had Pris back in his life, if not exactly sharing the friendship they'd enjoyed before. For now, they had the friendship, plus a little bit more.

"You can't let it go any further," Jeanette said flatly.

"I know that," he agreed, even as he wished it weren't true. Even as he dreamed of how Pris felt in his arms, how her mouth fit his like she was made for him, how he knew that he could make her happier than any other man could.

For a little while.

"Do you want to do to her what your father did to your mother? It's going to happen, if you don't end this, now and completely."

"I know that!" he snapped, even as everything inside him kicked hard in protest.

"Do you? Then why haven't you done something to stop it?"

He thought of the way his mother had looked at his father, her eyes full of disappointment and bitterness and raw hatred. Imagined Pris looking at him that way, and everything in him that could feel, everything that mattered, hurt just at the thought, and he knew he'd do anything to avoid it.

"What am I supposed to do?" he asked. "I'm supposed to tell her I don't want her? It would hurt her, just the saying of it. I'm not sure I could do that."

"Better now than later."

"Maybe." He shifted in his chair and caught her watching him, her gaze drifting down from his hands to his lap, and he flushed, uncomfortable. He'd always loved women looking at him with the same honest appreciation he showed for them, but this was Jeanette, and it felt all wrong. "I've never lied to her. I'm not sure I can. And I'm not at all sure she wouldn't know immediately if I tried to."

Her eyes, wide and gleaming green, so like Pris's, lifted to his face. "Would it be a lie?" she asked softly.

He swallowed hard, knowing that admitting it out loud to another person would somehow make it real and irrevocable in a way it hadn't been before. "Yes."

She rose, skirts swishing as she moved toward him in a rustle of silk and femininity.

"She's not like all the rest, Lucas."

"I know that."

"Do you?" Her skirts frothed between his spread knees. "She couldn't just take the pleasure without needing everything else. Couldn't guard her heart. Not from anyone, and especially not from you. And you couldn't give her anything more. It would be cruel to let her think otherwise, to hope otherwise. She's starting to hope, Lucas. You know that."

Her soft words wove a steel trap around him, tight and inescapable though spoken in a soft, seductive voice, closing in even as his throat constricted.

"She's no match for you, Lucas." Jeanette bent and he caught a glimpse of her face, wild eyes belying the steadiness of her voice. "Not like I am."

Then she pressed her mouth against his throat. He jolted up from the chair, unbalancing Jeanette. She wavered until he put a hand on her arm to steady her.

"Jeanette, I—"

"Please." Desperation edged that single word before her mouth curved into a familiar, beguiling smile. "Have you really never thought of it?"

Her arm trembled where he touched her. There was strong emotion there, but how much of it was for him? He didn't know whether she'd been moved to this by hatred of her husband or love for her sister.

Did it matter? It was an answer. Sleeping with Jeanette would be the one absolute and irrevocable way to make certain that Priscilla Wentworth would never allow him to lay one finger on her. If it hurt her now, perhaps it was the greatest kindness he could ever do her.

He didn't know if it would be the most noble act he ever did, or the most despicable. His gut tightened. Who was he to know the right thing? The son of William Garrett? He almost laughed at the absurdity.

He moved forward, testing. Her head fit beneath his chin; they were the same height, she and her sister. He inhaled deeply, letting the scent of Priscilla's soap cloud his mind. He touched her hair, the same thick softness, only a few shades brighter than Pris's beautiful brown, like a fawn's coat. It was as close as he was ever going to get to holding Pris like this.

"Lucas." She shook against him, in fear as much as passion, and lifted her head for his kiss. He stared down at her. The same green eyes. A pretty mouth, parted and waiting. A delicate, fine-boned nose, which struck him now as bland and indecisive.

Do it! He told himself. As he'd done a thousand times before.

"Oh, damn you, you stupid man!" Jeanette smacked him on the chest with the flat of her palm. "Don't tell me you've decided to dredge up a scruple at this late date!"

"I—" Deciding on the wiser course, he shut his mouth. Scruples didn't have a lot to do with it. He didn't know what did, just that while his mind might insist it was the right thing to do, it still *felt* all wrong.

"Oh, damn!" she repeated, a sob breaking through the curse. She crumpled against him. For a moment, he wondered if he could trust her tears, or if they were one more attempt to seduce him, a tactic that a month or two ago probably would have worked like a charm. But her breath stuttered, ragged and thready, and her tears weren't stirring anything but sympathy anyway, so he brought his arms around her to hold her up.

"Why can't I even do this right?" she wailed. "Every other woman in town barely has to blink in your direction, and here I'm throwing myself in your arms to no effect."

"I wouldn't exactly say *every* woman in town."

"*Me*," she went on, as if he hadn't spoken. "I used to be able to waggle my little finger and have men promise to bring me the world. Why not you?"

She snuffled loudly against his shirt, thoroughly dampening the sleeve.

"I don't know. Maybe because I remember you as that runny-nosed little brat who used to scream for her daddy every time I waved a worm in your direction. Most other men don't have that memory to call on to help them resist you."

She chuckled despite herself. "Such a charmer, aren't you?" She sighed, easing more comfortably against him as if she were settling in for the duration. When she spoke again, her voice was small and tentative, muffled by his shoulder. "What's Robert's excuse, then?"

Damn. Lucas sucked in a breath and blew it out slowly. He wasn't the one to be mucking around in somebody else's marriage. And he sure as hell didn't approve of what he regarded as Robert's cowardly approach to the problems in his. But it wasn't his place to comment, and he figured Jeanette needed explanations more than advice or another condemnation of her errant husband.

"A man's pride is a delicate thing," he said. "Some would rather hide and try and hang on to it, rather than face losing it. Especially in front of his woman."

"Pride!" The disdain in that one word would have been enough to make Robert shrivel, had he been within ten miles. Lucas could almost pity him, if he ever thought to return to his wife. "I gave too much allowance to his pride as it was. Where's the pride in running away? And what does it matter, anyway?"

"It matters. And don't ask me to explain it, because it just does."

"It's stupid," she said again, but there was no more anger behind it. She rubbed her cheek against his chest. "This is nice, Lucas. You do it well. Since it appears there's no chance of me exploring any of those other talents I keep hearing whispered about, do you suppose that maybe you'd just give me a hug now and then?"

He laughed. It was a novelty for him, too, to hold a woman close without even a tiny spark of sexual interest flaring. He felt rather as if he'd just gained himself a younger sister, and it warmed him enough to make him wonder what else he'd been missing out on in pursuing one thing with such single-minded enthusiasm all those years. "Anytime, darlin'. Anytime. Happy to be of service. It's a sacrifice for me, you know, to hold a beautiful woman in my arms."

"I'm sorry to interrupt," Priscilla said crisply, and all his warm feelings froze into bitter ice. "But you two might consider closing the door next time."

She stood just inside the doorway, holding herself tall and rigid, one hand curled tightly around the back of the nearest chair, that strong nose tilted high. He had to admire her fierce control even as he took in the stark paleness of her face, so white against the stormy emotion in her eyes.

"It's not what it looks like." The words were out before he thought, and he winced at their weakness, the banal excuse. He'd avoided uttering that phrase his whole life, mostly because it almost always *was* what it looked like. Shut up, he told himself. Let Pris believe what she saw, and she'd be free of him, once and for all.

"Don't be ridiculous." Jeanette turned, backing up against him so it looked like she couldn't bear to leave his embrace. "It's exactly what it looks like."

Priscilla hung on to the chair as if it were the only thing between her and the bottom of a fathomless pit. Pleased with her afternoon's work, she'd tripped happily into the room and found her sister in Lucas's arms, and her heart had plunged to her belly, which was now giving every indication of wanting to eject it out her throat.

I didn't know. Foolish words that kept whirling around in her brain, spinning by, crowding out any more sensible thoughts. She hadn't once suspected that there could ever be anything between the two of them—and had never had the slightest notion of what it would really feel like to find Lucas with another woman. While she'd always known it was theoretically possible, even likely, she hadn't *known.* Hadn't known that fury and agony and humiliation could all surge together, threaten to swamp her and pull her down to a place she might never crawl out of.

She knew she was staring, but she couldn't help it. Lucas just stood there, mouth open, looking as hopelessly dazed as if someone had just clubbed him with a dead walleye. Her smooth, glib, charming Lucas, more at a loss than she'd ever seen him, and she was distantly aware she might have been amused, if there had been room for another emotion besides the ones that churned wildly inside her.

And her sister, her beautiful sister, looking for all the world like she belonged there, so perfectly matched with him that Priscilla didn't know how she could have missed seeing it all along.

"I hope you know that this never would have happened," Jeanette said, looking so intently at her that Priscilla wondered what she could be seeing, "if you hadn't made it so clear that there was not and could never be anything romantic between you and Lucas. I *never* would have allowed it otherwise."

You should know me better than that! She wanted to shout it, scream it, beat it into her sister's head. Except that small corner of her that was still logical, a distant place hanging on to sanity by a fraying thread, reminded her that her sister was right. There was not, could not be anything more than friendship between her and Lucas, and this episode had just vividly demonstrated why.

She didn't want to look at him. Couldn't help but look at him, her gaze drawn back up to meet his as if pulled by a string.

She swallowed hard, willing the words to come out clear and strong. "I need to talk to Lucas."

"But—"

"Alone, Jeanette."

"Don't let him talk his way out of this one," Jeanette said, with the indulgent laugh of a woman discussing a flawed but still-cherished lover. "You know what he's like, once he gets that smooth tongue of his working."

It stabbed at her, sinking deep and lethal as an ice pick. Surely Jeanette hadn't meant it like that.

"Please," she said, grateful that it hadn't come out a whimper. "You owe me this much, Jeanette."

Jeanette spun, spearing Lucas with a warning look. "You do right by her," she snapped, before reluctantly gliding out. Priscilla turned and pulled the double doors shut, pausing there, her back to Lucas, her hands on the smooth cool metal of the doorknob. If she didn't turn around, if she didn't let go, maybe she could pretend it had never happened.

But Lucas wouldn't let her. "Pris?" he said, the way that only he could. She squeezed her eyes shut briefly before she faced him.

"Pris, I—"

"Don't talk," she said, even as her heart longed for him to talk it away, to convince her it was nothing like it had appeared. "Just answer."

"All right."

"Did you do it?"

"What, exactly, are you asking?" he asked, stalling, immediately sorry when she closed her eyes as if she couldn't even bear to look at him.

"Don't," she said pleadingly. "Just don't." Her lids fluttered open again, and he would have thrown himself off the top floor of the mill to avoid seeing that expression there. Hell, he'd spent most of the last month trying to avoid it, and here it was anyway.

"Did you lie with my sister?"

There it was. All he had to say was yes, and

Priscilla Wentworth was safe from him forever. While he'd likely never have her in his life again, he'd also avoid causing her more pain.

He wondered how his life had gotten into such a muddle that an outright lie to his best friend might be the most valiant thing he could do.

"No," he said anyway, on a wave of relief and remorse.

"Were you *going* to lie with my sister?"

"I—" A more complicated question. "I thought about it, maybe, for a moment or two. But no, I wasn't going to."

She gazed at him, mouth still firmly pressed into disapproval, eyes still swirling with something much darker than disapproval. "Fine," she clipped out. "Now then, about the—"

"Wait a minute," he said. "That's it?"

"That's it. What else do you want?"

"Don't you believe me?" he burst out. Pris always believed him, and he'd never given her reason not to.

"Oh, I believe you," she said.

"Then why are you still looking at me as if you don't?"

Because it doesn't matter, she thought. Because eventually, inevitably, someday his answer would be different. In her misguided way, and she and her sister would be discussing *that* later, as well, Jeanette had done her an enormous favor. She'd given her a sample of what awaited her, had she continued to build dreams around Lucas. And waiting, watching, anticipating its occurrence would be nearly as terrible as experiencing it.

"Leave it alone, Lucas," she said, shamed to find tears prickling when she should be grateful for her close escape. "There's nothing else to be said."

To someone who knew her well, Lucas thought, Pris never showed more emotion than when she was struggling mightily not to. Faint lines speared up from her brows, and her jaw was set at a sharp angle to her neck. He could draw her to him and kiss that tension away in an instant, soothe that harsh emotion with his touch. He'd never longed for anything so much in his life, and had never known with such certainty it would be the dumbest thing he'd ever done.

Hands fisted, nails cutting into his palms to keep from touching her, sweat breaking out on the back of his neck, Lucas Garrett did the right thing. He left her alone.

Even in his misbegotten life there had to be a first time for everything.

Chapter 19

❧

Over the previous weeks, Lucas had concluded he would probably never do anything more difficult than trying to hold himself aloof from Pris, making certain that she never suspected he wanted her, somehow finding the strength to resist the temptation to touch her again.

In the three weeks that followed her discovery of Jeanette in his arms, he found out just how wrong he'd been.

It was a thousand times harder to suffer her holding herself remote from *him* and not be able to do anything about it. She treated with him with distant courtesy, barely veiling a clear, unassailable coldness that he'd never seen her display to *anyone* before, much less him. In doing his utmost to avoid having her regard him with such disgust, it seemed he'd somehow promoted exactly that.

Worst of all, Pris had suddenly returned to her husband hunt with renewed vehemence. He argued that their energies should be devoted to the bottling enterprise rather than such frivolities.

Then he pointed out that if she was seen around town making eyes at men their secret would be revealed in no time. She insisted she'd be discreet, and demanded even more strongly that he bring forth the candidates he'd agreed on. In what even he knew was a weak attempt to gain her favor, he tried.

First there was the mill owner from Sauk Center, whom he'd hauled over to Maple Falls on the slight excuse of looking over some slightly flood-damaged—and therefore cheap—equipment still rusting on the factory floor. Pris had appeared to like him well enough. But something about his hearty laughter and determined bonhomie had set Lucas's teeth on edge, and he was unaccountably relieved when, over lunch, the soup vegetables kept getting caught in the man's lavish mustache in a most unattractive manner.

Then there was the hugely muscular fur trader who came to town every fall for supplies. But when Lucas had gone to the storeroom to finish filling his substantial order, the trader had turned his long-starved attentions on Pris in a very insistent manner. While her well-placed knee had cooled his ardor effectively, it hadn't satisfied Lucas, who had quietly visited the fellow before he left town and demonstrated his opinion in an enjoyably bloody way. Lucas had been all prepared, with heroic reluctance, to let Priscilla pry the story out of him, but she'd only glanced at his bruised and scraped knuckles, pursed her lips together firmly, and never mentioned it.

And worst of all had been the handsome

young hotelier whom Lucas had called on in St. Cloud, thinking he might become a steady customer for Maple Falls Spring Water—and he'd never even gotten so far as *meeting* Priscilla. Because unfortunately for all three of them, he'd turned out to be far more interested in Lucas than he'd ever be in any woman, something Lucas was trying very hard to forget happened.

He'd been forced to resort, after all, to Obadiah Rockwell, who, overcome during a slow stroll through town, had propped himself up against the nearest wall and gone promptly to sleep in a cloud of rumbling snores and whiskey fumes. A glimmer of Pris's old good humor leaked through at that, and he'd thought, "Aha! *Finally,*" only to have it disappear as quickly as a doused flame at the sight of Lucas's relieved smile.

The tension between the two of them was inevitably noticed by the town, prompting a few hopeful overtures. Lucas had mumbled something about a lover's quarrel and moped about in a way designed to indicate that spending time with him simply wouldn't be any fun. This led to somewhat fewer offers to console him, which he'd finally turned aside by the last-ditch measure of hinting that not only would he not be consoled, he *could* not be consoled.

All in all, he was miserably grateful to be getting the hell out of town.

He'd already hitched a buckboard behind Charger, the reliable gray gelding he'd owned for years, and loaded a half-dozen crates of samples. Now, with the October sun smiling down with unusual benevolence, he stripped off his jacket and tossed it over the seat, calculating that he'd need at least three more crates. To make this escape to St. Anthony a worthwhile trip, he intended to call on every single restaurant, saloon, hotel, and store in the entire town.

"Here you go!" Mick dragged the bag into which Lucas had shoved a handful of clothes through the front door of the store and let it slam shut behind him. "Found it right on your bed, just like you said."

"I knew I could count on you."

"Is there anything else?" Mick deposited the sack at Lucas's feet and looked at him expectantly.

"Nope." Maybe next time, Lucas thought, he'd see if he could talk Mick's mother into letting the boy come along. Mick would be completely thrilled by the city. "Except you promised me you'll check the store every day, right? I'm depending on you to keep the robbers away."

Mick puffed out a chest that Lucas was pleased to see was a bit more sturdy than it had been a few weeks ago. "I promise."

"There were a few things that I didn't get eaten up in time, so I left them on the counter. I expect them gone by the time I get back."

"You don't have to—"

"That's an order, Mick. If you don't eat them, it'll just bring mice, you know."

"Yes, sir!"

Lucas wondered if Mick's young male pride would be too damaged if he gave the boy a hug.

Aw, what the hell.

"Hey!" As soon as Lucas let him go, Mick patted down his hair and quickly checked to make sure no one had seen. But the corners of his mouth kept turning up.

"I'll see you when I get back."

"Yeah." The grin broke free. "I'll see you then." He waved and headed on down the street. Lucas waved after him.

Two blocks away, he saw Pris struggling along, lugging a large satchel topped by no fewer than three hatboxes, which she was having a hell of a time trying to crane her neck around in an attempt to see where she was going. The huge red flowers on her hat bobbed limply above the top box.

She made directly for him and dumped the entire pile on the ground. "You could have helped me!"

"I—" What in the world . . . ? "I know how you feel about empty chivalrous gestures toward independent women. I wouldn't dream of insulting you like that."

"I've changed my mind. Empty chivalrous gestures have their uses." Finally catching a breath, she blew it out in relief, then slanted him a wry look. "Like men. *Some* men," she amended.

She looked particularly . . . good this morning. Better than good. She tugged at the hem of her jacket to straighten it and patted her skirts into place. She wore a new suit, fashioned of black-and-white checked wool that he vaguely remembered selling to her mother years ago. It nipped in sharply at her waist before erupting out over extravagant crinolines. Black cording had been sewn in a pattern of deep swirls at the hem and

bodice, and a dash of scarlet silk peeked out between the lapels.

He couldn't remember the last time he'd seen
her in new clothes. He should know; he'd tried
hard enough to sell her some over the years. And
now all he wanted to do was start peeling her
out of them.

Look higher, he told himself. Above entice-
ments like hooks and buttons and silk. He focused on her hat, a huge wheel of black straw
with drapings of white silk and big, flat, deep-
red flowers that quivered like slices of liver every
time she moved her head. He shuddered.

"Well? Aren't you at least going to help me
load my luggage?"

He stared at her blankly. Beside him, Charger
stamped and snorted in frustration, impatient to
be on his way. Lucas knew exactly how he felt.
"Excuse me?"

"I'm going with you."

His already susceptible heart stopped, then
kicked into double-time. "You are not."

"Yes. I am," she said firmly, her nod setting
the scarlet poppies a-tremble.

Alone. In a hotel. Just the two of them. The
thought played around and around in his head,
and even that hideous hat began to have possibilities. If he tore off the silk, for instance . . .

"You can't!" he said, panicked, knowing that
whatever meager self-control he possessed
would fail miserably if he ended up in a hotel in
St. Anthony alone with Pris. Dear Lord, how
could she expect it of him?

"Of course I can."

"But—but—" He grabbed at feeble straws.

"Your mother! She would never allow you go off with me unchaperoned."

"My mother and I have come to something of an agreement as to whether she can *allow* me to do something or not. Besides, she is once again convinced that I am in no danger of falling for your, ah, charms." She looked down her long nose at him. "As well she should be."

His hands started to sweat. She couldn't go with him, she could *not* go with him.

"Also, there is the fact that she considers my reason for going . . ." She paused before finishing delicately, "Worthy."

He'd never got the impression that Mrs. Wentworth was still all that enamored of the bottling venture.

She looked pointedly at the satchel and boxes at her feet, then back at him.

"I can handle this trip myself," he said, struggling for a good reason why she shouldn't accompany him. Any reason except the real reason. "The sales will go better if there's only one of us there. Otherwise we might . . . contradict each other. Get in each other's way. And I'm already acquainted with many of the people I'm planning to see. Nothing like the personal touch."

She pinkened slightly. "So I've been told."

"You must trust me on this. This is my area of expertise."

She speared him with a look of simmering disdain. Hell, he thought, he'd been celibate—terrible monkish word. Abstinent was better; there was a certain high-minded idealism and nobility in the term. Choice, rather than lack of opportunity—he'd been *abstinent* for the longest stretch of his adult life, and she still looked at him as if he'd decided to hold an orgy on her front lawn.

"Sales," he added.

"I knew that." She suddenly took an extreme interest in the left front wheel of his wagon. "But I'm not precisely going along on bottling business."

"You're not?"

She shook her head.

"Why do you want to go, then?"

"It's personal," she said, so quietly he could barely hear her.

"What?"

"Personal business," she said, louder.

"What personal business?"

She tossed him a disgruntled glare and snapped, "You didn't really think I was going to depend on *you* to find me a husband, did you?"

"I—" He paused, swallowed hard. "You found yourself a husband?"

She poked at the fingers of her gloves, smoothing them on more firmly. "I found myself an excellent candidate," she qualified.

"Who is he?"

"His name is Reuben Morse. *Dr.* Reuben Morse, a widower with several children. His letters . . . he seems quite well spoken. And most respectful." She looked up at him at last. "Do you know him?"

"No."

"Oh. I thought perhaps . . . well, no matter."

"How did you find him?" Lucas heard himself saying the words, wondered where they came from, because surely his brain wasn't working well enough to make sensible conversation; it was still stuck back there where Pris had said she'd found herself a husband.

"In the newspaper." Color bloomed on her cheeks, bright as those stupid poppies. She lifted her chin, daring him to comment. "We've been corresponding for some time now. He is very . . . charming." Her eyes glowed, shimmering like sunshine on wet leaves, and all he could think was that he wished he'd been the one to put that look there.

Damn. Damn, damn, damn. Lucas bent and started pitching her boxes into the back of his wagon.

"What are you doing?"

"What does it look like? I'm loading your stuff." He heaved the satchel over the side of the wagon, nearly crushing one of the hatboxes, ignoring Pris's shriek of protest. She should be so lucky. "I guess we'd better get you to St. Anthony, then, shouldn't we?"

The sooner, the better, he thought. *The sooner you'll be safe from me.*

It was a miserably long trip for Priscilla. Oh, not that the weather wasn't perfect. Minnesota was at its best in autumn, the land ripe and golden. The air held a promising briskness, just cool enough to make one feel energetic and optimistic.

At least, that was how it had always affected her in the past. However, Lucas's stiff, frowning, and uncommunicative presence on the seat beside her dampened her spirits more effectively than a dozen rain showers could have.

Despite herself, she kept waiting for him to break out with a quip or relate some funny little story about whatever town they were passing through. To set himself to being the entertaining and charming companion she was used to. It didn't help to know that it was her own chilly treatment of him over the past weeks that had likely spawned his own, nor that she knew she should be grateful for his forbidding—and therefore safe—demeanor. She still missed the Lucas she'd known for so long.

And so she'd perched uncomfortably on the seat, her back going stiff with the long days on the road, her stomach jumping with nerves. Nerves that should have been over her impending meeting with the man who might become her husband, but which she was depressingly aware had far more to do with the man who sat not more than six inches from her hip. Now and then she'd look down at his hands on the reins, completely in control of the horse with only the subtlest of movements. His hands were still battered, scabs cracking across the knuckles as his fingers flexed, and she had to bite her lip to keep silent.

She strongly suspected those injuries had not come in the course of stocking his shelves, though she'd tried to convince herself they had. They'd come from banging into the unyielding head of that beastly fur trader, and she should have been annoyed. It was such a typically male reaction, to interject further violence into a situation she'd already handled competently. And yet it touched her ridiculously that he'd been so angered on her behalf, making her feel safe and

warm and cared for. Once, lulled into a thoughtless stupor by the hours of motion and sunshine,
she'd reached for him, catching herself the instant before brushing her fingers over the largest
scrape on the back of his hand.

Stupor, indeed.

Lucas was an unprincipled, lustful, faithless
seducer of women. But he was so very much
more than that, which was precisely her problem.

After two days of such thoughts; of long hours
staring at Charger's sweating rump; of rushed,
silent, unsatisfying meals; and of an inordinately
brief night in a marginally acceptable inn, she
was pitiably thankful when they pulled to a stop
in front of the River House Hotel in St. Anthony.
A grand limestone structure catering to the lumber trade, it presided over a bluff high above the
Mississippi, which was already much more impressive here than it was in Maple Falls.

Though Lucas steadfastly ignored any of her
suggestions that they stop and rest, it was long
after sundown by the time they reached the hotel. She was tired, hungry, and grimy. And
somewhat off-balance by the realization that Lucas looked absolutely *magnificent* at sunset.

Lucas vaulted from his seat, snagging the reins
around a nearby post and tying them off. He
stomped around the wagon and reached up a
hand to help her down. She stared at it for a
moment, wondering if she should accept his assistance, vibrantly aware that it had been weeks
since she'd touched him in even this innocent a
way. And wanting to with the kind of longing
she'd always before reserved for her deepest,

most cherished dreams. Knowing that was precisely why she shouldn't, but too exhausted by the trip—and, she admitted, too tired of circumspect self-preservation—to resist.

She shouldn't have worried. He held her hand for only a second, dropping it the instant her feet hit the ground.

"I'll get our rooms," he said.

"I can get my own." She was not technically here on bottling company business.

"I said I'd do it!" She blinked at his unwarranted vehemence. "For God's sake, don't tell me you're going to argue this point, too. It's not a threat to your competence or independence if I engage your room for you. It's just goddamn common courtesy."

Well. Under normal circumstances, his diatribe would have been more than enough to raise her hackles and force her to insist on reserving her own room. But after a long day, having Lucas take care of things for her had a certain appeal. His jaw was set at a determined angle, his eyes blazing. She knew he wasn't going to budge an inch without fierce struggle, and her own shoulders sagged.

"All right. But please, don't swear again. I'm not up to wrangling with you about it."

It took him a moment to realize she'd agreed. He spun on his heel and headed for the large double doors that fronted the hotel, leaving her to trail along behind him.

He got halfway there.

He turned and stomped back to her. "Come on," he said, and grabbed her elbow. He escorted her inside and surveyed the room quickly before thrusting her into the most comfortable chair, a big, over-cushioned wing chair by the empty fireplace, next to a table holding a large arrangement of late chrysanthemums. He disappeared through a door on the far side of the room, returning a few minutes later with a cup of tea and a plate of cookies, which he dumped on the table, sloshing tea over the side of the cup.

"Here," he said ungraciously. "Eat." Then he strode off to the front desk to arrange their rooms.

Priscilla snuggled into the soft cushions of the chair, fingering a deep bronze blossom while she sipped her tea and watched him across the room. His white shirt and gray wool pants were rumpled; his hair was in even worse shape. Yet he clearly belonged in this stylish, luxurious room, as comfortable here as he was in his store, his elegance a matter of innate confidence and masculinity rather than impeccable clothing. His grudging care of her warmed her in a way that all of his adroit and automatic courtesies never had.

Oh yes, he was an unprincipled rogue with women.

Unfortunately, she was having a harder and harder time remembering why that was such an unforgivable offense.

Chapter 20

〜〜✦〜〜

Priscilla's first meeting with Reuben Morse was set for Thursday evening. Which left her most of two whole days with little to do but pace the length of her room and think. Thinking about Reuben had her skittish with nerves and anticipation. Thinking about Lucas made her jumpy and warm, as she vacillated between what even she had to admit was infatuated fascination and hopeless despair. Oh, she was so *tired* of thinking!

And so very tired of her hotel room. Not that it wasn't a perfectly lovely hotel room, far nicer, actually, than she'd expected, given Lucas's innate frugality and the bottling venture's limited resources. The room was larger than she needed, sunny, with the light admitted through a wide, paned window that faced the river. Delicate blue flowers sprigged the white wallpaper, a deep blue spread neatly covered the large brass bed, and crisp white lace swooped at the windows.

But Priscilla was not accustomed to being confined, and after all that time, even the grandest of palaces would have seemed like a meager cell.

It didn't help that she hardly saw Lucas; he was far too busy running from one establishment to another to bother with her. Probably too well entertained by saloon girls, she thought resentfully.

The polite young man at the front desk had assured her that she couldn't do better than their own dining room for meals. This noon, convinced she would dissolve in a screaming fit if she had to spend one more moment confined by the hotel walls, she had ignored his advice and tried a small restaurant a short walk down the street.

It did not help her mood at all to discover the young man was right.

The streets and the restaurant teemed with men—traders, lumbermen, and businessmen of all sorts. At first it reminded her in some ways of Maple Falls when they'd first moved there, but the speculative and sometimes downright lewd looks cast her way effectively discouraged her from exploring further on her own.

A clock on the mantel chimed. Only one o'clock, giving her another five hours to pace and worry before she was to meet Reuben Morse.

She'd never survive it. Snagging her favorite hat from a nearby chair, she rushed through the door and down the stairs, determined to beg Lucas, if she must, to take her along on his afternoon's business.

She would promise, she decided as she scurried along, to say nothing. And surely it was important for her to learn how to sell their merchandise, as well as manage all other aspects of the business. What if at some point he were unable to continue to do so? She was sure she could learn to curb her tendency to speak her mind long enough to flatter the prospective customers properly.

She skidded to a stop in front of his door. She knew it was his, although she hadn't been to it before; he'd told her where to find him. *Just in case you need me*, he'd said, his seducer's voice roughening on the words, a low, rumbling tone that had strummed an answering chord deep within her. Right then she had decided to avoid coming to his room at all costs.

Desperate times, she thought. But still she hesitated, her hand hovering near the wood panel. An unescorted woman, knocking on the hotel room door of an unencumbered male, was so patently improper a thing to do she could hardly believe she was considering it. And that very impropriety sent a dangerous thrill rippling down her spine, warning her to run far and fast.

But they'd spent endless hours together on the trip here, sometimes miles from any sign of other humans, and he'd not so much as touched her—something about which she was not at *all* disappointed, she'd convinced herself. Obviously her virtue was safe in his hands . . . though perhaps *in his hands* wasn't the wisest choice of phrase.

Oh, he'd probably left already, anyway. She rapped on the door and it flew open before she'd even finished the last knock.

"Pris! I was just coming to find you." Lucas grinned hugely and scooped her up, drawing a startled gasp. He stepped back into the room and whirled about, laughing. When her set her back

on her feet, her heart was knocking in her throat
and she put a hand up to stop her spinning head.

"Pris, we are going to make *so* much money
from selling water we got for nothing!"

"Are we?" she asked, breathless with the motion. And with him.

"Oh, yes!" His enthusiasm was infectious, and
she found herself smiling. This was a Lucas she
knew well, caught with an idea and triumphant
at its success, and oh, she couldn't help but be
happy to see him again. Though mostly she was
pleased about the apparent success of their venture, she quickly amended.

"I think I'll go to Chicago next," he went on.
"I still know lots of people there. Some of the
boys I went to school with have even turned out
to be worth something."

"Do you think we can bottle enough?"

"We'll manage. By next summer, at least." The
room was too small to contain his energy; he
started to pace, back and forth across the bare
floor in two big strides.

A room, she finally noticed, that didn't even
look like it belonged in the same hotel as hers.
A narrow bunk was shoved against the stark
whitewashed walls. A simple pine bureau, the
only other furniture, half-blocked the tiny uncurtained window.

"What happened to your room?" she asked,
wondering if he'd been given employees' quar-
ters by mistake.

"My room?" A suspicious flush tinged his
neck. "Place is full up, this was the last of the
cheap rooms. Had to stick you in the one up-
stairs."

"Hmm." She'd spent enough time here the last two days to know that the hotel was half-filled at best.

"Let's go celebrate," he put in quickly.

"Don't you have more appointments this afternoon?"

"Nope. Saw everybody already. Got a yes out of almost every last one of them, too."

She couldn't face one more afternoon in her room. For no other reason than that, she would go out with him. Not that she was *going out* with him, exactly.

"Where are we going?"

"Wait and see."

"A panorama?" she asked. The boldly lettered banner, *A Panorama of the Mighty Mississippi— painted on three miles of canvas!*, covered the upper half of the plain frame building; advertisements and posters were tacked so thickly over the rest that at a distance it looked like wallpaper.

"Yes. Have you ever been?"

"No. Father claimed he could never sit still that long, and Mother would never go without him."

"Good." He was strangely—probably much too—pleased to be the first to show her.

The journey to St. Anthony had been a struggle. Constantly plagued with visions of pulling Charger off the road, finding the nearest private glade, and keeping Pris there until their strength gave out, he'd scarcely dared to look at her. He managed to resist only by constantly tormenting himself with the name of Reuben Morse. It worked, but it also spurred a dark mood that had been relieved only when he'd opened his door to find her standing on the other side.

"Shall we?" he said, formally presenting his arm.

Priscilla hesitated only a moment. It was a courtly gesture, one he'd offered before only when trying to impress their relationship upon the town of Maple Falls.

But this afternoon seemed set apart, bound by its own rules, its own possibilities. As if she could do anything, *be* anyone, and it would exist only in this place and time.

Today doesn't count, she told herself, and surrendered to it, slipping her arm through his where it fit as if it had always belonged.

At the doorway, he paid their admission, a quarter apiece, and ushered her into the darkened hall.

"I'm proud of you," she said. "Fifty cents for mere entertainment, and you didn't even wince."

He tried to scowl at her. His smile broke out instead, potent as a benevolent sun bestowing its favor. "Only the best for my best girl."

Today doesn't count. She could allow herself to be flattered by his words—even believe them a little, as he led her down the aisle flanked by rows of roughly fashioned benches in search of the best seats.

The matinee was uncrowded, attended mostly by children and their mothers, a clutch of adolescent boys, and a few elderly couples. The room itself was dim; angled reflectors threw lantern light onto the stage. The heavy red curtains were pulled back, revealing an enormous scroll, perhaps twelve feet high, mounted upright on a black-painted metal mechanism, already unfurled to the first scene.

"Look!" She pointed with the orientation pamphlet they'd been handed as they entered. "It's the falls!"

The falls of St. Anthony spilled across the first section of canvas, deep, gray-green water churning violently to white at its base as the soft, muted pink of a sunrise edged over the trees on the far shore.

Just as they slipped into their seats, a hidden pianoforte squawked to life and a man stepped onto the left side of the stage. Dressed in the dapper suit of a traveling peddler, he began to describe the scene before them as if none of them were familiar with it, and the immense scroll began to roll.

"There," Pris squealed in the delighted tones of a young girl, leaning against his arm in her excitement, and his breath caught. "That's our hotel. And there, right there! It's the window in my room. Lucas, do you see it?"

"I see it," he murmured, ignoring the show on the stage. It was far more fun to watch her, and the delight that flickered across her face. She'd removed her hat and her hair shone darkly. As she turned her head, it captured faint glimmers of light that leaked from the stage. He found himself waiting, patient and fascinated, for another flash of light to dance over her.

She still leaned against his arm, and his whole body tensed with her nearness. With the scent and smell and sight of her, and with the memory of sitting beside her for two whole days on a wagon seat. And the knowledge that there were two more whole days like that to come.

He took her hand, pressed his palm to hers, and wove their fingers together so they were linked. It wasn't enough, but it would have to do.

"Lucas?" she asked, tentative and hopeful.

"Watch the show," he murmured. "I wouldn't want you to miss anything."

She was spellbound for the next hour and a half, ignoring the speaker's words and allowing herself to be swept away by the music, completely drawn into the illusion of floating downstream on a riverboat, dense forests giving way to cultivated farmland, humble cabins and abandoned wigwams yielding to bustling towns. Their journey appeared to take three days, the sun and the moon alternately taking turns illuminating the river.

She pointed out things she thought Lucas might otherwise overlook—a fat sheep standing affronted in a meadow as a small girl tied a pink bow around his neck, an Indian brave peering out from the leafy boughs of a giant oak. In turn, he told her of the vessels that drifted by, great steamships and humble rafts, showboats and store boats dwarfing birch-bark canoes. The only thing better, she dared to think, would actually to be on that riverboat with Lucas beside her.

Once, to make certain he noticed the giant, yellow-eyed alligator lurking in the tangled swamp along the river's edge, she looked up to find him watching her, his dark eyes glittering as warmly as the lanterns. The dimness refined his face, turned bluntly good-looking features into sharp angles and keen, shadowy planes, made him seem like someone she barely knew.

"You're not watching the show," she whispered breathlessly.

"Yes, I am."

Warmth surged through her, carried on a wave of deep longing. *Today doesn't count.* But it felt as if it counted. It felt very much as if it counted.

He hadn't let go of her hand once. Maybe he never would, she thought. Maybe they'd stay right here, where nobody knew them, where there was no past and no future. Where she could believe everything she saw in his smile.

The pianoforte crashed into another key, swung into a gay rhythm. Priscilla pulled her gaze away from Lucas's as the river rolled into color-splashed New Orleans.

The show was over; the music faded as the rear doors were thrown open and curtains drawn back, flooding the room with light, leaching color from the painting that had seemed so vivid, ruining the magic.

A gnarled finger tapped Priscilla's shoulder. Behind her, an old man, stray gray wisps of hair bobbing above an elfin face, leaned forward, looking as if he might tip over at any moment. His elbow was clasped firmly by a woman nearly twice his size, her faded blue eyes beaming above deeply rounded cheeks.

"Watching the two of you . . . it was almost as good as the stage. Reminded us of ourselves. How long you been married?"

"Oh." Heat crawled up Priscilla's face. She

shot a guilty glance at Lucas and hastily dropped his hand. "We're not married."

"No?" He pondered for a moment, frowning, then cackled gleefully. "All I can say, young man, is, you'd better get this one to a preacher but quick, if you plan on acting on that gleam in your eye. If you know what's good for you."

Lucas cleared his throat. "I'll keep that in mind."

The man creaked to his feet, helped his wife up, and shuffled out between the rows of benches. Before she followed him, the woman bent to Priscilla. "Don't you worry, miss. Man who's got that look about him's a goner for sure. He'll come up to scratch in no time, mark my words." Her pale eyes twinkled. "After all, George did, even though all my friends kept telling me I'd bet on the wrong horse." She tapped her abundant chest. "A reformed scoundrel's the best husband, 'cause he knows what he's got instead of wonderin' what he's missin'."

Priscilla's cheeks burned. Thankfully, their row had cleared out, and she made a beeline for the exit, her head down to discourage any other unwelcome advice.

The air had cooled while they were inside; the wind freshened off the river and sparked chillbumps up her arms. She plunked her hat on her head, feeling a little better under its sheltering brim, and tied the bow with jerky emphasis.

"Well." It was terribly ungracious not to meet the eyes of one's host when expressing appreciation. Too bad. "I enjoyed it. The panorama, I mean. Thank you for taking me."

Tucking his hands in his pockets, Lucas

rocked back on his heels and squinted into the sunlight. "Sure." He dared a glance at her, though he knew perfectly well he was safer staring directly into the sun. The limp edge of her bedraggled hat flopped against her sweet neck; the silken ribbon bow emphasized the lovely curve of her jaw; and damned if he wasn't getting bizarrely fond of those idiotic hats.

"How about dinner?" he asked, unwilling to let the afternoon end.

"Oh." The wind fluttered the ends of the ribbon around her collarbone. "I can't."

She sounded truly sorry, so he figured it wouldn't take much to lure her into it.

"Why not?"

She captured the errant ends with her hand, holding them clenched in one gloved fist just where the curve of her breasts began. Given the chance—not that he would ever have the chance, he added hastily—it would be the first place he would kiss her.

"I'm having dinner with Reuben Morse tonight."

At first, he'd tried to talk her out of it. It was foolishly risky to run off alone to meet a man you knew so little about. Dangerous, even. When she'd deflected that argument—they were meeting in a public restaurant, which she'd been assured was quite busy, and she'd have her own driver, already arranged through the hotel—he'd turned to convincing her to allow him to go along. To ensure her safety, and to offer his own opinion of the fine doctor, a man's opinion, one more logical and objective than her own. Her appalled and vehement response had only hardened his resolve, and it had taken her threat of a full-blown weeping fit to keep him at the hotel that evening. Even then, he'd briefly considered following her, until he realized she had carefully avoided giving him the name of the restaurant, and had instructed the hotel staff that he was not to be told, either. The looks he received in reply to his insistent questions made him decide that he really didn't want to know what story she'd concocted to ensure the staff's compliance.

He skipped dinner, unwilling to choke down dry chicken by himself while Pris dined lavishly with her suitor. Instead, he positioned himself in the bar to await her return and learn the outcome of her engagement. No, her *appointment*. He swilled watered whiskey as if it were just water and allowed himself to be soothed by the bright-eyed interest of an attractive barmaid, even as his mind tortured him with images of Pris and Reuben Morse, laughing over candlelight. *Dr.* Reuben Morse, he amended bitterly, whose mental image he gleefully revised with a bulbous, dripping nose and a hairy mole on one florid cheek.

He stayed until the candle on his table sputtered into a puddle of wax and had to be replaced. How long did an introductory meeting take, anyway? But he'd kept his eyes glued to the doorway the entire time; to get to the staircase, she'd had to have gone right by him. He couldn't have missed her.

He tipped the barmaid generously, which thoroughly eased her disappointment, and paid for a full bottle. He tucked the whiskey beneath his elbow and staggered to his feet, pleased to find his balance within seconds. There, now— never let it be said that Lucas Garrett couldn't hold his liquor.

Pris had to be back by now; the sky outside the damask-draped windows was gloomy with approaching dusk. It seemed like a wonderful idea to go to her room and demand all the sordid details; surely it was expected of him, a concerned friend?

He made his way up the stairs with exaggerated care, tripping only once, which he blamed on a careless carpenter and a stair rise that had to be an inch too short.

Her doorway loomed in front of him, brass numbers gleaming with promise. His *friend* was on the other side, and he was absolutely determined to stop her from making the mistake of marrying some puffed-up doctor. He juggled the bottle, jamming it more firmly into its niche, and pounded on the door.

"Pris!" he bellowed. "Open up, it's me!"

Down the hall, a woman with scarlet curls piled on top of her head, painted lips gleaming a matching red, popped out of a doorway. "Quiet! Some of us are trying to sleep."

"Oops." He held his finger to his lips and grinned. Red Curls was *not* trying to "sleep." He'd bet his bottle on it. "Sorry."

He knocked on the door again. This time, in deference to Pris's touchy neighbor, he refrained from calling her name.

Still no answer. Where could she be? He knew his Pris better than to believe she was going to throw away years of carefully guarded virtue on some pompous doctor she'd just met. Hell, if she was the sort of woman to do that, she could have slept with *him* years ago. It occurred to him to be such a wonderful idea, he couldn't remember why they hadn't done exactly that.

Maybe he should raise a posse and start scouring the city just to make sure the good doctor hadn't dragged her off to have his wicked way with her. But he didn't think Pris would appreciate his concern, if it turned out she was fine, and anyway, she'd seemed to have things pretty well thought out. He supposed it wasn't all *that* late; Pris certainly could yammer on for a while, once she got going. She was probably fine. Probably.

What the hell was he going to do?

Chapter 21

⟶◦◦◦◦◦◦◦◦◦◦◦◦◦◦◦◦⟵

Priscilla walked slowly down the hallway, the hem of her skirt whispering over the navy-and-cream carpet runner, steps hushed by the thick rug. High on the walls, flames flickered in ornate brass sconces, sending her shadow dancing on the ivory walls.

Her meeting with Dr. Morse—Reuben, as he'd asked her to call him—had gone well. Though she had to admit that forty-eight seemed somewhat older in the flesh than she'd imagined. *Twice her age.* But he was still an attractive man, dark hair thickly shot with silver, a lush, matching mustache sprouting beneath a noble nose. Firm jaw, wide brow; the pouching beneath his deep gray eyes spoke of a man with too many responsibilities and too little sleep. A man who needed a woman to take charge of his life, to care for him as he cared for his patients.

As he spoke over dinner, it became obvious that his heart still belonged to his wife, dead more than two years. That was a point in his favor; he knew how to commit wholly to a relationship. He was kind and soft-spoken,

considerate of Priscilla's wishes, and deeply ded-
icated to his work.

Their meeting had been so successful, in fact,
that he'd invited her to stop by his home on her
way back to the hotel to meet his children. A
somewhat bold and precipitous invitation, he
admitted sheepishly, but he did not have the luxury of abundant time. And he was somewhat
anxious to be home, to see them before they were
all tucked in for the night.

Six children! Four girls, two boys. The youngest, Emily, a towheaded, red-cheeked toddler
six months shy of her third birthday, had dimpled at the sight of Priscilla, reached giggling for
the flowers on her hat, and stolen Priscilla's heart
completely.

Julie was the eldest, sixteen and clearly somewhat suspicious of the strange woman her father
had brought home. Priscilla was not disheart-
ened by her cool reception; she remembered sixteen well enough, and could admire the girl's
need to protect her father and family.

Yes, the family was all she'd hoped for, all
she'd ever dreamed of. The rather stilted formality between Reuben and herself was to be
expected; they'd only just met, and were
contemplating a serious and lifelong commitment.

She should have been excited. Jubilant, even.
But doubt shadowed her footsteps, anxiety tightening her stomach as if the mussels she'd eaten
at dinner didn't agree with her. Only natural, she
told herself. It was a big decision, and potentially
a massive change in her life.

And, she supposed, it had not been wise to

meet Reuben immediately after spending a magical afternoon with Lucas. What man could compare? The fact that with Lucas she felt she *belonged*, a deep and persistent sense that this was the place she was meant to be, was undoubtedly a product of their years of history together. She would feel the same with Reuben someday.

If she married him, she added hastily. She was putting her cart before her horse.

Jittery fingers fumbled in her handbag, searching for her key. Ah, there it was. A quick turn of her wrist, and the lock snicked open. She stepped inside, pulling the door shut behind her.

"Where have you been?"

Hand fluttering to her throat, she jumped. "Oh, Lucas, it's you. You startled me."

"Did I?" he said, a strange note shading his rich voice.

"Yes," she said, as uneasiness wound through her.

He'd dragged a chair into the center of the room. He sprawled there, facing the door, big body dwarfing the delicate carved chair, knees wide and lax, a whiskey bottle propped on the left one. Priscilla had left the draperies open, and the windowpanes diced moonlight into luminous squares, patches of light and dark falling across his face and chest.

"What are you doing here?"

"Waiting for you."

A day's growth of beard scraped darkly across his jaw. His wore a loose white shirt, rumpled and open at the throat. His dark eyes glinted dangerously, as if they'd captured a bit of the moonlight and honed it to a lethal edge. It felt as if she'd walked into her room and found a menacing stranger there, and her heart lodged high in her throat.

"How did you get in here?"

His teeth flashed in a lazy, confident smile. "I asked the maid."

"You did, did you?" Her anger spurred, a twin of the anxiety, emotion leaping in her veins. "And what did you tell her to get her to let you in?" she clipped out, accusation clear in her voice.

"I told her I wanted to surprise you. She thought it was very . . . romantic."

"I'll just bet she did." He had no right! And she refused to be unsettled by Lucas Garrett's presence in her room. She turned away from him, slipping the thick woolen shawl off her shoulders and folding it carefully before placing it in a drawer.

"How was your . . . dinner?" he asked, a sneer streaking through his voice.

"It was fine. Not that it's any of your business." Slamming the drawer shut with her hip, she groped along the edge of the bureau top, looking for matches. She needed to see him in the light, see him as something other than this threatening stranger concocted of moonlight and whiskey.

She didn't hear him move. A whisper of air stirred the fine hairs on the back of her neck, and then his hand clamped over hers, holding it flat against the bureau top. *He* hadn't needed to grope in the darkness, she thought resentfully.

"Don't," he said, his breath sighing harsh in

her ear, though he touched her nowhere else but his warm, big hand lying over hers. "There's enough light."

Like heck there was. But it seemed such a risky weapon to put in his hands right now, that suddenly she was afraid to remain in the moon-gilded night with him. "Excuse me. I'd like to put my hat away. *If* you don't mind."

He released her hand and stepped away, and she felt the absence of his heat keenly, as if she'd just dipped her hand in cool water. She tugged at the ribbons, pulled her hat off, and tossed it in the direction of the straight-backed chair beside the door.

"So." He dropped into the armchair, leaning back like a lazy panther, watching her with predatory eyes. "Tell me all about it."

How *dared* he? "As I was saying," she went on coolly, "it was a perfectly lovely evening. Reu—Dr. Morse is all I could have hoped for, exactly as I pictured him. And more."

As he listened to her extol the apparently many virtues of the redoubtable Dr. Morse, Lucas felt his muscles tense, his hands fisting. So, they were on a first-name basis already, were they?

The boozy, warm first wave of the whiskey had abandoned him an hour ago, and he'd kicked right into a mean drunk. Strange, because he'd never been a mean drunk. Or much of a drunk at all, for that matter. But as he sat in Pris's room, catching faint vapors of her soap and powder and perfume, seeing the rumpled spot on her bedcovers where she'd sat, to tug on her boots, maybe, and thought about her smiling at another man, he'd developed a definite mean streak.

"Are you going to marry him?" He flung the question out like the grimmest accusation.

Her head snapped up, eyes glittering. Her chin climbed. "Maybe I am going to marry him. *Probably* I'm going to marry him."

He bit back a snarl. "Did he kiss you?"

Her nose pointed toward the ceiling. Sitting below her as she stood, he had a clear view of the underside of her jaw, the segue into long, slender neck, fragile shadows dancing on elegant skin. His anger rose like whitecaps before a storm.

"Now, that is *absolutely* none of your business."

Reaching up, he caught her wrist in one quick motion, his grip unbreakable as a vise, yet gentle as one holding a newborn. *"Did he kiss you?"*

She tried to tug away; his hold merely tightened. How dared he ask? He, who'd kissed a hundred women, a thousand women, and so much more than kissed them—what right did he have to interrogate her about whether a pleasant gentleman had given her a simple kiss?

"Yes!" The answer cracked through the air like the snap of a whip. "Yes, he kissed me." She gave her wrist another yank, and he let go so quickly she had to step back to keep from stumbling.

The room was as quiet as a tomb; all she could hear was his breathing, low and harsh and ragged. And maybe that was his heartbeat, strong and wild, pulsing beneath her own.

"And how was it?" he asked, soft words stripped of all inflection.

"It was . . . fine," she said, and could have kicked herself for the mild answer. But it had been fine, a brief, respectful, and somewhat awkward peck on her cheek, delivered after a polite request, and over before she could even register the feel of it. "*Wonderful*," she amended, too late.

"Fine?"

She refused to respond to the heavy disgust that bled from his voice; there was nothing wrong with fine. Fine was . . . fine.

"For God's sake, Pris, if you insist on going through with this stupidity, at least you can do better than *fine*."

Stupidity? She stifled the urge to snap back, to bare her teeth and howl at the man like a wounded she-wolf. But she would not stoop to his beastly level.

"If you're going to marry somebody for convenience sake, the very least you can get out of the deal is good sex."

She clamped control hard around the fury he ignited. "Some of us count a fair number of things more important than the weak indulgence of a mere biological urge."

"Which only goes to show how little you know about it." He vaulted to his feet, a dark form towering over her. Why hadn't she ever before noticed just how much taller than her he was? "You should at least know what you're missing."

"I'm not missing anything," she insisted.

"I'll show you *fine*, by damn."

"Don't sw—"

His mouth swooped, unerring as a falcon falling on its prey.

His kiss was like the whiskey he tasted of: a first hard jolt of intoxicating heat, then a slight easing, a slow mellowing into potent warmth. And then another kiss, another sip, taking her deeper each time, further from sanity, drowning her in the sensation he drew from her, again and again.

To find an anchor in a reeling world, she reached for him, laid a hand along his face. She felt his jaw shift, the muscles working in rhythm as he tilted his head to take the kiss deeper, his new beard rasping her palm. His mouth nudged hers open so smoothly it seemed natural, and when his tongue came inside, there wasn't shock but a realization. *Now I know how it's supposed to feel.* His hot breath sighed along her cheek while he licked inside her mouth, shallow and deep, drawing her tongue into a slow, erotic dance.

She wasn't sure how she'd gotten so close to him. Had he pulled her there? Had she thrown herself near of her own accord? All she knew was they were pressed so tightly that if there'd been no clothes between them, every inch of their skin would have touched. The thought of being naked in his arms drew a low sound from her, and Lucas tightened his arms in response, drawing her up to fit better until their hearts thundered against each other.

Finally he drew back, lifting his head enough to look clearly in her face while his arms remained firmly linked around her back. "It's a lot to give up, Pris."

She knew he meant this wild churning of sensation inside her, the even more powerful feelings she knew lurked just beyond her reach, like a filament of sunshine peeking over the horizon just before dawn, hinting at what awaited her. Taunting her, tempting her, promising the blaze to come.

But *he* was even more to give up. His dark eyes gleamed, only inches away, and in them she saw everything, years of friendship and memories and light-hearted battles. Years of caring, of knowing they held a sturdy place in each other's lives, no matter what.

But *here* was the *what* she'd never anticipated. If she married, when she married, it would end. There was no place for a man like Lucas Garrett in that life.

Impending loss swamped her, drowned her more deeply than the passion had, even as they coexisted in her. As if she had two hearts: one aching for what she would lose, one beating for the pleasure it might gain in this one night.

She swallowed hard, drunken butterflies spun from anxiety and anticipation whirling in her stomach.

"Maybe I should know," she whispered. "What I'm giving up, I mean."

"Pris," he said, because he didn't know what else *to* say. He stared down at her, trying to read whether she knew what she said and if she meant it. Her eyes were wide behind the crystalline silver of her spectacle lenses, her mouth open and trembling.

"This'll change things," he warned.

"They've already changed."

And because it was true, and because the feel of her breasts pushing firm and warm against his chest drove reason and logic from his brain, he brought her into the lee between his legs, cupping her rump through layers of wool and cotton that hid more than they revealed.

And most of all because it was Pris, to whom he'd never been able to say no. Whose scent filled his nose and fogged his brain, whose mouth tasted sweet and hot and eager. Whose image had filled his dreams and nights for weeks. Or maybe, he thought dimly, for forever, and he just hadn't recognized her there before.

His body recognized her now, the way it recognized home. Hooking an arm firmly around her waist, he cradled one big palm beneath her rear and lifted her a few inches, walking backward to the bed while her booted toes scraped the floor and her body lay limp and compliant against him.

He bent, laying her back against a coverlet the color of midnight, and braced himself above her. His mouth went roaming, searching out spots that made her sigh and tremble. There, behind her ear, where the scent of her was strong. The corner of her mouth, ripe and plump and curving into a languid smile. The side of her neck, a thready pulse stuttering against his tongue.

He drew the scrap of red silk scarf away, exposing the hollow at the base of her throat, a soft indentation perfectly formed for the caress of his tongue, hinting at other recesses, other strokes that awaited them.

He battled to rein in the commands that beat in him. *Now, now, now! Take her now!* Each shudder he drew from her gave the demands stronger voice.

To ease her into the touch of a man's hands—*his* hands, he thought fiercely—he stroked her through her clothes. Rubbing her through the thin layers at her ribs, settling his hand over the checked wool that swelled over her breasts. His thumb whisked over the peak, back and forth, back and forth, a whispering scratch of sound miming the rhythm.

Lord, he would drive her mad! Lucas's hands moved over her, slow and light, a touch so bare Priscilla could hardly tell whether it was there at all or if she imagined it, making her yearn for more and arch into each light caress. Never satiating, only making her crave. *More.* A whisk over her breasts, a steady, tantalizing scrape over the tip. *More.* Feathery touches down her ribs, an easy exploration of her limbs. *More.* And once, an easy stroke straight down her center, brushing over her belly and further yet, and her hips surged up.

"More!"

At last he plucked at the buttons of her jacket, and she sighed, any anxiety she might have felt having been driven from her by those skillful hands, which left no room for anything but the want. No room for any thought but Lucas.

His expert fingers should have removed her clothes with practiced ease. He found himself unexpectedly clumsy, struggling with tapes and buttons that should have given way with a touch. But they were Pris's buttons, Pris's clothes, and it took longer than he expected. Especially since he had to stop after each fastening gave way, to kiss and stroke and admire.

Finally she lay naked beneath him, soft and yielding, but with her breath coming hard. Her arms lay at her sides, palms up, and he reached for her hand, pressing it against his waistband.

"Your turn."

She worked at his buttons, fingers fumbling, knuckles bumping his belly, nudging further down, an eternity before the first one came free. Then further down, the back of her hand pressing his erection, and the air hissed out of him.

"Maybe I'd better do it after all," he said through clamped teeth. "Stay here."

He levered up, leaving her sprawled like the most reckless wanton across the bed, a gleam of alabaster flesh against midnight blue. He thought she might roll away, to try and cover herself modestly. But she only watched him, her gaze following his hands as they went to the fastenings of his shirt, so he got to look his fill in return.

A small body, neat and firm, not the slightest bit showy, but oh, so pretty. He saw all the places he planned to kiss later, a shadow carving beneath her arm and slanting along the narrow slope of her ribs into her waist, curving moon-shaped crescents beneath each breast. Her nipples were dark in the dim room, a rose so deep it was one shade shy of brown, and the sweetness called to him. He yanked his shirt over his head, tossing it away. She gasped, her hips shifting restlessly, and between her thighs he caught a glistening of moisture peeking through the dark tangle of hair. His blood thundered.

This she had never imagined. To lie on her bed, silken fabric cool against her nude back, and watch him strip off his clothes for her. He stood right in the middle of the silvered checkerboard of moonlight, and she could hardly believe she was so lucky, to get to view him so clearly. She'd known he was strong. But so much better to see it. Broad planes of muscle banded his chest and corrugated his stomach. He toed off his boots, stripped off his socks, and then jerked at the remaining buttons of his pants, the ones that had defeated her, and she held her breath.

He shucked his pants and drawers in one quick motion, bending at the waist so for a moment she could see only the top of his head and shoulders. Hands on his hips, he straightened, and she realized he stayed there, waiting, to let her look as she wished. Realized, too, that he was studying her just as intently, and her skin heated. She lifted her arms in instinctive invitation.

He put his knee on the bed and the mattress dipped beneath his weight. Gently, he unhooked the earpieces of her glasses, slipped them off her nose, and set them on the tiny mahogany table beside the bed.

The room blurred instantly, edges fuzzing, shapes bleeding into one another. But Lucas himself remained distinct, each line of his face as sharp as if it had been etched into glass. Perhaps, she thought, because it *had* been etched, in her mind, which filled in the details now with effortless recall.

But then he lowered himself over her and her

mind ceased to work, bowing to the much more insistent demands of her body. He plucked the pins from her hair, smoothing it over her shoulders, down over her breasts, the cool, silken texture over her skin another new sensation, the tip of a nipple peaking through shiny strands.

His hands, his mouth . . . she ceased to keep track where they explored, the places they touched and heated and called to full attention. It blended together, a shimmer of passion here, a shudder of need there, until it seemed to her that he must be everywhere at once, touching all of her, tasting all of her. Dimly, she thought perhaps she should return the favor, but her body was no longer hers to command, so she simply lay, arms looped over her head where he'd put them, body taut and waiting. *Wanting.* Now and then she felt it . . . *him* . . . nudge her, a searing prod against her thigh, a heated brush against her belly as he bent to suck at her breast, and each time she jerked involuntarily, trying to get closer, wanting more.

Shadows chased through the room, there and gone in seconds. There was only the sound of skin whispering over silk, expectant sighs and sharp, indrawn breaths, the low, keening cry that broke from the back of her throat when he lifted himself over her and laid his weight upon her at last.

Their bellies pressed together, damp skin clinging. Lucas held his chest away, taking the weight on his arms, so he could see her. Eyes squeezed tightly shut, her face was drawn with strain, fierce and very beautiful. Her legs were only slightly apart, just enough to wedge in between, and he pressed his erection, full length, at the juncture of her thighs. She jerked against him, hips rising. He stroked her that way, sliding over her most sensitive place, helping her learn the rhythm and the pleasure without having to worry about the pain.

Her body stiffened, her thighs squeezed his hips. Sweat beaded his brow and trickled down his temple. He watched her nostrils flare, alert for the first, quivering signs of release. Almost there . . . almost. He pulled away a bit and her whole body jerked. And then he nudged inside her, only a little, pressing her legs wider, opening her to him.

His every muscle and tendon was painfully rigid, locked between the two desires, the need to ease his way for her sake and the compulsion to surge inside and make her his own. Slowly, he slid back and edged further again, a fraction more each time, a gradual and deliberate progress that threatened to drive him mad.

"Are you . . . does it hurt?" he asked through clenched teeth.

Her answer threaded high and faint. "I don't know."

She'd lost track of which was which, pleasure and pain. She wasn't even sure she cared; both drove her on, called to her, pulled her toward a completion she could only guess at.

He never faltered, in and back, deeper, deeper each time, her body echoing each thrust, sending the reverberations spiking through each nerve. Until at last he was fully inside, perfectly still,

body so deeply embedded in hers there seemed
no clear demarcation between the two of them.

"I can feel your heartbeat," she murmured.

Smiling, he placed his hand on her left breast,
fingers spread wide. "So can I."

"No. Not there." Unthinking, she reached between them, touching low on her belly. "Here."

Her fingertips brushed where they joined and
his severe control shattered like a glass vase
pitched from the sheerest cliff. He surged into
her, fast and quick and hard, spurring the breath
from her chest and all thought from her mind.
He no longer lured the sensations from her; now
he propelled them, commanded them, pushed
her so swiftly she was afraid she couldn't keep
up.

"Lucas?"

"I'm here," he said, and her fear disappeared.
"I'll catch you."

She strained against him. Greedy, hungry,
searching. He canted a shade to one side, wedging a hand between them where hers had been,
pressing his thumb right above their joining. She
went still, then arched, quivering like a bow-
string, internal muscles clenching around his
erection as her hands clutched fistfuls of blue
satin. He held on for an agonizing instant, long
enough to memorize the look on her face, to
burn the image of Pris lost to ecstasy deeply into
his brain. He let his eyes close, and it seemed as
if he hadn't, for he could still see her, cheeks
suffused with color, tendrils of hair curling
damp and dark at her temples, features drawn
with strain and pleasure.

"Pris!" he shouted, and let go, releasing control, releasing the world.

But hanging on to Priscilla Wentworth with every ounce of strength he owned.

Chapter 22

Lucas lay beside her on the bed, motionless and breathing deep ... sleeping? ... in the exact position in which he'd fallen when he'd rolled from her body. Priscilla had no idea how much time had passed—a few minutes? An hour? She'd been dozing herself. Or maybe, she thought, smiling inside, she'd been out cold, had fainted dead away. For surely no human body could feel *that* and remain conscious. It would overwhelm one's nervous system.

Summoning all her strength, she turned over, snuggling up against his side. It was almost as hard to open her eyelids, which seemed to weigh a stone apiece. They hadn't even managed to pull back the covers and were crosswise on the bed. Lucas took up more than his share of space. He sprawled like a lion king, his legs too long on one side, wrists dangling over the other edge. He looked so thoroughly satisfied, so pleased with the world, that pride surged within her.

She had made him look like that. She, Priscilla Wentworth, and no one else. Though the details were a little hazy, especially at the end there, she was almost certain she'd made him shout. *Just let him try and call me prissy now.* A giggle bubbled out of her, and he cracked one eye open.

"I guess I don't have to ask if you're okay."

"Nope."

He'd been lying there, worrying, wondering how Pris was going to react, steeling himself to deal with tears or recriminations, keeping his eyes securely shut until he was prepared. But instead she was looking smug as a cat that had holed up in a dairy.

He was feeling mighty smug himself. As if he might throw open the windows, beat his chest, and roar at the world: *I made Pris Wentworth happy!* Of course, that would require actually moving, something he figured he just might be able to do again someday. In a week or two.

"C'mere, love." He hooked an arm around her and settled her closer against his side.

Love. Everything inside Priscilla stilled, quiet as a becalmed pool waiting for a stone to break its surface. He'd called her *love*, the word tripping easily out of his mouth, as if he said it every day.

But then, maybe he did. Vague specters lurked at the back of her mind, long, snaking queues of other women . . . other bedmates. Resolutely, she locked the images away. There was no taking back what had already been done. She was determined to enjoy every last second of it, untainted. Time enough to worry tomorrow.

She laid a hand on his chest, feeling his heart thump against her palm, absently circling his nipple with her forefinger. Outside the moon had shifted in the sky, angling the light over the bed, allowing her to observe him, memorize him, without the fuzzy pulse of desire clouding her impressions. Her gaze traced down his body.

"It looks different now," she murmured without thinking.

Laughter burst out of him. "That it does." He flattened her hand against him. "If you keep on doing that, I can guarantee it'll be changing again soon."

"Really?" She settled in to watch, wondering just how that particular feat would be achieved.

"Assuming you're talking about my—" Amusement rumbled his diaphragm. "My *male chicken* part." His laughter grew louder, his torso shaking.

How dare he laugh at her now, the wretch! She thumped his side in warning. "Yes I was," she said primly.

"Oh, Lord. I should be insulted, shouldn't I?" He laughed louder. "Wherever did you come up with that?"

"I certainly wasn't going to use *that* word," she said, disgruntled. Of course *he* hadn't been insulted, because he'd known the truth of the matter. She'd been trying to show her sophistication, not retreating into a missish word like *privates* or *unmentionables*, and instead she'd only shown her innocence all the more. "What else was I supposed to call it?"

"Well, um—" Lucas cleared his throat.

"And I do *not* want to hear what you're about to suggest."

"You don't even know what I was going to say."

"I don't need to. I know you, and that's good enough."

"But you asked," he reminded her.

"It was a rhetorical question." Her indelicate nose swiveled toward the shadowed ceiling. He gave in to temptation and kissed her, a big loud smack.

"What was that for?" she asked suspiciously, waiting for him to start chuckling again.

"I don't know." He just *liked* the woman so damn much. But he'd learned long ago not to say such things in the heat of the moment, or the after-moment, as it were. The words meant too little, and women put far too much stock in them. So he confined his conversation to things like how beautiful they were or how sweet they were, phrases that satisfied without raising unwanted hopes. But none of those pat phrases were right for Pris. He felt himself floundering, out of his element, and thought about what an odd predicament that was. Imagine Lucas Garrett not knowing what to say in bed.

"How'd you know what Flora meant, anyway?" he asked, for lack of a better topic. And because he didn't think it was a word that would ever have sullied Priscilla Wentworth's delicate ears.

"Oh." It seemed a most inappropriate topic of conversation at the moment. Wasn't he supposed to be whispering glib, pretty words in her ear, assuring her how utterly desirable he'd found her? But suddenly the thought of him automatically spouting tired old lines turned her stomach, and she was grateful he hadn't. Besides, the warm feel of his fingers drifting in circles between her shoulders, thumb sliding down her spine, was better than any words could have been. "I overheard it, once. It was clear from the context what, ah—what they were referring to."

"Where?" he asked, curiosity prodding him. How'd she get herself into a situation where she'd overhear someone talking about a man's cock? And without him knowing about it?

Debating, Priscilla contemplated his ear, a whirl of dark hair curling beneath the lobe. The last thing she wanted at this moment was to rouse bad memories. But weren't they supposed to be closer than ever now? And she'd always wondered.

"Remember the cook you had in Chicago? The one who spent more time in our kitchen, drinking tea with Mrs. Bundleman, than she did cooking in yours?"

"I remember. Made yeast breads like a dream, but she never could cook a roast without turning it to charcoal."

"That's the one."

"You overheard Mrs. Macaffee talking about a *lover?*" It was mind-boggling to credit, that the stiff, disapproving woman had ever bent enough to allow a man entrance to her body.

"Not exactly." Priscilla tucked her tongue in her cheek. This was probably a really bad idea.

"What, then? She had a secret penchant for ribald jokes?" Or his mother's books, he thought, carefully skating away from an idea he really did not want to probe in any detail.

"No."

He waited. A door slammed down the hall. On

the street beneath Pris's window, someone wove by carrying a lantern; orange light jolted briefly across the ceiling. Pris edged up against his side, her belly cradling his hip, and flickering passion burst into full, roaring life. But it wasn't like Pris to keep her own counsel on any topic, and maybe he should find out what was bothering her first. After all, sex didn't solve everything . . . and now where the hell had *that* thought come from?

Her head rested against his shoulder, and she rubbed her cheek against him, chin tracing a slow arc. Her hair slipped over his pectorals and tickled his neck. Maybe it was his mother's novels, after all, and she figured he didn't know about them. Or . . .

"They were talking about how my father died, weren't they?"

Though loath to move—surely a man's shoulder had to be designed especially to cushion a woman's head, it fit so well—she lifted up to study him, wondering if he could really be as emotionless and unaffected as he sounded. He returned her gaze calmly, the corners of his mouth slanting up, hinting at a mocking smile. But beneath her fingers the muscles of his chest tightened.

"Yes," she admitted.

"And you're wondering if what you heard was true."

"You don't have to tell me," she said quickly.

"It's not a pretty story, Pris."

No, it wouldn't be. But it felt like there was a gap in her otherwise thorough knowledge of him, a great, gaping hole where this important event should reside. With all the whispers and sly innuendos, the leering comments and raised eyebrows that had swirled around Chicago in the weeks after William Garrett's death, sometimes she felt like she'd been the only person in the city who *didn't* know the truth.

"And this is probably not the right place to tell it," he continued.

"Where would the right place be?"

Lucas snorted derisively. "Good point."

His face was fixed toward the ceiling. Shadows purpled half moons beneath his eyes, deepened the lines around his mouth. Right now his easy smile seemed very far away.

"I'm sorry this topic was ever raised," she said. "My curiosity is not a good enough reason to dredge this up again."

His shoulders lifted and fell, a careless shrug that wasn't careless at all. "I stopped hiding things for my father's sake when I was ten, and got over being affected by his actions when I was fourteen. It's unimportant either way."

A prudent survival tactic for a man with a father like his. She wondered if it could possibly be that simple.

In the end, the desire to know this part of him won out. "I'd like to know. If you don't mind."

"All right. But let's get you under the covers first; wouldn't do to have you catch a chill."

He tucked her in among fine linen sheets and big fluffy pillows, sliding in beside her and wrapping her close. There'd been decadence before, with them lying naked and wanton on top of the silk; this was something different entirely, sharing a bed in truth. Comfortable, intentional, the sheets trapping his heat and wrapping her in it. Like longtime lovers, and it tugged at her heart even as having Lucas, naked, beside her renewed a slow, building simmer of desire.

"It was August," he said. "Hot."

"I remember."

"Like the night I came in your window. Humid, heavy, thunderstorms lurking in the west. All you had to do was move and you were soaking, like you'd put on clothes right out of the washtub."

He'd spent a restless night, he remembered. Gotten home late and spent from a sweaty evening with . . . what was her name? He couldn't remember. He'd flopped on his bed, hoping to catch a few hours of sleep, but the weather had kept him from doing more than just drifting in and out.

"You remember Mrs. Harriman?"

"Two doors down," Pris answered promptly. "Three yipping little dogs and a tongue like a viper."

"She was taking her morning constitutional in the square, along with two of her friends and a maid apiece." He voice was even, almost warm. But her hand rested on his stomach, and she could feel his flesh ripple, his muscles tightening and easing and cramping up again. "They rounded the bend in the path—at least, that's what I was told. You know the one, right before the statue of Jolliet? Heard that four of them screamed and fainted dead away at the sight."

He chuckled, a sound that was nothing like his usual laughter. This one was stripped of mirth, tainted with bitterness and old wounds.

"One of the maids had enough sense to go scurrying for me. Unfortunately, it was it was too late to recover his body quietly. The screams had roused half the neighborhood. Can't say that I blame them. He was quite a sight."

I should never have asked, she thought, wondering suddenly if she really wanted to know this. Easier to think of Lucas as a carelessly light-hearted scoundrel rather than a man who lived with difficult memories.

"Lucas, I—"

But it was too late; the images of that morning had been released and there was no stopping them now. She wasn't even sure if Lucas remembered who he was talking to, except that he gripped her hand as if it mattered. She squeezed back and hung on.

"Old fool." He shook his head, rolling back and forth against the deep pillows. "Tied up to that statue like a trussed chicken. Bet old Jolliet would've been shocked at that."

Enough, he decided abruptly, a taste in his mouth like burned soda powder. The rest of the details were not for Pris's ears. His father had been a pitiful and absurd figure in death, blindfolded, wearing nothing more than an outsized version of a women's leather corset done up in black leather, a coil of whip, and a tangle of chains and rope at his feet, his cock still at half-mast. No doubt his partner—or, knowing William's preferences, his *partners*—had hightailed it out of the square as soon as they'd realized that old, blackened heart had given out. You could hardly blame them, either.

"Have to give him one thing," Lucas said.

"The bastard died how he lived." That horrible chuckle again. "And he would have been elated to know he'd humiliated my mother one last time."

He'd was still sparing her the gruesome details, Priscilla realized. She was supposed to be comforting him, and instead he was still watching out for her. She turned and dropped a kiss on one broad shoulder that insisted on taking on too much, and she felt muscles leap at that slight touch.

"Anyway, we got out of there before the dirt settled on his grave. Wasn't much to keep us there."

"Does that bother you?" She'd wondered that, as well. She'd longed to continue her father's legacy and salvage the business he built. But Mr. Garrett's holdings had been liquidated immediately after his death.

"No. He made a lot of money, and he spent a lot of money. At least he didn't leave me any debts, which is more than a lot of sons can say."

He spoke more easily this time, without undercurrents or shadings. Obviously he told the truth; he didn't care that there'd been nothing for him to inherit.

"Besides, if there'd been anything left, all we'd have done was argue about it. I'd have said Mother should have it for what he'd put her through. And she would have wanted nothing that came from him and would have spent all her time trying to give it back to me. Just as well."

That first kiss had gone so well she tried another. She'd been the one to darken his mood in the first place, so she should be the one to distract him. She stretched, pecked the side of his neck this time, and he sucked in air on a long hiss.

"Besides, money has never been my problem." His voice had tightened again. But this time, Priscilla judged, the strain was from an entirely different source.

"What *are* your problems?" she murmured. Just a flick of her tongue over his earlobe, she decided. It really had been most unfair of her to make him do all the work the first time.

The man was slick, you had to give him that. He flipped her on top of him, her hips settled over his—and what a part that was, as he'd promised, changing by the moment—his mouth hovering near her breast, before her startled exclamation faded.

"What problems?"

Things were supposed to look better in the morning.

It was an accepted fact that things always seemed their worst in the dark, lonely hours in the middle of the night, and that optimism and energy returned with the rising sun.

Priscilla awoke at her usual early hour, just as the sun crept over the horizon. She hummed low under her breath, cuddling drowsily into a very comfortable nest, the softest and warmest bed she could remember.

She got to enjoy it for only an instant before she remembered exactly why the bed was so snug and so very warm. Her lids popped open.

She was nestled up against Lucas's side, one

leg thrown wantonly over his thighs, her cheek plastered against his shoulder. She eased away slowly, wincing when he snorted and rolled her way. Cold air rushed over her bare skin, and she wished she had a wrapper, a shawl, anything. One of the blankets had gotten pushed down to the foot of the bed, so she grabbed it, wrapping it around her as she stood beside the bed and looked down at him.

The gray, new light pearled the room, as if the air held the remains of a thin fog. Her skirt lay in a rumpled pile in the middle of the rug. Her hat, crown dented, ribbons hanging limp, had landed in the far corner. Lucas's wadded shirt lumped at the foot of the bed, crushed as if bodies had rolled across it.

He looked very fine in the morning, there was no doubt about that. His lashes, short and thick and shades darker than his hair, lay in a dense semicircle against the dark skin beneath his eyes. New beard shadowed his jaw, and his hair had acquired more of a wave than usual at some point during the night. Apparently the chill in the room bothered him not at all, for the sheets dipped low on his belly, leaving a wide expanse of thick muscle and bronze skin for her inspection. His forearms and hands were darker still, a clear line of demarcation where he'd rolled up his sleeves as he worked in the sun. And all she could think of was: *How many women have seen him like this?*

The ghosts she battled back successfully during the night were more persistent now. Oh, he'd learned all those skills somewhere, and he'd used them on her to such wonderful advantage that even now, as recriminations and regrets swamped her, desire throbbed low in her belly and twinged even further down just at the memory of what he'd done to her. And of the look of him in her bed.

Possessiveness seized her with the swift, complete violence of a summer cyclone. She wanted to be the only one who'd seen him like this, the only one whose name he shouted in a rush of blind ecstasy. There was about as much chance of that happening as there was of her capturing the moon.

Shivering, she tugged the blanket tighter around her shoulders and turned her back on the vision of him in a sex-mussed bed. She quietly tiptoed around the room, gathering her clothes in a careless ball before stuffing them deeply in the corner of her satchel. She dressed quickly and simply before going back to stand by the bed.

He still hadn't moved.

Dear God, what have we done? It was an endless litany, a repetitive chant that spun round and round in her brain, taking up so much space that any other thoughts had to squeeze in around the edges.

She regretted it all. Not just last night, but way back to that first night, when he'd climbed into her window and set them on the path that had landed them here. So foolish of them both. So irreparable.

She'd been so proud—too proud, she realized now—confident and complacent in the conviction that she held a place in his life that no other woman had, or ever would. A place she'd always have. And now, in one moment of surrender, she'd relinquished it completely, had thrust herself into those lines of women she'd imagined, become another interchangeable face among hundreds. And there was no going back.

She'd given in to an ordinary physical urge. Though it had felt anything but ordinary at the time, assigning it such a mild appellation as an *urge* was minimizing its power.

And she knew only one way to make sure she never did such an irrational and risky thing again.

"Lucas." She kept her voice low, though why she worried about what the neighbors might hear at this late date was beyond her. It made her feel all the more guilty and chastened.

The corner of his eye twitched.

"Lucas," she hissed.

He sighed and flopped over, flinging an arm across the shallow indention where she had lain.

She settled on that arm as the safest place to touch him and prodded him in one unyielding biceps. "Lucas!"

His mouth curved up, and he slid into the morning with the same leisurely, sensual ease as he'd sank into her last night.

"Good morning," he said simply. But his eyes said, *Come back to bed.*

"You have to go. Now." Before she was tempted beyond bearing.

He sat up, the sheet sagging further, threatening to expose even more. It didn't seem to concern him at all, but Priscilla had to fight to keep her gaze up where it belonged. Apparently having her curiosity satisfied was not enough to allow her to get her baser instincts under firm control. In fact, it seemed to have had the opposite effect.

He ran a hand through his hair, leaving it even more disordered. She wondered if there was a woman alive who could see it and not want to smooth it down.

Well, she'd just have to be the first.

"I was afraid of this," he said.

He wouldn't let her avoid the subject. She tried anyway. "Afraid of what?"

"This. Your waking up this morning and wallowing in guilt and embarrassment." In no mood to listen to her chide him about his language, he bit back the curse he wanted to let fly. Inside, though, it was damn, damn, damn. *Damn, I knew I never should have touched her. Damn, why'd you do that, fool?*

Easy to blame it on the whiskey. And a lie. All he had to do was look at her beside the bed, hair tumbled down around her shoulders, mouth rose and ripe in the morning light, and he knew why. She'd dressed hurriedly; her buttons were off by one, and her blouse tucked unevenly into her skirt. All the more inviting because he'd never seen her less than perfectly pressed and fastened.

He slid to the side of the bed, reached out, and took her hand, pressing his mouth to her palm, to the inside of her wrist, and Priscilla's stomach fluttered.

She wasn't guilty. And until a moment ago,

when he'd moved and left the covers completely behind, she hadn't been the slightest bit embarrassed.

Instead, she mourned, facing the unexpected, inalterable loss of something that was so very precious to her. Because she knew now, as his mouth drifted up her forearm and her knees softened, that she could never spend one second alone with Lucas Garrett again. And this, this shimmer of heat that followed his kiss to the inside of her elbow, the potent rise of desire, was exactly why.

"Please." She yanked her arm away, stepped back out of his reach.

He furrowed his brow, his eyes snapping with intensity, and she closed her own eyes to avoid the plea she saw there. "We have to leave right now," she begged. "Before we make any more mistakes."

"We can fix this. We can forget, we can go back . . ."

But they couldn't, and they both knew it.

"At least we won't make it worse," she whispered.

"What do you mean?"

"Like your parents. We won't . . . there won't be . . ." Her hand drew an awkward circle across her stomach.

"What makes you say that?"

She opened her eyes to find skin angling sharply over his cheekbones, pulling tight over his jaw. "But you—you said you always made sure! That you wouldn't let—I thought you'd take care of—"

"I didn't," he said, sharp as a fresh-stoned blade.

And why hadn't he? There were so many ways, various devices he'd stocked profitably—and illegally—in the back of his store. But even those weren't always reliable, so over the years he'd taken fewer and fewer chances, preferring sexual creativity to any chance of getting trapped as his father had. He'd rather enjoyed the challenge—how strongly could he bring pleasure to a woman, and himself, without spilling his seed inside her?

But last night, as he'd slid into Pris, it had never once occurred to him to pull back. Only the novelty of being deeply, fully embedded in a woman, having her body close tight around him, without barriers or vigilance had made him forget caution, he told himself, afraid to examine it any more closely.

"Oh, no," she moaned, worry pinching her brows together over her nose, bleaching her skin.

The idea bothered her so much, did it? "You'd better wait a month or so before you marry that doctor of yours."

She flinched.

"You are going to marry him, aren't you?"

The gray light hollowed out her cheeks, made her look fragile and colorless. He should apologize for the cruelty in his tone, should take her in his arms and shelter her and remember all the joy they'd shared.

But she didn't say no. He waited, sitting on the bed that still held the fragrance of their loving, staring across the room that held the vivid memories of it, hoping for one tiny sign that somehow, in some way, they could put this all to rights.

And she still didn't say no.

Chapter 23

〜〜∽◯◯∽〜〜

Dear Miss Wentworth,

*Please do not fret any longer. I read your con-
fession of the prank that you and your friend
perpetrated on the town with amusement and
no small amount of nostalgia, for in my youth,
I confess to having gotten myself in a tight spot
now and then, and even resorted to shading the
truth to escape. It is to my everlasting dismay
that Julie is showing signs of the same tendency.*

*I must admit, however, that I am having some
difficulty sympathizing with Mr. Garrett's
plight, as being plagued by women has never
been one of my problems . . . unless one counts
the leagues of women who descend upon me to
tell me graphic details of their latest suffering
with gout.*

*Returning to your concerns, however—
please, do not apologize! In fact, it speaks well
of your character that you would wish to help
him out of his difficulties, and that you feel a
need to see the matter through. I would never
ask you to go back on an agreement.*

Though I had harbored some hopes when I received your letter that your answer would be a quick and unequivocal yes, I can certainly understand that you feel the need to know me better before undertaking such a momentous decision. Therefore, what I propose is this.

I will come to see you three weeks from now. I know you are reluctant to take me away from my home and family, but my sister would be happy to stay with the children during my absence in the name of such a good cause. As to my patients . . . well, they will simply have to struggle along without me for a while. I have an old friend from the medical college who owes me a few days of filling in for me. Though I do not see as how I can manage to squeeze in more than two or three days in Maple Falls, I hope that will be sufficient to quiet your concerns.

Now, as to my reasons for being in Maple Falls in the company of your family and yourself without arousing suspicion—and here I will again confess, this time to taking some pleasure in creating a character for me to portray—perhaps I should be an "old friend of the family," one who had been abroad for some time and therefore unable to come immediately at your bereavement. On my return, however, let us say I felt it incumbent upon me to assure myself of your welfare in person. Is that enough, do you think? From what you have told me of the current residents of the town, my presence will be rather obvious.

> *Looking forward to your reply,*
> *yours most sincerely,*
> *Dr. Reuben Morse*

Priscilla sat at the small desk in her room, reading over the letter for the third time. The window was cracked open, admitting a crisp wind that belled the lace curtains like a hooped crinoline.

She was so very lucky to have found Reuben. The admission of her foolish charade with Lucas had bothered him not a whit. He was so understanding. Agreeable, steadfast, gentlemanly—all the qualities she'd hoped for in a husband.

A curtain flapped against the wall and she shivered, tugging the corners of her shawl more tightly around her shoulders.

She dipped her pen in the ink, bent over her desk, and began to write.

"So am I forgiven yet? I told Pris nothing happened, after all."

Lucas dug another pot out of the new crate of tinware he was unpacking and slapped it down on a shelf with a clang. Jeanette, having delivered the message about label glue with which Priscilla had sent her to the store, had now been perched on a stool for the last ten minutes flipping through a pattern book, shooting hopeful—and, in his opinion, not nearly remorseful enough—glances his way.

He banged down the lid on the pot. "I'm talking to you, aren't I?"

"If you call growling speaking to me." Shrugging, she flipped another page. "I was just trying to help Priscilla."

"So you said." Where were the stupid bread pans? Shredded paper spilled from the crate like foam on an over-fermented beer.

Jeanette gave him a dark look. "I still think it would have been better if you'd just gone along with me."

A pan ricocheted off the shelf where he'd tossed it and crashed to the floor. "If this is your version of an apology, Jeanette, you're not very good at it."

"As good as you." She thwapped the book shut. "I mean, look at the two of you! You prowl around like a wounded grizzly, practically taking the head off anyone who says one word to you—"

"I am not grouchy!"

Jeanette humphed. "And then there's Priscilla, moping around the house, mumbling over bottling company books until the wee hours, scarcely eating a thing—"

His head came up. "She all right?"

"No thanks to you—"

"Is she all right?" The only way he'd gotten through that silent, agonizing trip back from St. Anthony, and the two miserable weeks since, was by believing that this was what she wanted. Him out of her life, completely, permanently, absolutely. If he had to rip his guts out to do it— well, by damn, he owed her that.

"I suppose so," Jeanette said grudgingly. "But really, how long do you think you can keep this up? Lover's quarrel my a—uh, no one's going to believe that spiel much longer."

Kicking aside the empty crate, he attacked the next one, a metallic shriek pealing through the room as he pried out the nails fastening the top. "I don't care what they believe."

"I thought that was the whole point—"

"They can believe whatever they damn well want."

Lucas looked like he wanted to tear that crate apart with his bare hands, Jeanette thought. "What exactly happened between you and my sister when you were in St. Anthony?"

He ripped the cover free and tossed it aside. "Nothing happened."

"If you'd gone along with my plan in the first place, none of this—"

"I said nothing happened!" He stabbed the air with the handle of the hammer he'd been using. "Honest to God, Jeanette, you're relentless. No wonder that husband of yours ran off to—aw shit, Jeanette. I'm sorry."

Swallowing hard, she waved off his apology. "It doesn't matter."

"I'm an ass."

"Well, that's true." She smiled lamely. "But it still doesn't matter. I won't *let* it matter."

She slipped off the stool, going to the counter to replace the pattern book next to the piles of fabric and a multicolored pyramid of thread. Only a few feet away a half-dozen bottles of Maple Falls Spring Water were carefully arranged and she brushed her fingers over the portrait of herself on the label.

"It's a good selling point," Lucas told her. "To men, for the obvious reasons. And to women, hoping that all the good stuff in the water will make them look like you."

She smiled sadly, mildly appeased. "Do you

suppose we'll ship to the Jefferson Territory some day?"

"Why? Want Robert to know what he's missing?"

"Something like that."

"So go show him."

"What?" she asked, truly shocked.

"Go out there and show him."

"Don't be ridiculous. I could never do that."

"Why not?" He tossed the hammer on top of the next crate and started digging through the one he'd just opened. "He ran away from you, didn't he? Why are you letting him get away with it?"

"Go west? All by myself? Why would I do a thing like that?"

"So you can settle it one way or another and get on with your life instead of waiting around here for *him* to do something."

"I couldn't." But she was standing straighter, in a semblance of the regal bearing he'd always associated with her returning. "No one else is running after their men; how could I possibly . . ."

"You're not anyone else."

"I couldn't," she said automatically. But oh, surely she could imagine the look on Robert's face when she stepped off the stage in . . . wherever he was now. It might almost be worth the danger and the trouble of the journey, to show him that he couldn't just leave and forget her like a soiled collar.

The bell tinkled. Pamelia Fletcher and Louisa Rockwell strolled in, flashing hopeful smiles in Lucas's direction, their vivacity dimmed a shade

at finding Jeanette already there. They drifted
over to inspect the calicoes, talking in low un-
dertones.

"I'd better get back," Jeanette said. Then, with
a cheeky look at the other women, she asked in
a loud, clear voice, "Is there a message you'd like
me to deliver to my sister?"

He scowled at her. Served him right for planting absurd notions like running off to find Robert in her head, Jeanette thought, and for
whatever he'd done in St. Anthony that was
making both him and her sister so purely miserable.

"No."

"Really?" Pamelia and Louisa had stopped
chattering, bending their ears in her direction in
a way that, though meant to be subtle, was in
fact anything but. "A personal message? Something you didn't want the boy to hear?"

"No," he barked.

"The way you've had Mick running back and
forth between the two of you, one would think
you had a *few* things to say to her."

"That was business." He slammed a teapot
down so hard the bottom dented. "Bottling business, every last time."

"Of course it was."

The women had sidled closer. Couldn't bear
to miss a word, Jeanette supposed. Rounding on
them, Lucas speared them with an impatient
glare. "Can I help you with something?"

"Well!" Pamelia huffed, affronted.

"That's not a particularly friendly way to treat
your customers, Lucas," Jeanette reproached, unable to resist a slight needle. After watching her

sister mope around, she was determined that Lucas should suffer right along with her.

The baking sheet Lucas was unpacking bowed, nearly bent in half. Jeanette figured he was wishing that was her neck.

"Maybe you should let Mick wait on all the customers, after all. Until you can at least be pleasant, if not your usual charming self."

"I am always pleasant!" His brows lowered threateningly.

"Of course you are." He was remarkably easy to upset. It seemed he was more disturbed by his quarrel—or whatever it was—with her sister than she ever would have expected.

Nodding his head as if determined to show her, he stretched his lips wide, baring his teeth, and turned to his customers. "Is there something I can help you with, ladies?" he asked, the courteous words ruined by the tone he delivered them in.

"I . . . ah . . ." Louisa scrambled for a reason to account for their presence.

"We were looking for the hair rats!" Pamelia suggested triumphantly. "Do you have some?"

"Yes," he said flatly.

"Were are they, then?"

"In the stock room."

She waited for some encouragement that never came. "Can we see them, please?"

He scowled further. "No."

Jeanette smothered a giggle. "Oh yes, a model storekeeper, that's you."

"Mick helped me 'organize' the stock room last week, and I haven't been able to find a single thing since."

"Where is he, anyway? Priscilla sent me with the message when he didn't stop by this morning as usual."

"I don't know that, either! I've been trying for weeks to tell him that he really doesn't have to get here an hour before we open. Today he's an hour late."

"Are you talking about that boy? The little 'breed?" Louisa put in tentatively, clearly hoping to please. "I saw him on the way here."

"You did? Where is he?"

She bloomed under his concentrated interest. "He was playing by the old sawmill. Ducked inside just as I passed."

"You *let* him go in there?"

"I—" She blinked in confusion. "Why shouldn't I?"

"Because it's dangerous, that's why." Lucas shoved the crates aside and came around the case, causing Louisa to step back beneath his accusing glare. "It's never been repaired after the flood. The floors are weak, the walls need propping up, and there's a damn big hole over the drop to the river. Didn't you know that?"

"Well, of course I did, but—"

"And you didn't tell him to get out of there?"

"Well, I—"

"Or tell *me* right away, so I could get him out? You knew he worked here."

"Well, yes, but . . ." she sputtered. "He's not mine! I didn't want to interfere."

"Of course not."

She relaxed slightly, and Jeaneatte thought how the poor girl had no idea what was coming. Not that she didn't deserve it.

"Let me ask you this," Lucas said, dangerously soft. "If it had been Timothy Tuttle or Ernie Churchill, what would you have done?"

"I would have told them to get out—" She stopped, blanched.

"But he's a 'breed, is that it? Who cares what happens to him?"

"I—"

"Now, Lucas." Pamelia stepped in to rescue her friend. "You know that those little savages can take of themselves. And if they can't, who's to say they won't be better off?"

Raw red crept up Lucas's neck, the cords standing out starkly. But Pamelia wasn't worth the time right now.

He dashed for the door, calling to Jeanette over his shoulder. "Will you go tell Pris, ask her to meet me at the mill? If he's not there, she'll want to help look. And if he—" He yanked the door open, the crash when it met the wall drowning the sound of the bell. "She'll want to be there."

He ran through the streets full speed, head down, ignoring greetings, leaving gapemouthed, bewildered women staring after him.

He skidded to a stop by the sawmill, ears alert, eyes searching. Half-bare branches drew a tracery of shadow on the weather-grayed walls that no one had ever bothered to whitewash. Wind gusted, spraying brown leaves to pile against the stairway. High under the eaves, pale sunlight dashed over one of the few remaining panes of glass, giving the suggestion of motion behind the surface reflection.

"Mick!" he shouted, mounting the stairs. Inside, light pierced haphazardly boarded windows and poured through the open hole torn by the flood which still yawned in the back corner. The giant saw blade was splotched red and brown with rust. Stacks of broken, rotting lumber piled against the walls, and cobwebs shrouded the corners. Something, a mouse or a squirrel, probably, skittered along the far wall, and the air reeked with droppings and damp, moldering sawdust.

Layers of dust lay thickly over windowsills and along the top of machinery. Old leaves and dirt piled around the edges of the room, covering dark stains on the floors and walls. But beneath his feet the warped floor was scuffed and scraped bare, and by bigger feet than those of the rodents who'd claimed the building. Children exploring, he supposed; and who could blame them? Despite the danger, the place would have been irresistible to him when he was young.

"Mick!" The room echoed. Hollow, empty. An open staircase lurched up to the second floor. Steep and hazardous even in good repair, it was downright dangerous now. Lucas raced up it.

Used mostly for storage and offices, the second floor was tidier and dimmer. The floor creaked unsettlingly beneath his feet and he slowed.

"Mick!" Maybe he'd wasn't here. Maybe he was already back at the store, polishing off the rest of the sweet crackers Lucas had set aside for him.

Or maybe he *was* here, but unable to answer.

Lucas edged between a couple of splintering crates and eased by an old filing cabinet with torn, mildewed papers spilling out of an open drawer. The window he'd seen from below had no one behind it, after all. But across the room a window had been broken completely out. Quickly as he dared, he approached the window. It overlooked the river and the great mill wheel. When the dam had spanned the river, the water brushed the stone foundations. Now the river had receded and the wheel stood abandoned by its source of power. Its bottom hung three feet above the thin veiling of water that flowed over a tumble of rocks beneath it, the deeper waters rushing by uselessly a good six feet beyond.

"Mick!"

A small sound squeaked over his head, and he looked up, peering through the fretwork of wood. On the highest curve of the wheel, Mick huddled in the angle between a wide paddle and the spokes supporting it, his eyes huge and scared in his pale, set face. Lucas's breath froze in his lungs.

"There you are! My best employee, late for work. What am I to do with you?"

Mick's mouth worked, but no sound came out, every other muscle held rigidly still.

"Hiding out from me, are you? I would have let you out of cleaning the pickle barrel if I'd known you'd do something like this to avoid it."

Moisture brimmed in the boy's eyes.

"Okay, Mick, I'm here now. Everything's going to be okay. But you've got to breathe first."

The boy's chest shuddered.

"Again."

He sucked in another breath, deeper this time, and his chalky color eased a bit.

"Can't move," he whispered, looking down at his fingers, curled around a board as if he could dig the tips right into the wood and hang on. "My foot's stuck."

"I don't want you to move yet," Lucas said calmly. The wheel was held in place by inertia and two years of rust; no telling when it would decide to start turning.

"But—"

"Hey, this way I don't have to pay you for an hour, do I?" he said, his mind churning for the safest way to get the boy down.

"I'm not fired?" The wheel creaked and Mick gasped, wedging further back into his precarious perch.

"No, you're not fired." *What to do, what to do?* "Climbing trees got too tame for you, did it? Needed a fresh challenge?" he said, relieved when Mick smiled weakly. He'd need the boy relaxed enough to follow instructions when the time came.

"I suppose so."

"What's the good of climbing up there all by yourself, though? No point if there's no one to admire your bravery." He mentally sifted through the things he'd seen in the mill. What could he use? Had there been rope? A ladder? He didn't dare leave long enough to fetch anything but what was already at hand.

"Wasn't alone."

"What?" Lucas's attention snapped back. "Who was with you?"

A sullen set to his mouth, Mick avoided his

eyes. Lucas recognized what he was up against—
the code of all boys: *Never tattle.*

"Did they tell you to climb up there, Mick?"

"It was a dare! We were playing."

"And then they left you?" So as not to startle
the boy, he kept his voice soft, but inside he
screamed, *Worthless little brats!*

"What else were they supposed to do?" His
chin thrust out stubbornly, but fear and hurt
shone in Mick's eyes.

Lucas's heart went out to him. Mick had few
children to play with and longed for friends. But
most of the children in town were unlikely to see
him as anything but a half-Indian bastard, an obvious target to torment. He'd be easy prey for
anything they'd suggest, no matter how reckless.

"Mick, I'm going to go get some wood and
brace the wheel, make sure it doesn't go anywhere we don't want it to. You'll be all right here
for a minute more?"

"I think so."

"Sure you will."

A quick search turned up little of any use. He
collected a couple of small timbers and a half-
dozen thick boards, returning to find that Mick,
who hadn't moved a muscle, was staring down
at the rocks beneath him.

"Mick, there's no sense in looking down there.
You're up here, and here's where you're staying,
okay?"

"Okay."

Hanging half out the window, Lucas jammed
wood between the wheel and the wall of the
mill, shoving it in with his foot. Despite the cool

day, sweat trickled between his shoulder down his back and made his shirt stick.

"I'm going back down for a moment now, Mick, to prop it up at the bottom, too. Just to make sure."

Mick swallowed, nodded.

Five more minutes of work, while *Hurry, hurry* pounded at the back of his brain. He longed for a dozen strong men to grab hold of the wheel and hang on. But there was no one near to help, and few who cared what happened to this inconvenient boy.

He returned and hitched one hip up on the windowsill. "I used to be one hell of a climber when I was a kid. Let's see if I still know how, huh?"

"Don't come out here," Mick pleaded. "I don't want anything to happen to you."

Taking a deep breath, Lucas recited a fervent mental prayer for the stability of his makeshift propping. "Nothing's going to happen to me," he promised, and swung his legs over the ledge.

Chapter 24

The wagon bounced through a rut in the road. The wheels rattled, the seat chattered beneath Priscilla's rear. The horse's hooves pounded and it felt as if each hoofbeat resonated on her chest.

Please. She couldn't think enough to form a more coherent prayer. Just please, please, let the boy be safe.

She tried not to get ahead of herself; there was no reason to believe he wasn't all right. But the blue mood that had haunted her the last weeks had sharpened and hardened when Jeanette had told her that Mick was missing. Mick, who would have dragged himself from a sickbed rather than disappoint Lucas by showing up late for work.

The low gray clouds depressed her, the wind chilled her, and she couldn't shake the feeling that something was very wrong.

She'd sent Jeanette to find Mick's mother while she took the wagon to the mill in case . . . well, just in case.

She pulled the horse to the left, angling tightly

314

around the corner. Even before she halted the
wagon in front of the mill, she was hollering.

"Lucas! Mick!"

"We're here!" The answer was faint but un-
mistakably Lucas. He didn't sound upset, and
her tension eased.

"Lucas?"

"Around the back!"

She hurried around the side of the mill, along
the path that followed the bank. Rocks had
crumbled along the edge. Half of the overlook,
where her father had liked to take his lunch
while viewing the waterwheel and the river, had
been washed away.

"Lucas?"

"Up here."

She looked up, and her heart speared into her
throat. "How—"

"We seem to have a slight problem," Lucas
told her calmly. "Mick has grown overfond of
his view, put his foot through a board, and gotten stuck so he can stay here."

A burst of wind blew off the river and it
seemed to Priscilla that the wheel wobbled in
place. "What should I do?"

"You wouldn't happen to have a rope?" he
asked, in that same soft, collected voice, clearly
designed to keep Mick from panic.

Priscilla swallowed, trying to keep her own
words equally calm. "I'll get some."

She turned and ran. She found some in the
back of the wagon, right where she remembered—she thanked God she'd never gotten
around to clearing out the wagon bed. Looping
a thick coil over her shoulder, she tore back.

"Got it!"

"Come on up to the second floor. The window back here's all broken out. But be careful; the stairs and floorboards are weak in some spots."

Her bootheels clattered on the stairs; her breath panted out in short bursts.

She stuck her head out the window. Lucas was braced a foot from Mick, between a paddle and a crossbar, leaning back against a broad spoke, far more relaxed than he had any right to be. Mick, however, looked like all the blood had drained from his face.

"Hello, Mick. Really, this was rather an extreme measure to take just to get my full attention."

"Hey, Miz Wentworth," he managed weakly.

Priscilla tried to smile encouragingly, but then she looked down and her head spun dizzily.

"What do you want me to do?" she asked.

"I'm going to have to pry his foot out. I've braced the wheel as best I can, but most of those boards are half-rotted. Don't know how well it'll hold. If you can throw the rope over to me, maybe we can loop it around a spoke or two. Then I can toss the other end back, and you can—is there something in there you can wrap it around? Just to give a little extra support, in case this thing decides to start turning again?"

"I'll find something." A cross timber in the roof, maybe. Or she'd hang onto it herself, she thought, fresh determination surging. She simply refused to let anything happen to either one of her men. "Here we go."

Priscilla let three feet of rope dangle from her hand, and slowly swung that length back and forth, an increasing pendulum, bringing it closer to Lucas until he could snatch it in mid-swing.

"Let out a little more."

She doled out several more feet. Lucas bent to loop the length around a cross brace, bending slowly, slowly so as not to disturb the balance. The seconds crawled by, taking up five times their normal allotment of time.

As he bent further the wind shifted, strengthened. Leaves scattered; wood creaked. Then there was the screech of metal on metal and the wheel began to inch down.

"No!" Priscilla canted out the window, hands scrabbling for a hold on the wheel, splinters gouging her palms.

Lucas sprang to Mick. Feet braced on a lower paddle, one arm clutching higher, he yanked Mick's foot free and lifted him in his unencumbered arm. "Hang on!" he shouted. Mick obliged, locking both arms around Lucas's neck.

A boom shattered the air, the splintering of one of the timbers Lucas had used to try and lodge the wheel in place. The wheel eased around faster, dislodging the rest of the props, and picked up speed.

Lucas looked up and back at the window briefly, assessing, searching for any way to clamber back up to the window. His eyes briefly met Pris's, his grim expression showing he couldn't find another option.

And then he turned back, facing the water. He let go of his handhold and wrapped both arms around Mick.

He leaped.

To Pris they seemed to freeze in the air for an

instant, rendering the terrible image with permanent clarity in her brain. Bleak gray sky behind, the dull pewter surface of the water far below. Lucas and Mick, looking too small and fragile above the massive power of the river.

And then they plunged down, arrowing through the dark water, out where it was deeper and almost black. It closed over them, swallowing them completely.

"Dear God!" It was a prayer, an imprecation, a curse, a sob. In a blind panic, she tumbled down the stairway, out the door, to the bank of the river.

She'd spent suffering nights coming to terms with the knowledge that she'd lost Lucas. But that loss was tempered by knowing he was lost only to *her.* Not to the world. But this—to think that he would not be somewhere, laughing, teasing, making a woman smile . . . it was unimaginable.

And Mick. Mick, whose brief life had been such a struggle. He must have a chance to fashion something better out of it. He simply *must.*

She scanned the surface of the river. Water boiled at the base of the falls, just upstream from the mill, then smoothed out to sluggish brown ripples. The current was far more powerful than the surface revealed, but Lucas was a strong swimmer and the river had shrunk far below its spring torrents.

But it was cold now, a chill that could steal life in minutes. And she'd no idea if Lucas had jumped far enough to bring them to the deeper water beyond the rocks.

There . . . was it them? She squinted, eyes

glued to the spot where she'd glimpsed something bobbing above the surface. There again, Lucas's head, further downstream than she would have imagined, not more than fifteen feet from shore. He gasped, surged upward to bring Mick's head above the water. The current caught them and they spun, dipping briefly beneath the surface again.

"Lucas!" she shouted, running down the bank, stripping off her jacket and hat as she went. She could swim.

He struggled sideways, holding Mick's head on his shoulder above the water.

"Don't!" he shouted, working closer to the shore.

He was right and she knew it. She was of no use to him, would likely make his task all the harder. But standing there—waiting, hoping, nearly insensate with worry—was the hardest thing she'd ever done.

Come on, come on. A broken piece of wood surged by, the splintered remains of the props that had proved so inadequate. Lucas's progress stalled, the river sweeping them further downstream as he kicked toward the bank.

The Mississippi curved just ahead, depositing muck along the outside edge, a thin sandbar that disappeared in the spring floods. But it was enough now. He gave one last spurt of energy, found purchase for his feet. The water dragged at him, at the limp figure clinging to him, but it couldn't have them now. He staggered up, gently laying Mick safely above the waterline before collapsing himself, belly down, his legs still immersed in water to his knees.

"Lucas! Mick!"

Priscilla clambered down the bank, skidding on wet clay, bushes snagging her clothes, until she was beside them.

"Lucas?"

"Mick first," he muttered, face down in mud and sand.

Mick's dark hair plastered against his head, feathered wetly against his cheek. She laid a hand against his neck and his skin chilled her fingers. From the water, she told herself, not from death. There, she thought with relief, locating the faint, steady beat of his pulse. She rolled him on his side, gently slicking his hair from his forehead. He coughed, spewing water and mucus.

"Mick? Can you hear me?"

Eyes sealed shut, he nodded weakly.

"Good. Don't talk. I'm going to go get you some blankets, warm you up, okay? And then we'll work on getting you up the bank."

Another nod, followed by a deep sigh.

Priscilla hitched around to kneel by Lucas and bent down. He had his face turned sideways on the bank. Water glistened in his eyebrow, dripped from the dark ropes of his hair. Mud streaked his jaw. There was a bruise darkening his cheekbone, a faint purpling beneath the water-filmed skin.

"Oh, Lucas," she whispered, touched the growing welt, and the fear hit her with the force of a fist, all the clenching emotion that she hadn't had time to feel fully before. Her hand started to shake.

He opened one eye, bleary and tired, blinking

away the sting of the water that dripped into it, the brown of his iris so deep and rich that Priscilla thought she could drown in it as easily as she could in the river.

His lifted his hand, weakly curled his fingers around her trembling ones. "You didn't think you'd get rid of me that easily, did you?"

An hour past sunset, Priscilla was slumped on the wagon seat beside Lucas as he drove away from Mick's shack. She couldn't help but notice they were in very much the same positions that they'd occupied all the way home from St. Anthony, and her mood was every bit as dismal. Except this time she understood with startling precision just what the absence of this man would mean in her life, the hole that would be rent into the fabric they'd woven over the years.

But what choice did she have? She could have him, or she could have the family she'd always wanted. There was no way to have both, and the loss of either one would leave her so much poorer.

They'd spent the entire day with Mick. Jeanette had arrived with Lucas's mother shortly after Lucas had crawled out of the river, bringing blankets and towels as well as a cloak and gloves for Pris. They'd laid Mick in the back of the wagon and driven him home.

Priscilla tried mightily but unsuccessfully to persuade Lucas to go home, but why would she think he'd listen to her? So they'd both gone to Mick's, sending Jeanette home with a message for Clara not to expect Priscilla, for she'd stay as long as she was needed. She'd wrapped Mick's foot, plied him with blankets and hot drinks, until both she and Lucas were convinced he'd recover fully and Mick's mother had gratefully but firmly shooed them out the door.

Now the buildings of Maple Falls rolled by them. Here and there a light flared behind a curtain. Once a door opened and a woman called for her son to come in from his chores. But more buildings sat empty, unfriendly hulks stripped of their reason for existence. Priscilla wondered vaguely if she'd be like that someday, an old husk with her purpose long gone.

Wearily she sighed, her head wobbling on her neck. Though she knew it had only been one day, the ricocheting emotions had sapped her, making it seem as if three days had inched by. Lucas eased an arm around her, a comforting support. She battled the temptation for a moment before surrendering, letting her head fall to his shoulder.

"You'll be home soon," he murmured.

Home. And they'd be right back where they'd been this morning, sending messages through others, stilted notes that said nothing that mattered. Straining her ears over others' conversations, trying to catch a tidbit of gossip about him. Trying to find a way to forget him.

But she wasn't there yet.

"I don't want you to take me home."

"Pris." He clicked to her horse, drew the wagon to a stop in front of the newspaper offices, and turned on the seat. "You can't mean that."

The future yawned before her, unknowable,

uncertain. But empty of him; she knew that with terrible certainty. "Just tonight. Just once more, Lucas, before it all ends."

She touched his face, a feather-light brush that rocked him with the force of a gale wind. Dawning moonlight glistened in her eyes. How could he say no to her?

Slipping his hands beneath the muffling wool of her cloak, he bent his head and kissed her. Kissed her, while the autumn air nipped at their ears and the horse stamped and snorted impatiently. Kissed her, while his hands found swells and dips hidden beneath layers of clothing. Kissed her, while desire beat a tattoo in their blood that grew and strengthened with each passing second.

"I don't know where to take you," he murmured against her lips.

"Everywhere," she said, nipping the corner of his mouth. And then, "Oh," as she realized what he meant. Reluctantly, she suggested the obvious. "How about your—"

"No." He would not take her to his rooms, where so many others had been, to the bed built for sport.

It pleased her more than it should have, this small sign that she was not like all the others.

"Right out here, then." She smiled and wiggled close to him, their bodies creating a small cocoon of warmth beneath the heavy folds of her cloak.

"Out here? How bold of you, Miss Pris." It had a certain appeal, he admitted, as he dropped smiling kisses on her brow, her cheek, her neck. But he wanted more. More time, more space, without the urgency of cold and the threat of discovery. Another time, he thought, and then remembered there would not be another time. The knowledge hurt, a deep well of sorrow that burned an empty hole behind his heart.

"Let's go," he said. He reached behind her, came up with the hat her sister had included with the other things she'd brought, and plopped it on her head with the rapscallion's grin she loved so well. "Ready?"

No, she wasn't ready. Not ready for this all to end. But tomorrow was irrevocably waiting for her, whether she took this night or not. So she'd take this night and hoard it away in her heart for all the days without Lucas that were to come. "Ready."

Chapter 25

H e brought her to his store, the place he spent most of his time, where they'd plotted and planned Maple Falls Bottling together. The room was jammed with merchandise and supplies, illuminated only by moonlight and the small lantern he lit shortly after they arrived.

Lucas settled Pris on a small stool next to the unlit stove and placed the lantern on the floor beside her. "Cold? I could start a fire."

"No." She unfastened her cloak, folded it in a square, and set it on a nearby barrel.

"Wait here." He didn't move, but merely looked down at her, his face hard with intensity and an emotion that Priscilla couldn't name but felt all the same, deep inside where her feelings— the ones she didn't want to examine too closely— resided.

He cupped her face in both hands and dipped his head under the brim of her hat to kiss her. She felt his hands, cool and gentle on her cheeks. His mouth was neither. Hot and demanding, his tongue stroked deep, promising her the hundred things to come this night.

When he pulled back, she was breathless and dizzy with anticipation. "Hurry."

He grinned and hurried. She watched him as he strode about the dark room, his movements quick and purposeful, all male power and grace, and she thought: soon. Soon, he'll touch me again. He'll kiss me like before, and press deep inside me, and I'll feel . . . everything. I'll feel the world in one bright instant. An ache throbbed in her belly, and lower yet, and she shifted on the stool, pressing her legs together to ease it, impatient and hungry.

To ensure no one could see in, he tacked heavy cloth over the front windows. He double-checked the doors. Then he disappeared into the storeroom, returning with his arms full.

He cleared a space in the center of the room and she nearly jumped him right then, not caring that the floor would be hard and cold. Not caring about anything except having him deep inside her. But curiosity held her in check. That, and a lingering reluctance to hurry through this night.

He unrolled a spiral of cotton batting, then another, laying a feather-stuffed mattress over the top until the whole thing was a puff nearly a foot thick. An entire bolt of soft, striped flannel spread over the top. He gathered a box full of candles, a half-dozen lanterns, and arranged them around the bed, lighting each one as he went, bringing up the glow in the room, leaving the bed he'd made for her in a lake of shimmering gold.

His face very serious, he held a hand out to her as if he were a courtier and she his queen.

"I'm not sure my legs'll hold me up," she confessed.

"I won't let you fall."

She reached up to unpin her hat.

"Leave it," he told her. "The gloves, too."

"Why?"

He just smiled. Just once more, she'd told him. If this was all he was ever to have with her, Lucas was determined to live out every fantasy he could. To pack so much into one night that they both could live off the memories for the rest of their lives, he thought, swallowing hard.

But there was tonight, and he wasn't going to ruin it with worrying over the future.

His shirt was stiff and wrinkled—he hadn't wanted to leave Mick long enough to change, and his clothes had dried on his body, a crumpled reminder of just how close she'd come to losing him that afternoon. Her throat squeezed. He carried her hands to his bent, grayed collar and lifted his own to the tiny pearled buttons that marched down the front of her blouse. "Race you," he said.

"Unfair! I'm wearing gloves."

"But you've got lots more buttons for me to undo."

He was ahead already and she rushed to catch up. They finished even, laughing and breathless, gazes snagging on the flame-burnished skin bared between shirtfronts.

The more clothes they peeled back, the more their hands slowed. Impossible to hurry, when she had to draw her thumbs along the line of his waistband, dip her fingers below in the back. When he had to follow the lace edge of her chemise with his tongue. When every inch bared had to be touched and tasted and admired.

At last all their clothes lay in a pile at their feet and he stepped back to take in the view. Exactly how he'd imagined, the big hat shading her face, ribbons trailing over her shoulders, prim white gloves making her nakedness look all the more wanton. So Pris. So pretty and new.

He wished, suddenly, that he came to her with clean hands and a clean soul. That there'd been no one before, that they were evenly matched in this.

Her hips swaying, she stepped closer, where he could no longer see all of her at once. And then he laid his palms on her bare shoulders and knew it no longer mattered, for everything they made between them was new, fresh-sprung, unsullied as virgin snow.

"You don't want me to look at you?"

"No. Not right now," she said.

"You're embarrassed? You shouldn't be."

"No." She moved closer still, tight against him, her belly trapping his erection between them, forcing the breath from him. "You're just too far away like that."

She kissed his shoulder, his collarbone, her mouth hotter than any brand. More permanent, he realized; each kiss burned his skin, seared deep into his heart. Swiftly he lifted her in his arms.

"You don't have to carry me."

"Yes, I do. It's the easiest way I know to get you exactly where I want you."

"Wouldn't want to tire you out, though. Not

after such a strenuous day. I have plans for you, you know."

"I hope so." He lowered her to the makeshift bed, and she drifted into it as if she were falling into a cloud. "I wouldn't worry about it. I have a few plans of my own."

One of the hat ribbons lay over her shoulder, a stripe of ruby against her glowing gold-washed skin. Smoothing the ribbon over her breast, he rubbed her nipple through it with his thumb. She hummed a low sound, her head falling back. He tongued her through the fluid silk. The fabric was soft and smooth, but beneath he could feel her nipple pebbling up against his tongue.

"You do, hmm?" She liked the sound of that. Weak as though her bones were softening, bending to his will, she fell back into the puff of flannel. He followed her down, never taking his mouth from her breast, sucking right through the thin film of wet fabric. Another ribbon dangled below her jaw, and he brushed the tip of her other breast with it, a sensation too light to satisfy her. She arched, needing more.

His hand; that was what she'd needed, firm on her breast, kneading, stroking, molding her to his will, and she sighed into the pleasure he spun so effortlessly. Sensations purled over her skin, shimmered deep inside her, spreading outward like ripples on water until she thought that they would meet and grow and she would drown in the pleasure.

The dozens of flames circling the bed dazzled her eyes. Lucas dazzled *her*. His hands skimmed down her sides, angled over her hips. Her stomach quivered as he brushed his fingers over it.

Then lower, and the quivers strengthened, grew into soul-deep shudders as he stroked the sleek wetness between her legs. When he drew back, she bit her lip to keep from crying out.

Deliberately his gaze held hers as he lifted his hand into an oval of candlelight. Liquid gleamed on his fingertips and her skin burned. He touched her just below the collarbone, then drew a trail down, between her breasts, her ribs, all the way to the tangle of hair between her legs. She could feel the moisture on her skin, a cool line. But then his mouth was there, heating her, following the path he'd laid down, licking the taste of her from her skin.

His thumbs traced the valley where her thighs met her torso, brushing closer, closer. The sensation ratcheted through her, so strong she thought perhaps she could not bear it but instead would fly apart, shatter into a thousand pieces formed only of pleasure. His hands slid beneath her, lifted her, and she thought wildly no, he couldn't be . . . but he was, mouth against her, his tongue flicking lightly, stroking slow and quick, deeper, longer. And then his tongue thrust inside her and she cried out. She'd shattered as she'd feared, but she loved it, reveled in it, for she knew Lucas would hold her safe.

He let her drift down, ease only part way into relaxation. Her eyes were slumberous, her nipples deep colored and relaxed with her release, the tension in her body leaching away. The need to imprint himself on her surged. He worked both thumbs inside her and he felt her muscles close around them. He drove her higher this time, ruthlessly, tongue lashing, her climax fast and hard because she'd been only halfway down from the peak. And again, again, until the sobs shuddered from her throat, propelled by the need to use every second to make certain she would remember this, remember him, have these feelings—the ones that *he* had caused—imbed themselves in her body, brand her soul.

She was his. Her body responded to his every touch, every command, every wish. It seemed as if he could draw the pleasure from her with just a thought, before his body made his fantasies reality. Her skin was flushed, her limbs pliant. A moment, he thought. He would give her a moment before he began again. He slid up to lie beside her and soothed her with gentle strokes, letting her gather her strength.

But he'd underestimated her. She struggled up to kneel by his hip, crushed hat askew on her head, a loose skein of hair coiling beneath her ear.

"Just relax," he murmured. "Rest for a while."

"No." She removed her hat, shaking loose her hair to fall in glorious waves. The lamplight shone through from behind, a corona of gold and brown. "I want to . . . please, Lucas. Let me."

And because he understood the need to give pleasure as well as receive it, he steeled himself to let her do what she would. He lay back propped up on his elbows so he could watch her.

Hesitantly, she reached for him. "Tell me what to do."

"Do anything."

She touched his erection, lightly at first, a quick skating of her gloved fingers down his length, and the breath hissed out of him. The control he'd exerted by concentrating on her, seeking *her* pleasures, evaporated with that one bare touch.

"More."

She wrapped her hand around him and slid it up and down. He surged up into the rhythm. He saw his cock thrusting out of her dainty white-gloved hand, and desire crushed his resolve. He whipped forward to pull her to him.

"No," she said. "I'm not done yet."

A growl tore from his throat. His muscles clenched, wanting more, wanting her—but he would do as she'd asked, he swore to himself, or explode trying.

And then she bent down, her hair sliding over her shoulder, pooling on his belly like molten silk. Her mouth touched him, her tongue delicately tracing the full length, and he thought he would burst after all.

There was no world, Priscilla thought. Nothing but the two of them. No thought, no past, no future. Just the passion. Just this.

She took him into her mouth fully, as much as she could, feeling him shake with the thunder of desire. She could do this to him. She, Priscilla Wentworth, could make him shudder, make him groan, make him whisper her name in that hoarse voice. It filled her with power, gave her a kind of pleasure that was nothing like the physical one he'd caused but was no less satisfying. No less seductive.

She suckled gently, and he sprang up.

"I can't—"

He laid her back, kneeling upright between her legs, and lifted her hips to meet his. He plunged inside her, pushing deep, beyond any constraints of gentle control.

Deep, hard strokes. Her head lolled on the flannel, her face tightening with building strain. Her breasts quivered with each thrust. Again ... again. Her color deepened. Her breath quickened and he felt the first tiny quivers of release, her inner muscles gripping around him as her hand had earlier.

He needed her closer. He slid his hands beneath her back and lifted her up to him. She wrapped herself around him—legs linked behind his thighs, arms tight around his back, head pressed on his shoulder, chest and bellies sealed together. Only Pris, he thought. Surrounding him fully. Holding him. She sobbed his name.

Only Pris.

Near daybreak he surrendered to sleep, briefly and reluctantly. He'd made love to her over and over—he hadn't counted. It didn't matter; it seemed one continuous act. Even when his own flesh had been sated at last, he'd been compelled to continue, loving her with hands and mouth, until in her sharp pleasure he'd found himself hardening again, his body responding to her pleasure more strongly than it had ever responded to his own.

Somewhere in the back of his mind the thought was dimly formed, irrational, but powerful all the same: If he didn't sleep, the morning wouldn't come.

But it caught him anyway, stealing up on him as Pris had ridden him from above. She found her pleasure again and collapsed on him; he'd closed his eyes for a moment, and the sleep had stolen his night.

He'd thought it was only moments later when he opened his eyes again. But the slivers of light around the shrouds over the front window were blindingly bright. The lanterns had devoured their fuel and extinguished, the candles reduced to pools of lumpy wax. And Pris. Pris was fully dressed, sitting knees together and back straight on the small stool, waiting for him to awake. She'd been unable to punch her hat into a semblance of shape and so she clutched it in her hands before her like a shield, her expression serious and determined.

Oh shit, he thought. Here we go again.

She'd laid a corner of flannel across him while he slept, angling it over his waist. Deliberately he shoved it away and rolled to his feet. She averted her eyes demurely and his temper kicked like an old mule.

"A little late for prim and proper, isn't it?"

Her mouth thinned. She folded her hands tightly on her lap. "It would have been impolite to slip out while you were sleeping, but I really need to be going now—"

"*Polite?* For God's sake, Pris, you weren't worried about polite last night, when you put your mouth on my—"

"Stop it!" She flushed the color of the dawn. "All right, then, I—"

"Look at me!" She would not do this so easily, waltz out of here, as if there were nothing between them, without even meeting his eyes.

"All right." She didn't want to. She didn't know if she could do it, could look at him and

still say and do what she must. But he had the
right, didn't he? She'd given it to him, gleefully,
passionately, when she'd asked for him to take
her last night. She swallowed hard and turned
her gaze his way.

Oh, my. Her heart was a lump in her throat.
He was naked and beautiful, big feet planted
wide, fists jammed on his hips. Broad chest
planed with muscle, flat belly, the part of him
that she'd held in her mouth, taken into her
body, swelling even as she watched—oh, Lord,
she wanted him. Every fiber of her body
yearned, a physical craving as strong as it was
impossible.

But wanting wasn't enough. Hadn't she
learned that much, at least?

"I have to tell you—I don't want you to hear
it from someone else. Reuben is coming here; I
expect him in two weeks."

Damn it! How dared she do that, bring the
name of another man into this room where
they'd lost themselves in each other? Except it
had felt more like they'd found themselves in
each other.

Something tore inside him, a gaping, raw-
edged hole, and the words sprang from there,
unconscious, unbidden. Unthinkable.

"Marry me."

Her hands crushed the mangled hat. "You
can't mean that."

"Said it, didn't I?"

"I—" Her throat convulsed. "You don't want
to marry me. You just don't want me to marry
anybody else, do you?"

Because he wasn't sure if that wasn't a fair

part of the truth, he avoided the question. "So it's no."

Emotions buffeted her, an internal storm that roared in like a hurricane. Impossible to pick out any one, to examine it for truth. "I don't know what to say."

"Now, there's a first." Naked, he stamped over to her. "Why not me?" Even though it might be the biggest mistake he'd ever made, he was driven to state his case. "We like each other, work well together. We *know* each other."

"None of that was ever in doubt."

"We have spectacular lovemaking together."

"Do we?"

"Do you doubt it?"

"I have nothing to compare it to," she said soberly. Because she wanted to hear it from his wicked, wonderful mouth.

"Oh, yes. Better than spectacular. The best."

It shouldn't flatter her. But she was enormously, dangerously pleased.

"Tell me what more you could have with him."

"None of that is the problem, and you know it." They could talk around it all they wanted to; it was still there, a brick wall between them, one she could neither batter down nor ignore.

"I need to know, Lucas. Would you keep your vows?"

His expression turned to stone. "I've never lied to you."

Lie to me, she begged silently. *Tell me you'd never want another but me.*

"I would try," he said, even as he knew she needed to hear more than good intentions. Had his father made these promises to his mother? How could he say what he'd do in a decade or two? Hell, a year ago he could never have envisioned *this*.

"Try," she repeated flatly. *Try* was an easy word, a weak word.

What was the truth and what was a lie? If he meant it at this moment, was it a lie if he could not follow it for a lifetime? He tried to force the words out, but they kept getting blocked by echoes of the past.

"*Don't marry him,*" he said instead.

But she didn't know what else to do. She needed to plan out her life as best she could, eliminate as many risks as possible. There might be no peaks with Reuben, but there would also be none of the plummeting lows she was sure awaited her if she married Lucas.

"Damn it, Pris!" He waited for her admonishment. When it didn't come, he knew with a sinking feeling that she'd relinquished the right to scold him, given up any claim on his behavior. Any claim on *him*.

"You don't trust me."

"Oh, Lucas." Her eyes burned. Her *heart* burned. "I would trust you with my life."

He reached out, laid his hand on her bodice, just over her left breast. "But not with your heart."

Oh, God. "No," she whispered.

He pulled back his hand. It hovered in the chasm between them and they both knew with awful certainty that it was the last time he would ever touch her.

Chapter 26

Reuben Morse arrived in Maple Falls on the fifteenth of November and promptly captivated the town. He thoroughly charmed both Clara and Jeanette, who welcomed him with exultation and thinly disguised relief. And as for the rest of the women . . . here was an attractive and unattached man, and as such, he was treated with the acclaim usually reserved for a returning hero.

It was to his credit that all the attention seemed to amuse and befuddle him rather than turn his head. He was unfailingly polite to all the women he met and properly attentive to Priscilla and her family. He was particularly considerate of her mother, often drawing from her the kind of genuine smile that had been mostly absent the last three years. Priscilla was happy that she'd been able to provide her mother, who'd seemed so lonely, with an appealing new friend.

Priscilla found herself able to envision her life with Reuben clearly. It would be a friendly, affectionate partnership. She would be fully entrusted with the care of the children and the house, freeing Reuben to concentrate on his work. They would be united in their common goals.

He would never disappoint her. He would never hurt her. When he came home late she would never worry that he was doing anything but caring for a patient.

But a man like Reuben deserved equal consideration from her. She couldn't recall ever before being disturbed by a guilty conscience. It haunted her now, ruining her appetite, bedeviling her sleep with dreams.

Honesty compelled her to admit that perhaps some of her anxiety was due to Lucas. But she'd made the only wise decision possible; she was convinced of it. No, it was the fact that she'd broken faith with Reuben that was bothering her. She was not everything he believed her to be.

He'd been here two days and would be leaving tomorrow. Tonight, she must give him her decision; it was unfair to ask him to wait any longer. It was for the best, anyway; she needed to have the matter decided. It was only the uncertainty that had made her vulnerable to Lucas, allowed her to bend what she knew was right and give him her body.

Reuben had come for dinner. To her relief he'd seemed to sense that she needed some time with her own thoughts, and he took the chair beside her mother. He'd entertained them with tales of his most demanding and healthiest patients, who he claimed were often one and the same. He'd earned Priscilla's deep gratitude for surprising a rare, bright trill of laughter out of her mother.

After polishing off three apple fritters, he expressed an interest in seeing the spring he'd heard so much about. It went without saying he also wanted an opportunity to speak to Priscilla alone.

When she and Reuben stepped outside, evening had brought a thin mist to the air. It dulled the remaining autumn colors of the trees and grayed the evening sky.

"Would you like to take my buggy?" Reuben suggested. "It's quite comfortable, and there are blankets."

"Actually, I'd enjoy the walk." Not to mention give herself a little more time. "If you don't mind, of course."

After a moment's hesitation, he turned his collar up and said, "Of course I don't mind."

Priscilla strode through town, a half step ahead of Reuben, nervously pointing out every interesting, and in all honesty, a few uninteresting, points along the way. They finally achieved the spring, the glade looking worse for wear due to all the traffic it had received recently, and she stopped. Reuben puffed up behind her, his face reddened, as she felt a pang of guilt for having forced such exertion on him.

"I'm sorry," she said. "I shouldn't have insisted we walk. I forget that not everyone enjoys it as much as I do."

Reuben smiled weakly. "Don't mind a bit." He thumped a fist against his chest. "Good for the body, good for the soul. Prescribe a daily constitutional for my patients all the time. Just can't seem to work one into my schedule."

His smile grew, lifted into his eyes. It would

be a wife's responsibility to make sure that Reuben took better care of himself.

He took her hands, the layers of leather and cotton ensuring she detected none of his physical warmth. "My dear Priscilla—"

"I'm sorry." She pulled her hands away and turned. The spring bubbled over mossy boulders. A brown leaf spiraled down and landed in it, the water carrying it away into the deeper marshes. Lucas had knelt right there, near the gray rock, and held his hands out for her to drink from. She closed her eyes.

"Sorry?" She felt Reuben step nearer. "I should not bother with the speech I have prepared, then?"

"No! No, it's not that." She worried the fuzzy woolen fringe of her knitted shawl. "I . . . have a confession to make. *Another* one."

"You do?"

"I . . ." She squeezed her eyelids tighter. "I am not a virgin."

"I see."

He said nothing more for a long time; the water kept up its merry burble. A blue jay screamed harshly at her foolishness. Finally she peeked at him. His hands were tucked behind his back, his expressionless face turned toward the spring.

"I'm sorry," she said.

"I suppose there's only one thing to say, then." He cocked his head in her direction, water beading on his silvering hair and his mustache. "You see, neither am I."

"I—" Her back teeth clicked together, as if her mouth had intended to form words but was too surprised to decide on any.

"Maybe you'd guessed that," he said.

She smiled. "I had a suspicion, yes."

This time, when he took her hand, she let it remain. "You'd intend to keep your vows if you married, wouldn't you?"

"Of course, but—"

"Then I don't think that this particular issue requires any more discussion."

"I—" His eyes were gray as the sky, but infinitely warmer. There was no judgment in this man. Perhaps, she thought, having such intimate daily traffic with life and death made him more tolerant of human failings. A woman could do far worse than Reuben Morse.

"Should I try my pretty speech, then, Priscilla?"

She waited for the wave of relief. Instead, she felt curiously empty, as if the events of the past months had used up all her emotions. But that was much less painful than the intensity she'd been experiencing.

Priscilla sucked in the chilly, mist-laden air. "Yes, sir, I do believe I'd like to hear your speech."

Lydia Garrett had been arguing with herself for weeks.

Lucas was a grown man. A man needed to make his own decisions, lead his own life. Having a mother mucking around in it was usually a sure way to get a young man to do the wrong thing out of pure contrariness. And if Lucas was too pigheaded to see what was right in front of him, well, she had faith in Priscilla, who was not only bright but sensible. They'd work it out.

But as the weeks went on, she worried. Worried more, and fussed, and managed to write only twenty pages worth spit the entire time. She finally came to the irrefutable conclusion that it was her motherly duty to slap some sense into the boy.

The child who worked for Lucas was minding the store when she came charging in on a cold, bright November afternoon. In answer to her question, he'd hooked a thumb in the direction of the back door and proceeded to talk her into buying a skein of royal blue yarn. A natural salesman, that one.

She walked through the storeroom—and just how Lucas managed to find anything in there she'd never know. The back door was open a fraction, admitting the scent of impending winter, crisp pine and the thin coating of snow they'd had earlier in the week. She heard the irregular, vicious *thwack* of an ax slicing through wood and followed it out the door.

Lucas, dressed in a faded blue shirt and old pants in sore need of an ironing, was balancing a wedge of wood on an old stump. Around her was stacked the evidence of many other afternoons spent doing the same thing. Pieces were piled three deep against the back of the store, well over her head. Five other rows trailed off between the store and the stable. Lucas had a good start on a sixth.

"Trying to provide winter fuel for the entire town, are you?"

"Somebody's got to." Frowning, he swung the ax high over his head, sun sheering off the edge, and brought it down with rabid force. The chopped logs spurted off in opposite directions.

"Hmm." She refrained from pointing out that most of the women in town had been chopping wood for a good part of their lives. And that he was going to reduce that pile of oak to splinters and he still wouldn't be able to work off what was bothering him.

"I want to talk to you."

"So talk." He set the ax on top of the stump and tossed the two newly split chunks toward a growing pile.

"About you and Priscilla."

One of the two oak wedges went wide. He stomped over to pick it up and jam it where it belonged. "It's none of your business."

"Oh?" He was her son, and that made it her business. "Just like it was none of your business when you and Clara decided to spirit me out of Chicago after William died?"

He paused in the act of picking up the ax. "I don't know what you're talking about."

"Please." He was so transparent she couldn't help but laugh. "I know perfectly well you and Clara cooked it up between you, your sudden desire to go to work for Maple Falls Manufacturing and move up here to open the store."

"Why'd you go along with it?"

"I had my reasons." She huddled deeper into her cloak. "Just because something is the obvious solution, Lucas, doesn't mean it's not the correct one. People waste a lot of energy kicking against a thing only because it's not their own idea. Pure stubbornness."

He stared, then shrugged. "What were your reasons?"

"After I was widowed, George kept making suggestions about the two of us getting married. I don't ever want to get married again."

"There, you see?"

"My reasons for not getting married have nothing to do with you and Priscilla."

"They have *everything* to do with it."

She contemplated her son for a moment and tried another tack. "I met her Dr. Morse."

Lucas scowled and brought the ax down so hard the head bit through the wood and wedged in the stump beneath. "Good for you."

"He's very pleasant. Thoughtful."

"So why don't you try and charm the man yourself, if you like him so much?"

"Lucas! I'm quite happy with George; you know that."

Lucas shot her a dark look and put his effort into freeing the ax from the stump.

"He's leaving shortly, I believe. But I think he'll be back soon; I'm sure that Priscilla and Dr. Morse will come to a perfectly satisfactory arrangement."

He grunted, levering his arm beneath the handle of the ax in an attempt to pry it out. The handle gave first, breaking free from the head and wheeling off to land a good fifteen feet away. Lucas swore.

"Though really, an arrangement is not what one would hope for such a lovely girl as Priscilla. She deserves better," Lydia went on.

"She likes arrangements." He glowered at the ax head as if he could split the stump with a look. "Pris is highly in favor of arrangements. She *wants* an arrangement. I'm sure she'll be absolutely delighted with her goddamned bloody-wonderful *arrangement.*"

Lydia abandoned subtlety. She wasn't sure why she ever thought it would work with Lucas anyway. "Lucas, surely you cannot tell me you're going to sit around and let that girl marry some—"

"I asked her, all right!" Lucas braced one foot on the side of the trunk and shoved hard. The trunk toppled over with a thud and a plume of sawdust.

"But—"

Hands jammed on his hips, he looked up at her finally. His eyes were dark, haunted, an expression she'd never seen there before, and her mother's heart wept for him.

"I asked her," he repeated softly.

Lydia mentally backstepped, wheeled around to approach this dilemma from this new, unexpected angle. "She said no?"

"She sure as hell didn't say yes, did she?"

Not saying yes was not the same as saying no, Lydia thought. Perhaps all was not lost.

"What did you say, precisely?"

"I said, 'Marry me,' *precisely.*"

"And?"

"And what?"

"Nothing more?"

"I thought that about covered it."

"Oh, Lucas." Laughing sadly, Lydia shook her head. "I suppose you snapped it out in just about that tone, too, didn't you?"

"Shit!" The curse was so satisfying he said it again just for good measure. No prissy, interfering woman around to tell him to clean up his language. Perfectly good language, cuss words. Very useful.

"You should have known she would need a little more than that. You're so good at pretty words, Lucas. Whatever possessed you to leave them out this time?"

Lucas knew how to seduce a woman. He knew how to make her sigh his name, to scream it out in pleasure. How to make her knees go weak with a word. But he didn't know one damn thing about marrying one.

"A woman contemplating marriage needs promises, Lucas. Especially a woman like Pris."

"Which is exactly why it's a damn good thing she's not marrying *me*, isn't it?"

"I see," she said softly. "You don't believe you can make them to her, is that it?"

His eyes grew haunted, his voice ragged. "How can I?"

"You just do it."

He laughed, bitter, harsh. "And then break them in a year or two? Dear God, you know what that would do to her." His voice cracked. "And what doing that to her would do to me."

"Lucas, you are not your father."

"Aren't I?"

She stepped close, smiled up into his beloved face. He'd passed her in height when he was thirteen, and yet she was forever surprised when she had to look up to him. "You have his looks, that's true. His walk. His charm, and that mischievous smile."

Lucas's shoulders sagged with each trait she'd ticked off, as if hearing them confirmed by her had added an undeniable weight to an already heavy burden. She grasped his chin and tilted his head up.

"But you have my eyes. My frugality—your father never got so much as a penny in his palm without immediately looking for a place to spend it. And my heart."

"As if that's any better!" he burst out.

Pain stabbed. "Excuse me?"

"This is not an insult, Mother—but in this particular area, you are hardly a model citizen."

"Lucas." She shook her head sorrowfully. "You, of all people, should know that I am not my books. Far from it."

"I do know!" He'd never meant to tell her this. "I saw you. When I was young, I went to your room once—I'd been having nightmares again—and I saw them. *Both* of them, I remember them, they owned a house on Pecan Street—and you, and—" He couldn't look at her.

"Oh, Lucas. I am sorry, so very sorry that you saw that."

He attempted a careless laugh, failed miserably. "Me too."

How does one explain this to a son? It was not a thing for them to discuss, but somehow he had to know the truth. "I entered my marriage with great hopes, completely dazzled by your father. I knew of his reputation, of course, but I, foolish young girl that I was, was sure that my love would change him. That I would make him love me. I was wrong."

Each word made it worse, killing his heart piece by piece as they murdered his last weak hopes.

"For a long time, I thought perhaps the fault

was with me. I, in my innocence—and it was innocence, though not at all the kind the world recognizes—thought I could hold him by joining him. By becoming a partner in his adventures, by learning to be the kind of woman who could tempt him and intrigue him. I was very wrong, though it took me perhaps longer than it should have to realize it."

She sighed for the girl she'd been. "Since then, I have had exactly one . . ." She stopped, pleased to find that even after everything she'd done, she could not say the word *lover* to her son. "One *friend.* George. And I have been absolutely faithful to him for fifteen years. And I am *happy* with that, extraordinarily so. I can truly say I've never once been tempted."

"That's just because you're—" He snapped his mouth shut.

"Because I'm old?" She laughed merrily. "Oh, Lucas, you are so *young*. Luckily, you'll grow out of that."

"Why don't you marry him, then?"

"Because I enjoy my life the way it is. I am here, able to concentrate on my work and spend time with you. When I am with him, I am with him fully, but I am not willing to put my future in the hands of another man. Surely you can understand that."

"But—"

"No 'buts,' Lucas. Situations are different. *Lives* are different. Do not make the mistake of confusing yours with ours." Her voice gentled. "You have your own drive, your own kindness. A joy in your life that your father *never* had. You are your own man, Lucas. Every one of us, we all make our own choices. It would be cowardly to lay them at the feet of another."

Dreams, ruthlessly suppressed, half-realized dreams, stirred. "But how would I *know*?"

"You don't. But no one does, Lucas. You are no different, except that perhaps you realize the consequences of breaking those promises more fully than most. Maybe that would make you even more vigilant, more committed to them," she said. "A youthful indulgence of one's urges is not the same as being ruled by them."

"God, I wish I . . ." If only he could be sure.

"And there is one vast difference that you're overlooking. Your father never loved me. And you, of course, love Pris with all your heart." She smiled at his shock. "You do, you know."

"Of course I love her. Always have."

"No, not just that. You're *in* love with her as well."

Relief flooded him, joy at having the floodgates burst at last and letting the emotion roar through. "Yeah. That too."

"So honor her, too, by giving her decision to *her*. Let her decide with full knowledge of what she's giving up."

She wasn't sure he noticed when she left. He stood there, unmoving, staring thoughtfully at the old stump, as his breath smoked the air and swirled, forming clouds around a man lost to dreams.

His black bowler in his hand, Reuben Morse stood at the back door of the Wentworths' house. Milder weather had blown in an hour ago on a soft southern wind, and the sunshine felt good at his shoulders. Should be good traveling weather, he thought, anxious to return to his family.

He knocked.

"Come in!" a bright female voice called. He hesitated before reaching for the doorknob; it still seemed strange to him that he had the right to simply walk into this house.

At first he thought it was Priscilla, standing on the far side of the kitchen with her back to him, sloshing dishes in an enameled pan. For the back was trim, the hair, a shining upsweep of medium brown. But there was a frosting of silver in the hair, he noted just before she turned.

"Mrs. Wentworth," he said formally, dipping his head slightly. "I apologize for interrupting."

"Of course not!" She snatched a nearby dishrag and swiped her hands over it before tucking it into the waistband of her skirt. He remembered his wife making the same gesture and for an instant his heart squeezed. "I was just finishing the breakfast dishes." She waved a hand as if embarrassed to be caught. "We're a bit slow getting going this morning."

"Myself as well," he admitted. "I won't keep you long. I wished to say goodbye to Priscilla before I left town."

"Oh!" And then, "oh," with a little note of disappointment. "Priscilla is not here, I'm afraid. She went out to visit a family beyond town, the McCanns. I'm not certain when she'll be back."

"I suppose I'll be going, then."

"Please, let me offer you some coffee and some toast before you go."

He'd eaten an ample breakfast at the hotel. He

...ught of the long trip ahead, how much he
missed his children. And then he looked at this
woman who was to be his mother-in-law, with
that bright expectation on her face and a streak
of flour down the front of her checked shirt.
"Thank you. I'd like that."

He took a seat at the big linen-covered table
and laid his hat at his elbow. Mrs. Wentworth
bustled around, filling a crock with some deep
red preserves, pouring two cups of aromatic coffee. She worked with calm precision, the expertise born of long experience, her serene manner
an interesting contrast to her daughter's energy,
which sometimes he found rather tiring. But, he
reminded himself, energy would be a great asset
in dealing with his children. And the ones they
would undoubtedly have together, he thought,
frowning.

A cup in each hand, she paused by the table.
"Is something wrong?"

"No. No, of course not." When he took the cup
from her, his fingers brushed hers briefly. Entirely accidental. "It's simply been an eventful
few days."

"That it has."

She slid a plate in front of him, a half-dozen
slices of yeasty-smelling bread toasted to a lovely
brown that reminded him of her hair. She sat to
his right, her slender fingers wrapped around a
small cup patterned with pink roses. "I'm not
quite sure . . . if my husband were here, he'd be
interrogating you quite thoroughly."

"You're welcome to ask me whatever you'd
like." He relaxed and leaned back, spreading a
thick layer of chokecherry jelly on a piece of

toast. He breathed in the smell of coffee and
bread, the humid scent of the soap she'd used to
wash the dishes, and he felt a kind of peace that
had eluded him for two years. Odd, that he was
so comfortable with this woman he barely knew.
Much more so than he was with the daughter he
was to marry. But then, he had more reason to
be awkward with Priscilla.

"Thank you. I do have questions." She nodded, clearly determined to protect her offspring.
"Why did you feel you must go to such extremes
to find a wife? Surely there are many women in
St. Anthony who would be interested in the ...
position."

Position. A cold and impersonal term for com-
mitting to someone for all eternity. Yet he supposed it fit, he thought with a lonely pang. "I
suppose there are. I simply haven't had the
time—nor, I admit the interest—to search for
one."

Her lovely green eyes softened with sympathy. This was a woman who'd felt the same grief
he had, who'd endured the same losses.

"My sister Carol has lived with me since my
wife's death and has taken on the burden of raising my children and running the household. I
could never have managed it without her. However, I have recently learned that she's giving up
perhaps more than I realized, more than I want
to ask. She loves, quite deeply, I believe, a neighbor of ours, and he asked for her hand."

"She refused him?"

"Yes. Unwilling to leave me and the children
alone, I'm sure. I do not wish her to give up her
life for us, however. She's already helped us

enormously, has given more than I would have dared expect. I am hopeful my marriage will free her to follow her own heart."

"I understand," Clara said. "It is very thoughtful of you."

He shrugged. "It's family."

"That, too, I understand." She smiled ruefully. "I must admit that, while I am somewhat disconcerted by the idea of being called 'Grandmother,' I am very much looking forward to expanding our family."

Gulping, he ran a finger under his stiff collar.

She put down her teacup, her brow furrowing in concern. "You do not wish it? You don't want more children?"

"I . . . ah . . ."

"Priscilla will want more. You must be very clear on this point."

"Oh, I know that! I have every intention of . . ." He often discussed the most delicate of topics with his patients without the slightest hint of embarrassment. He couldn't recall ever feeling quite so discomposed. "She deserves children of her own, and we will surely have them, should we be so blessed. I had just thought . . . I had thought that part of my life was finished. It's a bit of an adjustment to realize it will begin again."

"But given the choice, you wouldn't choose them?"

"I will love them when they are here. You must have no fears on that point. It is simply . . . well, they are exhausting, you must give me that."

"That they are." Her expression grave, she

buttered another slice of toast. "But if you are not anxious to have more children, why didn't you look for an older woman? A widow, perhaps, with her own child-rearing years behind her?"

"I had considered that. But what woman who'd already raised her own would want to take on my brood?"

"You might be surprised," she said softly. "Take . . . yourself, for instance. You've earned a somewhat calmer and less strenuous life. Why would you give it up?"

"Me?" She touched the base of her neck, and unwillingly his gaze was drawn there. Her throat was slender, softened by age and lines. "There are women who might have welcomed that opportunity, Reuben—Mr. Morse," she added hastily.

"Reuben, please." He felt a tinge of impermissible pleasure at hearing her speak his name. "You wanted more children?"

"Oh, yes. It is the one great regret of my life— beyond losing Levi so early, of course. I would have loved the chance to have more children in my life. There is nothing I have ever found that brings me such joy. It's what women were meant to do."

Too late. The traitorous thought drifted through his mind before he locked it firmly away. He was set on a path now; he could not afford to waver.

"But now you are able to turn your efforts to your husband's business? Is there not some satisfaction there?"

She stilled the emotion flickering across her

features. And then, "I hate it!" With that admission, a torrent of words spilled out of her, what she saw as her responsibilities, her failures, delivered with a deep passion he wouldn't have expected from her.

He reached out, traced the path of a tear down her cheek, and wiped it off with his forefinger.

"We all have our regrets, Clara." *Clara.* He'd never called her by her given name before. A soft name, a dependable name, and the saying of it aloud was unexpectedly intimate to him.

She looked up at him, tears glazing her eyes, patiently waiting for him to continue.

"I . . . I am a physician." And because it had given him pleasure, he said her name again. "Clara, do you know what it's like? I am supposed to be a healer, the one who saves. Yet I couldn't save her."

He felt the burn of his own tears, ones he'd beaten back years ago. They hurt, but there was also relief in them, in letting them rise to the surface and flow out.

"Oh, Reuben." The hand she laid over his was warmly feminine, meant to comfort. But there was more here than comfort. It was as if he had no conscious control over his actions—he leaned toward her even as his mind told him *no.* Her beautiful eyes widened, but still she didn't pull away. Not even when his lips met hers.

Their bodies never touched. His hands lay flat on the surface of the table, his arms remained at his sides. But oh, what their mouths said. Loss and possibilities and a hundred what-ifs swirled above them, and a warmth that neither one had ever expected to feel again shimmered in them both.

He drew back. She was frozen in place. But not unaffected, he judged; her breath was quickened, her color high, her eyes misted with burgeoning passion.

"We shouldn't have done that," she whispered.

"I know."

"You must never tell her—anyone."

"But—"

"No!" Horror sprang into her eyes, chased all softer emotions. "You don't understand. She has lost . . . before, she lost a man she thought to marry. I cannot do that to her. We *will* not do that to her."

It would be foolish, he thought, to throw over all his careful plans for one brief conversation and one staggering kiss. There would never be more between them than this.

And yet . . . and yet. "Clara?"

Her mouth thinned, formed a rigid line like the one she would draw between them. Permanent, unbreachable, separating her from him as surely as death had separated him from his wife.

"You must never tell her."

Chapter 27

G lass tinkled brightly as Lucas carried the crate of unfilled bottles into the old chair factory. Above the door their brand new sign, still giving off paint fumes, claimed the place for the Maple Falls Bottling Cooperative.

It was a cold day, the last Saturday in November, and only two women were working. Mrs. Pugh and her daughter, huddled by a small stove, were gluing labels on the bottles filled during the week. The heat was welcome, as were the three filled crates stacked just inside the entry. He had a fancy restaurant in St. Paul clamoring for more of the water that was becoming their signature. *Zimmerman's fine dining—even our water is better!*

He set down the empty bottles and went over to check on the Pughs' progress. He ran a thumb over the smooth curve of a bottle, the pale tan label with Jeanette's face etched above the fancy lettering. The surge of pride surprised him. If nothing else, he and Priscilla were building something here, something important to the town and the people in it.

If nothing else. The only thing he'd done for days was think about it. Everything they'd said to each other, everything his mother had said to him, every single thing that had happened.

Mrs. Pugh slapped paste on a label and fit it to a bottle, smoothing the paper with her fingers. "I still don't know," she said to her daughter, "why they're having such a *small* wedding. One would think they'd realize that we'd all like to share in the celebration. Not to mention we could use a party after everything's that happened. And heaven knows they can afford to throw a nice one!"

"Mother," Harriet hissed, glancing worriedly at Lucas.

Mrs. Pugh shrugged. Since she'd finally accepted that Lucas wasn't going to rescue Harriet from spinsterhood, she was completely indifferent to his presence.

"Perhaps they wanted it that way, all things considered," Harriet ventured.

"Pshaw!" Mrs. Pugh jammed a finished bottle into a divided crate and reached for another. "It's just inconsiderate of them, that's all."

With a quick prayer of thanks that Mrs. Pugh would never be his mother-in-law, Lucas checked the straw packing around a crate of bottles ready for shipment and began hammering on the lid. One could hardly blame whatever distant acquaintance or relative had overlooked inviting her to their wedding.

"Well, it was rather rushed." Harriet methodically worked her way through her allotment of bottles. "Perhaps there simply wasn't time to plan a large party."

"Rushed it is." Mrs. Pugh sniffed. "I have my suspicions about the *speed* of this entire affair, too."

"Mother!"

Lucas hefted the finished crate.

"I believe," Harriet was going on, "that the wedding was, ah, so hurried because Jeanette is leaving for the territories shortly."

Crash.

The straw, Lucas thought dimly, was only partially effective. "What wedding?"

Mouths open, the women stared at him.

"But . . ." Harriet fumbled, looked to her mother for help.

Mrs. Pugh drew herself up. "We assumed you knew, considering how *close* you are to the family. Or perhaps I should say, how close you *were?*"

A pit, deep and black and yawning, opened up at his feet.

"And I still say—"

"When is it?" he demanded.

"The wedding?"

"Of course, the goddamned wedding!"

"Well, I never—"

"It was supposed to start at noon," Harriet told him kindly.

"Where?"

"At their house, I think."

"Rude as they were. All of you, never thinking of—" Mrs. Pugh rattled on, spewing complaints at Lucas's broad back as he charged out of the factory.

"Oh, hush, Mother," Harriet said at last, earning a shocked gasp of disbelief as she scrambled to her feet.

"Where are you going?" Mrs. Pugh sputtered.

"I'm going to watch the fun," she said, grinning, and followed Lucas.

Lucas tore open the Wentworths' heavy front door. He sped through, not bothering to close it behind him, and raced down the hallway. He turned sharply at the door to the parlor, sending the floor runner shooting off to crumple against the opposite wall.

He'd run all through town, and he had to gulp air before he could speak. The small wedding party was clumped near the fireplace. A bent, balding old man, black Bible open in his palms, faced a row of people. He saw a man's straight back, clad in a somber, distinguished gray wool suit. Arrayed beside him were three women, heads bent, brown hair dappled by cool sunlight falling through lace curtains. Other people gathered around the perimeter of the room. He saw his mother, and a clutch of stair-step children he assumed belonged to the groom.

He finally drew enough breath into his lungs, and used it all for one word. "Stop!" he hollered.

They all turned as one, as if their heads were linked together, controlled by the same puppeteer.

Reuben Morse looked exactly as his suit had predicted, graying and mature and sensible. Exactly what Pris had wanted. *Shit*. Lucas figured he'd simply beat the man to pulp if he had to. *Healthy* had been one of Pris's requirements, hadn't it?

Pris was dressed in soft royal blue wool, a flurry of lace at her throat. She carried a bunch of pale dried flowers tied with white ribbons that trailed to the floor, and looked so pretty and happy that his heart stopped. Jeanette was to her left, beaming and beautiful in sea green. And there, between Pris and Reuben, her hand firmly in his, was . . . Mrs. Wentworth?

He blinked.

"Lucas?" Pris asked.

"You're—" He stepped into the room. "You're not marrying him?"

"No."

The fear that had sprung full-blown and torturous in the factory gave way to swelling hope. "But I thought—"

Her flowers trembled, the ribbons fluttering as if a brisk breeze had sighed through the room. "I did, too."

"Is there a problem here?" the preacher asked, in a voice designed to ring through a cathedral.

"No. There's no problem." Not anymore. He was unaware of moving his feet; he just knew he was getting closer. Closer to Pris.

"Now see here—" Reuben began.

"Shhh." Clara squeezed his hand. They could wait; let her daughter have her chance to find what they had.

"Tell me what happened," Lucas said. It was the least of the things he had to ask her. But he needed time, to accept, to believe. And to anticipate.

"Oh." She couldn't believe he'd come charging in here. He'd come for her. For *her*. "I decided I couldn't marry Reuben after all. It . . . just wasn't right."

It wasn't you.

"But I'd figured he'd be a bit upset at my changing my mind. Imagine my surprise when he turned right around and asked my mother!"

"Imagine." They were grinning at each other. Stupid, silly grins, the kind of joyfully foolish expressions neither had ever worn before. Nothing had ever felt so good.

Smile lines hugged the corners of his mouth. A disobedient lock of dark hair fell over the chicken pox scar. How had she, however briefly, thought she could let another man touch her? How had she ever considered pledging herself to anyone but Lucas?

She knew there'd be no other man for her. But a fading shadow of uncertainty still hovered over a day that was rapidly becoming gilded; was she the only woman for him? "What are you doing here?"

And there, before everyone, was a sight that no female west of the Mississippi had ever thought to see.

Lucas Garrett went down on one knee.

Priscilla heard gasps, a chorus of shrieked "oohs," and looked up. The women who'd seen him racing hell-for-leather through town, Harriet Pugh sprinting after him, had followed and were now clustered in the doorway, jostling for position, their faces dreamy with the romance of it all. It reminded Priscilla of the scene at the schoolhouse, that first night Lucas had kissed her. She'd rued that day a hundred times since;

now she blessed it with a fervor that resounded in her soul.

"Wait." Her flowers were in the way, so she gave them a toss. They sailed through the air, shedding petals like giant snowflakes, and flew straight into the arms of Carol Morse.

For once in her life Priscilla didn't care if she flashed her ankles at the entire town. She hitched up her skirts and knelt down right in front of Lucas. Knee to knee, face to face. Soul to soul. "There. That's better."

"Pris." The gesture rocked him, told him better than any other how their lives would be. Eyes bright as gems behind her lenses, her nose strong and proudly high, she was as beautiful to him as any woman could hope to be. He wondered how he could possibly have been so blind all these years.

"Pris." He enfolded both her hands in his. "I love you, Pris."

Joy and tears sprang into her eyes. "Oh, Lucas, I—"

He kissed her. Because once she got started, he'd never have a chance to get it all out. Because it was the easiest way he knew to make her be quiet. And because he wanted to. So he kissed her, right there, kneeling on her mother's parlor rug. The first time he'd wanted the town to see them; now he wished it was the whole world, so they'd all know he'd laid claim to Pris as she had to him.

She was flushed and hazy when he lifted his head.

"Good," he said. "You listen, now. And then you can talk. You can talk all you want." He squeezed her hands. "You can talk for the rest of our lives."

She opened her mouth, then closed it again, bobbed her chin in agreement.

"I love you. I'm in love with you. Wildly in love with you. Madly in love with you. I love you with every beat of my heart."

The breath sighed out of her, along with all the worries, any last uncertainties. Pushed out of the way by all the happiness, all the love that seemed to grow, expand, take up her whole self.

"I don't know how to promise you the next fifty years. Don't know how to make you *know* that I can't imagine ever wanting anyone but you. But I know this." He took their folded hands and tapped them against his chest. "My heart has always been yours. It's been steadfast all these years. It's always belonged to you. Give me a chance to prove the rest of me does, too."

He smiled, and this one was only for her. "Marry me. We've got a preacher. We've got your family. Marry me now, before we waste one single second more. Marry me, Pris."

How could she do anything else?

"Yes."

Epilogue

April, 1862

The stagecoach thundered down Center Street, spewing mud over the new pine boardwalks. More black muck coated the sides of the coach and added a thick layer to the wheels. Johnny Merced, three inches taller and a good thirty pounds heavier, shouted to his team and drew them to a flashy stop in front of the Great Northern Hotel.

The door of the coach banged open. A man's head and shoulders emerged slowly and swung back and forth, looking both ways. Then he gingerly crawled out, legs wobbly from being cramped in the stage for hundreds of miles.

His clothes fit him worse than a scarecrow's, hanging on a frame that had given up more pounds than Johnny had gained. A thick, wild beard hid his face and merged with the bush of dark hair sprouting from his head. He stood smack dab in the middle of the street, slowly turning around and around, as if he couldn't believe what he was seeing.

People bustled in and out of buildings gleam-

ing with fresh paint and new windows. A half
dozen wagons and carriages awaited their owners along the street. There was the sound of hammering in the air, the smell of fresh-cut lumber
and new whitewash.

Across the street, in the offices of Maple Falls
Enterprises, Lucas Garrett dropped the curtain
he'd peeled back when he heard the stage approach. "There's another one back," he commented to his wife.

"Who is it?"

"Hard to tell." He turned to take in the sight
of his wife, lying naked and hugely pregnant in
the daybed he'd insisted on installing in their
offices. For her to rest while she carried their
child, he'd said. But Pris's energy constantly
amazed him, and more often than not the bed
was used for relaxation of a different sort entirely. "He doesn't look like the goldfields were
too kind to him."

"Tom Fergus, maybe," she suggested. "In her
last letter, Jeanette said she'd heard he might be
headed back."

"Well, he'll be in for a surprise, won't he?"

"He sure will." Tom would find his wife gone,
for one thing. Off to Chicago this time, for Priscilla had discovered a year ago that Flora owned
true genius for salesmanship, particularly with
the saloon owners. She'd taken to the task with
great gusto, allowing Lucas to stay home more
often.

But then, most of the returning men of Maple
Falls had been in for a shock when they'd come
staggering back. The bleak, failing town they'd

fled had become quietly prosperous. The wives they'd left behind were different women now, changed by the struggle to survive and keep their families together. More than one man had discovered his wife had no intention of taking him back. Others learned that they had to develop new relationships with women who welcomed them back out of love and not necessity.

Many men had not returned at all. Some had made their wives widows, in truth, finding their final reward at the bottom of a mine shaft. A few had gone off to join the Union Army rather than return home and admit defeat. Still others had simply disappeared, becoming one of the vast numbers of men who'd fled their old lives in the west.

The only man who'd actually struck it rich in the gold fields had been Michael McCann. He'd sent for Jenny, who'd promptly repaid Lucas, packed up her children, and left Maple Falls behind. Last they'd heard, Michael was building his wife the grandest mansion smack in the middle of the new town of Denver in what was now called the Colorado Territories.

Lucas crossed the neat, spare room and sat down on the bed next to his wife.

"Do you suppose there will be letters today?" she asked. "I haven't heard from Jeanette for a month."

"Don't worry. If there is one, Mick will run it right over." Mick and his mother lived in Lucas's former rooms over the store. Many of the other unwanted children and their mothers had returned to their tribes. Lucas often wondered if he'd done the boy a disservice by encouraging them to remain in a town that still had little liking for an illegitimate half-breed boy. But he couldn't imagine sending him back to a life that seemed destined mostly for hunger and war, either. It was perhaps the only real worry in his and Pris's life.

"I'd better get some clothes on, then." Made ungainly by her pregnancy, she struggled to sit up. Her changed body had required a certain amount of creativity a few minutes ago, a challenge he confessed to enjoying.

"Not yet." He grinned and set a palm on each side of her ripening belly. It was a continual source of amazement to him that his child—their child!—grew inside her.

"You would have me naked all the time if you could," she complained. But she smiled and eased back against the pillows.

"True." It gave him great pleasure that she felt comfortable like this, to be pregnant and bare in the daylight and not feel the slightest residual shyness. His Pris, he'd discovered, had been hiding a powerful wicked streak all those years.

"Well, I do hope there is a letter from her. I worry."

"I know you do. But she seems to be managing quite well. Do you suppose she's taken Robert back yet?"

"Not a chance," Pris told him. "She's having far too much fun running the saloon, being toasted as the prettiest woman in the territories. He's going to have to suffer for years even to have a chance."

"Wentworth women are worth a little suffering now and then."

"Thank you. Oh, and as I was telling you before you so *rudely* distracted me"—she grinned—"we need to go over the projected costs for the expansion."

After Clara had married Reuben and moved to St. Anthony, she'd turned all management of Maple Falls Manufacturing over to Priscilla, who had promptly sold off what she could, paid off the remaining creditors, and dismantled most of the business. Lucas had at first been surprised that she'd felt no reluctance to close down the business her father had built, but she'd assured him that her father would most of all want her to be a *good* businesswoman, which dictated concentrating on the enterprise with the greatest profit potential—Maple Falls Bottling Cooperative. Those earnings had allowed them cautiously to rebuild some of what was lost—the window factory was due to reopen in four weeks.

"Do you ever regret that we couldn't save more of Maple Falls Manufacturing?"

"I'm not sorry about one single thing, Lucas." To prove it, she grabbed his face in both hands and kissed him, hard and long and sweet.

Just for the joy of hearing her answer, he asked, "So you would have married me anyway? Even if I hadn't been the last man in town?"

Her eyes sparkled at him.

"You're damn right I would have."

Dear Reader,

If you love westerns the way that I love westerns, then you won't want to miss Connie Mason's latest love story, *To Tempt a Rogue*. When Ryan Delaney—the third Delaney brother—leaves the family ranch on what he hopes will be a great adventure, he never expects to get mixed up with Kitty Johnson. Is Kitty really running from the law, or is this a case of mistaken identity? And as passion flares between them, Ryan must determine if he's thinking with his head...or his heart.

Lovers of contemporary romance won't want to miss Hailey North's delightful, delicious *Pillow Talk*! Meg Cooper has always believed in what she calls "possibles," but is it possible to become engaged to a stranger for only two weeks? Sexy, wealthy Jules Ponthier woos Meg with promises of this "innocent" proposition—but how long can she resist this irresistible man? If you haven't yet become a fan of Hailey North, I guarantee this will make you one.

Karen Kay has thrilled countless readers with her sensuous, unforgettable love stories with Native American heroes. Her latest, *Night Thunder's Bride*, highlights her heartfelt brand of storytelling as a young pioneer woman must become the wife of Night Thunder, a Blackfoot warrior.

Eileen Putman makes her Avon debut with the wonderful *King of Hearts*, a Regency rake who is plucked from a hangman's noose and unexpectedly rescued by Louisa Peabody, a golden-haired beauty who seems to be the only woman in England who can resist his many charms.

Until next month, enjoy!

Lucia Macro
Lucia Macro
Senior Editor

AEL 0699

Avon Romantic Treasures

*Unforgettable, enthralling love stories,
sparkling with passion and adventure
from Romance's bestselling authors*

****

A RAKE'S VOW	*by Stephanie Laurens*
	79457-8/$5.99 US/$7.99 Can
SO WILD A KISS	*by Nancy Richards-Akers*
	78947-7/$5.99 US/$7.99 Can
UPON A WICKED TIME	*by Karen Ranney*
	79583-3/$5.99 US/$7.99 Can
ON BENDED KNEE	*by Tanya Anne Crosby*
	78573-0/$5.99 US/$7.99 Can
BECAUSE OF YOU	*by Cathy Maxwell*
	79710-0/$5.99 US/$7.99 Can
SCANDAL'S BRIDE	*by Stephanie Laurens*
	80568-5/$5.99 US/$7.99 Can
HOW TO MARRY A MARQUIS	*by Julia Quinn*
	80081-0/$5.99 US/$7.99 Can
THE WEDDING NIGHT	*by Linda Needham*
	79635-X/$5.99 US/$7.99 Can

Avon Romances—
the best in exceptional authors and unforgettable novels!

ELIZABETH LOWELL

THE NEW YORK TIMES *BESTSELLING AUTHOR*

"A law unto herself in the world of romance!"

Amanda Quick

America Loves Lindsey!
The Timeless Romances
of #1 Bestselling Author

KEEPER OF THE HEART	77493-3/$6.99 US/$8.99 Can
THE MAGIC OF YOU	75629-3/$6.99 US/$8.99 Can
ANGEL	75628-5/$6.99 US/$8.99 Can
PRISONER OF MY DESIRE	75627-7/$6.99 US/$8.99 Can
ONCE A PRINCESS	75625-0/$6.99 US/$8.99 Can
WARRIOR'S WOMAN	75301-4/$6.99 US/$8.99 Can
MAN OF MY DREAMS	75626-9/$6.99 US/$8.99 Can
SURRENDER MY LOVE	76256-0/$6.50 US/$7.50 Can
YOU BELONG TO ME	76258-7/$6.99 US/$8.99 Can
UNTIL FOREVER	76259-5/$6.50 US/$8.50 Can
LOVE ME FOREVER	72570-3/$6.99 US/$8.99 Can
SAY YOU LOVE ME	72571-1/$6.99 US/$8.99 Can
ALL I NEED IS YOU	76260-9/$6.99 US/$8.99 Can

And Now in Hardcover
THE PRESENT: A MALORY HOLIDAY NOVEL
97725-7/$16.00 US/21.00 CAN